HEIR of FIRE

SARAH J. MAAS

BLOOMSBURY
LONDON NEW DELHI NEW YORK SYDNEY

Bloomsbury Publishing, London, New Delhi, New York and Sydney

First published in Great Britain in September 2014 by
Bloomsbury Publishing Plc
50 Bedford Square, London WC1B 3DP

First published in the USA in September 2014 by
Bloomsbury Children's Books
1385 Broadway, New York, New York 10018

www.sarahjmaas.com
www.bloomsbury.com

Bloomsbury is a registered trademark of Bloomsbury Publishing Plc

A CIP catalogue record for this book is available from the British Library

ISBN 978 1 4088 3912 6

MIX
Paper from responsible sources
FSC® C020471

Printed and bound in Great Britain by CPI Group (UK) Ltd, Croydon CR0 4YY

7 9 10 8 6

HEIR *of* FIRE

BOOKS BY SARAH J. MAAS

Throne of Glass
Crown of Midnight

The Assassin's Blade

Again, for Susan—
whose friendship changed my life for the better
and gave this book its heart.

Amaroth
Frozen Wastes
The Ruins of Morla
Jungle of Morla
The Western Wastes
The Witch Kingdom
Briarcliff
Erilea
Bogdano Jun
The Deserted Land
Gulf of Oro
The Singing Sands
Yurpa
The Red Desert
Silent Assassins
Oasis of Barg
The Cleaver
Xandria
Noll
The Black Dunes
The Black Sands of Roth
volcano flows

Terrasen
North Sea
N
Wolf Tribe
Staghorn Mountains
Allsbrook
Rosamel
Orynth
Suria
Anascaul Mountains
Perranth Mountains
Perranth
Frozen Wastes
Endovier
Salt Mines
Ruhnn Mountains
Meah
Great Ocean
Adarlan
Mountains of Ararat
Oakwald Forest
The Ferian Gap
The Silver Lake
Anielle
Rifthold
Avery River
To Wendlyn
White Fang Mountains
Morath
Fenharrow
Bellhaven
Melisande
Dead Islands
Skull's Bay
Calaculla
Leriba
Eyllwe
Grasslands of Eyllwe
Banjali
Stone Marshes

PART ONE

HEIR OF ASH

1

Gods, it was boiling in this useless excuse for a kingdom.

Or maybe it felt that way because Celaena Sardothien had been lounging on the lip of the terra-cotta roof since midmorning, an arm flung over her eyes, slowly baking in the sun like the loaves of flatbread the city's poorest citizens left on their windowsills because they couldn't afford brick ovens.

And gods, she was sick of flatbread—*teggya*, they called it. Sick of the crunchy, oniony taste of it that even mouthfuls of water couldn't wash away. If she never ate another bite of teggya again, it would be too soon.

Mostly because it was all she'd been able to afford when she landed in Wendlyn two weeks ago and made her way to the capital city, Varese, just as she'd been ordered by his Grand Imperial Majesty and Master of the Earth, the King of Adarlan.

She'd resorted to swiping teggya and wine off vendors' carts since her money ran out, not long after she'd taken one look at the heavily fortified limestone castle, at the elite guards, at the cobalt banners flapping so proudly in the dry, hot wind and decided *not* to kill her assigned targets.

So it had been stolen teggya . . . and wine. The sour red wine from the vineyards lining the rolling hills around the walled capital—a taste she'd initially spat out but now very, very much enjoyed. Especially since the day when she decided that she didn't particularly care about anything at all.

She reached for the terra-cotta tiles sloping behind her, groping for the clay jug of wine she'd hauled onto the roof that morning. Patting, feeling for it, and then—

She swore. Where in hell was the wine?

The world tilted and went blindingly bright as she hoisted herself onto her elbows. Birds circled above, keeping well away from the white-tailed hawk that had been perched atop a nearby chimney all morning, waiting to snatch up its next meal. Below, the market street was a brilliant loom of color and sound, full of braying donkeys, merchants waving their wares, clothes both foreign and familiar, and the clacking of wheels against pale cobblestones. But where in hell was the—

Ah. There. Tucked beneath one of the heavy red tiles to keep cool. Just where she'd stashed it hours before, when she'd climbed onto the roof of the massive indoor market to survey the perimeter of the castle walls two blocks away. Or whatever she'd thought sounded official and useful before she'd realized that she'd rather sprawl in the shadows. Shadows that had long since been burned away by that relentless Wendlyn sun.

Celaena swigged from the jug of wine—or tried to. It was empty, which she supposed was a blessing, because *gods* her head was spinning. She needed water, and more teggya. And perhaps something for the gloriously painful split lip and scraped cheekbone she'd earned last night in one of the city's *tabernas*.

Groaning, Celaena rolled onto her belly and surveyed the street forty feet below. She knew the guards patrolling it by now—had marked their faces and weapons, just as she had with the guards atop the high castle walls. She'd memorized their rotations, and how they opened the three massive gates that led into the castle. It seemed that the Ashryvers and their ancestors took safety very, very seriously.

It had been ten days since she'd arrived in Varese itself, after hauling ass from the coast. Not because she was particularly eager to kill her targets, but because the city was so damn large that it seemed her best chance of dodging the immigration officials, whom she'd given the slip instead of registering with their oh-so-benevolent work program. Hurrying to the capital had also provided welcome activity after weeks at sea, where she hadn't really felt like doing anything other than lying on the narrow bed in her cramped cabin or sharpening her weapons with a near-religious zeal.

You're nothing but a coward, Nehemia had said to her.

Every slice of the whetting stone had echoed it. *Coward, coward, coward.* The word had trailed her each league across the ocean.

She had made a vow—a vow to free Eyllwe. So in between moments of despair and rage and grief, in between thoughts of Chaol and the Wyrdkeys and all she'd left behind and lost, Celaena had decided on one plan to follow when she reached these shores. One plan, however insane and unlikely, to free the enslaved kingdom: find and obliterate the Wyrdkeys the King of Adarlan had used to build his terrible empire. She'd gladly destroy herself to carry it out.

Just her, just him. Just as it should be; no loss of life beyond their own, no soul stained but hers. It would take a monster to destroy a monster.

If she had to be here thanks to Chaol's misplaced good intentions, then at least she'd receive the answers she needed. There was one person in Erilea who had been present when the Wyrdkeys were wielded by a conquering demon race that had warped them into three tools of such mighty power that they'd been hidden for thousands of years and nearly wiped from memory. Queen Maeve of the Fae. Maeve knew everything—as was expected when you were older than dirt.

So the first step of her stupid, foolish plan had been simple: seek out Maeve, get answers about how to destroy the Wyrdkeys, and then return to Adarlan.

It was the least she could do. For Nehemia—for . . . a lot of other people. There was nothing left in her, not really. Only ash and an abyss and the unbreakable vow she'd carved into her flesh, to the friend who had seen her for what she truly was.

When they had docked at the largest port city in Wendlyn, she couldn't help but admire the caution the ship took while coming to shore—waiting until a moonless night, then stuffing Celaena and the other refugee women from Adarlan in the galley while navigating the secret channels through the barrier reef. It was understandable: the reef was the main defense keeping Adarlan's legions from these shores. It was also part of her mission here as the King's Champion.

That was the other task lingering in the back of her mind: to find a way to keep the king from executing Chaol or Nehemia's family. He'd promised to do it should she fail in her mission to retrieve Wendlyn's naval defense plans and assassinate its king and prince at their annual midsummer ball. But she'd shoved all those thoughts aside when they'd docked and the refugee women had been herded ashore for processing by the port's officials.

Many of the women were scarred inside and out, their eyes gleaming with echoes of whatever horrors had befallen them in Adarlan. So even after she'd vanished from the ship during the chaos of docking, she'd lingered on a nearby rooftop while the women were escorted into a building—to find homes and employment. Yet Wendlyn's officials could later bring them to a quiet part of the city and do whatever they wanted. Sell them. Hurt them. They were refugees: unwanted and without any rights. Without any voice.

But she hadn't lingered merely from paranoia. No—Nehemia would have remained to ensure they were safe. Realizing that, Celaena had wound up on the road to the capital as soon as she was certain the women were all right. Learning how to infiltrate the castle was merely something to occupy her time while she decided how to execute the first steps of her plan. While she tried to stop thinking about Nehemia.

It had all been fine—fine and easy. Hiding in the little woods and barns along the way, she passed like a shadow through the countryside.

Wendlyn. A land of myths and monsters—of legends and nightmares made flesh.

The kingdom itself was a spread of warm, rocky sand and thick forest, growing ever greener as hills rolled inland and sharpened into towering peaks. The coast and the land around the capital were dry, as if the sun had baked all but the hardiest vegetation. Vastly different from the soggy, frozen empire she'd left behind.

A land of plenty, of opportunity, where men didn't just take what they wanted, where no doors were locked and people smiled at you in the streets. But she didn't particularly care if someone did or didn't smile at her—no, as the days wore on, she found it suddenly very difficult to bring herself to care about anything at all. Whatever determination, whatever rage, whatever *anything* she'd felt upon leaving Adarlan had ebbed away, devoured by the nothingness that now gnawed at her.

It was four days before Celaena spotted the massive capital city built across the foothills. Varese, the city where her mother had been born; the vibrant heart of the kingdom.

While Varese was cleaner than Rifthold and had plenty of wealth spread between the upper and lower classes, it was a capital city all the same, with slums and back alleys, whores and gamblers—and it hadn't taken too long to find its underbelly.

On the street below, three of the market guards paused to chat, and Celaena rested her chin on her hands. Like every guard in this kingdom, each was clad in light armor and bore a good number of weapons.

Rumor claimed the Wendlynite soldiers were trained by the Fae to be ruthless and cunning and swift. And she didn't want to know if that was true, for about a dozen different reasons. They certainly seemed a good deal more observant than the average Rifthold sentry—even if they hadn't yet noticed the assassin in their midst. But these days, Celaena knew the only threat she posed was to herself.

Even baking in the sun each day, even washing up whenever she could in one of the city's many fountain-squares, she could still feel Archer Finn's blood soaking her skin, into her hair. Even with the constant noise and rhythm of Varese, she could still hear Archer's groan as she gutted him in that tunnel beneath the castle. And even with the wine and heat, she could still see Chaol, horror contorting his face at what he'd learned about her Fae heritage and the monstrous power that could easily destroy her, about how hollow and dark she was inside.

She often wondered whether he'd figured out the riddle she'd told him on the docks of Rifthold. And if he had discovered the truth . . . Celaena never let herself get that far. Now wasn't the time for thinking about Chaol, or the truth, or any of the things that had left her soul so limp and weary.

Celaena tenderly prodded her split lip and frowned at the market guards, the movement making her mouth hurt even more. She'd deserved that particular blow in the brawl she'd provoked in last night's taberna—she'd kicked a man's balls into his throat, and when he'd caught his breath, he'd been enraged, to say the least. Lowering her hand from her mouth, she observed the guards for a few moments. They didn't take bribes from the merchants, or bully or threaten with fines like the guards and officials in Rifthold. Every official and soldier she'd seen so far had been similarly . . . good.

The same way Galan Ashryver, Crown Prince of Wendlyn, was good..

Dredging up some semblance of annoyance, Celaena stuck out her tongue. At the guards, at the market, at the hawk on the nearby chimney, at the castle and the prince who lived inside it. She wished that she had not run out of wine so early in the day.

It had been a week since she'd figured out how to infiltrate the castle, three days after arriving in Varese itself. A week since that horrible day when all her plans crumbled around her.

A cooling breeze pushed past, bringing with it the spices from the vendors lining the nearby street—nutmeg, thyme, cumin, lemon verbena. She inhaled deeply, letting the scents clear her sun-and-wine-addled head. The pealing of bells floated down from one of the neighboring mountain towns, and in some square of the city, a minstrel band struck up a merry midday tune. Nehemia would have loved this place.

That fast, the world slipped, swallowed up by the abyss that now lived within her. Nehemia would never see Wendlyn. Never wander through the spice market or hear the mountain bells. A dead weight pressed on Celaena's chest.

It had seemed like such a perfect plan when she'd arrived in Varese. In the hours she'd spent figuring out the royal castle's defenses, she'd debated how she'd find Maeve to learn about the keys. It had all been going smoothly, flawlessly, until . . .

Until that gods-damned day when she'd noted how the guards left a hole in their defense in the southern wall every afternoon at two o'clock, and grasped how the gate mechanism operated. Until Galan Ashryver had come riding out through those gates, in full view of where she'd been perched on the roof of a nobleman's house.

It hadn't been the sight of him, with his olive skin and dark hair, that had stopped her dead. It hadn't been the fact that, even from a distance, she could see his turquoise eyes—*her* eyes, the reason she usually wore a hood in the streets.

No. It had been the way people cheered.

Cheered for him, their prince. Adored him, with his dashing smile and his light armor gleaming in the endless sun, as he and the soldiers behind him rode toward the north coast to continue blockade running. *Blockade running.* The prince—her target—was a gods-damned blockade runner against Adarlan, and his people *loved* him for it.

She'd trailed the prince and his men through the city, leaping from rooftop to rooftop, and all it would have taken was one arrow through those turquoise eyes and he would have been dead. But she followed him all the way to the city walls, the cheers growing louder, people tossing flowers, everyone beaming with pride for their perfect, perfect prince.

She'd reached the city gates just as they opened to let him through. And when Galan Ashryver rode off into the sunset, off to war and glory and to fight for good and freedom, she lingered on that roof until he was a speck in the distance.

Then she had walked into the nearest taberna and gotten into the bloodiest, most brutal brawl she'd ever provoked, until the city guard was called in and she vanished moments before everyone was tossed into the stocks. And then she had decided, as her nose bled down the front of her shirt and she spat blood onto the cobblestones, that she wasn't going to do *anything.*

There was no point to her plans. Nehemia and Galan would have led the world to freedom, and Nehemia should have been breathing. Together the prince and princess could have defeated the King of Adarlan. But Nehemia was dead, and Celaena's vow—her stupid, pitiful vow—was worth as much as mud when there were beloved heirs like Galan who could do so much more. She'd been a fool to make that vow.

Even Galan—Galan was barely making a dent against Adarlan, and he had an entire armada at his disposal. She was one person, one complete waste of life. If Nehemia hadn't been able to stop the king . . . then that plan, to find a way to contact Maeve . . . that plan was absolutely useless.

Mercifully, she still hadn't seen one of the Fae—not a single damn one—or the faeries, or even a lick of magic. She'd done her best to avoid it. Even before she'd spotted Galan, she'd kept away from the market stalls that offered everything from healing to trinkets to potions, areas that were usually also full of street performers or mercenaries trading their gifts to earn a living. She'd learned which tabernas the magic-wielders liked to frequent and never went near them. Because sometimes she felt a trickling, writhing *thing* awaken in her gut if she caught a crackle of its energy.

It had been a week since she'd given up her plan and abandoned any attempt to care at all. And she suspected it'd be many weeks more before she decided she was truly sick of teggya, or brawling every night just to feel something, or guzzling sour wine as she lay on rooftops all day.

But her throat was parched and her stomach was grumbling, so Celaena slowly peeled herself off the edge of the roof. Slowly, not because of those vigilant guards, but rather because her head was well and truly spinning. She didn't trust herself to care enough to prevent a tumble.

She glared at the thin scar stretching across her palm as she shimmied down the drainpipe and into the alley off the market street. It was now nothing more than a reminder of the pathetic promise she'd made at Nehemia's half-frozen grave over a month ago, and of everything and everyone else she'd failed. Just like her amethyst ring, which she gambled away every night and won back before sunrise.

Despite all that had happened, and Chaol's role in Nehemia's death, even after she'd destroyed what was between them, she hadn't been able to forfeit his ring. She'd lost it thrice now in card games, only to get it back—by whatever means necessary. A dagger poised to slip between the ribs usually did a good deal more convincing than actual words.

Celaena supposed it was a miracle she made it down to the alley, where the shadows momentarily blinded her. She braced a hand on the cool stone wall, letting her eyes adjust, willing her head to stop spinning. A mess—she was a gods-damned mess. She wondered when she'd bother to stop being one.

The tang and reek of the woman hit Celaena before she saw her. Then wide, yellowed eyes were in her face, and a pair of withered, cracked lips parted to hiss, "Slattern! Don't let me catch you in front of my door again!"

Celaena pulled back, blinking at the vagrant woman—and at her door, which . . . was just an alcove in the wall, crammed with rubbish and what had to be sacks of the woman's belongings. The woman herself was hunched, her hair unwashed and teeth a ruin of stumps. Celaena blinked again, the woman's face coming into focus. Furious, half-mad, and filthy.

Celaena held up her hands, backing away a step, then another. "Sorry."

The woman spat a wad of phlegm onto the cobblestones an inch from Celaena's dusty boots. Failing to muster the energy to be disgusted or furious, Celaena would have walked away had she not glimpsed herself as she raised her dull gaze from the glob.

Dirty clothes—stained and dusty and torn. Not to mention, she smelled *atrocious*, and this vagrant woman had mistaken her for . . . for a fellow vagrant, competing for space on the streets.

Well. Wasn't that just *wonderful*. An all-time low, even for her. Perhaps it'd be funny one day, if she bothered to remember it. She couldn't recall the last time she'd laughed.

At least she could take some comfort in knowing that it couldn't get worse.

But then a deep male voice chuckled from the shadows behind her.

2

The man—male—down the alley was Fae.

After ten years, after all the executions and burnings, a Fae male was prowling toward her. Pure, solid Fae. There was no escaping him as he emerged from the shadows yards away. The vagrant in the alcove and the others along the alley fell so quiet Celaena could again hear those bells ringing in the distant mountains.

Tall, broad-shouldered, every inch of him seemingly corded with muscle, he was a male blooded with power. He paused in a dusty shaft of sunlight, his silver hair gleaming.

As if his delicately pointed ears and slightly elongated canines weren't enough to scare the living shit out of everyone in that alley, including the now-whimpering madwoman behind Celaena, a wicked-looking tattoo was etched down the left side of his harsh face, the whorls of black ink stark against his sun-kissed skin.

The markings could easily have been decorative, but she still remembered enough of the Fae language to recognize them as words, even in such an artistic rendering. Starting at his temple, the tattoo flowed over his jaw and down his neck, where it disappeared beneath the pale surcoat and cloak he wore. She had a feeling the markings continued down the rest of him, too, concealed along with at least half a dozen weapons. As she reached into her cloak for her own hidden dagger, she realized he might have been handsome were it not for the promise of violence in his pine-green eyes.

It would have been a mistake to call him young—just as it would have been a mistake to call him anything but a warrior, even without the sword strapped across his back and the vicious knives at his sides. He moved with lethal grace and surety, scanning the alley as if he were walking onto a killing field.

The hilt of the dagger was warm in her hand, and Celaena adjusted her stance, surprised to be feeling—fear. And enough of it that it cleared the heavy fog that had been clouding her senses these past few weeks.

The Fae warrior stalked down the alley, his knee-high leather boots silent on the cobblestones. Some of the loiterers shrank back; some bolted for the sunny street, to random doorways, anywhere to escape his challenging stare.

Celaena knew before his sharp eyes met hers that he was here for her, and who had sent him.

She reached for her Eye amulet, startled to find it was no longer around her neck. She'd given it to Chaol—the only bit of protection she could grant him upon leaving. He'd probably thrown it away as soon as he figured out the truth. Then he could go back to the haven of being her enemy. Maybe he'd tell Dorian, too, and the pair of them would both be safe.

Before she could give in to the instinct to scuttle back up the drainpipe and onto the roof, she considered the plan she'd abandoned. Had some god remembered she existed and decided to throw her a bone? She'd needed to see Maeve.

Well, here was one of Maeve's elite warriors. Ready. Waiting.

And from the vicious temper emanating from him, not entirely happy about it.

The alley remained as still as a graveyard while the Fae warrior surveyed her. His nostrils flared delicately, as if he were—

He was getting a whiff of her scent.

She took some small satisfaction in knowing she smelled horrific, but it wasn't that smell he was reading. No, it was the scent that marked her as *her*—the smell of her lineage and blood and what and who she was. And if he said her name in front of these people . . . then she knew that Galan Ashryver would come running home. The guards would be on high alert, and *that* was not part of her plan at all.

The bastard looked likely to do such a thing, just to prove who was in charge. So she summoned her energy as best she could and sauntered over to him, trying to remember what she might have done months ago, before the world had gone to hell. "Well met, my friend," she purred. "Well met, indeed."

She ignored the shocked faces around them, focusing solely on sizing him up. He stood with a stillness that only an immortal could achieve. She willed her heartbeat and breathing to calm. He could probably hear them, could probably smell every emotion raging through her. There'd be no fooling him with bravado, not in a thousand years. He'd probably lived that long already. Perhaps there'd be no beating him, either. She was Celaena Sardothien, but he was a Fae warrior and had likely been one for a great while.

She stopped a few feet away. Gods, he was huge. "What a lovely surprise," she said loudly enough for everyone to hear. When was the last time she'd sounded that pleasant? She couldn't even remember the last time she'd spoken in full sentences. "I thought we were to meet at the city walls."

He didn't bow, thank the gods. His harsh face didn't even shift. Let him think what he wanted. She was sure she looked nothing like what he'd been told to expect—and he'd certainly laughed when that woman mistook her for a fellow vagrant.

"Let's go," was all he said, his deep, somewhat bored voice seeming to echo off the stones as he turned to leave the alley. She'd bet good money that the leather vambraces on his forearms concealed blades.

She might have given him a rather obnoxious reply, just to feel him out a bit more, but people were still watching. He prowled along, not deigning to look at any of the gawkers. She couldn't tell if she was impressed or revolted.

She followed the Fae warrior into the bright street and through the bustling city. He was heedless of the humans who paused their working and walking and milling about to stare. He certainly didn't wait for her to catch up as he strode up to a pair of ordinary mares tied by a trough in a nondescript square. If memory served her correctly, the Fae usually possessed far finer horses. He had probably arrived in another form and purchased these here.

All Fae possessed a secondary animal form. Celaena was currently in hers, her mortal human body as animal as the birds wheeling above. But what was his? He could have been a wolf, she thought, with that layered surcoat that flowed to midthigh like a pelt, his footfalls so silent. Or a mountain cat, with that predatory grace.

He mounted the larger of the mares, leaving her to the piebald beast that looked more interested in seeking out a quick meal than trekking across the land. That made two of them. But they'd gone far enough without any explanation.

She stuffed her satchel into a saddlebag, angling her hands so that her sleeves hid the narrow bands of scars on her wrists, reminders of where the manacles had been. Where *she* had been. It was none of his business. None of Maeve's business, either. The less they knew about her, the less they could use against her. "I've known a few brooding warrior-types in my day, but I think you might be the broodiest of them all." He whipped his head to her, and she drawled, "Oh, hello. I think you know who I am, so I won't bother introducing myself. But before I'm carted off to gods-know-where, I'd like to know who *you* are."

His lips thinned. He surveyed the square—where people were now watching. And everyone instantly found somewhere else to be.

When they'd scattered, he said, "You've gathered enough about me at this point to have learned what you need to know." He spoke the common tongue, and his accent was subtle—lovely, if she was feeling generous enough to admit it. A soft, rolling purr.

"Fair enough. But what am I to call you?" She gripped the saddle but didn't mount it.

"Rowan." His tattoo seemed to soak up the sun, so dark it looked freshly inked.

"Well, Rowan—" Oh, he did *not* like her tone one bit. His eyes narrowed slightly in warning, but she went on, "Dare I ask where we're going?" She had to be drunk—still drunk or descending to a new level of apathy—if she was talking to him like this. But she couldn't stop, even as the gods or the Wyrd or the threads of fate readied to shove her back toward her original plan of action.

"I'm taking you where you've been summoned."

As long as she got to see Maeve and ask her questions, she didn't particularly care how she got to Doranelle—or whom she traveled with.

Do what has to be done, Elena had told her. In her usual fashion, Elena had omitted to specify *what* had to be done once she arrived in Wendlyn. At least this was better than eating flatbread and drinking wine and being mistaken for a vagrant. Perhaps she could be on a boat back to Adarlan within three weeks, possessing the answers that would solve everything.

It should have energized her. But instead she found herself silently mounting her mare, out of words and the will to use them. Just the past few minutes of interaction had drained her completely.

It was better that Rowan didn't seem inclined to speak as she followed him out of the city. The guards merely waved them through the walls, some even backing away.

As they rode on, Rowan didn't ask why she was here and what she'd been doing for the past ten years while the world had gone to hell. He pulled his pale hood over his silver hair and moved ahead, though it was still easy enough to mark him as different, as a warrior and law unto himself.

If he was truly as old as she suspected, she was likely little more than a speck of dust to him, a fizzle of life in the long-burning fire of his immortality. He could probably kill her without a second thought—and then move on to his next task, utterly untroubled by ending her existence.

It didn't unnerve her as much as it should have.

3

For a month now, it had been the same dream. Every night, over and over, until Chaol could see it in his waking hours.

Archer Finn groaning as Celaena shoved her dagger up through his ribs and into his heart. She embraced the handsome courtesan like a lover, but when she gazed over Archer's shoulder, her eyes were dead. Hollow.

The dream shifted, and Chaol could say nothing, do nothing as the golden-brown hair darkened to black and the agonized face wasn't Archer's but Dorian's.

The Crown Prince jerked, and Celaena held him tighter, twisting the dagger one final time before she let Dorian slump to the gray stones of the tunnel. Dorian's blood was already pooling—too fast. But Chaol still couldn't move, couldn't go to his friend or the woman he loved.

The wounds on Dorian multiplied, and there was blood—so much blood. He knew these wounds. Though he'd never seen the body, he'd combed through the reports detailing what Celaena had done to the rogue assassin Grave in that alley, the way she'd butchered him for killing Nehemia.

Celaena lowered her dagger, each drop of blood from its gleaming blade sending ripples through the pool already around her. She tipped back her head, breathing in deep. Breathing in the death before her, taking it into her soul, vengeance and ecstasy mingling at the slaughter of her enemy. Her true enemy. The Havilliard Empire.

The dream shifted again, and Chaol was pinned beneath her as she writhed above him, her head still thrown back, that same expression of ecstasy written across her blood-splattered face.

Enemy. Lover.

Queen.

The memory of the dream splintered as Chaol blinked at Dorian, who was sitting beside him at their old table in the Great Hall—and waiting for an answer to whatever he had said. Chaol gave an apologetic wince.

The Crown Prince didn't return Chaol's half smile. Instead, Dorian quietly said, "You were thinking about her."

Chaol took a bite from his lamb stew but tasted nothing. Dorian was too observant for his own good. And Chaol had no interest in talking about Celaena. Not with Dorian, not with anyone. The truth he knew about her could jeopardize more lives than hers.

"I was thinking about my father," Chaol lied. "When he returns to Anielle in a few weeks, I'm to go with him." It was the price for getting Celaena to the safety of Wendlyn: his father's support in exchange for his return to the Silver Lake to take up his title as the heir of Anielle. And he'd been willing to make that sacrifice; he'd make any sacrifice to keep Celaena and her secrets safe. Even now that he knew who—

what she was. Even after she'd told him about the king and the Wyrdkeys. If this was the price he had to pay, so be it.

Dorian glanced toward the high table, where the king and Chaol's father dined. The Crown Prince should have been eating with them, but he'd chosen to sit with Chaol instead. It was the first time Dorian had done so in ages—the first time they had spoken since their tense conversation after the decision was made to send Celaena to Wendlyn.

Dorian would understand if he knew the truth. But Dorian couldn't know who and what Celaena was, or what the king was truly planning. The potential for disaster was too high. And Dorian's own secrets were deadly enough.

"I heard the rumors you were to go," Dorian said warily. "I didn't realize they were true."

Chaol nodded, trying to find something—anything—to say to his friend.

They still hadn't spoken of the other thing between them, the other bit of truth that had come out that night in the tunnels: Dorian had magic. Chaol didn't want to know anything about it. If the king decided to interrogate him . . . he hoped he'd hold out, if it ever came to that. The king, he knew, had far darker methods of extracting information than torture. So he hadn't asked, hadn't said one word. And neither had Dorian.

He met Dorian's gaze. There was nothing kind in it. But Dorian said, "I'm trying, Chaol."

Trying, because Chaol's not consulting him on the plan to get Celaena out of Adarlan had been a breach of trust, and one that shamed him, though Dorian could never know that, either. "I know."

"And despite what happened, I'm fairly certain we're not enemies." Dorian's mouth quirked to the side.

You will always be my enemy. Celaena had screamed those words at Chaol the night Nehemia had died. Screamed it with ten years' worth of conviction and hatred, a decade spent holding the world's greatest secret so deep within her that she'd become another person entirely.

Because Celaena was Aelin Ashryver Galathynius, heir to the throne and rightful Queen of Terrasen.

It made her his mortal enemy. It made her Dorian's enemy. Chaol still didn't know what to do about it, or what it meant for them, for the life he'd imagined for them. The future he'd once dreamed of was irrevocably gone.

He'd seen the deadness in her eyes that night in the tunnels, along with the wrath and exhaustion and sorrow. He'd seen her go over the edge when Nehemia died, and knew what she'd done to Grave in retribution. He didn't doubt for one heartbeat that she could snap again. There was such glittering darkness in her, an endless rift straight through her core.

Nehemia's death had shattered her. What *he* had done, his role in that death, had shattered her, too. He knew that. He just prayed that she could piece herself back together again. Because a broken, unpredictable assassin was one thing. But a queen . . .

"You look like you're going to be sick," Dorian said, bracing his forearms on the table. "Tell me what's wrong."

Chaol had been staring at nothing again. For a heartbeat, the weight of everything pressed so heavily upon him that he opened up his mouth.

But the boom of swords striking shields in salute echoed from the hallway, and Aedion Ashryver—the King of Adarlan's infamous General of the North and cousin to Aelin Galathynius—stalked into the Great Hall.

The hall fell silent, including his father and the king at the high table. Before Aedion was halfway across the room, Chaol was positioned at the bottom of the dais.

It wasn't that the young general was a threat. Rather, it was the way Aedion prowled toward the king's table, his shoulder-length golden hair gleaming in the torchlight as he smirked at them all.

Handsome was a light way of describing what Aedion was. Overwhelming was more like it. Towering and heavily muscled, Aedion was every inch the warrior rumor claimed him to be. Even though his clothes were mostly for function, Chaol could tell that the leather of his light armor was of fine make and exquisitely detailed. A white wolf pelt was slung across his broad shoulders, and a round shield had been strapped to his back—along with an ancient-looking sword.

But his face. And his eyes . . . Holy gods.

Chaol put a hand on his sword, schooling his features to remain neutral, disinterested, even as the Wolf of the North came close enough to slaughter him.

They were Celaena's eyes. Ashryver eyes. A stunning turquoise with a core of gold as bright as their hair. Their hair—even the shade of it was the same. They could have been twins, if Aedion weren't twenty-four and tanned from years in the snow-bright mountains of Terrasen.

Why had the king bothered to keep Aedion alive all those years ago? Why bother to forge him into one of his fiercest generals? Aedion was a prince of the Ashryver royal line and had been raised in the Galathynius household—and yet he served the king.

Aedion's grin remained as he stopped before the high table and sketched a bow shallow enough that Chaol was momentarily stunned. "Majesty," the general said, those damning eyes alight.

Chaol looked at the high table to see if the king, if anyone, noticed the similarities that could doom not only Aedion but also Chaol and Dorian and everyone he cared about. His father just gave him a small, satisfied smile.

But the king was frowning. "I expected you a month ago."

Aedion actually had the nerve to shrug. "Apologies. The Staghorns were slammed with a final winter storm. I left when I could."

Every person in the hall held their breath. Aedion's temper and insolence were near-legendary—part of the reason he was stationed in the far reaches of the North. Chaol had always thought it wise to keep him far from Rifthold, especially as Aedion seemed to be a bit of a two-faced bastard, and the Bane—Aedion's legion—was notorious for its skill and brutality, but now . . . why had the king summoned him to the capital?

The king picked up his goblet, swirling the wine inside. "I didn't receive word that your legion was here."

"They're not."

Chaol braced for the execution order, praying he wouldn't be the one to do it. The king said, "I told you to bring them, General."

"Here I was, thinking you wanted the pleasure of my company." When the king growled, Aedion said, "They'll be here within a week or so. I didn't want to miss any of the fun." Aedion again shrugged those massive shoulders. "At least I didn't come empty-handed." He snapped his fingers behind him and a page rushed in, bearing a large satchel. "Gifts from the North, courtesy of the last rebel camp we sacked. You'll enjoy them."

The king rolled his eyes and waved a hand at the page. "Send them to my chambers. Your *gifts*, Aedion, tend to offend polite company." A low chuckle—from Aedion, from some men at the king's table. Oh, Aedion was dancing a dangerous line. At least Celaena had the good sense to keep her mouth shut around the king.

Considering the trophies the king had collected from Celaena as Champion, the items in that satchel wouldn't be mere gold and jewels. But to collect heads and limbs from Aedion's own people, Celaena's people . . .

"I have a council meeting tomorrow; I want you there, General," the king said.

Aedion put a hand on his chest. "Your will is mine, Majesty."

Chaol had to clamp down on his terror as he beheld what glinted on Aedion's finger. A black ring—the same that the king, Perrington, and most of those under their control wore. *That* explained why the king allowed the insolence: when it came down to it, the king's will truly was Aedion's.

Chaol kept his face blank as the king gave him a curt nod—dismissal. Chaol silently bowed, now all too eager to get back to his table. Away from the king—from the man who held the fate of their world in his bloodied hands. Away from his father, who saw too much. Away from the general, who was now making his rounds through the hall, clapping men on the shoulder, winking at women.

Chaol had mastered the horror roiling in his gut by the time he sank back into his seat and found Dorian frowning. "Gifts indeed," the prince muttered. "Gods, he's insufferable."

Chaol didn't disagree. Despite the king's black ring, Aedion still seemed to have a mind of his own—and was as wild off the battlefield as he was on it. He usually made Dorian look like a celibate when it came to finding debauched ways to amuse himself. Chaol had never spent much time with Aedion, nor wanted to, but Dorian had known him for some time now. Since—

They'd met as children. When Dorian and his father had visited Terrasen in the days before the royal family was slaughtered. When Dorian had met Aelin—met Celaena.

It was good that Celaena wasn't here to see what Aedion had become. Not just because of the ring. To turn on your own people—

Aedion slid onto the bench across from them, grinning. A predator assessing prey. "You two were sitting at this same table the last time I saw you. Good to know some things don't change."

Gods, that face. It was Celaena's face—the other side of the coin. The same arrogance, the same unchecked anger. But where Celaena crackled with it, Aedion seemed to . . . pulse. And there was something nastier, far more bitter in Aedion's face.

Dorian rested his forearms on the table and gave a lazy smile. "Hello, Aedion."

Aedion ignored him and reached for a roast leg of lamb, his black ring glinting. "I like the new scar, Captain," he said, jerking his chin toward the slender white line across Chaol's cheek. The scar Celaena had given to him the night Nehemia died and she'd tried to kill him—now a permanent reminder of everything he'd lost. Aedion went on, "Looks like they didn't chew you up just yet. And they finally gave you a big-boy sword, too."

Dorian said, "I'm glad to see that storm didn't dim your spirits."

"Weeks inside with nothing to do but train and bed women? It was a miracle I bothered to come down from the mountains."

"I didn't realize you bothered to do anything unless it served your best interests."

A low laugh. "There's that charming Havilliard spirit." Aedion dug into his meal, and Chaol was about to demand why he was bothering to sit with them—other than to torment them, as he'd always liked to do when the king wasn't looking—when he noticed that Dorian was staring.

Not at Aedion's sheer size or armor, but at his face, at his eyes . . .

"Shouldn't you be at some party or other?" Chaol said to Aedion. "I'm surprised you're lingering when your usual enticements await in the city."

"Is that your courtly way of asking for an invitation to my gathering tomorrow, Captain? Surprising. You've always implied that you were above my sort of party." Those turquoise eyes narrowed and he gave Dorian a sly grin. "You, however—the last party I threw worked out *very* well for you. Redheaded twins, if I recall correctly."

"You'll be disappointed to learn I've moved on from that sort of existence," Dorian said.

Aedion dug back into his meal. "More for me, then."

Chaol clenched his fists under the table. Celaena had not exactly been virtuous in the past ten years, but she'd never killed a natural-born citizen of Terrasen. Had refused to, actually. And Aedion had always been a gods-damned bastard, but now . . . Did he know what he wore on his finger? Did he know that despite his arrogance, his defiance and insolence, the king could *make* him bend to his will whenever he pleased? He couldn't warn Aedion, not without potentially getting himself and everyone he cared about killed should Aedion truly have allegiance to the king.

"How are things in Terrasen?" Chaol asked, because Dorian was studying Aedion again.

"What would you like me to tell you? That we are well-fed after a brutal winter? That we did not lose many to sickness?" Aedion snorted. "I suppose hunting rebels is always fun, if you've a taste for it. Hopefully His Majesty has summoned the Bane to the South to finally give them some real action." As Aedion reached for the water, Chaol glimpsed the hilt of his sword. Dull metal flecked with dings and scratches, its pommel nothing more than a bit of cracked, rounded horn. Such a simple, plain sword for one of the greatest warriors in Erilea.

"The Sword of Orynth," Aedion drawled. "A gift from His Majesty upon my first victory."

Everyone knew that sword. It had been an heirloom of Terrasen's royal family, passed from ruler to ruler. By right, it was Celaena's. It had belonged to her father. For Aedion to possess it, considering what that sword now did, the lives it took, was a slap in the face to Celaena and to her family.

"I'm surprised you bother with such sentimentality," Dorian said.

"Symbols have power, Prince," Aedion said, pinning him with a stare. Celaena's stare—unyielding and alive with challenge. "You'd be surprised by the power this still wields in the North—what it does to convince people not to pursue foolhardy plans."

Perhaps Celaena's skills and cunning weren't unusual in her bloodline. But Aedion was an Ashryver, not a Galathynius—which meant that his great-grandmother had been Mab, one of the three Fae-Queens, in recent generations crowned a goddess and renamed Deanna, Lady of the Hunt. Chaol swallowed hard.

Silence fell, taut as a bowstring. "Trouble between you two?" Aedion asked, biting into his meat. "Let me guess: a woman. The King's Champion, perhaps? Rumor has it she's . . . interesting. Is that why you've moved on from my sort of fun, princeling?" He scanned the hall. "I'd like to meet her, I think."

Chaol fought the urge to grip his sword. "She's away."

Aedion instead gave Dorian a cruel smile. "Pity. Perhaps she might have convinced me to move on as well."

"Mind your mouth," Chaol snarled. He might have laughed had he not wanted to strangle the general so badly. Dorian merely drummed his fingers on the table. "And show some respect."

Aedion chuckled, finishing off the lamb. "I am His Majesty's faithful servant, as I have always been." Those Ashryver eyes once more settled on Dorian. "Perhaps I'll be your whore someday, too."

"If you're still alive by then," Dorian purred.

Aedion went on eating, but Chaol could still feel his relentless focus pinned on them. "Rumor has it a Matron of a witch clan was killed on the premises not too long ago," Aedion said casually. "She vanished, though her quarters indicated she'd put up a hell of a fight."

Dorian said sharply, "What's your interest in that?"

"I make it my business to know when the power brokers of the realm meet their end."

A shiver spider-walked down Chaol's spine. He knew little about the witches. Celaena had told him a few stories—and he'd always prayed they were exaggerated. But something like dread flickered across Dorian's face.

Chaol leaned forward. "It's none of your concern."

Aedion again ignored him and winked at the prince. Dorian's

nostrils flared, the only sign of the rage that was rising to the surface. That, and the air in the room shifted—brisker. Magic.

Chaol put a hand on his friend's shoulder. "We're going to be late," he lied, but Dorian caught it. He had to get Dorian out—away from Aedion—and try to leash the disastrous storm that was brewing between the two men. "Rest well, Aedion." Dorian didn't bother saying anything, his sapphire eyes frozen.

Aedion smirked. "The party's tomorrow in Rifthold if you feel like reliving the good old days, Prince." Oh, the general knew exactly what buttons to push, and he didn't give a damn what a mess it made. It made him dangerous—deadly.

Especially where Dorian and his magic were concerned. Chaol forced himself to say good night to some of his men, to look casual and unconcerned as they walked from the dining hall. Aedion Ashryver had come to Rifthold, narrowly missing running into his long-lost cousin.

If Aedion knew Aelin was still alive, if he knew who and what she had become or what she had learned regarding the king's secret power, would he stand with her, or destroy her? Given his actions, given the ring he bore . . . Chaol didn't want the general anywhere near her. Anywhere near Terrasen, either.

He wondered how much blood would spill when Celaena learned what her cousin had done.

Chaol and Dorian walked in silence for most of the trek to the prince's tower. When they turned down an empty hallway and were certain no one could overhear them, Dorian said, "I didn't need you to step in."

"Aedion's a bastard," Chaol growled. The conversation could end there, and part of him was tempted to let it, but he made himself say, "I was worried you'd snap. Like you did in the passages." He loosed a tight breath. "Are you . . . stable?"

"Some days are better than others. Getting angry or frightened seems to set it off."

They entered the hallway that ended in the arched wooden door to Dorian's tower, but Chaol stopped him with an arm on his shoulder. "I don't want details," he murmured so the guards posted outside Dorian's door couldn't hear, "because I don't want my knowledge used against you. I know I've made mistakes, Dorian. Believe me, I know. But my priority has always been—and still is—keeping you protected."

Dorian stared at him for a long moment, cocking his head to the side. Chaol must have looked as miserable as he felt, because the prince's voice was almost gentle as he said, "Why did you really send her to Wendlyn?"

Agony punched through him, raw and razor-edged. But as much as he yearned to tell the prince about Celaena, as much as he wanted to unload all his secrets so it would fill the hole in his core, he couldn't. So he just said, "I sent her to do what needs to be done," and strode back down the hall. Dorian didn't call after him.

4

Manon pulled her bloodred cloak tightly around herself and pressed into the shadows of the closet, listening to the three men who had broken into her cottage.

She'd tasted the rising fear and rage on the wind all day and had spent the afternoon preparing. She'd been sitting on the thatched roof of the whitewashed cottage when she spotted their torches bobbing over the high grasses of the field. None of the villagers had tried to stop the three men—though none had joined them, either.

A Crochan witch had come to their little green valley in the north of Fenharrow, they'd said. In the weeks that she'd been living amongst them, carving out a miserable existence, she'd been waiting for this night. It was the same at every village she'd lived in or visited.

She held her breath, keeping still as a deer as one of the men—a tall, bearded farmer with hands the size of dinner plates—stepped into her bedroom. Even from the closet, she could smell the ale on his breath—and the bloodlust. Oh, the villagers knew exactly what they planned to do with the witch who sold potions and charms from her back door, and who could predict the sex of a babe before it was due. She was surprised it had taken these men so long to work up the nerve to come here, to torment and then destroy what petrified them.

The farmer stopped in the middle of the room. "We know you're here," he coaxed, even as he stepped toward the bed, scanning every inch of the room. "We just want to talk. Some of the townsfolk are spooked, you see—more scared of you than you are of them, I bet."

She knew better than to listen, especially as a dagger glinted behind his back while he peered under the bed. Always the same, at every backwater town and uptight mortal village.

As the man straightened, Manon slipped from the closet and into the darkness behind the bedroom door.

Muffled clinking and thudding told her enough about what the other two men were doing: not just looking for her, but stealing whatever they wanted. There wasn't much to take; the cottage had already been furnished when she'd arrived, and all her belongings, by training and instinct, were in a sack in the corner of the closet she'd just vacated. Take nothing with you, leave nothing behind.

"We just want to talk, witch." The man turned from the bed, finally noticing the closet. He smiled—in triumph, in anticipation.

With gentle fingers, Manon eased the bedroom door shut, so quietly the man didn't notice as he headed for the closet. She'd oiled the hinges on every door in this house.

His massive hand gripped the closet doorknob, dagger now angled at his side. "Come out, little Crochan," he crooned.

Silent as death, Manon slid up behind him. The fool didn't even know she was there until she brought her mouth close to his ear and whispered, "Wrong kind of witch."

The man whirled, slamming into the closet door. He raised the dagger between them, his chest heaving. Manon merely smiled, her silver-white hair glinting in the moonlight.

He noticed the shut door then, drawing in breath to shout. But Manon smiled broader, and a row of dagger-sharp iron teeth pushed from the slits high in her gums, snapping down like armor. The man started, hitting the door behind him again, eyes so wide that white shone all around them. His dagger clattered on the floorboards.

And then, just to really make him soil his pants, she flicked her wrists in the air between them. The iron claws shot over her nails in a stinging, gleaming flash.

The man began whispering a plea to his soft-hearted gods as Manon let him back toward the lone window. Let him think he stood a chance while she stalked toward him, still smiling. The man didn't even scream before she ripped out his throat.

When she was done with him, she slipped through the bedroom door. The two men were still looting, still believing that all of this belonged to her. It had merely been an abandoned house—its previous owners dead or smart enough to leave this festering place.

The second man also didn't get the chance to scream before she gutted him with two swipes of her iron nails. But the third farmer came looking for his companions. And when he beheld her standing there, one hand twisted in his friend's insides, the other holding him to her as she used her iron teeth to tear out his throat, he ran.

The common, watery taste of the man, laced with violence and fear, coated her tongue, and she spat onto the wooden floorboards. But Manon didn't bother wiping away the blood slipping down her chin as she gave the remaining farmer a head start into the field of towering winter grass, so high that it was well over their heads.

She counted to ten, because she wanted to hunt, and had been that way since she tore through her mother's womb and came roaring and bloody into this world.

Because she was Manon Blackbeak, heir to the Blackbeak Witch-Clan, and she had been here for weeks, pretending to be a Crochan witch in the hope that it would flush out the real ones.

They were still out there, the self-righteous, insufferable Crochans, hiding as healers and wise-women. Her first, glorious kill had been a Crochan, no more than sixteen—the same age as Manon at the time. The dark-haired girl had been wearing the bloodred cloak that all Crochans were gifted upon their first bleeding—and the only good it had done was mark her as prey.

After Manon left the Crochan's corpse in that snow-blasted mountain pass, she'd taken the cloak as a trophy—and still wore it, over a hundred years later. No other Ironteeth witch could have done it—because no other Ironteeth witch would have dared incur the wrath of the three Matrons by wearing their eternal enemy's color. But from the day Manon stalked into Blackbeak Keep wearing the cloak and holding that Crochan heart in a box—a gift for her grandmother—it had been her sacred duty to hunt them down, one by one, until there were none left.

This was her latest rotation—six months in Fenharrow while the rest of her coven was spread through Melisande and northern Eyllwe under similar orders. But in the months that she'd prowled from village to village, she hadn't discovered a single Crochan. These farmers were the first bit of fun she'd had in weeks. And she would be damned if she didn't enjoy it.

Manon walked into the field, sucking the blood off her nails as she went. She slipped through the grasses, no more than shadow and mist.

She found the farmer lost in the middle of the field, softly bleating with fear. And when he turned, his bladder loosening at the sight of the blood and the iron teeth and the wicked, wicked smile, Manon let him scream all he wanted.

5

Celaena and Rowan rode down the dusty road that meandered between the boulder-spotted grasslands and into the southern foothills. She'd memorized enough maps of Wendlyn to know that they'd pass through them and then over the towering Cambrian Mountains that marked the border between mortal-ruled Wendlyn and the immortal lands of Queen Maeve.

The sun was setting as they ascended the foothills, the road growing rockier, bordered on one side by rather harrowing ravines. For a mile, she debated asking Rowan where he planned to stop for the night. But she was tired. Not just from the day, or the wine, or the riding.

In her bones, in her blood and breath and soul, she was so, so tired. Talking to anyone was too taxing. Which made Rowan the perfect companion: he didn't say a single word to her.

Twilight fell as the road brought them through a dense forest that spread into and over the mountains, the trees turning from cypress to oak, from narrow to tall and proud, full of thickets and scattered mossy boulders. Even in the growing dark, the forest seemed to be breathing. The warm air hummed, leaving a metallic taste coating her tongue. Far behind them, thunder grumbled.

Wouldn't that be wonderful. Especially since Rowan was finally dismounting to make camp. From the look of his saddlebags, he didn't have a tent. Or bedrolls. Or blankets.

Perhaps it was now fair to assume that her visit with Maeve wasn't to be pleasant.

Neither of them spoke as they led their horses into the trees, just far enough off the road to be hidden from any passing travelers. Dumping their gear at the camp he'd selected, Rowan brought his mare to a nearby stream he must have heard with those pointed ears. He didn't falter one step in the growing dark, though Celaena certainly stubbed her toes against a few rocks and roots. Excellent eyesight, even in the dark—another Fae trait. One she could have if she—

No, she wasn't going to think about that. Not after what had happened on the other side of that portal. She'd shifted then—and it had been awful enough to remind her that she had no interest in ever doing it again.

After the horses drank, Rowan didn't wait for her as he took both mares back to the camp. She used the privacy to see to her own needs, then dropped to her knees on the grassy bank and drank her fill of the stream. Gods, the water tasted . . . new and ancient and powerful and delicious.

She drank until she understood the hole in her belly might very well be from hunger, then staggered back to camp, finding it by the gleam of Rowan's silver hair. He wordlessly handed her some bread and cheese, then returned to rubbing down the horses. She muttered a thank-you, but didn't bother offering to help as she plunked down against a towering oak.

When her belly had stopped hurting so much and she realized just how loudly she'd been munching on the apple he'd also tossed her while feeding the horses, she mustered enough energy to say, "Are there so many threats in Wendlyn that we can't risk a fire?"

He sat against a tree and stretched his legs, crossing his ankles. "Not from mortals."

His first words to her since they'd left the city. It could have been an attempt to spook her, but she still did a mental inventory of all the weapons she carried. She wouldn't ask. Didn't want to know what manner of thing might crawl toward a fire.

The tangle of wood and moss and stone loomed, full of the rustling of heavy leaves, the gurgling of the swollen brook, the flapping of feathered wings. And there, lurking over the rim of a nearby boulder, were three sets of small, glowing eyes.

The hilt of her dagger was in her palm a heartbeat later. But they just stared at her. Rowan didn't seem to notice. He only leaned his head against the oak trunk.

They had always known her, the Little Folk. Even when Adarlan's shadow had covered the continent, they still recognized what she was. Small gifts left at campsites—a fresh fish, a leaf full of blackberries, a crown of flowers. She'd ignored them, and stayed out of Oakwald Forest as much as she could.

The faeries kept their unblinking vigil. Wishing she hadn't downed the food so quickly, Celaena watched them back, ready to spring to a defensive position. Rowan hadn't moved.

What ancient oaths the faeries honored in Terrasen might be disregarded here. Even as she thought it, more eyes glowed between the trees. More silent witnesses to her arrival. Because Celaena was Fae, or something like a mongrel. Her great-grandmother had been Maeve's sister, proclaimed a goddess when she died. Ridiculous, really. Mab had been very much mortal when she tied her life to the human prince who loved her so fiercely.

She wondered how much these creatures knew about the wars that had destroyed her land, about the Fae and faeries that had been hunted down, about the burning of the ancient forests and the butchering of the sacred stags of Terrasen. She wondered if they had ever learned what became of their brethren in the West.

She didn't know how she found it in herself to care. But they seemed so . . . curious. Surprising even herself, Celaena whispered into the humming night, "They still live."

All those eyes vanished. When she glanced at Rowan, he hadn't opened his eyes. But she had the sense that the warrior had been aware the entire time.

6

Dorian Havilliard stood before his father's breakfast table, his hands held behind his back. The king had arrived moments ago but hadn't told him to sit. Once Dorian might have already said something about it. But having magic, getting drawn into whatever mess Celaena was in, seeing that other world in the secret tunnels . . . all of that had changed everything. The best he could do these days was maintain a low profile—to keep his father or anyone else from looking too long in his direction. So Dorian stood before the table and waited.

The King of Adarlan finished off the roast chicken and sipped from whatever was in his bloodred glass. "You're quiet this morning, Prince." The conqueror of Erilea reached for a platter of smoked fish.

"I was waiting for you to speak, Father."

Night-black eyes shifted toward him. "Unusual, indeed."

Dorian tensed. Only Celaena and Chaol knew the truth about his magic—and Chaol had shut him out so completely that Dorian didn't feel like attempting to explain himself to his friend. But this castle was full of spies and sycophants who wanted nothing more than to use whatever knowledge they could to advance their position. Including selling out their Crown Prince. Who knew who'd seen him in the hallways or the library, or who had discovered that stack of books he'd hidden in Celaena's rooms? He'd since moved them down to the tomb, where he went every other night—not for answers to the questions that plagued him but just for an hour of pure silence.

His father resumed eating. He'd been in his father's private chambers only a few times in his life. They could be a manor house of their own, with their library and dining room and council chamber. They occupied an entire wing of the glass castle—a wing opposite from Dorian's mother. His parents had never shared a bed, and he didn't particularly want to know more than that.

He found his father watching him, the morning sun through the curved wall of glass making every scar and nick on the king's face even more gruesome. "You're to entertain Aedion Ashryver today."

Dorian kept his composure as best he could. "Dare I ask why?"

"Since General Ashryver failed to bring his men here, it appears he has some spare time while awaiting the Bane's arrival. It would be beneficial to you both to become better acquainted—especially when your choice of friends of late has been so . . . common."

The cold fury of his magic clawed its way up his spine. "With all due respect, Father, I have two meetings to prepare for, and—"

"It's not open for debate." His father kept eating. "General Ashryver has been notified, and you will meet him outside your chambers at noon."

Dorian knew he should keep quiet, but he found himself asking, "Why do you tolerate Aedion? Why keep him alive—why make him a general?" He'd been unable to stop wondering about it since the man's arrival.

His father gave a small, knowing smile. "Because Aedion's rage is a useful blade, and he is capable of keeping his people in line. He will not risk their slaughter, not when he has lost so much. He has quelled many a would-be rebellion in the North from that fear, for he is well aware that it would be his own people—the civilians—who suffered first."

He shared *blood* with a man this cruel. But Dorian said, "It's still surprising that you'd keep a general almost as a captive—as little more than a slave. Controlling him through fear alone seems potentially dangerous."

Indeed, he wondered if his father had told Aedion about Celaena's mission to Wendlyn—homeland of Aedion's royal bloodline, where Aedion's cousins the Ashryvers still ruled. Though Aedion trumpeted about his various victories over rebels and acted like he practically owned half the empire himself . . . How much did Aedion remember of his kin across the sea?

His father said, "I have my ways of leashing Aedion should I need to. For now, his brazen irreverence amuses me." His father jerked his chin toward the door. "I will not be amused, however, if you miss your appointment with him today."

And just like that, his father fed him to the Wolf.

Despite Dorian's offers to show Aedion the menagerie, the kennels, the stables—even the damned library—the general only wanted to do one thing: walk through the gardens. Aedion claimed he was feeling restless and sluggish from too much food the night before, but the smile he gave Dorian suggested otherwise.

Aedion didn't bother talking to him, too preoccupied with humming bawdy tunes and inspecting the various women they passed. He'd dropped the half-civilized veneer only once, when they'd been striding down a narrow path flanked by towering rosebushes—stunning in the summer, but deadly in the winter—and the guards had been a turn behind, blind for the moment. Just enough time for Aedion to subtly trip Dorian into one of the thorny walls, still humming his lewd songs.

A quick maneuver had kept Dorian from falling face-first into the thorns, but his cloak had ripped, and his hand stung. Rather than give the general the satisfaction of seeing him hiss and inspect his cuts, Dorian had tucked his barking, freezing fingers into his pockets as the guards rounded the corner.

They spoke only when Aedion paused by a fountain and braced his scarred hands on his hips, assessing the garden beyond as though it were a battlefield. Aedion smirked at the six guards lurking behind, his eyes bright—so bright, Dorian thought, and so strangely familiar as the general said, "A prince needs an escort in his own palace? I'm insulted they didn't send more guards to protect you from me."

"You think you could take six men?"

The Wolf had let out a low chuckle and shrugged, the scarred hilt of the Sword of Orynth catching the near-blinding sunlight. "I don't think I should tell you, in case your father ever decides my usefulness is not worth my temperament."

Some of the guards behind them murmured, but Dorian said, "Probably not."

And that was it—that was all Aedion said to him for the rest of the cold, miserable walk. Until the general gave him an edged smile and said, "Better get that looked at." That was when Dorian realized his right hand was still bleeding. Aedion just turned away. "Thanks for the walk, Prince," the general said over his shoulder, and it felt more like a threat than anything.

Aedion didn't act without a reason. Perhaps the general had convinced his father to force this excursion. But for what purpose, Dorian couldn't grasp. Unless Aedion merely wanted to get a feel for what sort of man Dorian had become and how well Dorian could play the game. He wouldn't put it past the warrior to have done it just to assess a potential ally or threat—Aedion, for all his arrogance, had a cunning mind. He probably viewed court life as another sort of battlefield.

Dorian let Chaol's hand-selected guards lead him back into the wonderfully warm castle, then dismissed them with a nod. Chaol hadn't come today, and he was grateful—after that conversation about his magic, after Chaol refused to speak about Celaena, Dorian wasn't sure what else was left for them to talk about. He didn't believe for one moment that Chaol would willingly sanction the deaths of innocent men, no matter whether they were friends or enemies. Chaol had to know, then, that Celaena wouldn't assassinate the Ashryver royals, for whatever reasons of her own. But there was no point in bothering to talk to Chaol, not when his friend was keeping secrets, too.

Dorian mulled over his friend's puzzle-box of words again as he walked into the healers' catacombs, the smell of rosemary and mint wafting past. It was a warren of supply and examination rooms, kept far from the prying eyes of the glass castle high above. There *was* another ward high in the glass castle, for those who wouldn't deign to make the trek down here, but this was where the best healers in Rifthold—and Adarlan—had honed and practiced their craft for a thousand years. The pale stones seemed to breathe the essence of centuries of drying herbs, giving the subterranean halls a pleasant, open feeling.

Dorian found a small workroom where a young woman was hunched over a large oak table, a variety of glass jars, scales, mortars, and pestles before her, along with vials of liquid, hanging herbs, and bubbling pots over small, solitary flames. The healing arts were one of the few that his father hadn't completely outlawed ten years ago—though once, he'd heard, they'd been even more powerful. Once, healers had used magic to mend and save. Now they were left with whatever nature provided them.

Dorian stepped into the room and the young woman looked up from the book she was scanning, a finger pausing on the page. Not beautiful, but—pretty. Clean, elegant lines, chestnut hair woven in a braid, and golden-tan skin that suggested at least one family member came from Eyllwe. "Can I—" She got a good look at him, then, and dropped into a bow. "Your Highness," she said, a flush creeping up the smooth column of her neck.

Dorian held up his bloodied hand. "Thornbush." *Rosebush* made his cuts seem that much more pathetic.

She kept her eyes averted, biting her full bottom lip. "Of course." She gestured a slender hand toward the wooden chair before the table. "Please. Unless—unless you'd rather go to a proper examination room?"

Dorian normally hated dealing with the stammering and scrambling, but this young woman was still so red, so soft-spoken that he said, "This is fine," and slid into the chair.

The silence lay heavy on him as she hurried through the workroom, first changing her dirty white apron, then washing her hands for a good long minute, then gathering all manner of bandages and tins of salve, then a bowl of hot water and clean rags, and then finally, finally pulling a chair around the table to face his.

They didn't speak, either, when she carefully washed and then examined his hand. But he found himself watching her hazel eyes, the sureness of her fingers, and the blush that remained on her neck and face. "The hand is—very complex," she murmured at last, studying the cuts. "I just wanted to make sure that nothing was damaged and that there weren't any thorns lodged in there." She swiftly added, "Your Highness."

"I think it looks worse than it actually is."

With a feather-light touch, she smeared a cloudy salve on his hand, and, like a damn fool, he winced. "Sorry," she mumbled. "It's to disinfect the cuts. Just in case." She seemed to curl in on herself, as if he'd give the order to hang her merely for that.

He fumbled for the words, then said, "I've dealt with worse."

It sounded stupid coming out, and she paused for a moment before reaching for the bandages. "I know," she said, and glanced up at him.

Well, damn. Weren't those eyes just stunning. She quickly looked back down, gently wrapping his hand. "I'm assigned to the southern wing of the castle—and I'm often on night duty."

That explained why she looked so familiar. She'd healed not only him that night a month ago but also Celaena, Chaol, Fleetfoot . . . had been there for *all* of their injuries these past seven months. "I'm sorry, I can't remember your name—"

"It's Sorscha," she said, though there was no anger in it, as there should have been. The spoiled prince and his entitled friends, too absorbed in their own lives to bother learning the name of the healer who had patched them up again and again.

She finished wrapping his hand and he said, "In case we didn't say it often enough, thank you."

Those green-flecked brown eyes lifted again. A tentative smile. "It's an honor, Prince." She began gathering up her supplies.

Taking that as his cue to leave, he stood and flexed his fingers. "Feels good."

"They're minor wounds, but keep an eye on them." Sorscha dumped the bloodied water down the sink in the back of the room. "And you needn't come all the way down here the next time. Just—just send word, Your Highness. We're happy to attend to you." She curtsied low, with the long-limbed grace of a dancer.

"You've been responsible for the southern stone wing all this time?" The question within the question was clear enough: *You've seen everything? Every inexplicable injury?*

"We keep records of our patients," Sorscha said softly—so no one else passing by the open doorway could hear. "But sometimes we forget to write down everything."

She hadn't told anyone what she'd seen, the things that didn't add up. Dorian gave her a swift bow of thanks and strode from the room. How many others, he wondered, had seen more than they let on? He didn't want to know.

Sorscha's fingers, thankfully, had stopped shaking by the time the Crown Prince left the catacombs. By some lingering grace of Silba, goddess of healers and bringer of peace—and gentle deaths—she'd managed to keep them from trembling while she patched up his hand, too. Sorscha leaned against the counter and loosed a long breath.

The cuts hadn't merited a bandage, but she'd been selfish and foolish and had wanted to keep the beautiful prince in that chair for as long as she could manage.

He didn't even know who she was.

She'd been appointed full healer a year ago, and had been called to attend to the prince, the captain, and their friend countless times. And the Crown Prince still had no idea who she was.

She hadn't lied to him—about failing to keep records of everything. But she remembered it all. Especially that night a month ago, when the three of them had been bloodied up and filthy, the girl's hound injured, too, with no explanation and no one raising a fuss. And the girl, their friend . . .

The King's Champion. That's who she was.

Lover, it seemed, of both the prince and his captain at one time or another. Sorscha had helped Amithy tend to the young woman after the brutal duel to win her title. Occasionally, she'd checked on the girl and found the prince holding her in bed.

She'd pretended it didn't matter, because the Crown Prince was notorious where women were involved, but . . . it hadn't stopped the sinking ache in her chest. Then things had changed, and when the girl was poisoned with gloriella, it was the captain who stayed with her. The captain who had acted like a beast in a cage, prowling the room until Sorscha's own nerves had been frayed. Not surprisingly, several weeks later, the girl's handmaid, Philippa, came to Sorscha for a contraceptive tonic. Philippa hadn't said whom it was for, but Sorscha wasn't an idiot.

When she'd attended the captain a week after that, four brutal scratches down his face and a dead look in his eyes, Sorscha had understood. And understood again the last time, when the prince, the captain, and the girl were all bloodied along with the hound, that whatever had existed between the three of them was broken.

The girl especially. *Celaena*, she'd heard them say accidentally when they thought she was already out of the room. Celaena Sardothien. World's greatest assassin and now the King's Champion. Another secret Sorscha would keep without them ever knowing.

She was invisible. And glad of it, most days.

Sorscha frowned at her table of supplies. She had half a dozen tonics and poultices to make before dinner, all of them complex, all of them dumped on her by Amithy, who pulled rank whenever she could. On top of it, she still had her weekly letter to write to her friend, who wanted every little detail about the palace. Just thinking of all the tasks gave her a headache.

Had it been anyone other than the prince, she would have told them to go find another healer.

Sorscha returned to her work. She was certain he'd forgotten her name the moment he left. Dorian was heir to the mightiest empire in the world, and Sorscha was the daughter of two dead immigrants from a village in Fenharrow that had been burned to ash—a village that no one would ever remember.

But that didn't stop her from loving him, as she still did, invisible and secret, ever since she'd first laid eyes on him six years ago.

7

Nothing else approached Celaena and Rowan after that first night. He certainly didn't say anything to her about it, or offer his cloak or any sort of protection against the chill. She slept curled on her side, turning every other minute from some root or pebble digging into her back or jolting awake at the screech of an owl—or something worse.

By the time the light had turned gray and mist drifted through the trees, Celaena felt more exhausted than she'd been the night before. After a silent breakfast of bread, cheese, and apples, she was nearly dozing atop her mare as they resumed their ride up the forested foothill road.

They passed few people—mostly humans leading wagons down to some market, all of whom glanced at Rowan and gave them the right of way. Some even muttered prayers for mercy.

She'd long heard the Fae existed peacefully with the humans in Wendlyn, so perhaps the terror they encountered was due to Rowan himself. The tattoo didn't help. She had debated asking him what the words meant, but that would involve talking. And talking meant building some sort of . . . relationship. She'd had enough of friends. Enough of them dying, too.

So she'd kept her mouth shut the entire day they rode through the woods up into the Cambrian Mountains. The forest turned lusher and denser, and the higher they rode, the mistier it became, great veils of fog drifting past to caress her face, her neck, her spine.

Another cold, miserable night camped off the road later and they were riding again before dawn. By then, the mist had seeped into her clothes and skin, and settled right along her bones.

On the third evening, she'd given up hoping for a fire. She'd even embraced the chill and the insufferable roots and the hunger whose edge she couldn't dull no matter how much bread and cheese she ate. The aches and pains were soothing somehow.

Not comforting, but . . . distracting. Welcome. Deserved.

She didn't want to know what that meant about her. She couldn't let herself look that far inward. She'd come close, that day she'd seen Prince Galan. And it had been enough.

They veered from the path in the dwindling afternoon hours, cutting across mossy earth that cushioned each step. She hadn't seen a town in days, and the granite boulders were now carved with whorls and patterns. She supposed they were markers—a warning to humans to stay the hell away.

They had to be another week from Doranelle, but Rowan was heading along the mountains, not over them, climbing higher still, the ascent broken by occasional plateaus and fields of wildflowers. She hadn't seen a lookout, so she had no sense of where they were, or how high. Just the endless forest, and the endless climb, and the endless mist.

She smelled smoke before she saw the lights. Not campfires, but lights from a building rising up out of the trees, hugging the spine of the mountain slope. The stones were dark and ancient—hewn from something other than the abundant granite. Her eyes strained, but she didn't fail to note the ring of towering rocks woven between the trees, surrounding the entirety of the fortress. It was hard *not* to notice them when they rode between two megaliths that curved toward each other like the horns of a great beast, and a zinging current snapped against her skin.

Wards—magic wards. Her stomach turned. If they didn't keep out enemies, they certainly served as an alarm. Which meant the three figures patrolling each of the three towers, the six on the outer retaining wall, and the three at the wooden gates would now know they were approaching. Men and women in light leather armor and bearing swords, daggers, and bows monitored their approach.

"I think I'd rather stay in the woods," she said, her first words in days. Rowan ignored her.

He didn't even lift an arm in greeting to the sentries. He must be familiar with this place if he didn't stoop to hellos. As they drew closer to the ancient fortress—which was little more than a few watchtowers woven together by a large connecting building, splattered with lichen and moss—she did the calculations. It had to be some border outpost, a halfway point between the mortal realm and Doranelle. Perhaps she'd finally have a warm place to sleep, even if just for the night.

The guards saluted Rowan, who didn't spare them a passing glance. They all wore hoods, masking any signs of their heritage. Were they Fae? Rowan might not have spoken to her for most of their journey—he'd shown as much interest in her as he would in a pile of shit on the road—but if she were staying with the Fae . . . others might have questions.

She took in every detail, every exit, every weakness as they entered the large courtyard beyond the wall, two rather mortal-looking stable hands rushing to help them dismount. It was so still. As if everything, even the stones, was holding its breath. As if it had been waiting. The sensation only worsened when Rowan wordlessly led her into the dim interior of the main building, up a narrow set of stone stairs, and into what looked to be a small office.

It wasn't the carved oak furniture, or the faded green drapes, or the warmth of the fire that made her stop dead. It was the dark-haired woman seated behind the desk. Maeve, Queen of the Fae.

Her aunt.

And then came the words she had been dreading for ten years.

"Hello, Aelin Galathynius."

8

Celaena backed away, knowing exactly how many steps it would take to get into the hall, but slammed into a hard, unyielding body just as the door shut behind them. Her hands were shaking so badly she didn't bother going for her weapons—or Rowan's. He'd cut her down the instant Maeve gave the order.

The blood rushed from Celaena's head. She forced herself to take a breath. And another. Then she said in a too-quiet voice, "Aelin Galathynius is *dead*." Just speaking her name aloud—the damned name she had dreaded and hated and tried to forget . . .

Maeve smiled, revealing sharp little canines. "Let us not bother with lies."

It wasn't a lie. That girl, that princess had died in a river a decade ago. Celaena was no more Aelin Galathynius than she was any other person.

The room was too hot—too small, Rowan a brooding force of nature behind her.

She was not to have time to gather herself, to make up excuses and half truths, as she should have been doing these past few days instead of free-falling into silence and the misty cold. She was to face the Queen of the Fae as Maeve wanted to be faced. And in some fortress that seemed far, far beneath the raven-haired beauty watching her with black, depthless eyes.

Gods. *Gods.*

Maeve was fearsome in her perfection, utterly still, eternal and calm and radiating ancient grace. The dark sister to the fair-haired Mab.

Celaena had been fooling herself into thinking this would be easy. She was still pressed against Rowan as though he were a wall. An impenetrable wall, as old as the ward-stones surrounding the fortress. Rowan stepped away from her with his powerful, predatory ease and leaned against the door. She wasn't getting out until Maeve allowed her.

The Queen of the Fae remained silent, her long fingers moon-white and folded in the lap of her violet gown, a white barn owl perched on the back of her chair. She didn't bother with a crown, and Celaena supposed she didn't need one. Every creature on earth would know who she was—what she was—even if they were blind and deaf. Maeve, the face of a thousand legends . . . and nightmares. Epics and poems and songs had been written about her, so many that some even believed she was just a myth. But here was the dream—the nightmare—made flesh.

This could work to your advantage. You can get the answers you need right here, right now. Go back to Adarlan in a matter of days. Just—breathe.

Breathing, as it turned out, was rather hard when the queen who had been known to drive men to madness for amusement was observing every flicker of her throat. That owl perched on Maeve's chair—*Fae or true beast?*—was watching her, too. Its talons were curled around the back of the chair, digging into the wood.

It was somewhat absurd, though—Maeve holding court in this half-rotted office, at a desk stained with the Wyrd knew what. Gods, the fact that Maeve was seated at a *desk*. She should be in some ethereal glen, surrounded by bobbing will-o'-the-wisps and maidens dancing to lutes and harps, reading the wheeling stars like they were poetry. Not here.

Celaena bowed low. She supposed she should have gotten on her knees, but—she already smelled awful, and her face was likely still torn and bruised from her brawling in Varese. As Celaena rose, Maeve remained smiling faintly. A spider with a fly in its web.

"I suppose that with a proper bath, you'll look a good deal like your mother."

No exchanging pleasantries, then. Maeve was going right for the throat. She could handle it. She could ignore the pain and terror to get what she wanted. So Celaena smiled just as faintly and said, "Had I known who I would be meeting, I might have begged my escort for time to freshen up."

She didn't feel bad for one heartbeat about throwing Rowan to the lions.

Maeve's obsidian eyes flicked to Rowan, who still leaned against the door. She could have sworn there was approval in the Fae Queen's smile. As if the grueling travel were a part of this plan, too. But why? Why get her off-kilter?

"I'm afraid I must bear the blame for the pressing pace," Maeve said. "Though I suppose he could have bothered to at least find you a pool to bathe in along the way." The Queen of Faedom lifted an elegant hand, gesturing to the warrior. "Prince Rowan—"

Prince. She swallowed the urge to turn to him.

"—is from my sister Mora's bloodline. He is my nephew of sorts, and a member of my household. An extremely distant relation of yours; there is some ancient ancestry linking you."

Another move to get her on uneven footing. "You don't say."

Perhaps that wasn't the best reply. She should probably be on the floor, groveling for answers. And she had a feeling she'd likely get to that point very, very soon. But . . .

"You must be wondering why it is I asked Prince Rowan to bring you here," Maeve mused.

For Nehemia, she'd play this game. Celaena bit her tongue hard enough to keep her gods-damned smart-ass mouth shut.

Maeve placed her white hands on the desk. "I have been waiting a long, long while to meet you. And as I do not leave these lands, I could not see you. Not with my eyes, at least." The queen's long nails gleamed in the light.

There were legends whispered over fires about the other skin Maeve wore. No one had lived to tell anything beyond *shadows and claws and a darkness to devour your soul.*

"They broke my laws, you know. Your parents disobeyed my commands when they eloped. The bloodlines were too volatile to be mixed, but your mother promised to let me see you after you were born." Maeve cocked her head, eerily similar to the owl behind her. "It would seem that in the eight years after your birth, she was always too busy to uphold her vow."

If her mother had broken a promise . . . if her mother had kept her from Maeve, it had been for a damn good reason. A reason that tickled at the edges of Celaena's mind, a blur of memory.

"But now you are here," Maeve said, seeming to come closer without moving. "And a grown woman. My eyes across the sea have brought me such strange, horrible stories of you. From your scars and steel, I wonder whether they are indeed true. Like the tale I heard over a year ago, that an assassin with Ashryver eyes was spotted by the horned Lord of the North in a wagon bound for—"

"Enough." Celaena glanced at Rowan, who was listening intently, as if this was the first he was hearing of it. She didn't want him knowing about Endovier—didn't want that pity. "I know my own history." She

flashed Rowan a glare that told him to mind his own business. He merely looked away, bored again. Typical immortal arrogance. Celaena faced Maeve, tucking her hands into her pockets. "I'm an assassin, yes."

A snort from behind, but she didn't dare take her eyes off Maeve.

"And your other talents?" Maeve's nostrils flared—scenting. "What has become of them?"

"Like everyone else on my continent, I haven't been able to access them."

Maeve's eyes twinkled, and Celaena knew—knew that Maeve could smell the half truth. "You are not on your continent anymore," Maeve purred.

Run. Every instinct roared with the word. She had a feeling that the Eye of Elena would have been no use, but she wished she had it anyway. Wished the dead queen were here, for that matter. Rowan was still at the door—but if she was fast, if she outsmarted him . . .

A flash of memory blinded her, bright and uncontrollable, unleashed by the instinct begging her to flee. Her mother had rarely let Fae into their home, even with her heritage. A few trusted ones were allowed to live with them, but any Fae visitors had been closely monitored, and for the duration of their stay, Celaena had been sequestered in the family's private chambers. She'd always thought it was overprotective, but now . . . "Show me," Maeve whispered with a spider's smile. *Run. Run.*

She could still feel the burn of blue wildfire exploding out of her in that demon realm, still see Chaol's face as she lost control of it. One wrong move, one wrong *breath*, and she could have killed him and Fleetfoot.

The owl rustled its wings, the wood groaning beneath its talons, and the darkness in Maeve's eyes spread, reaching. There was a faint pulse in the air, a throbbing against her blood. A tapping, then a razor-sharp slicing against her mind—as if Maeve were trying to cleave open her skull and peer inside. Pushing, testing, tasting—

Fighting to keep her breathing steady, Celaena positioned her hands within easy reach of her blades as she pushed back against the claws in her mind. Maeve let out a low laugh, and the pressure in her head ceased.

"Your mother hid you from me for years," Maeve said. "She and your father always had a remarkable talent for knowing when my eyes were searching for you. Such a rare gift—the ability to summon and manipulate flame. So few exist who possess more than an ember of it; fewer still who can master its wildness. And yet your mother wanted you to stifle your power—though she knew that I only wanted you to submit to it."

Celaena's breath burned her throat. Another flicker of memory—of lessons not about starting fires but putting them out.

Maeve went on, "Look at how well that turned out for them."

Celaena's blood froze. Every self-preserving instinct went right out of her head. "And where were *you* ten years ago?" She spoke so low, from so deep in her shredded soul, that the words were barely more than a growl.

Maeve angled her head slightly. "I do not take kindly to being lied to."

The snarl on Celaena's face faltered. Dropped right into her gut. Aid had never come for Terrasen from the Fae. From Wendlyn. And it was all because . . . because . . .

"I do not have more time to spare you," Maeve said. "So let me be brief: my eyes have told me that you have questions. Questions that no mortal has the right to ask—about the keys."

Legend said Maeve could commune with the spirit world—had Elena, or Nehemia, told her? Celaena opened her mouth, but Maeve held up a hand. "I will give you those answers. You may come to me in Doranelle to receive them."

"Why not—"

A growl from Rowan at the interruption.

"Because they are answers that require time," Maeve said, then slowly added, as if she savored every word, "and answers you have not yet earned."

"Tell me what I can do to earn them and I will do it." Fool. A damned fool's response.

"A dangerous thing to offer without hearing the price."

"You want me to show you my magic? I'll show it to you. But not here—not—"

"I have no interest in seeing you drop your magic at my feet like a sack of grain. I want to see what you can *do* with it, Aelin Galathynius—which currently seems like not very much at all." Celaena's stomach tightened at that cursed name. "I want to see what you will become under the right circumstances."

"I don't—"

"I do not permit mortals or half-breeds into Doranelle. For a half-breed to enter my realm, she must prove herself both gifted and worthy. Mistward, this fortress"—she waved a hand to encompass the room—"is one of several proving grounds. And a place where those who do not pass the test can spend their days."

Beneath the growing fear, a flicker of disgust went through her. *Half-breed*—Maeve said it with such disdain. "And what manner of test might I expect before I am deemed worthy?"

Maeve gestured to Rowan, who had not moved from the door. "You shall come to me once Prince Rowan decides that you have mastered your gifts. He shall train you here. And you shall not set foot in Doranelle until he deems your training complete."

After facing the horseshit she'd seen in the glass castle—demons, witches, the king—training with Rowan, even in magic, seemed rather anticlimactic.

But—but it could take weeks. Months. Years. The familiar fog of nothing crept in, threatening to smother her once again. She pushed it back long enough to say, "What I need to know isn't something that can *wait*—"

"You want answers regarding the keys, heir of Terrasen? Then they shall be waiting for you in Doranelle. The rest is up to you."

"Truthfully," Celaena blurted. "You will truthfully answer my questions about the keys."

Maeve smiled, and it was not a thing of beauty. "You haven't forgotten *all* of our ways, then." When Celaena didn't react, Maeve added, "I will *truthfully* answer all your questions about the keys."

It might be easier to walk away. Go find some other ancient being to pester for the truth. Celaena breathed in and out, in and out. But Maeve had been there—had been there at the dawn of this world during the Valg wars. She had *held* the Wyrdkeys. She knew what they looked like, how they felt. Maybe she even knew where Brannon had hidden them—especially the last, unnamed key. And if Celaena could find a way to steal the keys from the king, to destroy him, to stop his armies and free Eyllwe, even if she could find just *one* Wyrdkey . . . "What manner of training—"

"Prince Rowan shall explain the specifics. For now, he will escort you to your chamber to rest."

Celaena looked Maeve straight in her death-dealing eyes. "You swear you'll tell me what I need to know?"

"I do not break my promises. And I have the feeling that you are unlike your mother in that regard, too."

Bitch. *Bitch*, she wanted to hiss. But then Maeve's eyes flicked to Celaena's right palm. She knew everything. Through whatever spies or power or guesswork, Maeve knew everything about her and the vow to Nehemia.

"To what end?" Celaena asked softly, the anger and the fear dragging her down into an inescapable exhaustion. "You want me to train only so I can make a spectacle of my talents?"

Maeve ran a moon-white finger down the owl's head. "I wish you to become who you were born to be. To become queen."

Become queen.

The words haunted Celaena that night—kept her from sleeping, even though she was so exhausted she could have wept for the dark-eyed Silba to put her out of her misery. *Queen.* The word throbbed right along with the fresh split lip that *also* made sleeping very uncomfortable.

She could thank Rowan for that.

After Maeve's command, Celaena hadn't bothered with good-byes before walking out. Rowan had only cleared the way because Maeve gave him a nod, and he followed Celaena into a narrow hallway that smelled of roasting meat and garlic. Her stomach grumbled, but she'd probably hurl her guts up the second she swallowed anything. So she trailed Rowan down the corridor, down the stairs, each footstep alternating between iron-willed control and growing rage.

Left. *Nehemia.*

Right. *You made a vow, and you will keep it, by whatever means necessary.*

Left. *Training. Queen.*

Right. *Bitch. Manipulative, cold-blooded, sadistic bitch.*

Ahead of her, Rowan's own steps were silent on the dark stones of the hallway. The torches hadn't been lit yet, and in the murky interior, she could hardly tell he was there. But she knew—if only because she could almost feel the ire radiating off him. Good. At least one other person wasn't particularly thrilled about this bargain.

Training. *Training.*

Her whole life had been training, from the moment she was born. Rowan could train her until he was blue in the face, and as long as it got her the answers about the Wyrdkeys, she'd play along. But it didn't mean that, when the time came, she had to *do* anything. Certainly not take up her throne.

She didn't even *have* a throne, or a crown, or a court. Didn't want them. And she could bring down the king as Celaena Sardothien, thank you very much.

She tightened her fingers into fists.

They encountered no one as they descended a winding staircase and started down another corridor. Did the residents of this fortress—Mistward, Maeve had called it—know who was in that study upstairs? Maeve probably got off on terrifying them. Maybe she had all of them—*half-breeds*, she'd called them—enslaved through some bargain or another. Disgusting. It was disgusting, to keep them here just for having a mixed heritage that was no fault of theirs.

Celaena finally opened up her mouth.

"You must be *very* important to Her Immortal Majesty if she put you on nurse duty."

"Given your history, she didn't trust anyone but her best to keep you in line."

Oh, the prince wanted to tangle. Whatever self-control he'd had on their trek to the fortress was hanging by a thread. Good.

"Playing warrior in the woods doesn't seem like the greatest indicator of talent."

"I fought on killing fields long before you, your parents, or your grand-uncle were even born."

She bristled—exactly like he wanted. "Who's to fight here except birds and beasts?"

Silence. Then—"The world is a far bigger and more dangerous place than you can imagine, girl. Consider yourself blessed to receive any training—to have the chance to prove yourself."

"I've seen plenty of this big and dangerous world, princeling."

A soft, harsh laugh. "Just wait, *Aelin*."

Another jab. And she let herself fall for it. "Don't call me that."

"It's your name. I'm not going to call you anything different."

She stepped in his path, getting right near those too-sharp canines. "No one here can know who I am. Do you understand?"

His green eyes gleamed, animal-bright in the dark. "My aunt has given me a harder task than she realizes, I think." *My* aunt. Not *our* aunt.

And then she said one of the foulest things she'd ever uttered in her life, bathing in the pure hate of it. "Fae like you make me understand the King of Adarlan's actions a bit more, I think."

Faster than she could sense, faster than anything had a right to be, he punched her.

She shifted enough to keep her nose from shattering but took the blow on her mouth. She hit the wall, whacked her head, and tasted blood. *Good*.

He struck again with that immortal speed—or would have. But with equally unnerving swiftness, he halted his second blow before it fractured her jaw and snarled in her face, low and vicious.

Her breathing turned ragged as she purred, "Do it."

He looked more interested in ripping out her throat than in talking, but he held the line he'd drawn. "Why should I give you what you want?"

"You're just as useless as the rest of your brethren."

He let out a soft, lethal laugh that raked claws down her temper. "If you're that desperate to eat stone, go ahead: I'll let you try to land the next punch."

She knew better than to listen. But there was such a roar in her blood that she could no longer see right, think right, breathe right. So she damned the consequences to hell as she swung.

Celaena hit nothing but air—air, and then his foot hooked behind hers in an efficient maneuver that sent her careening into the wall once more. Impossible—he'd tripped her as if she was nothing more than a trembling novice.

He was now a few feet away, arms crossed. She spat blood and swore. He smirked. It was enough to send her hurtling for him again, to tackle or pummel or strangle him, she didn't know.

She caught his feint left, but when she dove right, he moved so swiftly that despite her lifetime of training, she crashed into a darkened brazier behind him. The clatter echoed through the too-quiet hall as she landed face-first on the stone floor, her teeth singing.

"Like I said," Rowan sneered down at her, "you have a lot to learn. About everything."

Her lip already aching and swollen, she told him exactly what he could go do to himself.

He sauntered down the hall. "Next time you say anything like that," he said without looking over his shoulder, "I'll have you chopping wood for a month."

Fuming, hatred and shame already burning her face, Celaena got to her feet. He dumped her in a very small, very cold room that looked like little more than a prison cell, letting her take all of two steps inside before he said, "Give me your weapons."

"Why? And no." Like hell she'd give him her daggers.

In a swift movement, he grabbed a bucket of water from beside her door and tossed the contents onto the hall floor before holding it out. "Give me your weapons."

Training with him would be absolutely wonderful. "Tell me why."

"I don't have to explain myself to you."

"Then we're going to have another brawl."

His tattoo seeming impossibly darker in the dim hall, he stared at her beneath lowered brows as if to say, *You call* that *a brawl?* But instead he growled, "Starting at dawn, you'll earn your keep by helping in the kitchen. Unless you plan to murder everyone in the fortress, there is no need for you to be armed. Or to be armed while we train. So I'll keep your daggers until you've earned them back."

Well, that felt familiar. "The kitchen?"

He bared his teeth in a wicked grin. "Everyone pulls their weight here. Princesses included. No one's above some hard labor, least of all you."

And didn't she have the scars to prove it. Not that she'd tell him that. She didn't know what she'd do if he learned about Endovier and mocked her for it—or pitied her. "So my training includes being a scullery maid?"

"Part of it." Again, she could have sworn she could read the unspoken words in his eyes: *And I'm going to savor every damn second of your misery.*

"For an old bastard, you certainly haven't bothered to learn manners at any point in your long existence." Never mind that he looked to be in his late twenties.

"Why should I waste flattery on a child who's already in love with herself?"

"We're related, you know."

"We've as much blood in common as I do with the fortress pig-boy."

She felt her nostrils flare, and he shoved the bucket in her face. She almost knocked it right back into his, but decided that she didn't want a broken nose and began disarming herself.

Rowan counted every weapon she put in the bucket as though he'd already learned how many she'd been carrying, even the hidden ones. Then he tucked the bucket against his side and slammed the door without so much of a good-bye beyond "Be ready at dawn."

"Bastard. Old stinking bastard," she muttered, surveying the room.

A bed, a chamber pot, and a washbasin with icy water. She'd debated a bath, but opted to use the water to clean out her mouth and tend to her lip. She was starving, but going to find food involved meeting people. So once she'd mended her lip as best she could with the supplies in her satchel, she tumbled into bed, reeking vagrant clothes and all, and lay there for several hours.

There was one small window with no coverings in her room. Celaena turned over in bed to look through it to the patch of stars above the trees surrounding the fortress.

Lashing out at Rowan like that, saying the things she did, trying to *fight* with him . . . She'd deserved that punch. More than deserved it. If she was being honest with herself, she was barely passable as a human being these days. She fingered her split lip and winced.

She scanned the night sky until she located the Stag, the Lord of the North. The unmoving star atop the stag's head—the eternal crown—pointed the way to Terrasen. She'd been told that the great rulers of Terrasen turned into those bright stars so their people would never be alone—and would always know the way home. She hadn't set foot there in ten years. While he'd been her master, Arobynn hadn't let her, and afterward she hadn't dared.

She had whispered the truth that day at Nehemia's grave. She'd been running for so long that she didn't know what it was to stand and fight. Celaena loosed a breath and rubbed her eyes.

What Maeve didn't understand, what she could never understand, was just how much that little princess in Terrasen had damned them a decade ago, even worse than Maeve herself had. She had damned them all, and then left the world to burn into ash and dust.

So Celaena turned away from the stars, nestling under the threadbare blanket against the frigid cold, and closed her eyes, trying to dream of a different world.

A world where she was no one at all.

9

Manon Blackbeak stood on a cliff beside the snow-swollen river, eyes closed as the damp wind bit her face. There were few sounds she enjoyed more than the groans of dying men, but the wind was one of them.

Leaning into the breeze was the closest she came to flying these days—save in rare dreams, when she was again in the clouds, her iron-wood broom still functioning, not the scrap of useless wood it was now, chucked into the closet of her room at Blackbeak Keep.

It had been ten years since she'd tasted mist and cloud and ridden on the back of the wind. Today would have been a flawless flying day, the wind wicked and fast. Today, she would have soared.

Behind her, Mother Blackbeak was still talking with the enormous man from the caravan who called himself a duke. It had been more than coincidence, she supposed, that soon after she'd left that blood-soaked field in Fenharrow she'd received a summons from her grandmother.

And more than coincidence that she'd been not forty miles from the rendezvous point just over the border in Adarlan.

Manon was on guard duty while her grandmother, the High Witch of the Blackbeak clan, spoke to the duke beside the raging Acanthus River. The rest of her coven had taken their positions around the small encampment—twelve other witches, all around Manon's age, all of them raised and trained together. Like Manon, they had no weapons, but it seemed that the duke knew enough to realize Blackbeaks didn't need weapons to be deadly.

You didn't need a weapon at all when you were born one.

And when you were one of Manon's Thirteen, with whom she had fought and flown for the past hundred years . . . Often just the name of the coven was enough to send enemies fleeing. The Thirteen did not have a reputation for mercy—or making mistakes.

Manon eyed the armored guards around the camp. Half were watching the Blackbeak witches, the others monitoring the duke and her grandmother. It was an honor that the High Witch had chosen the Thirteen to guard her—no other coven had been summoned. No other coven was needed if the Thirteen were present.

Manon slid her attention to the nearest guard. His sweat, the faint tang of fear, and the heavy musk of exhaustion drifted toward her. From the look and smell of it, they'd been traveling for weeks. There were two prison wagons with them. One emitted a very distinct male odor—and perhaps a remnant of cologne. One was female. Both smelled wrong.

Manon had been born soulless, her grandmother said. Soulless and heartless, as a Blackbeak ought to be. She was wicked right down to the marrow of her bones. But the people in those wagons, and the duke, they smelled *wrong*. Different. Alien.

The nearby guard shifted on his feet. She gave him a smile. His hand tightened on the hilt of his sword.

Because she could, because she was growing bored, Manon cocked her jaw, sending her iron teeth snapping down. The guard took a step back, his breath coming faster, the acrid tang of fear sharpening.

With her moon-white hair, alabaster skin, and burnt-gold eyes, she'd been told by ill-fated men that she was beautiful as a Fae queen. But what those men realized too late was that her beauty was merely a weapon in her natural-born arsenal. And it made things so, so fun.

Feet crunched in the snow and bits of dead grass, and Manon turned from the trembling guard and the roaring brown Acanthus to find her grandmother approaching.

In the ten years since magic had vanished, their aging process had warped. Manon herself was well over a century old, but until ten years ago, she had looked no older than sixteen. Now, she looked to be in her midtwenties. They were aging like mortals, they had soon realized with no small amount of panic. And her grandmother . . .

The rich, voluminous midnight robes of Mother Blackbeak flowed like water in the crisp breeze. Her grandmother's face was now marred with the beginnings of wrinkles, her ebony hair sprinkled with silver. The High Witch of the Blackbeak Clan wasn't just beautiful—she was alluring. Even now, with mortal years pressing down upon her bone-white skin, there was something entrancing about the Matron.

"We leave now," Mother Blackbeak said, walking north along the river. Behind them, the duke's men closed ranks around the encampment. Smart for mortals to be so cautious when the Thirteen were present—and bored.

One jerk of the chin from Manon was all it took for the Thirteen to fall in line. The twelve other sentinels kept the required distance behind Manon and her grandmother, footsteps near silent in the winter grass. None of them had been able to find a single Crochan in the months they'd been infiltrating town after town. And Manon fully expected some form of punishment for it later. Flogging, perhaps a few broken fingers—nothing too permanent, but it would be public. That was her grandmother's preferred method of punishment: not the *how*, but the humiliation.

Yet her grandmother's gold-flecked black eyes, the heirloom of the Blackbeak Clan's purest bloodline, were bent on the northern horizon, toward Oakwald Forest and the towering White Fangs far beyond. The gold-speckled eyes were the most cherished trait in their Clan for a reason Manon had never bothered to learn—and when her grandmother had seen that Manon's were wholly of pure, dark gold, the Matron had carried her away from her daughter's still-cooling corpse and proclaimed Manon her undisputed heir.

Her grandmother kept walking, and Manon didn't press her to speak. Not unless she wanted her tongue ripped clean from her mouth.

"We're to travel north," her grandmother said when the encampment was swallowed up by the foothills. "I want you to send three of your Thirteen south, west, and east. They are to seek out our kith and kin and inform them that we will all assemble in the Ferian Gap. Every last Blackbeak—no witch or sentinel left behind."

Nowadays there was no difference—every witch belonged to a coven and was therefore a sentinel. Since the downfall of their western kingdom, since they had started clawing for their survival, every Blackbeak, Yellowlegs, and Blueblood had to be ready to fight—ready at any time to reclaim their lands or die for their people. Manon herself had never set foot in the former Witch Kingdom, had never seen the ruins or the flat, green expanse that stretched to the western sea. None of her Thirteen had seen it, either, all of them wanderers and exiles thanks to a curse from the last Crochan Queen as she bled out on that legendary battlefield.

The Matron went on, still staring at the mountains. "And if your sentinels see members of the other clans, they are to inform them to gather in the Gap, too. No fighting, no provoking—just spread the word." Her grandmother's iron teeth flashed in the afternoon sun. Like most of the ancient witches—the ones who had been born in the Witch Kingdom and fought in the Ironteeth Alliance to shatter the chains of the Crochan Queens—Mother Blackbeak wore her iron teeth permanently on display. Manon had never seen them retracted.

Manon bit back her questions. The Ferian Gap—the deadly, blasted bit of land between the White Fang and Ruhnn Mountains, and one of the few passes between the fertile lands of the east and the Western Wastes.

Manon had made the passage through the snow-crusted labyrinth of caves and ravines on foot—just once, with the Thirteen and two other covens, right after magic had vanished, when they were all nearly blind, deaf, and dumb with the agony of suddenly being grounded. Half of the other witches hadn't made it through the Gap. The Thirteen had barely survived, and Manon had almost lost an arm to an ice cavern cave-in. Almost lost it, but kept it thanks to the quick thinking of Asterin, her second in command, and the brute strength of Sorrel, her Third. The Ferian Gap; Manon hadn't been back since. For months now there had been rumors of far darker things than witches dwelling there.

"Baba Yellowlegs is dead." Manon whipped her head to her grandmother, who was smiling faintly. "Killed in Rifthold. The duke received word. No one knows who, or why."

"Crochans?"

"Perhaps." Mother Blackbeak's smile spread, revealing iron teeth spotted with rust. "The King of Adarlan has invited us to assemble in the Ferian Gap. He says he has a gift for us there."

Manon considered what she knew about the vicious, deadly king hell-bent on conquering the world. Her responsibility as both Coven leader and heir was to keep her grandmother alive; it was instinct to anticipate every pitfall, every potential threat. "It could be a trap. To gather us in one place, and then destroy us. He could be working with the Crochans. Or perhaps the Bluebloods. They've always wanted to make themselves High Witches of every Ironteeth Clan."

"Oh, I think not," Mother Blackbeak purred, her depthless ebony eyes crinkling. "For the king has made us an offer. Made all the Ironteeth Clans an offer."

Manon waited, even though she could have gutted someone just to ease the miserable impatience.

"The king needs riders," Mother Blackbeak said, still staring at the horizon. "Riders for his wyverns—to be his aerial cavalry. He's been breeding them in the Gap all these years."

It had been a while—too damn long—but Manon could feel the threads of fate twisting around them, tightening.

"And when we are done, when we have served him, he will let us keep the wyverns. To take our host to reclaim the Wastes from the mortal pigs who now dwell there." A fierce, wild thrill pierced Manon's chest, sharp as a knife. Following the Matron's gaze, Manon looked to the horizon, where the mountains were still blanketed with winter. To fly again, to soar through the mountain passes, to hunt down prey the way they'd been born to . . .

They weren't enchanted ironwood brooms.

But wyverns would do just fine.

10

After a grueling day of training new recruits, avoiding Dorian, and keeping well away from the king's watchful eye, Chaol was almost at his rooms, more than ready to sleep, when he noticed that two of his men were missing from their posts outside the Great Hall. The two remaining men winced as he stopped dead.

It wasn't unusual for guards to occasionally miss a shift. If someone was sick, if they had some family tragedy, Chaol always found a replacement. But two *missing* guards, with no replacement in sight . . .

"Someone had better start talking," he ground out.

One of them cleared their throats—a newer guard, who had just finished his training three months before. The other one was relatively new, too, which was why he'd assigned them to night duty outside the empty Great Hall. But he'd put them under the supposedly responsible and watchful eyes of the two *other* guards, both of whom had been there for years.

The guard who'd cleared his throat went red. "It—they said . . . Ah, Captain, they said that no one would really notice if they were gone, since it's the Great Hall, and it's empty and, ah—"

"Use your words," Chaol snapped. He was going to *murder* the two deserters.

"The general's party, sir," said the other. "General Ashryver walked past on his way into Rifthold and invited them to join him. He said it would be all right with you, so they went with him."

A muscle feathered in his jaw. Of course Aedion did.

"And you two," Chaol growled, "didn't think it would be useful to report this to anyone?"

"With all due respect, sir," said the second one, "we were . . . we didn't want them to think we were ratters. And it's just the Great Hall—"

"Wrong thing to say," Chaol snarled. "You're both on double duty for a month—in the gardens." Where it was still freezing. "Your leisure time is now nonexistent. And if you *ever* again fail to report another guard abandoning his post, you're both gone. Understood?"

When he got a mumbled confirmation, he stalked toward the front gate of the castle. Like hell he'd go to sleep now. He had two guards to hunt down in Rifthold . . . and a general to exchange some words with.

Aedion had rented out an entire tavern. Men were at the door to keep out the riffraff, but one glare from Chaol, one glimpse of the eagle-shaped pommel of his sword, had them stepping aside. The tavern was crammed with various nobles, some women who could have been courtesans or courtiers, and men—lots of drunk, boisterous men. Card games, dice, bawdy singing to the music made by the small quintet by the roaring fire, free-flowing taps of ale, bottles of sparkling wine . . . Was Aedion going to pay for this with his blood money, or was it on the king?

Chaol spotted his two guards, plus half a dozen others, playing cards, women in their laps, grinning like fiends. Until they saw him.

They were still groveling as Chaol sent them packing—back to the castle, where he would deal with them tomorrow. He couldn't decide whether they deserved to lose their positions, since Aedion had lied, and he didn't like making choices like that unless he'd slept on them first. So out they went, into the freezing night. And then Chaol began the process of hunting down the general.

But no one knew where he was. First, someone sent Chaol upstairs, to one of the tavern's bedrooms. Where he indeed found the two women someone said Aedion had slipped away with—but another man was between them. Chaol only demanded where the general had gone. The women said they'd seen him playing dice in the cellar with some masked, high-ranking nobles. So Chaol stormed down there. And indeed, there were the masked, high-ranking nobles. They were pretending to be mere revelers, but Chaol recognized them anyway, even if he didn't call them out by name. They insisted Aedion was last seen playing the fiddle in the main room.

So Chaol went back upstairs. Aedion was certainly not playing the fiddle. Or the drum, or the lute or the pipes. In fact, it seemed that Aedion Ashryver wasn't even at his own party.

A courtesan prowled up to him to sell her wares, and would have walked away at his snarl had Chaol not offered her a silver coin for information about the general. She'd seen him leave an hour ago—on the arm of one of her rivals. Headed off to a more *private* location, but she didn't know where. If Aedion was no longer here, then . . . Chaol went back to the castle.

But he did hear one more bit of information. The Bane would arrive soon, people said, and when the legion descended on the city, they planned to show Rifthold a whole new level of debauchery. All of Chaol's guards were invited, apparently.

It was the last thing he wanted or needed—an entire legion of lethal warriors wreaking havoc on Rifthold and distracting his men. If that happened, the king might look too closely at Chaol—or ask where he sometimes disappeared to.

So he needed to have more than just words with Aedion. He needed to find something to use against him so Aedion would agree *not* to throw these parties and swear to keep his Bane under control. Tomorrow night, he'd go to whatever party Aedion threw.

And see what leverage he could find.

11

Freezing and aching from shivering all night, Celaena awoke before dawn in her miserable little room and found an ivory tin sitting outside the door. It was filled with a salve that smelled of mint and rosemary, and beneath it was a note written in tight, concise letters.

You deserved it. Maeve sends her wishes for a speedy recovery.

Snorting at the lecture Rowan must have received, and how it must have ruffled his feathers to bring her the gift, Celaena smeared the salve onto her still-swollen lip. A glance in the speckled shard of mirror above the dresser revealed that she had seen better days. And was never drinking wine or eating teggya again. Or going more than a day without a bath.

Apparently Rowan agreed, because he'd also left a few pitchers of water, some soap, and a new set of clothes: white underthings, a loose shirt, and a pale-gray surcoat and cloak similar to what he had worn the day before. Though simple, the fabric was thick and of good quality.

Celaena washed as best she could, shaking with the cold leaking in from the misty forest beyond. Suddenly homesick for the giant bathing pool at the palace, she quickly dried and slid into the clothes, thankful for the layers.

Her teeth wouldn't stop chattering. Hadn't stopped chattering all night, actually. Having wet hair now didn't help, even after she braided it back. She stuffed her feet into the knee-high leather boots and tied the thick red sash around her waist as tightly as she could manage without losing the ability to move, hoping to give herself *some* shape, but . . .

Celaena scowled at the mirror. She'd lost weight—enough so that her face looked about as hollow as she felt. Even her hair had become rather dull and limp. The salve had already taken down the swelling in her lip, but not the color. At least she was clean again. If frozen to her core. And—completely overdressed for kitchen duty. Sighing, she unwrapped her sash and shrugged off the overcoat, tossing them onto the bed. Gods, her hands were so cold that the ring on her finger was slipping and sliding about. She knew it was a mistake, but she looked at it anyway, the amethyst dark in the early morning light.

What would Chaol make of all this? She was here, after all, because of him. Not just here in this physical place, but here inside this endless exhaustion, the near-constant ache in her chest. It was not his fault that Nehemia died, not when the princess had orchestrated everything. Yet he had kept information from her. He had chosen the *king*. Even though he'd claimed he loved her, he still loyally served that monster. Maybe she had been a fool for letting him in, for dreaming of a world where she could ignore the fact that he was captain to the man who had shattered her life again and again.

The pain in her chest sharpened enough that breathing became difficult. She stood there for a moment, pushing back against it, letting it sink into the fog that smothered her soul, and then trudged out the door.

The one benefit to scullery duty was that the kitchen was warm. Hot, even. The great brick oven and hearth were blazing, chasing away the morning mist that slithered in from the trees beyond the bay of windows above the copper sinks. There were only two other people in the kitchen—a hunched old man tending to the bubbling pots on the hearth and a youth at the wooden table that split the kitchen in half, chopping onions and monitoring what smelled like bread. By the Wyrd, she was hungry. That bread smelled divine. And what was in those pots?

Despite the absurdly early hour, the young man's merry prattling had echoed off the stones of the stairwell, but he'd fallen silent, both men stopping their work, when Rowan strode down the steps into the kitchen. The Fae prince had been waiting for her down the hall, arms crossed, already bored. But his animal-bright eyes had narrowed slightly, as if he'd been half hoping she would oversleep and give him an excuse to punish her. As an immortal, he probably had endless patience and creativity when it came to thinking up miserable punishments.

Rowan addressed the old man by the hearth—standing so still that Celaena wondered if the prince had learned it or been born with it. "Your new scullery maid for the morning shift. After breakfast, I have her for the rest of the day." Apparently, his lack of greeting wasn't personal. Rowan looked at her with raised brows, and she could see the words in his eyes as clearly as if he'd spoken them: *You wanted to remain unidentified, so go ahead, Princess. Introduce yourself with whatever name you want.*

At least he'd listened to her last night. "Elentiya," she choked out. "My name is Elentiya." Her gut tightened.

Thank the gods Rowan didn't snort at the name. She might have eviscerated him—or tried to, at least—if he mocked the name Nehemia had given her.

The old man hobbled forward, wiping his gnarled hands on a crisp white apron. His brown woolen clothes were simple and worn—a bit threadbare in places—and he seemed to have some trouble with his left knee, but his white hair was tied back neatly from his tan face. He bowed stiffly. "So good of you to find us additional help, Prince." He shifted his chestnut-brown eyes to Celaena and gave her a no-nonsense once-over. "Ever work in a kitchen?"

With all the things she had done, all the places and things and people she had seen, she had to say no.

"Well, I hope you're a fast learner and quick on your feet," he said.

"I'll do my best." Apparently that was all Rowan needed to hear before he stalked off, his footsteps silent, every movement smooth and laced with power. Just watching him, she knew he'd held back last night when punching her. If he'd wanted to, he could have shattered her jaw.

"I'm Emrys," the old man said. He hurried to the oven, grabbing a long, flat wooden shovel from the wall to pull a brown loaf out of the oven. Introduction over. Good. No wishy-washy nonsense or smiling or any of that. But his ears—

Half-breeds. Peeking up from Emrys's white hair were the markers of his Fae heritage.

"And this is Luca," the old man said, pointing to the youth at the worktable. Even though a rack of iron pots and pans hanging from the ceiling partially blocked her view of him, he gave Celaena a broad smile, his mop of tawny curls sticking up this way and that. He had to be a few years younger than her at least, and hadn't yet grown into his tall frame or broad shoulders. He didn't have properly fitting clothes, either, given how short the sleeves of his ordinary brown tunic were. "You and he will be sharing a lot of the scullery work, I'm afraid."

"Oh, it's absolutely miserable," Luca chirped, sniffling loudly at the reek of the onions he was chopping, "but you'll get used to it. Though maybe not the waking up before dawn part." Emrys shot the young man a glare, and Luca amended, "At least the company's good."

She gave him her best attempt at a civilized nod and took in the layout again. Behind Luca, a second stone staircase spiraled up and out of sight, and the two towering cupboards on either side of it were crammed with well-worn, if not cracked, dishes and cutlery. The top half of a wooden door by the windows was wide open, a wall of trees and mist swirling beyond a small clearing of grass. Past them, the ring of megaliths towered like eternal guardians.

She caught Emrys studying her hands and held them out, scars and all. "Already mangled and ruined, so you won't find me weeping over broken nails."

"Mother keep me. What happened?" But even as the old man spoke, she could see him putting the pieces together—see him deciphering Celaena's accent, taking in her swollen lip and the shadows under her eyes.

"Adarlan will do that to a person." Luca's knife thudded on the table, but Celaena kept her eyes on the old man. "Give me whatever work you want. Any work."

Let Rowan think she was spoiled and selfish. She was, but she wanted sore muscles and blistered hands and to fall into bed so exhausted she wouldn't dream, wouldn't think, wouldn't feel much of anything.

Emrys clicked his tongue. There was enough pity in the man's eyes that for a heartbeat, Celaena contemplated biting his head off. Then he said, "Just finish the onions. Luca, you mind the bread. I've got to start on the casseroles."

Celaena took up the spot that Luca had already vacated at the end of the table, passing the giant hearth as she did so—a mammoth thing of ancient stone, carved with symbols and odd faces. Even the posts of the brazier had been fashioned into standing figures, and displayed atop the thin mantel was a set of nine iron figurines. Gods and goddesses.

Celaena quickly looked away from the two females in the

center—one crowned with a star and armed with a bow and quiver, the other bearing a polished bronze disk upheld between her raised hands. She could have sworn she felt them watching her.

Breakfast was a madhouse.

As dawn filled the windows with golden light, chaos descended on the kitchen, people rushing in and out. There weren't any servants, just weathered people doing their chores or even helping because they felt like it. Great tubs of eggs and potatoes and vegetables vanished as soon as they were placed on the table, whisked up the stairs and into what had to be the dining hall. Jugs of water, of milk, of the gods knew what were hauled up. Celaena was introduced to some of the people, but most didn't cast a look in her direction.

And wasn't that a lovely change from the usual stares and terror and whispers that had marked the past ten years of her life. She had a feeling Rowan would keep his mouth shut about her identity, if only because he seemed to hate talking to others as much as she did. In the kitchen, chopping vegetables and washing pans, she was absolutely, gloriously nobody.

Her dull knife was a nightmare when it came to chopping mushrooms, scallions, and an endless avalanche of potatoes. No one, except perhaps Emrys with his all-seeing eyes, seemed to notice her perfect slices. Someone merely scooped them up and tossed them in a pot, then told her to cut something else.

Then—nothing. Everyone but her two companions vanished upstairs, and sleepy laughter, grumbling, and clinking silverware echoed down the stairwell. Famished, Celaena looked longingly at the food left on the worktable just as she caught Luca staring at her.

"Go ahead," he said with a grin before moving to help Emrys haul a massive iron cauldron over toward the sink. Even with the insanity of the past hour, Luca had managed to chat up almost every person who came into the kitchen, his voice and laughter floating over the clanging pots and barked orders. "You'll be at those dishes for a while and might as well eat now."

Indeed, there was a *tower* of dishes and pots already by the sinks. The cauldron alone would take forever. So Celaena plunked down at the table, served herself some eggs and potatoes, poured a cup of tea, and dug in.

Devouring was a better word for what she did. Holy gods, it was delicious. Within moments, she'd consumed two pieces of toast laden with eggs, then started on the fried potatoes. Which were as absurdly good as the eggs. She ditched the tea in favor of downing a glass of the richest milk she'd ever tasted. Not that she ever really drank milk, since she'd had her pick of exotic juices in Rifthold, but . . . She looked up from her plate to find Emrys and Luca gaping from the hearth. "Gods above," the old man said, moving to sit at the table. "When was the last time you ate?"

Good food like this? A while. And if Rowan was coming back at some point, she didn't want to be swaying from hunger. She needed her strength for training. Magic training. Which was sure to be horrific, but she would do it—to fulfill her bargain with Maeve and honor her vow to Nehemia. Suddenly not very hungry, she set down her fork. "Sorry," she said.

"Oh, eat all you like," Emrys said. "There's nothing more satisfying to a cook than seeing someone enjoy his food." He said it with enough humor and kindness that it chafed.

How would they react if they knew the things she'd done? What would they do if they knew about the blood she'd spilled, how she'd tortured Grave and taken him apart piece by piece, the way she'd gutted Archer in that sewer? The way she'd failed her friend. Failed a lot of people.

They were noticeably quieter as they sat down. They didn't ask her any questions. Which was perfect, because she didn't really want to start a conversation. She wouldn't be here for long, anyway. Emrys and Luca kept to themselves, chatting about the training Luca was to do with some of the sentries on the battlements that day, the meat pies Emrys would make for lunch, the oncoming spring rains that might ruin the Beltane festival like last year. Such ordinary things to talk about, worry about. And they were so easy with each other—a family in their own way.

Uncorrupted by a wicked empire, by years of brutality and slavery and bloodshed. She could almost see the three souls in the kitchen lined up beside each other: theirs bright and clear, hers a flickering black flame.

Do not let that light go out. Nehemia's last words to her that night in the tunnels. Celaena pushed around the food on her plate. She'd never known anyone whose life hadn't been overshadowed by Adarlan. She could barely remember her brief years before the continent had been enslaved, when Terrasen had still been free.

She could not remember what it was like to be free.

A pit yawned open beneath her feet, so deep that she had to move lest it swallow her whole.

She was about to get started on the dishes when Luca said from down the table, "So you either have to be very important or very unlucky to have Rowan training you to enter Doranelle." *Damned* was more like it, but she kept her mouth shut. Emrys was looking on with cautious interest. "That *is* what you're training for, right?"

"Isn't that why you're all here?" The words came out flatter than even she expected.

Luca said, "Yes, but I've got years until I learn whether I've met their qualifications."

Years. *Years?* Maeve couldn't mean for her to be here that long. She looked at Emrys. "How long have you been training?"

The old man snorted. "Oh, I was about fifteen when I came here, and worked for them for about . . . ten years, and I was never worthy enough. Too ordinary. Then I decided I'd rather have a home and my own kitchen here than be looked down upon in Doranelle for the rest of my days. It didn't hurt that my mate felt the same way. You'll meet him soon enough. He's always popping in to steal food for himself and his men." He chuckled, and Luca grinned.

Mate—not husband. The Fae had mates: an unbreakable bond, deeper than marriage, that lasted beyond death. Celaena asked, "So you're all—half-breeds?"

Luca stiffened, but flashed a smile as he said, "Only the pure-blooded Fae call us that. We prefer demi-Fae. But yes, most of us were born to mortal mothers, with the fathers unaware they'd sired us. The gifted ones usually get snatched away to Doranelle, but for us *common* offspring, the humans still aren't comfortable with us, so . . . we go here, we come to Mistward. Or to the other border outposts. Few enough get permission to go to Doranelle that most just come here to live among their own kind." Luca's eyes narrowed on her ears. "Looks like you got more human in you than Fae."

"Because I'm not half." She didn't want to share any more details than that.

"Can you shift?" Luca asked. Emrys shot him a warning look.

"Can *you*?" she asked.

"Oh, no. Neither of us can. If we could, we'd probably be in Doranelle with the other 'gifted' offspring that Maeve likes to collect."

Emrys growled. "Careful, Luca."

"Maeve doesn't deny it, so why should I? That's what Bas and the others are saying, too. Anyway, there are a few sentries here who have secondary forms, like Malakai—Emrys's mate. And they're here because they want to be."

She wasn't at all surprised that Maeve took an interest in the gifted ones—or that Maeve locked all the useless ones out. "And do either of you have—gifts?"

"You mean magic?" Luca said, his mouth quirking to the side. "Oh, no—neither of us got a lick of it. I heard your continent always had more wielders than we did, anyway, and more variety. Say, is it true that it's all gone over there?"

She nodded. Luca let out a low whistle. He opened his mouth to ask more, but she wasn't particularly in the mood to talk about it so she said, "Does anyone at this fortress have magic?" Maybe they'd be able to tell her what to expect with Rowan—and Maeve.

Luca shrugged. "Some. They've only got a hint of boring stuff, like encouraging plants to grow or finding water or convincing rain to come. Not that we need it here."

They'd be of no assistance with Rowan or Maeve, then. Wonderful.

"But," Luca chattered on, "no one here has any exciting or rare abilities. Like shape-shifting into whatever form they want, or controlling fire"—her stomach clenched at that—"or oracular sight. We *did* have a female wander in with raw magic two years ago—she could do anything she wanted, summon any element, and she was here a week before Maeve called her to Doranelle and we never heard from her again. A shame—she was so pretty, too. But it's the same here as it is everywhere else: a few people with a pathetic trace of elemental powers that are really only fun for farmers."

Emrys clicked his tongue. "You should pray the gods don't strike you with lightning for speaking like that." Luca groaned, rolling his eyes, but Emrys continued his lecture, gesturing at the youth with his teacup. "Those powers were gifts given to us by them long ago—gifts we needed to survive—and were passed down through the generations. Of course they'd be aligned with the elements, and of course they'd be watered down after so long."

Celaena glanced toward those iron figurines on the mantel. She contemplated mentioning that some believed the gods had also bred with ancient humans and given them magic that way, but . . . that would involve more talking than necessary. She tilted her head to the side. "What do you know about Rowan? How old is he?" The more she learned, the better.

Emrys wrapped his wrinkled hands around his teacup. "He's one of the few Fae we see around Mistward—he stops in every now and then to retrieve reports for Maeve, but he keeps to himself. Never stays the night. Occasionally he'll come with the others like him—there are six of them who closely serve the Queen as war leaders or spies, you see. They never talk to us, and all we hear are rumors about where they go and what they do. But I've known Rowan since I first came here. Not that I really know him, mind you. Sometimes he's gone for years, off serving Her Majesty. And I don't think anyone knows how old he is. When I was fifteen, the oldest people living here had known him since they were younglings, so . . . I'd say he's very old."

"And mean as an adder," Luca muttered.

Emrys gave him a warning look. "You'd best mind your tongue." He glanced toward the doors, as if Rowan would be lurking there. When his gaze fell again on Celaena, it was wary. "I'll admit that you're probably in for a good heap of difficulty."

"He's a stone-cold killer and a sadist is what he means," Luca added. "The meanest of Maeve's personal cabal of warriors, they say."

Well, that wasn't a surprise, either. But there were five others like him—*that* was an unpleasant fact. She said quietly, "I can handle him."

"We're not allowed to learn the Old Language until we enter Doranelle," Luca said, "but I heard his tattoo is a list of all the people he's slaughtered."

"Hush," Emrys said.

"It's not like he doesn't act like it." Luca frowned again at Celaena. "Maybe you should consider whether Doranelle is worth it, you know? It's not so bad living here."

She'd already had enough interacting. "I can handle him," she repeated. Maeve couldn't intend to keep her here for years. If that started to seem likely, Celaena would leave. And find another way to stop the king.

Luca opened his mouth but Emrys hushed him again, his gaze falling on Celaena's scarred hands. "Let her run her own course."

Luca started chattering about the weather, and Celaena headed to the mountain of dishes. As she washed, she fell into a rhythm, as she'd done while cleaning her weapons aboard that ship.

The kitchen sounds turned muffled as she let herself spiral down, contemplating that horrible realization again and again: she could not remember what it was like to be free.

12

The Blackbeak Clan was the last to fully assemble at the Ferian Gap.

As a result, they got the smallest and farthest rooms in the warren of halls carved into the Omega, the last of the Ruhnn Mountains and the northernmost of the sister-peaks flanking the snow-blasted pass.

Across the gap was the Northern Fang, the final peak of the White Fangs, which was currently occupied by the king's men—massive brutes who still didn't know quite what to make of the witches who had stalked in from every direction.

They'd been here for a day and Manon had yet to glimpse any sign of the wyverns the king had promised. She'd heard them, even though they were housed across the pass in the Northern Fang. No matter how deep you got into the Omega's stone halls, the shrieks and roars vibrated in the stone, the air pulsed with the boom of leathery wings, and the floors hissed with the scrape of talon on rock.

It had been five hundred years since all three Clans had assembled.

There had been over twenty thousand of them at one point. Now only three thousand remained, and that was a generous estimate. All that was left of a once-mighty kingdom.

Still, the halls of the Omega were a dangerous place to be. Already she'd had to pull apart Asterin and a Yellowlegs bitch who hadn't yet learned that Blackbeak sentinels—especially members of the Thirteen—didn't take lightly to being called soft-hearted.

There had been blue blood splattered on their faces, and though Manon was more than pleased to see that Asterin, beautiful, brash Asterin, had done most of the damage, she'd still had to punish her Second.

Three unblocked blows. One to the gut, so Asterin could feel her own powerlessness; one to the ribs, so she'd consider her actions every time she drew breath; and one to the face, so her broken nose would remind her that the punishment could have been far worse.

Asterin had taken them all without scream or complaint or plea, just as any of the Thirteen would have done.

And this morning, her Second, nose swollen and bruised at the bridge, had given Manon a fierce grin over their miserable breakfast of boiled oats. Had it been another witch, Manon would have dragged her by the neck to the front of the room and made her regret the insolence, but Asterin . . .

Even though Asterin was her cousin, she wasn't a friend. Manon didn't have friends. None of the witches, especially the Thirteen, had friends. But Asterin had guarded her back for a century, and the grin was a sign that she wouldn't put a dagger in Manon's spine the next time they were knee-deep in battle.

No, Asterin was just insane enough to wear the broken nose like a badge of honor, and would love her crooked nose for the rest of her not-so-immortal life.

The Yellowlegs heir, a haughty bull of a witch named Iskra, had merely given her offending sentinel a warning to keep her mouth shut and sent her down to the infirmary in the belly of the mountain. Fool.

All the coven leaders were under orders to keep their sentinels in line—to suppress the fighting between Clans. Or else the three Matrons would come down on them like a hammer. Without punishment, without Iskra making an example of her, the offending witch would keep at it until she got strung up by her toes by the new High Witch of the Yellowlegs Clan.

They'd held a sham of a memorial service last night for Baba Yellowlegs in the cavernous mess hall—lighting any old candles in lieu of the traditional black ones, wearing whatever hoods they could find, and going through the Sacred Words to the Three-Faced Goddess as though they were reading a recipe.

Manon had never met Baba Yellowlegs, and didn't particularly care that she'd died. She was more interested in *who* had killed her, and why. They all were, and it was those questions that were exchanged between the expected words of loss and mourning. Asterin and Vesta had done the talking, as they usually did, chatting up the other witches while Manon listened from nearby. No one knew anything, though. Even her two Shadows, concealed in the dark pockets of the mess hall as they'd been trained to do, had overheard nothing.

It was the not knowing that made her shoulders tight as Manon stalked up the sloped hallway to where the Matrons and all the Coven leaders were to assemble, Blackbeak and Yellowlegs witches stepping aside to let her pass. She resented not knowing anything that might be useful, that might give the Thirteen or the Blackbeaks an advantage. Of course, the Bluebloods were nowhere to be seen. The reclusive witches had arrived first and claimed the uppermost rooms in the Omega, saying they needed the mountain breeze to complete their rituals every day.

Religious fanatics with their noses in the wind, was what Mother Blackbeak had always called them. But it had been their insane devotion to the Three-Faced Goddess and their vision of the Witch Kingdom under Ironteeth rule that had mustered the Clans five centuries ago—even if it had been the Blackbeak sentinels who'd won the battles for them.

Manon treated her body as she would any other weapon: she kept it clean and honed and ready at any time to defend and destroy. But even her training couldn't keep her from being out of breath when she reached the atrium by the black bridge that connected the Omega to the Northern Fang. She hated the expanse of stone without even touching it. It smelled wrong.

It smelled like those two prisoners she'd seen with the duke. In fact, this whole place reeked like that. The scent wasn't natural; it didn't belong in this world.

About fifty witches—the highest-ranking coven leaders in each Clan—were gathered at the giant hole in the side of the mountain. Manon spotted her grandmother immediately, standing at the bridge entrance with what had to be the Blueblood and Yellowlegs Matrons.

The new Yellowlegs Matron was supposedly some half sister of Baba, and she certainly looked the part: huddled in brown robes, saffron ankles peeking out, white hair braided back to reveal a wrinkled, brutal face mottled with age. By rule, all Yellowlegs wore their iron teeth and nails on permanent display, and the new High Witch's were shining in the dull morning light.

Unsurprisingly, the Blueblood Matron was tall and willowy, more priestess than warrior. She wore the traditional deep blue robes, and a band of iron stars circled her brow. As Manon approached the crowd, she could see that the stars were barbed. Not surprising, either.

Legend had it that all witches had been gifted by the Three-Faced Goddess with iron teeth and nails to keep them anchored to this world when magic threatened to pull them away. The iron crown, supposedly, was proof that the magic in the Blueblood line ran so strong that their leader needed *more*—needed iron and pain—to keep her tethered in this realm.

Nonsense. Especially when magic had been gone these past ten years. But Manon had heard rumors of the rituals the Bluebloods did in their forests and caves, rituals in which pain was the gateway to magic, to opening their senses. Oracles, mystics, zealots.

Manon stalked through the ranks of the assembled Blackbeak coven leaders. They were the most numerous—twenty coven leaders, over which Manon ruled with her Thirteen. Each leader touched two fingers to her brow in deference. She ignored them and took up a spot at the front of the crowd, where her grandmother gave her an acknowledging glance.

An honor, for any High Witch to acknowledge an individual. Manon bowed her head, pressing two fingers to her brow. Obedience, discipline, and brutality were the most beloved words in the Blackbeak Clan. All else was to be extinguished without second thought.

She still had her chin high, hands behind her back, when she spotted the other two heirs watching her.

The Blueblood heir, Petrah, stood closest to the High Witches, her group in the center of the crowd. Manon stiffened but held her gaze.

Her freckled skin was as pale as Manon's, and her braided hair was as golden as Asterin's—a deep, brassy color that caught the gray light. She was beautiful, like so many of them, but grave. Above her blue eyes, a worn leather band rested on her brow in lieu of the iron-star crown. There was no way of telling how old she was, but she couldn't be much older than Manon if she looked this way after magic had vanished. There was no aggression, but no smile, either. Smiles were rare amongst witches—unless you were on the hunt or on a killing field.

The Yellowlegs heir, though . . . Iskra was grinning at Manon, bristling with a challenge that Manon found herself aching to meet. Iskra hadn't forgotten the brawl between their sentinels in the hallway yesterday. If anything, from the look in Iskra's brown eyes, it seemed that the brawl had been an invitation. Manon found herself debating how much trouble she'd get into for shredding the throat of the Yellowlegs heir. It would put an end to any fights between their sentinels.

It would also put an end to her life, if the attack were unprovoked. Witch justice was swift. Dominance battles could end in loss of life, but the claim had to be made up front. Without a formal provocation from Iskra, Manon's hands were tied.

"Now that we're assembled," the Blueblood Matron—Cresseida—said, drawing Manon's attention, "shall we show you what we've been brought here to do?"

Mother Blackbeak waved a hand to the bridge, black robes billowing in the icy wind. "We walk into the sky, witches."

The crossing of the black bridge was more harrowing than Manon wanted to admit. First, there was the miserable stone, which throbbed beneath her feet, giving off that reek that no one else seemed to notice. Then there was the screeching wind, which battered them this way and that, trying to shove them over the carved railing.

They couldn't even see the floor of the Gap. Mist shrouded everything below the bridge—a mist that hadn't vanished in the day they'd been here, or the days they'd hiked up the Gap. It was, she supposed, some trick of the king's. Contemplating it led only to more questions, none of which she bothered to voice, or really care about all that much.

By the time they reached the cavernous atrium of the Northern Fang, Manon's ears were frozen and her face was raw. She'd flown at high altitudes, in all kinds of weather, but not for a long while. Not without a fresh belly of meat in her, keeping her warm.

She wiped her runny nose on the shoulder of her red cloak. She'd seen the other coven leaders eyeing the crimson material—as they always did, with yearning and scorn and envy. Iskra had gazed at it the longest, sneering. It would be nice—really damn nice—to peel off the Yellowlegs heir's face one day.

They reached the gaping mouth into the upper reaches of the Northern Fang. Here the stone was scarred and gouged, splattered with the Triple Goddess knew what. From the tang of it, it was blood. Human blood.

Five men—all looking hewn from the same scarred stone themselves—met the three Matrons with grim nods. Manon fell into step behind her grandmother, one eye on the men, the other on their surroundings. The other two heirs did the same. At least they agreed on that.

As heirs, their foremost duty was to protect their High Witches, even if it meant sacrificing themselves. Manon glanced at the Yellowlegs Matron, who held herself just as proudly as the two Ancients as they walked into the shadows of the mountain. But Manon didn't take her hand off her blade, Wind-Cleaver, for a heartbeat.

The screams and wing beats and clank of metal were far louder here.

"This is where we breed and train 'em until they can make the Crossing to the Omega," one of the men was saying, gesturing to the many cave mouths they passed as they strode through the cavernous hall. "Hatcheries are in the belly of the mountain, a level above the forges for the armory—to keep the eggs warm, you see. Dens are a level above that. We keep 'em separated by gender and type. The bulls we hold in their own pens unless we want to breed 'em. They kill anyone in their cages. Learned that the hard way." The men chuckled, but the witches did not. He went on about the different types—the bulls were the best, but a female could be just as fierce and twice as smart. The smaller ones were good for stealth, and had been bred to be totally black against the night sky, or a pale blue to blend into daylight patrols.

The average wyvern's colors they didn't care about so much, since they wanted their enemies to drop dead from terror, the man claimed.

They descended steps carved into the stone itself, and if the reek of blood and waste didn't overwhelm every sense, then the din of the wyverns—a roaring and screeching and booming of wings and flesh on rock—nearly drowned out the man's words. But Manon stayed focused on her grandmother's position, on the positions of the others around her. And she knew that Asterin, one step behind her, was doing the same for her.

He led them onto a viewing platform in a massive cavern. The sunken floor was at least forty feet below, one end of the chamber wholly open to the cliff face, the other sealed with an iron grate—no, a door.

"This is one of the training pits," the man explained. "It's easy to sort out the natural-born killers, but we discover a lot of them show their mettle in the pits. Before you . . . ladies," he said, trying to hide his wince at the word, "even lay eyes on them, they'll be in here, fighting it out."

"And when," said Mother Blackbeak, pinning him with a stare, "will we select our mounts?"

The man swallowed. "We trained a brood of gentler ones to teach you the basics."

A growl from Iskra. Manon might also have snarled at the implied insult, but the Blueblood Matron spoke. "You don't learn to ride by hopping on a warhorse, do you?"

The man almost sagged with relief. "Once you're comfortable with the flying—"

"We were born on the back of the wind," said one of the coven leaders in the back. Some grunts of approval. Manon kept silent, as did her Blackbeak coven leaders. Obedience. Discipline. Brutality. They did not descend to boasting.

The man fidgeted and kept his focus on Cresseida, as if she were the only safe one in the room, even with her barbed crown of stars. Idiot. Manon sometimes thought the Bluebloods were the deadliest of them all.

"Soon as you're ready," he said, "we can begin the selection process. Get you on your mounts, and start the training."

Manon risked taking her eyes off her grandmother to study the pit. There were giant chains anchored in one of the walls, and enormous splotches of dark blood stained the stones, as if one of these beasts had been pushed against it. A giant crack spider-webbed from the center. Whatever hit the wall had been tossed hard.

"What are the chains for?" Manon found herself asking. Her grandmother gave her a warning look, but Manon focused on the man. Predictably, his eyes widened at her beauty—then stayed wide as he beheld the death lurking beneath it.

"Chains are for the bait beasts," he said. "They're the wyverns we use to show the others how to fight, to turn their aggression into a weapon. We're under orders not to put any of 'em down, even the runts and broken ones, so we put the weaklings to good use."

Just like dog fighting. She looked again to the splotch and the crack in the wall. The bait beast had probably been thrown by one of the bigger ones. And if the wyverns could hurl each other like that, then the damage to humans . . . Her chest tightened with anticipation, especially as the man said, "Want to see a bull?"

A glimmer of iron nails as Cresseida made an elegant gesture to continue. The man let out a sharp whistle. None of them spoke as chains rattled, a whip cracked, and the iron gate to the pit groaned as it lifted. And then, heralded by men with whips and spears, the wyvern appeared.

A collective intake of breath, even from Manon.

"Titus is one of our best," the man said, pride gleaming in his voice.

Manon couldn't tear her eyes away from the gorgeous beast: his mottled gray body covered in a leathery hide; his massive back legs, armed with talons as big as her forearm; and his enormous wings, tipped with a claw and used to propel him forward like a front set of limbs.

The triangular head swiveled this way and that, and his dripping maw revealed yellow, curved fangs. "Tail's armed with a venomous barb," the man said as the wyvern emerged fully from the pit, snarling at the men down there with him. The reverberations of the snarl echoed through the stone, into her boots and up her legs, right into her husk of a heart.

A chain was clamped around his back leg, undoubtedly to keep him from flying out of the pit. The tail, as long as his body and tipped with two curved spikes, flicked back and forth like a cat's.

"They can fly hundreds of miles in a day and still be ready to fight when they arrive," the man said, and the witches all hissed in a breath. That sort of speed and endurance . . .

"What do they eat?" asked Petrah, freckled face still calm and grave.

The man rubbed his neck. "They'll eat anything. But they like it fresh."

"So do we," said Iskra with a grin. Had anyone but the Yellowlegs heir said it, Manon would have joined in with the other grins around her.

Titus gave a sudden thrash, lunging for the nearest man while using his magnificent tail to snap the raised spears behind him. A whip cracked, but it was too late.

Blood and screams and the crunch of bone. The man's legs and head tumbled to the ground. The torso was swallowed down in one bite. The smell of blood filled the air, and every single one of the Ironteeth witches inhaled deeply. The man in front of them took a too-casual step away.

The bull in the pit was now looking up at them, tail still slashing against the floor.

Magic was gone, and yet this was possible—this creation of magnificent beasts. Magic was gone, and yet Manon felt the sureness of the moment settle along her bones. She was *meant* to be here. She'd have Titus or no other.

Because she'd suffer no creature to be her mount but the fiercest, the one whose blackness called to her own. As her eyes met with the endless dark of Titus's, she smiled at the wyvern.

She could have sworn he smiled back.

13

Celaena didn't realize how exhausted she was until all sounds—Emrys's soft singing from the table, the thud of dough as he kneaded it, the chopping of Luca's knife and his ceaseless chatter about everything and anything—stopped. And she knew what she'd find when she turned toward the stairwell. Her hands were pruny, fingers aching, back and neck throbbing, but . . . Rowan was leaning against the archway of the stairwell, arms crossed and violence beckoning in his lifeless eyes. "Let's go."

Though his features remained cold, she had the distinct impression that he was somewhat annoyed at her for not sulking in a corner, bemoaning the state of her nails. As she left, Luca drew a finger across his neck as he mouthed *good luck*.

Rowan led her through a small courtyard, where sentries tried to pretend they weren't watching their every move, and out into the forest. The ward-magic woven between the ring of megaliths again nipped at her skin as they passed, and nausea washed through her. Without the constant heat of the kitchen, she was half-frozen by the time they strode between the moss-coated trees, but even that was only a vague flicker of feeling.

Rowan trekked up a rocky ridge toward the highest reaches of the forest, still clouded in mist. She barely paused to take in the view of the foothills below, the plains before them, all green and fresh and safe from Adarlan. Rowan didn't utter a single word until they reached what looked like the weather-stained ruins of a temple.

It was now no more than a flat bed of stone blocks and columns whose carvings had been dulled by wind and rain. To her left lay Wendlyn, foothills and plains and peace. To her right arose the wall of the Cambrian Mountains, blocking any sight of the immortal lands beyond. Behind her, far down, she could make out the fortress snaking along the spine of the mountain.

Rowan crossed the cracked stones, his silver hair battered by the crisp, damp wind. She kept her arms loose at her sides, more out of reflex than anything. He was armed to the teeth, his face a mask of unyielding brutality.

She made herself give a little smile, her best attempt at a dutiful, eager expression. "Do your worst."

He looked her over from head to toe: the mist-damp shirt, now icy against her puckered skin, the equally stained and damp pants, the position of her feet . . .

"Wipe that smarmy, lying smile off your face." His voice was as dead as his eyes, but it had a razor-sharp bite behind it.

She kept her smarmy, lying smile. "I don't know what you're talking about."

He stepped toward her, the canines coming out this time. "Here's your first lesson, girl: cut the horseshit. I don't feel like dealing with it, and I'm probably the only one who doesn't give a damn about how angry and vicious and awful you are underneath."

"I don't think you particularly want to see how angry and vicious and awful I am underneath."

"Go ahead and be as nasty as you want, Princess, because I've been ten times as nasty, for ten times longer than you've been alive."

She didn't let it out—no, because he didn't truly understand a thing about what lurked under her skin and ran claws down her insides—but she stopped any attempt to control her features. Her lips pulled back from her teeth.

"Better. Now shift."

She didn't bother to sound pleasant as she said, "It's not something I can control."

"If I wanted excuses, I'd ask for them. *Shift*."

She didn't know how. She had never mastered it as a child, and there certainly hadn't been any opportunities to learn in the past decade. "I hope you brought snacks, because we're going to be here a long, long while if today's lesson is dependent upon my shifting."

"You're *really* going to make me enjoy training you." She had a feeling he could have switched out *training you* for *eating you alive*.

"I've already participated in a dozen versions of the master-disciple training saga, so why don't we cut that horseshit, too?"

His smile turned quieter, more lethal. "Shut your smart-ass mouth and shift."

A shuddering rush went through her—a spear of lightning in the abyss. *"No."*

And then he attacked.

She'd contemplated his blows all morning, the way he'd moved, the swiftness and angles. So she dodged the first blow, sidestepping his fist, strands of her hair snapping in the wind.

She even twisted far enough in the other direction to avoid the second strike. But he was so damn fast she could barely register the movements—so fast that she had no chance of dodging or blocking or anticipating the third blow. Not to her face but to her legs, just as he had the night before.

One sweep of his foot and she was falling, twisting to catch herself, but not fast enough to avoid thudding her brow against a weather-smooth rock. She rolled, the gray sky looming, and tried to remember how to breathe as the impact echoed through her skull. Rowan pounced with fluid ease, his powerful thighs digging into her ribs as he straddled her. Breathless, head reeling, and muscles drained from a morning in the kitchen and weeks of hardly eating, she couldn't twist and toss him—couldn't do anything. She was outweighed, outmuscled, and for the first time in her life, she realized she was utterly outmatched.

"*Shift*," he hissed.

She laughed up at him, a dead, wretched sound even to her own ears. "Nice try." Gods, her head throbbed, a warm trickle of blood was leaking from the right side of her brow, and he was now *sitting* on her chest. She laughed again, strangled by his weight. "You think you can trick me into shifting by pissing me off?"

He snarled, his face speckled with the stars floating in her vision. Every blink shot daggers of pain through her. It would probably be the worst black eye of her life.

"Here's an idea: I'm rich as hell," she said over the pounding in her head. "How about we pretend to do this training for a week or so, and then you tell Maeve I'm good and ready to enter her territory, and I'll give you all the gods-damned gold you want."

He brought his canines so close to her neck that one movement would have him ripping out her throat. "Here's an idea," he growled. "I don't know what the hell you've been doing for ten years, other than flouncing around and calling yourself an assassin. But I think you're used to getting your way. I think you have no control over yourself. No control, and no discipline—not the kind that counts, deep down. You are a *child*, and a spoiled one at that. And," he said, those green eyes holding nothing but distaste, "you are a coward."

Had her arms not been pinned, she would have clawed his face off right then. She struggled, trying every technique she'd ever learned to dislodge him, but he didn't move an inch.

A low, nasty laugh. "Don't like that word?" He leaned closer still, that tattoo of his swimming in her muddled vision. "*Coward*. You're a coward who has run for ten years while innocent people were burned and butchered and—"

She stopped hearing him.

She just—stopped.

It was like being underwater again. Like charging into Nehemia's room and finding that beautiful body mutilated on the bed. Like seeing Galan Ashryver, beloved and brave, riding off into the sunset to the cheers of his people.

She lay still, watching the churning clouds above. Waiting for him to finish the words she couldn't hear, waiting for a blow she was fairly certain she wouldn't feel.

"Get up," he said suddenly, and the world was bright and wide as he stood. *"Get up."*

Get up. Chaol had said that to her once, when pain and fear and grief had shoved her over an edge. But the edge she'd gone over the night Nehemia had died, the night she'd gutted Archer, the day she'd told Chaol the horrible truth . . . Chaol had helped shove her over that edge. She was still on the fall down. There was no getting up, because there was no bottom.

Powerful, rough hands under her shoulders, the world tilting and spinning, then that tattooed, snarling face in hers. Let him take her head between those massive hands and snap her neck.

"Pathetic," he spat, releasing her. "Spineless and pathetic."

For Nehemia, she had to try, had to *try*—

But when she reached in, toward the place in her chest where that monster dwelled, she found only cobwebs and ashes.

Celaena's head was still reeling, and dried blood now itched down the side of her face. She didn't bother to wipe it off, or to really care about the black eye that she was positive had blossomed during the miles they'd hiked from the temple ruins and into the forested foothills. But not back to Mistward.

She was swaying on her feet when Rowan drew a sword and a dagger and stopped at the edge of a grassy plateau, speckled with small hills. Not hills—barrows, the ancient tombs of lords and princes long dead, rolling to the other edge of trees. There were dozens, each marked with a stone threshold and sealed iron door. And through the murky vision, the pounding headache, the hair on the back of her neck rose.

The grassy mounds seemed to . . . breathe. To sleep. Iron doors—to keep the wights inside, locked with the treasure they'd stolen. They infiltrated the barrows and lurked there for eons, feeding on whatever unwitting fools dared seek the gold within.

Rowan inclined his head toward the barrows. "I had planned to wait until you had some handle on your power—planned to make you come at night, when the barrow-wights are *really* something to behold, but consider this a favor, as there are few that will dare come out in the day. Walk through the mounds—face the wights and make it to the other side of the field, Aelin, and we can go to Doranelle whenever you wish."

It was a trap. She knew that well enough. He had the gift of endless time, and could play games that lasted centuries. Her impatience, her mortality, the fact that every heartbeat brought her closer to death, was being used against her. To face the wights . . .

Rowan's weapons gleamed, close enough to grab. He shrugged those powerful shoulders as he said, "You can either wait to earn back your steel, or you can enter as you are now."

The flash of temper snapped her out of it long enough to say, "My bare hands are weapon enough." He just gave a taunting grin and sauntered into the maze of hills.

She trailed him closely, following him around each mound, knowing that if she fell too far behind, he'd leave her out of spite.

Steady breathing and the yawns of awakening things arose beyond those iron doors. They were unadorned, bolted into the stone lintels with spikes and nails that were so old they probably predated Wendlyn itself.

Her footsteps crunched in the grass. Even the birds and insects did not utter a too-loud sound here. The hills parted to reveal an inner circle of dead grass around the most crumbling barrow of all. Where the others were rounded, this one looked as if some ancient god had stepped on it. Its flattened top had been overrun with the gnarled roots of bushes; the three massive stones of the threshold were beaten, stained, and askew. The iron door was gone.

There was only blackness within. Ageless, breathing blackness.

Her heartbeat pounded in her ears as the darkness reached for her.

"I leave you here," Rowan said. He hadn't set one foot inside the circle, his boots just an inch shy of the dead grass. His smile turned feral. "I'll meet you on the other side of the field."

He expected her to bolt like a hare. And she wanted to. Gods, this place, that damned barrow only a hundred yards away, made her want to run and run and not stop until she found a place where the sun shone day *and* night. But if she did this, then she could go to Doranelle tomorrow. And those wights waiting in the other half of the field . . . they couldn't be worse than what she'd already seen, and fought, and found dwelling in the world and inside of herself.

So she inclined her head to Rowan, and walked onto the dead field.

14

Each step toward the central mound had Celaena's blood roaring. The darkness between the stained, ancient stones grew, swirling. It was colder, too. Cold and dry.

She wouldn't stop, not with Rowan still watching, not when she had so much to do. She didn't dare look too long toward the open doorway and the thing lurking beyond. A lingering shred of pride—stupid, mortal pride—kept her from bolting through the rest of the field. Running, she remembered, only attracted some predators. So she kept her steps slow and called on every bit of training she'd had, even as the wight slunk closer to the threshold, no more than a ripple of ravenous hunger encased in rags.

Yet the wight remained within its mound, even as she came near enough to drag into the barrow, as if it were . . . hesitating.

She was just passing the barrow when a pulsing, stale bit of air pushed against her ears. Maybe running was a good idea. If magic was the only weapon against wights, then her hands would be useless. Still, the wight lingered beyond the threshold.

The strange, dead air pushed against her ears again, a high-pitched ringing wending itself into her head. She hurried, grass crunching as she gathered every detail she could to wield against whatever assailant lurked nearby. Treetops swayed in the misty breeze on the other end of the field. It wasn't far.

Celaena passed the central mound, cracking her jaw against the ringing in her ears, worse and worse with each step. Even the wight cringed away. It hadn't been hesitating because of her, or Rowan.

The circle of dead grass ended a few steps away—just a few. Just a few, and then she could run from whatever it was that could make a wight tremble in fear.

And then she saw him. The man standing behind the barrow.

Not a wight. She glimpsed only a flash of pale skin, night-dark hair, unfathomable beauty, and an onyx torque around his strong column of a neck, and—

Blackness. A wave of it, slamming down on her.

Not oblivion but actual dark, as if he'd thrown a blanket over the two of them.

The ground *felt* grassy, but she couldn't see it. Couldn't see *anything*. Not beyond, not to the side, not behind. There was only her and the swirling black.

Celaena crouched, biting down on a curse as she scanned the dark. Whatever he was, despite his shape, he wasn't mortal. In his perfection, in those depthless eyes, there was nothing human.

Blood tickled her upper lip—a nosebleed. The pounding in her ears began to drown out her thoughts, any plan, as if her body were repulsed by the very essence of whatever this thing was. The darkness remained, impenetrable, unending.

Stop. Breathe.

But someone was breathing behind her. Was it the man, or something else?

The breathing was louder, closer, and a chill air brushed her nose, her lips, licking along her skin. Running—running was smarter than just waiting. She took several bounding steps that *should* have taken her toward the edge of the field, but—

Nothing. Only endless black and the breathing *thing* that was closer now, reeking of dust and carrion and another scent, something she hadn't smelled for a lifetime but could never forget, not when it had been coating that room like paint.

Oh, *gods*. Breath on her neck, snaking up the shell of her ear.

She whirled, drawing in what might very well be her last breath, and the world flashed bright. Not with clouds and dead grass. Not with a Fae Prince waiting nearby. The room . . .

This room . . .

The servant woman was screaming. Screaming like a teakettle. There were still puddles just inside the shut windows—windows Celaena herself had sealed the night before when they'd been flapping in the swift and sudden storm.

She had thought the bed was wet because of the rain. She'd climbed in because the storm had made her hear such horrible things, made her feel like there was something *wrong*, like there was someone standing in the corner of her room. It was not rain soaking the bed in that elegantly rugged chamber at the country manor.

It was not rain that had dried on her, on her hands and skin and nightgown. And that smell—not just blood, but something else . . . "This is not real," Celaena said aloud, backing away from the bed on which she was standing like a ghost. *"This is not real."*

But there were her parents, sprawled on the bed, their throats sliced ear to ear.

There was her father, broad-shouldered and handsome, his skin already gray.

There was her mother, her golden hair matted with blood, her face . . . her face . . .

Slaughtered like animals. The wounds were so vulgar, so gaping and deep, and her parents looked so—so—

Celaena vomited. She fell to her knees, her bladder loosening just before she vomited a second time.

"This is not real, this is not real," she gasped as a wet warmth soaked her pants. She couldn't breathe, couldn't breathe, couldn't—

And then she was pushing to her feet, bolting away from that room, toward the wood-paneled walls, through them like a wraith herself, until—

Another bedroom, another body.

Nehemia. Carved up, mutilated, violated and broken.

The *thing* lurking behind her slid a hand over her waist, along her abdomen, pulling her back against its chest with a lover's gentleness. Panic surged, so strong that she slammed her elbow back and up—hitting what felt like flesh and bone. It hissed, releasing her. That was all she needed. She ran, treading through the illusion of her friend's blood and organs, and then—

Watery sunlight and dead grass and a heavily armed silver-haired warrior whom she sprinted toward, not caring about the vomit on her clothes, her soiled pants, the gasping, shrieking noise coming out of her throat. She ran until she reached him and fell to the green grass, gripping it, shredding it, retching even though she had nothing left in her but a trickle of bile. She was screaming or sobbing or not making any sound at all.

Then she felt the shift and the surge, a well opening beneath her stomach and filling with burning, relentless fire.

No. No.

Agony cleaved her in a pulse, her vision jumping between crystal clarity and the muted eyesight of mortals, her teeth aching as the fangs punched out and retracted, ebb and flow, immortal and mortal,

mortal and immortal, shifting as fast as a hummingbird's flapping wings—

With each shift, the well deepened, that wildfire rising and falling and reaching up, up . . .

She really did scream then, because her throat burned, or maybe that was the magic coming out, at last unleashed.

Magic—

Celaena awoke under the canopy of the forest. It was still daylight, and from the dirt on her shirt and pants and boots, it seemed like Rowan had dragged her here from the barrows.

That was vomit on her shirt and pants. And then there was . . . She'd wet herself. Her face heated, but she shoved away the thoughts about *why* she had pissed herself, why she had hurled her guts up. And that last thought, about magic—

"No discipline, no control, and no courage," came a growling voice.

Head throbbing, she found Rowan sitting on a rock, his muscular arms braced on his knees. A dagger hung from his left hand, as if he'd been idly tossing the damn thing in the air while she lay in her own filth. "You failed," he said flatly. "You made it to the other side of the field, but I said to face the wights—not throw a magical tantrum."

"I will *kill* you," she said, the words raw and gasping. "How *dare*—"

"That was not a wight, Princess." He flicked his attention toward the trees beyond her. She might have roared about using specifics to escape his bargain to bring her to Doranelle, but when his eyes met hers again, he seemed to say, *That thing should not have been there.*

Then what in hell was it, you stupid bastard? she silently shot back.

He clenched his jaw before he said aloud, "I don't know. We've had skinwalkers on the prowl for weeks, roaming down from the hills to search for human pelts, but this . . . this was something different. I have never encountered its like, not in these lands or any other. Thanks to having to drag you away, I don't think I'll learn anytime soon." He gave a pointed look at her current state. "It was gone when I circled back. Tell me what happened. I saw only darkness, and when you emerged, you were . . . different." She dared a look at herself again. Her skin was bone-white, as if the little color she'd received lying on those rooftops in Varese had been leeched away, and not only by fright and sickness.

"No," she said. "And you can go to hell."

"Other lives might depend on it."

"I want to go back to the fortress," she breathed. She didn't want to know about the creatures or about the skinwalkers or about any of it. Each word was an effort. "Right now."

"You're done when I say you're done."

"You can kill me or torture me or throw me off a cliff, but I am *done* for today. In that darkness, I saw things that no one should be able to see. It dragged me through my memories—and not the decent ones. Is that enough for you?"

He spat out a noise, but got to his feet and began walking. She staggered and stumbled, knees trembling, and kept moving after him, all the way into the halls of Mistward, where she angled her body so that none of the passing sentries or workers could see her soiled pants, the vomit. There was no hiding her face, though. She kept her attention on the prince, until he opened a wooden door and a wall of steam hit her. "These are the female baths. Your room is a level up. Be in the kitchens at dawn tomorrow." And then he left her again.

Celaena trudged into the steamy chamber, not caring who was in there as she shucked off her clothes, collapsed into one of the sunken stone tubs, and did not stir for a long, long while.

15

Chaol wasn't at all surprised that his father was twenty minutes late to their meeting. Nor was he surprised when his father strode into Chaol's office, slid into the chair opposite his desk, and offered no explanation for his tardiness. With calculated cool and distaste, he surveyed the office: no windows, a worn rug, an open trunk of discarded weapons that Chaol had never found the time to polish or send for repairs.

At least it was organized. The few papers on his desk were stacked; his glass pens were in their proper holders; his suit of armor, which he rarely had occasion to wear, gleamed from its dummy in the corner. His father said at last, "This is what our illustrious king gives the Captain of his Guard?"

Chaol shrugged, and his father studied the heavy oak desk. A desk he'd inherited from his predecessor, and one on which he and Celaena had—

He shut down the memory before it could boil his blood, and instead smiled at his father. "There was a larger office available in the glass addition, but I wanted to be accessible to my men." It was the truth. He also hadn't wanted to be anywhere near the administrative wing of the castle, sharing a hallway with courtiers and councilmen.

"A wise decision." His father leaned back in the ancient wooden chair. "A leader's instincts."

Chaol pinned him with a long stare. "I'm to return to Anielle with you—I'm surprised you waste your breath on flattery."

"Is that so? From what I've seen, you have been making no move to prepare for this so-called return. You're not even looking for a replacement."

"Despite your low opinion of my position, it's one I take seriously. I won't have just anyone looking after this palace."

"You haven't even told His Majesty that you're leaving." That pleasant, dead smile remained on his father's face. "When I begged for my leave next week, the king made no mention of you accompanying me. Rather than land you in hot water, boy, I held my tongue."

Chaol kept his face bland, neutral. "Again, I'm not leaving until I find a proper replacement. It's why I asked you to meet me. I need time." It was true—partially, at least.

Just as he had for the past few nights, Chaol had dropped by Aedion's party—another tavern, even more expensive, even more packed. Aedion wasn't there again. Somehow everyone *thought* the general was there, and even the courtesan who'd left with him the first night said the general had given her a gold coin—without utilizing her services—and gone off to find more sparkling wine.

Chaol had stood on the street corner where the courtesan said she'd left him, but found nothing. And wasn't it fascinating that no one really seemed to know exactly when the Bane would arrive, or where they were currently camped—only that they were on their way. Chaol was too busy during the day to track Aedion down, and during the king's various meetings and luncheons, confronting the general was impossible. But tonight he planned to arrive at the party early enough that he'd see if Aedion even showed and where he slipped off to. The sooner he could get something on Aedion, the sooner he could settle all this nonsense and keep the king from looking too long in his direction before he turned in his resignation.

He'd only called this meeting because of a thought that had awoken him in the middle of the night—a slightly insane, highly dangerous plan that would likely get him killed before it even accomplished anything. He'd skimmed through all those books Celaena had found on magic, and found nothing at all about how he might help Dorian—and Celaena—by freeing it. But Celaena had once told him that the rebel group Archer and Nehemia had run claimed two things: one, that they knew where Aelin Galathynius was; and two, that they were close to finding a way to break the King of Adarlan's mysterious power over the continent. The first one was a lie, of course, but if there was the slightest chance that these rebels knew how to free magic . . . he had to take it. He was already going out to trail Aedion, and he'd seen all of Celaena's notes about the rebel hideouts, so he had an idea of where they could be found. This would have to be dealt with carefully, and he still needed as much time as he could buy.

His father's dead smile faded, and true steel, honed by decades of ruling Anielle, shone through. "Rumor has it you consider yourself a man of honor. Though I wonder what manner of man you truly are, if you do not honor your bargains. I wonder . . ." His father made a good show of chewing on his bottom lip. "I wonder what your motive was, then, in sending your woman to Wendlyn." Chaol fought the urge to stiffen. "For the noble Captain Westfall, there would be no question that he truly wanted His Majesty's Champion to dispatch our foreign enemies. Yet for the oath-breaker, the liar . . ."

"I am not breaking my vow to you," Chaol said, meaning every word. "I intend to go to Anielle—I will swear that in any temple, before any god. But only when I've found a replacement."

"You swore a month," his father growled.

"You're to have me for the rest of my damned life. What is a month or two more to you?"

His father's nostrils flared. What purpose, then, did his father have in wanting him to return so quickly? Chaol was about to ask, itching to make his father squirm a bit, when an envelope landed on his desk.

It had been years—years and years, but he still remembered his mother's handwriting, still recalled the elegant way in which she drew his name. "What is this?"

"Your mother sent a letter to you. I suppose she's expressing her joy at your anticipated return." Chaol didn't touch the envelope. "Aren't you going to read it?"

"I have nothing to say to her, and no interest in what she has to say to me," Chaol lied. Another trap, another way to unnerve him. But he had so much to do here, so many things to learn and uncover. He'd honor his vow soon enough.

His father snatched back the letter, tucking it into his tunic. "She will be most saddened to hear that." And he knew his father, well aware of Chaol's lie, would tell his mother exactly what he'd said. For a heartbeat, his blood roared in his ears, the way it always had when he'd witnessed his father belittling his mother, reprimanding her, ignoring her.

He took a steadying breath. "Four months, then I'll go. Set the date and it'll be done."

"Two months."

"Three."

A slow smile. "I could go to the king right now and ask for your dismissal instead of waiting three months."

Chaol clenched his jaw. "Name your price, then."

"Oh, there's no price. But I think I like the idea of you owing me a favor." That dead smile returned. "I like that idea very much. Two months, boy."

They did not bother with good-byes.

Sorscha was called up to the Crown Prince's chambers just as she was settling in to brew a calming tonic for an overworked kitchen girl. And though she tried not to seem too eager and pathetic, she found a way to very, very quickly dump the task on one of the lower-level apprentices and make the trek to the prince's tower.

She'd never been here, but she knew where it was—all the healers did, just in case. The guards let her pass with hardly a nod, and by the time she'd ascended the spiral staircase, the door to his chambers was already open.

A mess. His rooms were a mess of books and papers and discarded weapons. And there, sitting at a table with hardly a foot of space cleared for him, was Dorian, looking rather embarrassed—either at the mess, or at his split lip.

She managed to bow, even as that traitorous heat flooded her again, up her neck and across her face. "Your Highness summoned me?"

A cleared throat. "I—well, I think you can see what needs repairing."

Another injury to his hand. This one looked like it was from sparring, but the lip . . . getting that close to him would be an effort of will. Hand first, then. Let that distract her, anchor her.

She set down her basket of supplies and lost herself in the work of readying ointments and bandages. His scented soap caressed her nose, strong enough to suggest he'd just bathed. Which was a horrible thing to think about as she stood beside his chair, because she was a professional healer, and imagining her patients naked was not a—

"Aren't you going to ask what happened?" the prince said, peering up at her.

"It's not my place to ask—and unless it's relevant to the injury, it's nothing I need to know." It came out colder, harder than she meant. But it was true.

Efficiently, she patched up his hand. The silence didn't bother her; she'd sometimes spent days in the catacombs without speaking to anyone. She'd been a quiet child before her parents had died, and after the massacre in the city square, she'd become even more so. It wasn't until she'd come to the castle that she found friends—found that she sometimes *liked* talking. Yet now, with him . . . well, it seemed that the prince didn't like silence, because he looked up at her again and said, "Where are you from?"

Such a tricky question to answer, since the how and why of her journey to this castle were stained by the actions of his father. "Fenharrow," she said, praying that would be the end of it.

"Where in Fenharrow?"

She almost cringed, but she had more self-control than that after five years of tending gruesome injuries and knowing that one flicker of disgust or fear on her face could shatter a patient's control. "A small village in the south. Most people have never heard of it."

"Fenharrow is beautiful," he said. "All that open land, stretching on forever."

She did not remember enough of it to recall whether she had loved the flat expanse of farmland, bordered on the west by mountains and on the east by the sea.

"Did you always want to be a healer?"

"Yes," she said, because she was entrusted to heal the heir to the empire and could show nothing but absolute certainty.

A slash of a grin. "Liar."

She didn't mean to, but she met his gaze—those sapphire eyes so bright in the late afternoon sun streaming through the small window. "I did not mean any offense, Your—"

"I'm prying." He tested the bandages. "I was trying to distract myself."

She nodded, because she had nothing to say and could never come up with anything clever anyway. She drew out her tin of disinfecting salve. "For your lip, if you don't mind, Your Highness, I want to make sure there's no dirt or anything in the wound so it—"

"Sorscha." She tried not to let it show, what it did to her to have him remember her name. Or to hear him say it. "Do what you need to do."

She bit her lip, a stupid nervous habit, and nodded as she tilted his chin up so she could better see his mouth. His skin was so warm. She touched the wound and he hissed, his breath caressing her fingers, but didn't pull back or reprimand or strike her as some of the other courtiers did.

She applied the salve to his lip as quickly as she could. Gods, his lips were soft.

She hadn't known he was the prince the day she first saw him, striding through the gardens, the captain in tow. They were barely into their teenage years, and she was an apprentice in hand-me-down clothes, but for a moment, he'd looked at her and smiled. He'd *seen* her when no one else had for years, so she found excuses to be in the upper levels of the castle. But she'd wept the next month when she spied him again, and two apprentices had whispered about how handsome the prince was—Dorian, heir to the throne.

It had been secret and stupid, this infatuation with him. Because when she finally encountered him again, years later while helping Amithy with a patient, he did not look at her. She had become invisible, like many of the healers—invisible, just as she had wanted. "Sorscha?"

Her horror achieved new depths as she realized she'd been staring at his mouth, fingers still in her tin of salve. "I'm sorry," she said, wondering whether she should throw herself from the tower and end her humiliation. "It's been a long day." That wasn't a lie.

She was acting like a fool. She'd been with a man before—one of the guards, just once and long enough to know she wasn't particularly interested in letting another one touch her anytime soon. But standing so close, his legs brushing the skirt of her brown homespun dress . . .

"Why didn't you tell anyone?" he asked quietly. "About me and my friends."

She backed away a step but held his stare, even though training and instinct told her to avert her eyes. "You were never cruel to the healers—to anyone. I like to think that the world needs . . ." Saying that was too much. Because the world was his father's world.

"Needs better people," he finished for her, standing. "And you think my father would have used your knowledge of our . . . comings and goings against us."

So he knew that Amithy reported anything unusual. Amithy had told Sorscha to do the same, if she knew what was good for her. "I don't mean to imply that His Majesty would—"

"Does your village still exist? Are your parents still alive?"

Even years later, she couldn't keep the pain from her voice as she said, "No. It was burned. And no: they brought me to Rifthold and were killed in the city's immigrant purge."

A shadow of grief and horror in his eyes. "So why would you ever come here—work here?"

She gathered her supplies. "Because I had nowhere else to go." Agony flickered on his face. "Your Highness, have I—"

But he was staring as if he understood—and saw her. "I'm sorry."

"It wasn't your decision. Or your soldiers who rounded up my parents."

He only looked at her for a long moment before thanking her. A polite dismissal. And she wished, as she left that cluttered tower, that she'd never opened her mouth—because perhaps he'd never call on her again for the sheer awkwardness of it. She wouldn't lose her position, because he wasn't that cruel, but if he refused her services, then it might lead to questions. So Sorscha resolved, as she lay that night in her little cot, to find a way to apologize—or maybe find excuses to keep the prince from seeing her again. Tomorrow, she'd figure it out tomorrow.

The following day she didn't expect the messenger who arrived after breakfast, asking for the name of her village. And when she hesitated, he said that the Crown Prince wanted to know.

Wanted to know, so he could have it added to his personal map of the continent.

16

Of all the spaces in the Omega, the mess hall was by far the most dangerous.

The three Ironteeth Clans had been divided into rotating shifts that kept them mostly separated—training with the wyverns, training in the weapons room, and training in mortal warfare. It was smart to separate them, Manon supposed, since tensions were high, and would continue to run high until the wyverns were selected. Everyone wanted a bull. Though Manon fully expected to get one, perhaps even Titus, it didn't keep her from wanting to punch out the teeth of anyone who even whispered about coveting a bull of her own.

There were only a few overlapping minutes between their three-hour rotations, and the coven leaders did their best to keep them from running into each other. At least Manon did. Her temper was on a tight leash these days, and one more sneer from the Yellowlegs heir was likely to end in bloodshed. The same could be said of her Thirteen, two of whom—the green-eyed twins Faline and Fallon, more demon than witch—had gotten into a brawl with some Yellowlegs idiots, unsurprisingly. She'd punished them just as she'd punished Asterin: three blows each, public and humiliating. But, like clockwork, fights still broke out between other covens whenever they were in close quarters.

Which was what made the mess hall so deadly. The two daily meals were the only time they all shared together—and while they kept to their own tables, the tension was so thick Manon could slice it with her blade.

Manon stood in line for her bowl of slop—that was the best name she could give the doughy goop the mess hall served—flanked by Asterin, with the last of the Blueblood witches in the line ahead of her. Somehow, the Bluebloods were always first—first in line for food, first to ride the wyverns (the Thirteen had yet to get airborne), and likely to get first pick of the beasts. A growl rumbled deep in her throat, but Manon pushed her tray along the table, watching the pale-faced server heap a grayish-white ball of food into the bowl of the Blueblood in front of her.

She didn't bother to note the details of his features as the thick vein in his throat pulsed. Witches didn't need blood to survive, but humans didn't need wine, either. The Bluebloods were picky about whose blood they drank—virgins, young men, pretty girls—but the Blackbeaks didn't particularly care one way or another.

The man's ladle began shaking, tip-tapping along the side of the cauldron.

"Rules are rules," drawled a voice to her left. Asterin let out a warning snarl, and Manon didn't have to look to know that the Yellowlegs heir, Iskra, lurked there. "No eating the rabble," the dark-haired witch added, shoving her bowl in front of the man, cutting the line. Manon took in the iron nails and teeth, the calloused hand so blatantly making a show of dominance.

"Ah. I was wondering why no one's bothered to eat you," Manon said.

Iskra shouldered her way farther in front of Manon. Manon could feel the eyes in the room shifting toward them, but she reined in her temper, allowing the disrespect. Mess hall posturing meant nothing. "I hear your Thirteen are taking to the air today," said the Yellowlegs heir as Manon received her own ration.

"What business is it of yours?"

Iskra shrugged her toned shoulders. "They say you were once the best flier in all three Clans. It would be a shame if it were just more gossip."

It was true—she'd earned her spot as coven leader as much as she'd inherited it.

Iskra went on, sliding her plate along to the next server, who spooned some pale root vegetable onto her slop. "There's talk of skipping our training rotation so we can see the legendary Thirteen take to the skies for the first time in a decade."

Manon clicked her tongue in pretend thought. "I also heard there's talk that the Yellowlegs need all the help they can get in the sparring room. But I suppose any army needs its supply drivers."

A low laugh from Asterin, and Iskra's brown eyes flashed. They reached the end of the serving table, where Iskra faced Manon. With their trays in hand, neither could reach for the blades at their sides. The room had gone silent, even the high table at which the three Matrons sat.

Manon's gums stung as her iron teeth shot from their slits and snapped down. She said quietly, but loud enough for everyone to hear, "Any time you need a lesson in combat, Iskra, you just let me know. I'd be happy to teach you a few things about soldiering."

Before the heir could reply, Manon stalked across the room. Asterin gave Iskra a mocking bow of the head, followed by identical gestures from the rest of her Thirteen, but Iskra remained staring at Manon, simmering.

Manon plunked down at her table to find her grandmother smiling faintly. And when all of Manon's twelve sentinels were seated around her, Thirteen from now until the Darkness embraced them, Manon allowed herself a smile, too.

They were going to fly today.

As if the open cliff face weren't enough to make the two gathered Blackbeak covens shift on their feet, the twenty-six tethered wyverns in a tight space, none of them *that* docile, made even Manon twitchy.

But she showed no fear as she approached the wyvern at the center. Two lines of thirteen stood chained and ready. The Thirteen took the first. The other coven took the one behind. Manon's new riding gear was heavy and awkward—leather and fur, capped with steel shoulder-guards and leather wrist-braces. More than she was used to wearing, especially with her red cloak.

They'd already practiced saddling the mounts for two days, though they'd usually have handlers around to do it for them. Manon's mount for the day—a small female—was lying on her belly, low enough that Manon easily climbed her hind leg and hauled herself into the saddle at the spot where the long neck met the massive shoulders. A man approached to adjust the stirrups, but Manon leaned to do it herself. Breakfast had been bad enough. Coming close to a human throat now would only tempt her further.

The wyvern shifted, its body warm against her cold legs, and Manon tightened her gloved grip on the reins. Down the line, her sentinels mounted their beasts. Asterin was ready, of course, her cousin's gold hair tightly braided back, her fur collar ruffling in the biting wind from the open drop ahead of them. She flashed Manon a grin, her dark, gold-flecked eyes bright. Not a trace of fear—just the thrill.

The beasts knew what to do, the handlers had said. They knew how to make the Crossing on instinct alone. That's what they called the sheer plunge between the two mountain peaks, the final test for a rider and mount. If the wyverns couldn't make it, they'd splatter on the rocks far below. With their riders.

There was movement on the viewing platforms on either side, and the Yellowlegs heir's coven swaggered in, all of them smiling, none more broadly than Iskra.

"Bitch," Asterin murmured. As if it weren't bad enough that Mother Blackbeak stood on the opposite viewing platform, flanked by the other two High Witches. Manon lifted her chin and looked to the drop ahead.

"Just like we practiced," the overseer said, climbing from the open-faced pit to the viewing platform where the three Matrons stood. "Hard kick in the side sends 'em off. Let 'em navigate the Crossing. Best advice is to hold on like hell and enjoy the ride." A few nervous laughs from the coven behind her, but the Thirteen remained silent. Waiting. Just as they would faced with any army, before any battle.

Manon blinked, the muscles behind her golden eyes pulling down the clear film that would shield her vision from the wind. Manon allowed herself a moment to adjust to the thickness of the extra lid. Without it, they'd fly like mortals, squinting and streaming tears all over the place.

"Ready at your command, lady," the man called to her.

Manon studied the open gap ahead, the bridge barely visible above, the gray skies and mist. She looked down the line, into each of the six faces on either side. Then she turned ahead, to the drop and the world waiting beyond.

"We are the Thirteen, from now until the Darkness claims us." She said it quietly, but knew all could hear her. "Let's remind them why."

Manon kicked her mount into action. Three galloping, thunderous steps beneath her, surging forward, forward, forward, a leap into freezing air, the clouds and the bridge and the snow all around, and then the drop.

Her stomach shot right into her throat as the wyvern arced and angled down, wings tucked in tight. As she'd been instructed, Manon rose into a crouch over the neck, keeping her face close to the leathery skin, the wind screaming in her face.

The air rippled behind her, her Thirteen mere feet away, falling as one, past rock and snow, shooting for the earth.

Manon gritted her teeth. The blur of stone, the kiss of mist, her hair ripping out of her braid, waving like a white banner above her.

The mist parted, and Darkness embrace her, there was the Gap floor, so close, and—

Manon held on to the saddle, to the reins, to conscious thought as massive wings spread and the world tilted, and the body beneath her flipped up, up, riding the wind's current in a sheer climb along the side of the Northern Fang.

There were triumphant howls from below, from above, and the wyvern kept climbing, swifter than Manon had ever flown on her broom, past the bridge and up into the open sky.

That fast, Manon was back in the skies.

The cloudless, endless, eternal sky held them as Asterin and then Sorrel and Vesta flanked her, then the rest of the Thirteen, and Manon schooled her face into cool victory.

To her right, Asterin was beaming, her iron teeth shining like silver. To her left, red-haired Vesta was just shaking her head, gaping at the mountains below. Sorrel was as stone-faced as Manon, but her black eyes danced. The Thirteen were airborne again.

The world spread beneath them, and ahead, far to the West, was the home they would someday reclaim. But now, now . . .

The wind caressed and sang to her, telling her of its currents, more an instinct than a magical gift. An instinct that had made her the best flier in all three Clans.

"What now?" Asterin called. And though she'd never seen any of her Thirteen cry, Manon could have sworn there were tears shining in the corners of her cousin's eyes.

"I say we test them out," Manon said, keeping that wild exuberance locked up tight in her chest, and reined her mount toward where the first canyon run awaited them. The whoops and cackles of her Thirteen as they rode the current were finer than any mortal music.

Manon stood at attention in her grandmother's small room, staring at the far stone wall until she was spoken to. Mother Blackbeak sat at the wooden desk, her back to Manon as she pored over some document or letter. "You did well today, Manon," her grandmother said at last.

Manon touched two fingers to her brow, though her grandmother still studied the papers.

Manon hadn't needed to be told by the overseer that it was the best Crossing he had witnessed to date. She'd taken one look at the empty platform where the Yellowlegs coven had been and known they'd left as soon as Manon didn't splatter on the ground.

"Your Thirteen and all the Blackbeak covens did well," her grandmother went on. "Your work in keeping them disciplined these years is commendable."

Manon's chest swelled, but she said, "It's my honor to serve you, Grandmother."

Her grandmother scribbled something down. "I want you and the Thirteen to be Wing Leader—I want you leading all the Clans." The witch twisted to look at Manon, her face unreadable. "There are to be war games in a few months to decide the ranks. I don't care how you do it, but I expect to crown you victor."

Manon didn't need to ask why.

Her grandmother's eyes fell on Manon's red cloak and she smiled faintly. "We don't yet know who our enemies will be, but once we are done with the king's war and reclaim the Wastes, it will not be a Blueblood or Yellowlegs sitting on the Ironteeth throne. Understand?"

Become Wing Leader, command the Ironteeth armies, and keep control of those armies once the Matrons eventually turned on one another. Manon nodded. It would be done.

"I suspect the other Matrons will give similar orders to their heirs. Make sure your Second keeps close to you."

Asterin was already outside, guarding the door, but Manon said, "I can look after myself."

Her grandmother hissed. "Baba Yellowlegs was seven hundred years old. She tore down the walls of the Crochan capital with her bare hands. And yet someone slipped into her wagon and murdered her. Even if you live to be a thousand, you'll be lucky to be half the witch she was." Manon kept her chin high. "Watch your back. I will not be pleased if I have to find myself another heir."

Manon bowed her head. "As you will it, Grandmother."

17

Celaena awoke, freezing and groaning from a relentless headache. That, she knew, was from hitting her head on the temple stones. She hissed as she sat up, and every inch of her body, from her ears to her toes to her teeth, gave a collective burst of pain. It felt as if she'd been pummeled by a thousand iron fists and left to rot in the cold. *That* was from the uncontrolled shifting she'd done yesterday. The gods knew how many times she'd shuddered between one form and the other. From the tenderness of her muscles, it had to have been dozens.

But she hadn't lost control of the magic, she reminded herself as she rose, gripping the chipped bedpost. She pulled the pale robe tighter around her as she shuffled for the dresser and basin. After the bath, she'd realized she had nothing to change into and had stolen one of the many robes, leaving her reeking clothes heaped by the door. She'd barely made it to her room before she collapsed on the bed, pulled the scrap of blanket over her, and slept.

And slept. And slept. She didn't feel like talking with anyone. And no one came for her, anyway.

Celaena braced her hands on the dresser and grimaced at her reflection. She looked like shit, felt like shit. Even more grim and gaunt than yesterday. She picked up the tin of salve Rowan had given her, but then decided he should see what he'd done. And she'd looked worse—two years ago, when Arobynn had beaten her to a bloody pulp for disobeying his orders. This was nothing compared to how mangled she'd been then.

She opened the door to find that someone had left clothes—the same as yesterday, but fresh. Her boots had been cleaned of mud and dust. Either Rowan had left them, or someone else had noticed her filthy clothing. Gods—she'd *soiled* herself in front of him.

She didn't let herself wallow in the humiliation as she dressed and went to the kitchens, the halls dark in the moments before dawn. Already, Luca was prattling about the fighting knife a sentry had loaned him for his training, and on and on and on.

Apparently she had underestimated how horrific her face was, because Luca stopped his chattering midsentence to swear. Whirling, Emrys took one look at her and dropped his earthenware bowl before the hearth. "Great Mother and all her children."

Celaena went to the heap of garlic cloves on the worktable and picked up a knife. "It looks worse than it feels." A lie. Her head was still pounding from the cut on her brow, and her eye was deeply bruised beneath.

"I've got some salve in my room—" Luca started from where he was already washing dishes, but she gave him a long look.

She began peeling the cloves, her fingers instantly sticky. They were still staring, so she flatly said, "It's none of your business."

Emrys left his shattered bowl on the hearthstones and hobbled over, anger dancing in those bright, clever eyes. "It's my business when you come into my kitchen."

"I've been through worse," she said.

Luca said, "What do you mean?" He eyed her mangled hands, her black eye, and the ring of scars around her neck, courtesy of Baba Yellowlegs. She silently invited him to do the calculations: a life in Adarlan with Fae blood, a life in Adarlan as a woman . . . His face paled.

After a long moment, Emrys said, "Leave it alone, Luca," and stooped to pick up the fragments of the bowl.

Celaena went back to the garlic, Luca markedly quieter as he worked. Breakfast was made and sent upstairs in the same chaotic rush as yesterday, but a few more demi-Fae noticed her today. She either ignored them or stared them down, marking their faces. Many had pointed ears, but most seemed human. Some wore civilian clothing—tunics and simple gowns—while the sentries wore light leather armor and heavy gray cloaks with an array of weapons (many the worse for wear). The warriors looked her way the most, men and women both, wariness and curiosity mingling.

She was busy wiping down a copper pot when someone let out a low, appreciative whistle in her direction. "Now *that* is one of the most glorious black eyes I've ever beheld." A tall old man—handsome despite being around Emrys's age—strode through the kitchen, empty platter in his hands.

"You leave her be, too, Malakai," Emrys said from the hearth. His husband—mate. The old man gave a dashing grin and set down the platter on the counter near Celaena.

"Rowan doesn't pull punches, does he?" His gray hair was cropped short enough to reveal his pointed ears, but his face was ruggedly human. "And it looks like you don't bother using a healing salve." She held his gaze but gave no reply. Malakai's grin faded. "My mate works too much as it is. You don't add to that burden, understand?"

Emrys growled his name, but Celaena shrugged. "I don't want to bother with any of you."

Malakai caught the unspoken warning in her words—*so don't try to bother with me*—and gave her a curt nod. She heard, more than saw, him stride to Emrys and kiss him, then the rumble of some murmured, stern words, and then his steady footsteps as he walked out again.

"Even the demi-Fae warrior males push overprotective to a whole new level," Emrys said, the words laced with forced lightness.

"It's in our blood," Luca said, lifting his chin. "It is our duty, honor, and life's mission to make sure our families are cared for. Especially our mates."

"And it makes you a thorn in our side," Emrys clucked. "Possessive, territorial beasts." The old man strode to the sink, setting down the cool kettle for Celaena to wash. "My mate means well, lass. But you're a stranger—and from Adarlan. And you're training with . . . someone none of us quite understand."

Celaena dumped the kettle in the sink. "I don't care," she said. And meant it.

Training was horrible that day. Not just because Rowan asked if she was going to vomit or piss herself again, but also because for hours—*hours*—he made her sit amongst the temple ruins on the ridge, battered by the misty wind. He wanted her to shift—that was his only command.

She demanded to know why he couldn't teach her the magic without shifting, and he gave her the same answer again and again: no shift, no magic lessons. But after yesterday, nothing short of him taking his long dagger and cutting her ears into points would get her to change forms. She tried once—when he stalked into the woods for some privacy. She tugged and yanked and pulled at whatever lay deep inside her, but got nothing. No flash of light or searing pain.

So they sat on the mountainside, Celaena frozen to the bone. At least she didn't lose control again, no matter what insults he threw her way, either aloud or through one of their silent, vicious conversations. She asked him why he wasn't pursuing the creature that had been in the barrow-wights' field, and he merely said that he was looking into it, and the rest was none of her concern.

Thunderclouds clustered during the late afternoon. Rowan forced her to sit through the storm until her teeth were clattering in her skull and her blood was thick with ice, and then they finally made the trek to the fortress. He ditched her by the baths again, eyes glimmering with an unspoken promise that tomorrow would be worse.

When she finally emerged, there were dry clothes in her room, folded and placed with such care that she was starting to wonder whether she didn't have some invisible servant shadowing her. There was no way in hell an immortal like Rowan would have bothered to do that for a human.

She debated staying in her rooms for the rest of the night, especially as rain lashed at her window, lightning illuminating the trees beyond. But her stomach gurgled. She was light-headed again, and knew she'd been eating like an idiot. With her black eye, the best thing to do was eat—even if it meant going to the kitchens.

She waited until she thought everyone had gone upstairs. There were always leftovers after breakfast—there had to be some at dinner. Gods, she was bone-tired. And ached even worse than she had this morning.

She heard the voices long before she entered the kitchen and almost turned back, but—no one had spoken to her at breakfast save Malakai. Surely everyone would ignore her now, too.

She'd estimated a good number of people in the kitchen, but was still a bit surprised by how packed it was. Chairs and cushions had been dragged in, all facing the hearth, before which Emrys and Malakai sat, chatting with those gathered. There was food on every surface, as if dinner had been held in here. Keeping to the shadows atop the stairs, she observed them. The dining hall was spacious, if a bit cold—why gather around the kitchen hearth?

She didn't particularly care—not when she saw the food. She slipped in through the gathered crowd with practiced stealth and ease, filling up a plate with roast chicken, potatoes (gods, she was already sick of potatoes), and hot bread. Everyone was still chatting; those who didn't have seats were standing against the counters or walls, laughing and sipping from their mugs of ale.

The upper half of the kitchen door was open to let out the heat from all the bodies, the sound of rain filling the room like a drum. She caught a glimmer of movement outside, but when she looked, there was nothing there.

Celaena was about to slip back up the stairs when Malakai clapped his hands and everyone stopped talking. Celaena paused again in the shadows of the stairwell. Smiles spread, and people settled in. Seated on the floor in front of Emrys's chair was Luca, a pretty young woman pressed into his side, his arm casually draped around her shoulders—casually, but with enough of a grip to tell every other male in the room that she was his. Celaena rolled her eyes, not at all surprised.

Still, she caught the look Luca gave the girl, the mischief in his eyes that sent a pang of jealousy right through her. She'd looked at Chaol with that same expression. But their relationship had never been as unburdened, and even if she hadn't ended things, it never would have been like that. The ring on her finger became a weight.

Lightning flashed, revealing the grass and forest beyond. Seconds later, thunder shook the stones, triggering a few shrieks and laughs.

Emrys cleared his throat, and every eye snapped to his lined face. The ancient hearth illuminated his silver hair, casting shadows throughout the room. "Long ago," Emrys began, his voice weaving between the drumming rain and grumbling thunder and crackling fire, "when there was no mortal king on Wendlyn's throne, the faeries still walked among us. Some were good and fair, some were prone to little mischiefs, and some were fouler and darker than the blackest night."

Celaena swallowed. These were words that had been spoken in front of hearths for thousands of years—spoken in kitchens like this one. Tradition.

"It was those wicked faeries," Emrys went on, the words resonating in every crack and crevice, "that you always had to watch for on the ancient roads, or in the woods, or on nights like this, when you can hear the wind moaning your name."

"Oh, not that one," Luca groaned, but it wasn't heartfelt. Some of the others laughed—a bit nervously, even. Someone else protested, "I won't sleep for a week."

Celaena leaned against the stone wall, shoveling food down her throat as the old man wove his tale. The hair on her neck stood on end for the duration of it, and she could see every horrific moment of the story as clearly as if she had lived it.

As Emrys finished his tale, thunder boomed, and even Celaena flinched, almost upsetting her empty plate. There were some wary laughs, some taunts and gentle pushes. Celaena frowned. If she'd heard this story—with the wretched creatures who delighted in skin-sewing and bone-crunching and lightning-crisping—before traveling here with Rowan, she never would have followed him. Not in a million years.

Rowan hadn't lit a single fire on the journey here—hadn't wanted to attract attention. From these sorts of creatures? He hadn't known what that thing was the day before in the barrows. And if an immortal didn't know . . . She used breathing exercises to calm her pounding heart. Still, she'd be lucky if she slept tonight.

Though everyone else seemed to be waiting for the next story, Celaena stood. As she turned to leave, she looked again to that half-open kitchen door, just to make sure there was nothing lurking outside. But it was not some fell creature who waited in the rain. A large white-tailed hawk was perched in the shadows.

It sat absolutely still. But the hawk's eyes—there was something strange about them . . . She'd seen that hawk before. It had watched her for days as she'd lazed on that rooftop in Varese, watched her drink and steal and doze and brawl.

At least she now knew what Rowan's animal form was. What she didn't know was why he bothered to listen to these stories.

"Elentiya." Emrys was extending a hand from where he sat before the hearth. "Would you perhaps share a story from your lands? We'd love to hear a tale, if you'd do us the honor."

Celaena kept her eyes on the old man as everyone turned to where she stood in the shadows. Not one of them offered a word of encouragement, save for Luca, who said, "Tell us!"

But she had no right to tell those stories as if they were her own. And she could not remember them correctly, not as they had been told at her bedside.

She clamped down on the thought as hard as she could, shoving it back long enough to calmly say, "No, thank you," and walk away. No one came after her. She didn't give a damn what Rowan made of the whole thing.

The whispers died with each step, and it wasn't until she'd shut the door to her freezing room and slid into bed that she loosed a sigh. The rain stopped, the clouds cleared on a brisk wind, and through the window, a patch of stars flickered above the tree line.

She had no stories to tell. All the legends of Terrasen were lost to her, and only fragments were strewn through her memories like rubble.

She pulled her scrap of blanket higher and draped an arm over her eyes, shutting out the ever-watching stars.

18

Mercifully, Dorian wasn't forced to entertain Aedion again, and saw little of him outside of state dinners and meetings, where the general pretended he didn't exist. He saw little of Chaol, too, which was a relief, given how awkward their conversations had been of late. But he'd begun to spar with the guards in the mornings. It was about as fun as lying on a bed of hot nails, but at least it gave him something to do with the restless, anxious energy that hounded him day and night.

Not to mention all those cuts and scrapes and sprains gave him an excuse to go to the healers' catacombs. Sorscha, it seemed, had caught on to his training schedule, and her door was always open when he arrived.

He hadn't been able to stop thinking about what she'd said in his room, or wondering why someone who had lost everything would dedicate her life to helping the family of the man who had taken it all away. And when she'd said *Because I had nowhere else to go* . . . for a second, it hadn't been Sorscha but Celaena, broken with grief and loss and rage, coming to his room because there was no one else to turn to. He'd never known what that was like, that loss, but Sorscha's kindness to him—which he'd repaid so foully until now—hit him like a stone to the head.

Dorian entered her workroom, and Sorscha looked up from the table and smiled, broadly and prettily and . . . well, wasn't that exactly the reason he found excuses to come here every day.

He held up his wrist, already stiff and throbbing. "Landed on it badly," he said by way of greeting. She came around the table, giving him enough time to admire the long lines of her figure in her simple gown. She moved like water, he thought, and often caught himself marveling at the way she used her hands.

"There's not much I can do for that," she said after examining his wrist. "But I have a tonic for the pain—only to subdue it, and I can put your arm in a sling if—"

"Gods, no. No sling. I'll never hear the end of it from the guards."

Her eyes twinkled, just a bit—in that way they did when she was amused and tried hard not to be.

But if there was no sling, then he had no excuse to be here, and even though he had an inane council meeting in an hour and still needed to bathe . . . He stood. "What are you working on?"

She took a careful step back from him. She always did that, to keep the wall up. "Well, I have a few tonics and salves to make for some of the servants and guards today—to replenish their stocks." He knew he shouldn't, but he moved to peer over her narrow shoulder at the worktable, at the bowls and vials and beakers. She made a small noise in her throat, and he swallowed his smile as he leaned a bit closer. "This is normally a task for apprentices, but they were so busy today that I offered to take some of their workload." She usually talked like this when she was nervous. Which, Dorian had noticed with some satisfaction, was when he came near. And not in a bad way—if he'd sensed that she was truly uncomfortable, he'd have kept his distance. This was more . . . flustered. He liked flustered.

"But," she went on, trying to sidestep away, "I'll make your tonic right now, Your Highness."

He gave her the space she needed as she hurried about the table with graceful efficiency, measuring powders and crushing dried leaves, so steady and self-assured . . . He realized he'd been staring when she spoke again. "Your . . . friend. The King's Champion. Is she well?"

Her mission to Wendlyn was fairly secret, but he could get around that. "She's off on my father's errand for the next few months. I certainly hope she's well, though I have no doubt she can care for herself."

"And her hound—she's well?"

"Fleetfoot? Oh, she's fine. Her leg's healed beautifully." The hound now slept in *his* bed, of course, and bullied him for scraps and treats to no end, but . . . it was nice to have some piece of his friend while she was gone. "Thanks to you."

A nod, and silence fell as she measured and then poured some green-looking liquid. He sincerely hoped he wasn't going to drink that.

"They said . . ." Sorscha kept her spectacular eyes down. "They said there was some wild animal roaming the halls a few months ago—that's what killed all those people before Yulemas. I never heard whether they caught it, but then . . . your friend's dog looked like she'd been attacked."

Dorian willed himself to keep still. She'd truly put some things together, then. And hadn't told anyone. "Ask it, Sorscha."

Her throat bobbed, and her hands shook a little—enough that he wanted to reach out and cover them. But he couldn't move, not until she spoke. "What was it?" she breathed.

"Do you want the answer that will keep you asleep at night, or the one that might ensure you never sleep again?" She lifted her gaze to him, and he knew she wanted the truth. So he loosed a breath and said, "It was two different . . . creatures. My father's Champion dealt with the first. She didn't even tell the captain and me until we faced the second." He could still hear that creature's roar in the tunnel, still see it squaring off against Chaol. Still had nightmares about it. "The rest is a bit of a mystery." It wasn't a lie. There was still so much he didn't know. And didn't want to learn.

"Would His Majesty punish you for it?" A quiet, dangerous question.

"Yes." His blood chilled at the thought. Because if he knew, if his father learned Celaena had somehow opened a portal . . . Dorian couldn't stop the ice spreading through him.

Sorscha rubbed her arms and glanced at the fire. It was still burning high, but . . . Shit. He had to go. Now. Sorscha said, "He'd kill her, wouldn't he? That's why you said nothing."

Dorian slowly started backing out, fighting against the panicked, wild *thing* inside of him. He couldn't stop the rising ice, didn't even know where it was coming from, but he kept seeing that creature in the tunnels, kept hearing Fleetfoot's pained bark, seeing Chaol choose to sacrifice himself so they could get away—

Sorscha stroked the length of her dark braid. "And—and he'd probably kill the captain, too."

His magic erupted.

After Sorscha had been forced to wait in the cramped office for twenty minutes, Amithy finally paraded in, her tight bun making her harsh face even more severe. "Sorscha," she said, sitting down at her desk and frowning. "What am I to do with you? What example does this set for the apprentices?"

Sorscha kept her head down. She knew she'd been kept waiting in order to make her fret over what she'd done: accidentally knocking over her entire worktable and destroying not only countless hours and days of work, but also a good number of expensive tools and containers. "I slipped—I spilled some oil and forgot to wipe it up."

Amithy clicked her tongue. "Cleanliness, Sorscha, is one of our most important assets. If you cannot keep your own workroom clean, how can you be trusted to care for our patients? For His Highness, who was there to witness your latest bout of unprofessionalism? I've taken the liberty of apologizing in person, and offered to oversee his future care, but . . ." Amithy's eyes narrowed. "He said he would pay for the repair costs—and would still like you to serve him."

Sorscha's face warmed. It had happened so quickly.

As the blast of ice and wind and something *else* surged toward her, Sorscha's scream had been cut off by the door slamming shut. That had probably saved their lives, but all she could think of was getting out of the way. So she'd crouched beneath her table, hands over her head, and prayed.

She might have dismissed it as a draft, might have felt foolish, if the prince's eyes hadn't seemed to *glow* in that moment before the wind and cold, had the glasses on the table not all shattered, had ice not coated the floor, had he not just stayed there, untouched.

It wasn't possible. The prince . . . There was a choking, awful sound, and then Dorian was on his knees, peering under the worktable. "Sorscha. *Sorscha.*"

She'd gaped at him, unable to find the words.

Amithy drummed her long, bony fingers on the wooden desk. "Forgive me for being indelicate," she said, but Sorscha knew the woman didn't care one bit about manners. "But I'll also remind you that interacting with our patients outside of our duties is prohibited."

There could be no other reason for Prince Dorian to prefer Sorscha's services over Amithy's, of course. Sorscha kept her eyes on her clenched hands in her lap, still flecked with cuts from some of the small shards of glass. "You needn't worry about that, Amithy."

"Good. I'd hate to see your position compromised. His Highness has a reputation with women." A little, smug smile. "And there are many beautiful ladies at this court." *And you are not one of them*.

Sorscha nodded and took the insult, as she always did and had always done. That was how she survived, how she had remained invisible all these years.

It was what she'd promised the prince in the minutes after his explosion, when her shaking ceased and she'd *seen* him. Not the magic but the panic in his eyes, the fear and pain. He wasn't an enemy using forbidden powers, but—a young man in need of help. Her help.

She could not turn away from it, from him, could not tell anyone what she'd witnessed. It was what she would have done for anyone else.

In the cool, calm voice that she reserved for her most grievously injured patients, she had said to the prince, "I am not going to tell anyone. But right now, you are going to help me knock this table over, and then you are going to help me clean this up."

He'd just stared at her. She stood, noting the hair-thin slices on her hands that had already starting stinging. "I am not going to tell anyone," she said again, grabbing one corner of the table. Wordlessly, he went to the other end and helped her ease the table onto its side, the remaining glass and ceramic jars tumbling to the ground. For all the world, it looked like an accident, and Sorscha went to the corner to grab the broom.

"When I open this door," she had said to him, still quiet and calm and not quite herself, "we will pretend. But after today, after this . . ." Dorian stood rigid, as if he were waiting for the blow to fall. "After this," she said, "if you are all right with it, we will try to find ways to keep this from happening. Perhaps there's some tonic to suppress it."

His face was still pale. "I'm sorry," he breathed, and she knew he meant it. She went to the door and gave him a grim smile.

"I will start researching tonight. If I find anything, I'll let you know. And perhaps—not now, but later . . . if Your Highness has the inclination, you could tell me a bit about *how* this is possible. It might help me somehow." She didn't give him time to say yes, but instead opened the door, walked back to the mess, and said a little louder than usual, "I am *truly* sorry, Your Highness . . . there was something on the floor, and I slipped, and—"

From there, it had been easy. The snooping healers had arrived to see what the commotion was about, and one of them had scuttled off to Amithy. The prince had left, and Sorscha had been ordered to wait here.

Amithy braced her forearms on the desk. "His Highness was extraordinarily generous, Sorscha. Let it be a lesson for you. You're lucky you didn't injure yourself further."

"I'll make an offering to Silba today," Sorscha lied, quiet and small, and left.

Chaol pressed himself into the darkened alcove of a building, holding his breath as Aedion approached the cloaked figure in the alley. Of all the places he'd expected Aedion to go when he slipped out of his party at the tavern, the slums were not one of them.

Aedion had made a spectacular show of playing the generous, wild host: buying drinks, saluting his guests, ensuring everyone saw him doing something. And just when no one was looking, Aedion had walked right out the front, as if he were too lazy to go to the privy in the back. A staggering drunk, arrogant and careless and haughty.

Chaol had almost bought it. Almost. Then Aedion had gotten a block away, thrown his hood over his head, and prowled into the night, stone-cold sober.

He'd trailed from the shadows as Aedion left the wealthier district and strolled into the slums, taking alleys and crooked streets. He could have passed for a wealthy man seeking another sort of woman. Until he'd stopped outside this building and that cloaked figure with the twin blades approached him.

Chaol couldn't hear the words between Aedion and the stranger, but he could read the tension in their bodies well enough. After a moment, Aedion followed the newcomer, though not before he thoroughly scanned the alley, the rooftops, the shadows.

Chaol kept his distance. If he caught Aedion buying illicit substances, that might be enough to get him to calm down—to keep the parties at a minimum and control the Bane when it arrived.

Chaol tracked them, mindful of the eyes he passed, every drunk and orphan and beggar. On a forgotten street by the Avery's docks, Aedion and the cloaked figure slipped into a crumbling building. It wasn't just any building, not with sentries posted on the corner, by the door, on the rooftop, even milling about the street, trying to blend in. They weren't royal guards, or soldiers.

It wasn't a place to purchase opiates or flesh, either. He'd been memorizing the information Celaena had gathered about the rebels, and had stalked them as often as he'd trailed Aedion, mostly to no avail. Celaena had claimed they'd been looking for a way to defeat the king's power. Larger implications aside, if he could find out not only how the king had stifled magic but also how to liberate it before he was dragged back to Anielle, then Dorian's secret might be less explosive. It might help him, somehow. And Chaol would always help him, his friend, his prince.

He couldn't stop a shiver down his spine as he touched the Eye of Elena and realized the derelict building, with this pattern of guards, positively reeked of the rebels' habits. Perhaps it wasn't mere coincidence that had led him here.

He was so focused on his thundering heart that Chaol didn't have a chance to turn as a dagger pricked his side.

19

Chaol didn't put up a fight, though he knew he was as likely to receive death as he was answers. He recognized the sentries by their worn weapons and their fluid, precise movements. He'd never forget those details, not after he'd spent a day being held prisoner in a warehouse by them—and witnessed Celaena cut through them as though they were stalks of wheat. They'd never known that it had been their lost queen who came to slaughter them.

The sentries forced him to his knees in an empty room that smelled of old hay. Chaol found Aedion and a familiar-looking old man staring down at him. The one who had begged Celaena to stop that night in the warehouse. There was nothing remarkable about the old man; his worn clothes were ordinary, his body lean but not yet withered. Beside him stood a young man Chaol knew by his soft, vicious laugh: the guard who had taunted him when he'd been held prisoner. Shoulder-length dark hair hung loose around a face that was more cruel than handsome, especially with the wicked scar slashing through his eyebrow and down his cheek. He dismissed the sentries with a jerk of his chin.

"Well, well," Aedion said, circling Chaol. His sword was out, gleaming in the dim light. "Captain of the Guard, heir of Anielle, *and* spy? Or has your lover been giving you some tricks of the trade?"

"When you throw parties and convince my men to leave their posts, when you're *not* at those parties because you're sneaking through the streets, it's my duty to know why, Aedion."

The scarred young man with the twin swords stepped closer, circling with Aedion now. Two predators, sizing up their prey. They'd probably fight over his carcass.

"Too bad your Champion isn't here to save you this time," the scarred one said quietly.

"Too bad you weren't there to save Archer Finn," Chaol said.

A flare of nostrils, a flash of fury in cunning brown eyes, but the young man fell silent as the old man held out a hand. "Did the king send you?"

"I came because of *him*." Chaol jerked his chin at Aedion. "But I've been looking for you two—and your little group—as well. Both of you are in danger. Whatever you think Aedion wants, whatever he offers you, the king keeps him on a tight leash." Perhaps that bit of honesty would buy him what he needed: trust and information.

But Aedion barked out a laugh. "What?" His companions turned to him, brows raised. Chaol glanced at the ring on the general's finger. He hadn't been mistaken. It was identical to the ones the king, Perrington, and others had worn.

Aedion caught Chaol's look and stopped his circling.

For a moment, the general stared at him, a glimmer of surprise and amusement darting across his tan face. Then Aedion purred, "You've turned out to be a far more interesting man than I thought, Captain."

"Explain, Aedion," the old man said softly, but not weakly.

Aedion smiled broadly as he yanked the black ring off his finger. "The day the king presented me with the Sword of Orynth, he also offered me a ring. Thanks to my heritage, my senses are . . . sharper. I thought the ring smelled strange—and knew only a fool would accept that kind of gift from him. So I had a replica made. The real one I chucked into the sea. But I always wondered what it did," he mused, tossing the ring with one hand and catching it. "It seems the captain knows. And disapproves."

The man with the twin swords ceased his circling, and the grin he gave Chaol was nothing short of feral. "You're right, Aedion," he said without taking his eyes off Chaol. "He *is* more interesting than he seems."

Aedion pocketed the ring as if it were as if it were indeed a fake. And Chaol realized that he'd revealed far more than he'd ever intended.

Aedion began circling again, the scarred young man echoing the graceful movements. "A magical leash—when there is no magic left," the general mused. "And yet you still followed me, believing I was under the king's spell. Thinking you could use me to win the rebels' favor? Fascinating."

Chaol kept his mouth shut. He'd already said enough to damn himself.

Aedion went on, "These two said your assassin friend was a rebel sympathizer. That she handed over information to Archer Finn without thinking twice—that she allowed rebels to sneak out of the city when she was commanded to put them down. Was she the one who told you about the king's rings, or did you discover that tidbit all on your own? What, exactly, is going on in that glass palace when the king isn't looking?"

Chaol clamped down on his retort. When it became clear he wouldn't speak, Aedion shook his head.

"You know how this has to end," Aedion said, and there wasn't anything mocking in it. Just cold calculation. The true face of the Northern

Wolf. "The way I see it, you signed your own death warrant when you decided to trail me, and now that you know so much . . . You have two options, Captain: we can torture it out of you and then we'll kill you, or you can tell us what you know and we'll make it quick for you. As painless as possible, on my honor."

They stopped circling.

Chaol had faced death a few times in the past months. Had faced and seen and dealt it. But *this* death, where Celaena and Dorian and his mother would never know what happened to him . . . It disgusted him, somehow. Enraged him.

Aedion stepped closer to where Chaol knelt.

He could take out the scarred one, then hope he could stand against Aedion—or at least flee. He *would* fight, because that was the only way he could embrace this sort of death.

Aedion's sword was at the ready—the sword that belonged to Celaena by blood and right. Chaol had assumed he was a two-faced butcher. Aedion *was* a traitor. But not to Terrasen. Aedion had been playing a very dangerous game since arriving here—since his kingdom fell ten years ago. And tricking the king into thinking that he'd been wearing his ring all this time—that was indeed information Aedion would be willing to kill to keep safe. Yet there was other information Chaol could use, perhaps, to get out of this alive.

Regardless of how shattered she'd been when she left, Celaena was safe now. She was away from Adarlan. But Dorian, with his magic, with the threat he secretly posed, was not. Aedion took a readying breath to kill him. Keeping Dorian protected was all he had left, all that had ever really mattered. If these rebels did indeed know something—*anything*—about magic that might help to free it, if he could use Aedion to get that information . . .

It was a gamble—the biggest gamble he'd ever made. Aedion raised his sword.

With a silent prayer for forgiveness, Chaol looked straight at Aedion. "Aelin is alive."

Aedion Ashryver had been called Wolf, general, prince, traitor, and murderer. And he was all of those things, and more. Liar, deceiver, and trickster were his particular favorites—the titles only those closest to him knew.

Adarlan's Whore, that's what the ones who didn't know him called him. It was true—in so many ways, it was true, and he had never minded it, not really. It had allowed him to maintain control in the North, to keep the bloodshed down to a minimum and a lie. Half the Bane were rebels, and the other half sympathizers, so many of their "battles" in the North had been staged, the body count a deceit and an exaggeration—at least, once the corpses got up from the killing field under cover of darkness and went home to their families. Adarlan's Whore. He had not minded. Until now.

Cousin—that had been his most beloved title. Cousin, kin, protector. Those were the secret names he harbored deep within, the names he whispered to himself when the northern wind was shrieking through the Staghorns. Sometimes that wind sounded like the screams of his people being led to the butchering blocks. And sometimes it sounded like Aelin—Aelin, whom he had loved, who should have been his queen, and to whom he would have one day sworn the blood oath.

Aedion stood on the decaying planks of an empty dock in the slums, staring at the Avery. The captain was beside him, spitting blood into the water thanks to the beating given to him by Ren Allsbrook, Aedion's newest conspirator and yet another dead man risen from the grave.

Ren, heir and Lord of Allsbrook, had trained with Aedion as a child—and had once been his rival. Ten years ago, Ren and his grandfather, Murtagh, had escaped the butchering blocks thanks to a diversion started by Ren's parents that cost them their lives and gave Ren the nasty scar down his face. But Aedion hadn't known—he'd thought them dead, and had been stunned to learn that *they* were the secret rebel group he'd hunted down upon arriving in Rifthold. He'd heard the claims that Aelin was alive and raising an army and had dragged himself down from the north to get to the bottom of it and destroy the liars, preferably cutting them up piece by piece.

The king's summons had been a convenient excuse. Ren and Murtagh had instantly admitted that the rumors had been spread by a former member of their rebel group. They had never had or heard of any contact with their dead queen. But seeing Ren and Murtagh, he'd since wondered who else might have survived. He had never allowed himself to hope that Aelin . . .

Aedion set his sword on the wooden rail and ran his scarred fingers down it, taking in the nicks and lines, each mark a tale of legendary battles fought, of great kings long dead. The sword was the last shred of proof that a mighty kingdom had once existed in the North.

It wasn't his sword, not really. In those initial days of blood and conquest, the King of Adarlan had snatched the blade from Rhoe Galathynius's cooling body and brought it to Rifthold. And there it had stayed, the sword that should have been Aelin's.

So Aedion had fought for years in those war camps and battlefields, fought to prove his invaluable worth to the king, and had taken everything that was done to him, again and again. When he and the Bane won that first battle and the king had proclaimed him the Northern Wolf and offered him a boon, Aedion had asked for the sword.

The king attributed the request to an eighteen-year-old's romanticism, and Aedion had swaggered about his own glory until everyone believed that he was a traitorous, butchering bastard who made a mockery of the sword just by touching it. But winning back the sword didn't erase his failure.

Even though he'd been thirteen, and even though he'd been forty miles away in Orynth when Aelin had been killed on the country estate, he should have stopped it. He'd been sent to her land upon his mother's death to become Aelin's sword and shield, to serve in the court she was supposed to have ruled, that child of kings. So he should have ridden out when the castle erupted with news that Orlon Galathynius had been assassinated. By the time anyone did, Rhoe, Evalin, and Aelin were dead.

It was that reminder he'd carried with him on his back, the reminder of who the sword belonged to, and to whom, when he took his last breath and went to the Otherworld, he'd finally give it.

But now the sword, that weight he'd embraced for years, felt . . . lighter and sharper, far more fragile. Infinitely precious. The world had slipped from beneath his feet.

No one had spoken for a moment after the Captain of the Guard made his claim. *Aelin is alive.* Then the captain had said he'd only speak with Aedion about it.

Just to show they weren't bluffing about torturing him, Ren had bloodied him up with a cool precision that Aedion grudgingly admired, but the captain had taken the blows. And whenever Ren paused, Murtaugh looking on disapprovingly, the captain said the same thing. After it became clear that the captain would either tell only Aedion or die, he'd called off Ren. The heir of Allsbrook bristled, but Aedion had dealt with plenty of young men like him in the war camps. It never took much to get them to fall in line. Aedion gave him a long, hard stare, and Ren backed down.

Which was how they wound up here, Chaol cleaning off his face with a scrap of his shirt. For the past few minutes, Aedion had listened to the most unlikely story he'd ever heard. The story of Celaena Sardothien, the infamous assassin, being trained by Arobynn Hamel, the story of her downfall and year in Endovier, and how she'd wound up in the ridiculous competition to become the King's Champion. The story of Aelin, his Queen, in a death camp, and then serving in her enemy's house.

Aedion braced his hands on the rail. It couldn't be true. Not after ten years. Ten years without hope, without proof.

"She has your eyes," Chaol said, working his jaw. If this assassin—an *assassin*, gods above—was truly Aelin, then she was the King's Champion. Then she was the captain's—

"You sent her to Wendlyn," Aedion said, his voice ragged. The tears would come later. Right now, he was emptied. Gutted. Every lie, every rumor and act and party he'd thrown, every battle, real or faked, every life he'd taken so more could live . . . How would he ever explain that to her? Adarlan's Whore.

"I didn't know who she was. I just thought she would be safer there because of what she is."

"You realize you've only given me a bigger reason to kill you." Aedion clenched his jaw. "Do you have any idea what kind of risk you took in telling me? I could be working for the king—you *thought* I was in thrall to him, and all you had for proof against it was a quick story. You might as well have killed her yourself." Fool—stupid, reckless fool. But the captain still had the upper hand here—the king's noble captain, who was now toeing the line of treason. He'd wondered about the captain's allegiance when Ren told him about the involvement of the King's Champion with the rebels, but—damn. Aelin. *Aelin* was the King's Champion, *Aelin* had helped the rebels, and gutted Archer Finn. His knees threatened to buckle, but he swallowed the shock, the surprise and terror and glimmer of delight.

"I know it was a risk," the captain said. "But the men who have those rings—something changes in their eyes, a kind of darkness that sometimes manifests physically. I haven't seen it in you since you've been here. And I've never seen someone throw so many parties, but only attend for a few minutes. You wouldn't go to such lengths to hide your meetings with the rebels if you were enslaved to the king, especially when during all this time the Bane still hasn't come, despite your assurances that it will be here soon. It doesn't add up." The captain met his stare. Perhaps not quite a fool, then. "I think she'd want you to know."

The captain looked down the river toward the sea. This place reeked. Aedion had smelled and seen worse in war camps, but the slums of Rifthold certainly gave them a run for their money. And Terrasen's capital, Orynth, its once-shining tower now a slab of filthy white stone, was well on its way to falling into this level of poverty and despair. But maybe, someday soon . . .

Aelin was *alive*. Alive, and as much of a killer as he was, and working for the same man. "Does the prince know?" He'd never been able to speak with the prince without remembering the days before Terrasen's downfall; he'd never been able to hide that hatred.

"No. He doesn't even know why I sent her to Wendlyn. Or that she's—you're both . . . Fae."

Aedion had never possessed a fraction of the power that had smoldered in her veins, which had burned libraries and caused such general worry that there had been talk—in those months before the world went to hell—of sending her somewhere so that she could learn to control it. He'd overheard debate over packing her off to various academies or tutors in distant lands, but never to their aunt Maeve, waiting like a spider in a web to see what became of her niece. And yet she'd wound up in Wendlyn, on her aunt's doorstep.

Maeve had either never known or never cared about his inherited gifts. No, all he had were some of the physical traits of their immortal kin: strength, swiftness, sharp hearing, keen smell. It had made him a formidable opponent on the battlefield—and saved his life more than once. Saved his very soul, if the captain was right about those rings.

"Is she coming back?" Aedion asked quietly. The first of the many, many questions he had for the captain, now that he'd proved himself to be more than a useless servant of the king.

There was enough agony in the captain's eyes that Aedion knew that he loved her. Knew, and felt a tug of jealousy, if only because the captain knew her that well. "I don't know," Chaol admitted. If he hadn't been his enemy, Aedion would have respected the man for the sacrifice implied. But Aelin had to come back. She *would* come back. Unless that return only earned her a walk to the butchering block.

He would sort through each wild thought when he was alone. He gripped the damp rail harder, fighting the urge to ask more.

But then the captain gave him a weighing look, as if he could see through every mask Aedion had ever worn. For a heartbeat, Aedion considered putting the blade right through the captain and dumping his body in the Avery, despite the information he possessed. The captain glanced at the blade, too, and Aedion wondered if he was thinking the same thing—regretting his decision to trust him. The captain *should* regret it, should curse himself for a fool.

Aedion said, "Why were you tracking the rebels?"

"Because I thought they might have valuable information." It had to be truly valuable, then, if he'd risk revealing himself as a traitor to get it.

Aedion had been willing to torture the captain—to kill him, too. He'd done worse before. But torturing and killing his queen's lover wouldn't go over well if—*when* she returned. And the captain was now his greatest source of information. He wanted to know more about Aelin, about her plans, about what she was like and how he could find her. He wanted to know everything. Anything. Especially where the captain now stood on the game board—and what the captain knew about the king. So Aedion said, "Tell me more about those rings."

But the captain shook his head. "I want to make a bargain with you."

20

The black eye was still gruesome, but it improved over the next week as Celaena worked in the kitchens, tried and failed to shift with Rowan, and generally avoided everyone. The spring rains had come to stay and the kitchen was packed every night, so Celaena took to eating dinner on the shadowed steps, arriving just before the Story Keeper began speaking.

Story Keeper—that's what Emrys was, a title of honor amongst both Fae and humans in Wendlyn. What it meant was that when he began telling a story, you sat down and shut up. It also meant that he was a walking library of the kingdom's legends and myths.

By that time, Celaena knew most of the fortress's residents, if only in the sense that she could put names to faces. She'd observed them out of instinct, to learn her surroundings, her potential enemies and threats. She knew they observed her, too, when they thought she wasn't paying attention. And any shred of regret she felt at not approaching them was burned up by the fact that no one bothered to approach her, either.

The only person who made an effort was Luca, who still peppered Celaena with questions as they worked, still prattled on and on about his training, the fortress gossip, the weather. He'd only talked to her once about anything else—on a morning when it had taken a monumental effort to peel herself out of bed, and only the scar on her palm had made her plant her feet on the icy floor. She'd been washing the breakfast dishes, staring out the window without seeing anything, too heavy in her bones, when Luca had dumped a pot in the sink and quietly said, "For a long while, I couldn't talk about what happened to me before I came here. There were some days I couldn't talk at all. Couldn't get out of bed, either. But if—when you need to talk . . ."

She'd shut him down with a long look. And he hadn't said anything like it since.

Thankfully, Emrys gave her space. Lots of space, especially when Malakai arrived during breakfast to make sure Celaena hadn't caused any trouble. She usually avoided looking at the other fortress couples, but here, where she couldn't walk away . . . she hated their closeness, the way Malakai's eyes lit up every time he saw him. Hated it so much that she choked on it.

She never asked Rowan why he, too, came to hear Emrys's stories. As far as they were each concerned, the other didn't exist outside of training.

Training was a generous way to describe what they were doing, as she had accomplished *nothing*. She didn't shift once. He snarled and sneered and hissed, but she couldn't do it. Every day, always when Rowan disappeared for a few moments, she tried, but—nothing. Rowan threatened to drag her back to the barrows, as that seemed to be the only thing that had triggered any sort of response, but he'd backed off—to her surprise—when she told him that she'd slit her own throat before entering that place again. So they swore at each other, sat in brooding silence on the temple ruin, and occasionally had those unspoken shouting matches. If she was in a particularly nasty mood, he made her chop wood—log after log, until she could hardly lift the ax and her hands were blistered. If she was going to be pissed off at the whole damn world, he said, if she was going to waste his time by not shifting, then she might as well be useful in some way.

All this waiting—for her. For the shift that made her shudder to think about.

It was on the eighth day after her arrival, after scrubbing pots and pans until her back throbbed, that Celaena stopped in the middle of their hike up the now-familiar ridge. "I have a request." She never spoke to him unless she needed to—mostly to curse at him. Now she said, "I want to see *you* shift."

A blink, those green eyes flat. "You don't have the privilege of giving orders."

"Show me how you do it." Her memories of the Fae in Terrasen were foggy, as if someone had smeared oil over them. She couldn't remember seeing one of them change, where their clothes had gone, how fast it had been . . . He stared her down, seeming to say, *Just this once*, and then—

A soft flash of light, a ripple of color, and a hawk was flapping midair, beating for the nearest tree branch. He settled on it, clicking his beak. She scanned the mossy earth. No sign of his clothes, his weapons. It had taken barely more than a few heartbeats.

He gave a battle cry and swooped, talons slashing for her eyes. She lunged behind the tree just as there was another flash and shudder of color, and then he was clothed and armed and growling in her face. *"Your turn."*

She wouldn't give him the satisfaction of seeing her tremble. It was—incredible. Incredible to see the shift. "Where do your clothes go?"

"Between, somewhere. I don't particularly care." Such dead, joyless eyes. She had a feeling she looked like that these days. She *knew* she had looked like that the night Chaol had caught her gutting Archer in the tunnel. What had left Rowan so soulless?

He bared his teeth, but she didn't submit. She'd been watching the demi-Fae warrior males at the fortress, and they growled and showed their teeth about *everything*. They were not the ethereal, gentle folk that legend painted, that she vaguely remembered from Terrasen. No holding hands and dancing around the maypole with flowers in their hair. They were predators, the lot of them. Some of the dominant females were just as aggressive, prone to snarling when challenged or annoyed or even hungry. She supposed she might have fit in with them if she'd bothered to try.

Still holding Rowan's stare, Celaena calmed her breathing. She imagined phantom fingers reaching down, pulling her Fae form out. Imagined a wash of color and light. *Pushed* herself against her mortal flesh. But—nothing.

"Sometimes I wonder whether this is a punishment for *you*," she said through her teeth. "But what could you have done to piss off her Immortal Majesty?"

"Don't use that tone when you talk about her."

"Oh, I can use whatever tone I want. And you can taunt and snarl at me and make me chop wood all day, but short of ripping out my tongue, you can't—"

Faster than lightning, his hand shot out and she gagged, jolting as he grabbed her tongue between his fingers. She bit down, *hard*, but he didn't let go. "Say that again," he purred.

She choked as he kept pinching her tongue, and she went for his daggers, simultaneously slamming her knee up between his legs, but he shoved his body against hers, a wall of hard muscle and several hundred years of lethal training trapping her against a tree. She was a joke by comparison—a *joke*—and her *tongue*—

He released her tongue, and she gasped for breath. She swore at him, a filthy, foul name, and spat at his feet. And that's when he bit her.

She cried out as those canines pierced the spot between her neck and shoulder, a primal act of aggression—the bite so strong and claiming that she was too stunned to move. He had her pinned against the tree and clamped down harder, his canines digging deep, her blood spilling onto her shirt. Pinned, like some weakling. But that was what she'd become, wasn't it? Useless, pathetic.

She growled, more animal than sentient being. And *shoved*.

Rowan staggered back a step, teeth ripping her skin as she struck his chest. She didn't feel the pain, didn't care about the blood or the flash of light.

No, she wanted to rip his throat out—rip it out with the elongated canines she bared at him as she finished shifting and roared.

21

Rowan grinned. "There you are." Blood—her blood—was on his teeth, on his mouth and chin. And those dead eyes glowed as he spat her blood onto the earth. She probably tasted like a sewer to him.

There was a shrieking in her ears, and Celaena lunged at him. Lunged, and then stopped as she took in the world with stunning clarity, smelled it and tasted it and breathed it like the finest wine. Gods, this place, this kingdom smelled *divine*, smelled like—

She had shifted.

She panted, even though her lungs were telling her she was no longer winded and did not need as many breaths in this body. There was a tickling at her neck—her skin slowly beginning to stitch itself together. She was a faster healer in this form. Because of the magic . . . *Breathe. Breathe.*

But there it was, rising up, wildfire crackling in her veins, in her fingertips, the forest around them so much kindling, and then—

She shoved back. Took the fear and used it like a battering ram inside herself, against the power, shoving it down, down.

Rowan prowled closer. "Let it out. Don't fight it."

A pulse beat against her, nipping, smelling of snow and pine. Rowan's power, taunting hers. Not like her fire, but a gift of ice and wind. A freezing zap at her elbow had her falling back against the tree. The magic bit her cheek now. Magic—attacking her.

The wildfire exploded in a wall of blue flame, rushing for Rowan, engulfing the trees, the world, herself, until—

It vanished, sucked out into nothing, along with the air she was breathing.

Celaena dropped to her knees. As she clutched at her neck as if she could claw open an airway for herself, Rowan's boots appeared in the field of her vision. He'd pulled the air out—suffocated her fire. Such power, such control. Maeve had not given her an instructor with similar abilities—she'd instead sent someone with power capable of smothering her fire, someone who wouldn't mind doing it should she become a threat.

Air rushed down her throat in a whoosh. She gasped it down in greedy gulps, hardly registering the agony as she shifted back into her mortal form, the world going quiet and dull again.

"Does your lover know what you are?" A cold question.

She lifted her head, not caring how he'd found out. "He knows everything." Not entirely true.

His eyes flickered—with what emotion, she couldn't tell. "I won't be biting you again," he said, and she wondered just what he'd tasted in her blood.

She growled, but the sound was muted. Fangless. "Even if it's the only way to get me to shift?"

He walked uphill—to the ridge. "You don't bite the women of other males."

She heard, more than felt, something die from her voice as she said, "We're not—together. Not anymore. I let him go before I came here."

He looked over his shoulder. "Why?" Flat, bored. But still, slightly curious.

What did she care if he knew? She'd curled her hand into a fist in her lap, her knuckles white. Every time she glanced at the ring, rubbed it, caught it gleaming, it punched a hole right through her.

She should take the damn thing off. But she knew she wouldn't, if only because that near-constant agony felt deserved. "Because he's safer if he's as repulsed by me as you are."

"At least you've already learned one lesson." When she cocked her head, he said, "The people you love are just weapons that will be used against you."

She didn't want to recall how Nehemia had been used—had used *herself*—against her, to force her to act. Wanted to pretend she wasn't starting to forget what Nehemia had looked like.

"Shift again," Rowan ordered, jerking his chin at her. "This time, try to—"

She was forgetting what Nehemia looked like. The shade of her eyes, the curve of her lips, the smell of her. Her laugh. The roaring in Celaena's head went quiet, silenced by that familiar nothingness.

Do not let that light go out.

But Celaena didn't know how to stop it. The one person she could have told, who might have understood . . . She was buried in an unadorned grave, so far from the sun-warmed soil that she had loved.

Rowan gripped her by the shoulders. *"Are you listening?"*

She gave him a bored stare, even as his fingers dug into her skin. "Why don't you just bite me again?"

"Why don't I give you the lashing you deserve?"

He looked so dead set on it that she blinked. "If you *ever* take a whip to me, I will skin you alive."

He let go of her and stalked around the clearing, a predator assessing its prey. "If you don't shift again, you're pulling double duty in the kitchens for the next week."

"Fine." At least working in the kitchens had some quantifiable results. At least in the kitchens, she could tell up from down and knew what she was doing. But this—this promise she'd made, the bargain she'd struck with Maeve . . . She'd been a fool.

Rowan paused his stalking. "You're worthless."

"Tell me something I don't know."

He went on, "You would probably have been more useful to the world if you'd actually died ten years ago."

She just looked him in the eye and said, "I'm leaving."

Rowan didn't stop her as she returned to the fortress and packed. It took all of a minute, as she hadn't even unloaded her satchel and had no weapons left. She supposed she could have ripped the fortress apart to find where Rowan had stashed them, or stolen them from the demi-Fae, but both would require time and bring more attention than she wanted. She didn't talk to anyone as she walked out.

She'd find another way to learn about the Wyrdkeys and destroy the King of Adarlan and free Eyllwe. If she kept going like this, she'd have nothing left inside to fight with.

She'd marked the paths they'd taken on the way in, but as she entered the tree-covered slopes, she mostly relied on the position of the cloud-veiled sun to navigate. She'd make the trip back, find food along the way, and figure out something else. This had been a fool's errand from the start. At least she hadn't been too long delayed—though she might now have to be quicker about finding the answers she needed, and—

"Is this what you do? Run away when things get hard?" Rowan was standing between two trees directly in her path, having undoubtedly flown here.

She brushed past him, her legs burning with the downhill walk.

"You're free of your obligation to train me, so I have nothing more to say to you, and you have nothing more to say to me. Do us both a favor and go to hell."

A growl. "Have you ever had to fight for anything in your life?"

She let out a low, bitter laugh and walked faster, veering westward, not caring about the direction as much as getting away from him. But he kept up easily, his long, heavily muscled legs devouring the mossy ground. "You're proving me right with every step you take."

"I don't care."

"I don't know what you want from Maeve—what answers you're looking for, but you—"

"You don't know what I want from her?" It was more of a shout than a question. "How about saving the world from the King of Adarlan?"

"Why bother? Maybe the world's not worth saving." She knew he meant it, too. Those lifeless eyes spoke volumes.

"Because I made a *promise*. A promise to my friend that I would see her kingdom freed." She shoved her scarred palm into his face. "I made an unbreakable vow. And you and Maeve—all you gods-damned bastards—are getting in the way of that." She went off down the hill-side again. He followed.

"And what of your own people? What of your own kingdom?"

"They are better off without me, just as you said."

His tattoo scrunched as he snarled. "So you'd save another land, but not yours. Why can't your friend save her own kingdom?"

"Because she is *dead*!" She screamed the last word so loudly it burned in her throat. "Because she is dead, and I am left with my *worthless* life!"

He merely stared at her with that animal stillness. When she walked away, he didn't come after her.

She lost track of how far she walked and in what direction she traveled. She didn't really care. She hadn't spoken the words—*she is dead*—since the day after Nehemia had been taken from her. But she *was* dead. And Celaena missed her.

Night swept in earlier due to the cloud cover, the temperature plummeting as thunder grumbled in the distance. She made weapons as she went, finding a sharp stone to whittle down branches into rudimentary spears: the longer one she used as a walking stick, and though they were little more than stakes, she told herself the two short ones were daggers. Better than nothing.

Each step was heavier than the last, and she had enough of a sense of self-preservation left to start looking for a place to spend the night. It was almost dark when she found a decent spot: a shallow cave in the side of a granite ledge.

She swiftly gathered enough wood for a fire. The irony of it wasn't wasted on her. If she had any control over her magic—she shut down that thought before it finished. She hadn't made a fire in years, so it took a few tries, but it worked. Just as thunder cracked above her little cave and the skies opened up.

She was hungry, and thankfully found some apples at the bottom of her satchel, along with old teggya from Varese that was still edible, if hard to chew. After she ate as much of it as she could stand, she pulled her cloak around herself and nestled into the side of the cave.

She didn't fail to notice the small, glowing eyes that gathered, peering through the brambles or over boulders or around trees. None of them had bothered her since that first night, and they didn't come closer. Her instincts, warped as they had felt these last few weeks, didn't raise any alarms, either. So she didn't tell them off, and didn't really mind them at all.

With the fire and the pounding rain, it was almost cozy—not like her freezing room. Though she was exhausted, she felt somewhat clearheaded. Almost like herself again, with her makeshift weapons. She'd made a smart choice to leave. *Do what needs to be done*, Elena had told her. Well, she'd needed to leave before Rowan shredded her into so many pieces that she would never stand a chance of putting herself back together.

Tomorrow, she'd start over. She'd spotted what looked like a crumbling, forgotten road that she could follow downhill. As long as she kept going toward the plains, she could find her way back to the coast. And come up with a new plan as she went.

It was good she had left.

Exhaustion hit her so thoroughly that she was asleep moments after she sprawled beside the fire, one hand clasped around her spear. She probably would have dozed until dawn had a sudden silence not jerked her awake.

22

Celaena's fire was still crackling, the rain still pounding beyond the cave mouth. But the forest had gone quiet. Those little watching eyes had vanished.

She uncoiled to her feet, spear in one hand and a stake in the other, and crept to the narrow cave entrance. With the rain and the fire, she couldn't make out anything. But every hair on her body was standing, and a growing reek was slithering in from the forest beyond. Like leather and carrion. Different from what she'd whiffed at the barrows. Older and earthier and . . . hungrier.

Suddenly, the fire seemed like the stupidest thing she had ever done.

No fires. That had been Rowan's only rule while trekking to the fortress. And they had stayed off the roads—veering away entirely from the forgotten, overgrown ones. Ones like the path she'd spied nearby.

The silence deepened.

She slipped into the drenched forest, stubbing her toes on rocks and roots as her eyes adjusted to the dark. But she kept moving ahead—curving down and away from the ancient path.

She'd made it far enough that her cave was little more than a glow on the hill above, a flicker of light illuminating the trees. A gods-damned beacon. She angled her stake and spear into better positions, about to continue on when lightning flashed.

Three tall, lanky silhouettes lurked in front of her cave.

Though they stood like humans, she knew, deep in her bones from some collective mortal memory, that they were not. They were not Fae, either.

With expert quiet, she took another step, then another. They were still poking around the cave entrance, taller than men, neither male nor female.

Skinwalkers are on the prowl, Rowan had warned that first day they'd trained, *searching for human pelts to bring back to their caves.* She had been too dazed to ask or care. But now—now that carelessness, that wallowing, was going to get her killed. Skinned.

Wendlyn. Land of nightmares made flesh, where legends roamed the earth. Despite years of stealth training, each step felt like a snap, her breathing too loud.

Thunder grumbled, and she used the cover of the sound to take a few bounding steps. She stopped behind another tree, breathing as quietly as she could, and peered around it to survey the hillside behind her. Lightning flashed again.

The three figures were gone. But the leathery, rancid smell swarmed all around her now. *Human pelts.*

She eyed the tree she'd ducked behind. The trunk was too slick with moss and rain to scale, the branches too high. The other trees weren't any better. And what good was being stuck up a tree in a lightning storm?

She darted to the next tree, carefully avoiding any sticks or leaves, cursing silently at the slowness of her pace, and— *Damn it all to hell.* She burst into a run, the mossy earth treacherous underfoot. She could make out the trees, some larger rocks, but the slope was steep. She kept her feet under her, even as undergrowth cracked behind, faster and faster.

She didn't dare take her focus off the trees and rocks as she hurtled down the slope, desperate for any flat ground. Perhaps their hunting territory ended somewhere—perhaps she could outrun them until dawn. She veered eastward, still going downhill, and grabbed on to a trunk to swing herself around, almost losing her balance as she slammed into something hard and unyielding.

She slashed with her stake—only to be grabbed by two massive hands.

Her wrists sang in agony as the fingers squeezed hard enough that she couldn't stab either weapon into her captor. She twisted, bringing up a foot to smash into her assailant, and caught a flash of fangs before— Not fangs. Teeth.

And there was no gleam of flesh-pelts. Only silver hair, shining with rain.

Rowan dragged her against him, pressing them into what appeared to be a hollowed-out tree.

She kept her panting quiet, but breathing didn't become any easier when Rowan gripped her by the shoulders and put his mouth to her ear. The crashing footsteps had stopped.

"You are going to listen to every word I say." Rowan's voice was softer than the rain outside. "Or else you are going to die tonight. Do you understand?" She nodded. He let go—only to draw his sword and a wicked-looking hatchet. "Your survival depends entirely on you." The smell was growing again. "You need to shift *now*. Or your mortal slowness will kill you."

She stiffened, but reached in, feeling for some thread of power. There was nothing. There had to be some trigger, some *place* inside her where she could command it . . . A slow, shrieking sound of stone on metal sounded through the rain. Then another. And another. They were sharpening their blades. "Your magic—"

"They do not breathe, so have no airways to cut off. Ice would slow them, not stop them. My wind is already blowing our scent away from them, but not for long. *Shift*, Aelin."

Aelin. It was not a test, not some elaborate trick. The skinwalkers did not need air.

Rowan's tattoo shone as lightning filled their little hiding spot. "We are going to have to run in a moment. What form you take when we do will determine our fates. So *breathe*, and *shift*."

Though every instinct screamed against it, she closed her eyes. Took a breath. Then another. Her lungs opened, full of cool, soothing air, and she wondered if Rowan was helping with that, too.

He was helping. And he was willing to meet a horrible fate in order to keep her alive. He hadn't left her alone. She hadn't been alone.

There was a muffled curse, and Rowan slammed his body against hers, as if he could somehow shield her. No, not shield her. Cover her, the flash of light.

She barely registered the pain—if only because the moment her Fae senses snapped into place, she had to shove a hand against her own mouth to keep from retching. Oh, gods, the festering *smell* of them, worse than any corpse she'd ever dealt with.

With her delicately pointed ears, she could hear them now, each step they took as the three of them systematically made their way down the hill. They spoke in low, strange voices—at once male and female, all ravenous.

"There are two of them now," one hissed. She didn't want to know what power it wielded to allow it to speak when it had no airways. "A

Fae male joined the female. I want him—he smells of storm winds and steel." Celaena gagged as the smell shoved down her throat. "The female we'll bring back with us—dawn's too close. Then we can take our time peeling her apart."

Rowan eased off her and said quietly, not needing to be near for her to hear while he assessed the forest beyond, "There is a swift river a third of a mile east, at the base of a large cliff." He didn't look at her as he extended two long daggers, and she didn't nod her thanks as she silently discarded her makeshift weapons and gripped the ivory hilts. "When I say *run*, you run like hell. Step where I step, and don't turn around for any reason. If we are separated, run straight—you'll hear the river." Order after order—a commander on the battlefield, solid and deadly. He peered out of the tree. The smell was nearly overpowering now, swarming from every angle. "If they catch you, you cannot kill them—not with a mortal weapon. Your best option is to fight until you can get free and run. Understand?"

She gave another nod. Breathing was hard again, and the rain was now torrential.

"On my mark," Rowan said, smelling and hearing things that were lost even to her heightened senses. "Steady . . ." She sank onto her haunches as Rowan did the same.

"Come out, come out," one of them hissed—so close it could have been inside the tree with them. There was a sudden rustling in thebrush to the west, almost as if two people were running. Instantly, the reek of the skinwalkers lessened as they raced after the cracking branches and leaves that Rowan's wind led in the other direction.

"Now," Rowan hissed, and burst out of the tree.

Celaena ran—or tried to. Even with her sharpened vision, the brush and stones and trees proved a hindrance. Rowan raced toward the rising roar of the river, swollen from the spring rains, his pace slower than she'd expected, but . . . but he was slowing for her. Because this Fae body was different, and she was adjusting wrong, and—

She slipped, but a hand was at her elbow, keeping her upright. "Faster," was all he said, and as soon as she'd found her footing, he was off again, shooting through the trees like a mountain cat.

It took all of a minute before the force of that smell gnawed on her heels and the snapping of the brush closed in. But she wouldn't take her eyes off Rowan, and the brightening ahead—the end of the tree line. Not much farther until they could jump, and—

A fourth skinwalker leapt out of where it had somehow been lurking undetected in the brush. It lunged for Rowan in a flash of leathery, long limbs marred with countless scars. No, not scars—*stitches.* The stitches holding its various hides together.

She shouted as the skinwalker pounced, but Rowan didn't falter a step as he ducked and twirled with inhuman speed, slashing down with his sword and viciously slicing with the hatchet.

The skinwalker's arm severed at the same moment its head toppled off its neck.

She might have marveled at the way he moved, the way he killed, but Rowan didn't stop sprinting, so Celaena raced after him, glancing once at the body the Fae warrior had left in pieces.

Sagging bits of leather on the wet leaves, like discarded clothes. But still twitching and rustling—as if waiting for someone to stitch it back together.

She ran faster, Rowan still bounding ahead.

The skinwalkers closed in from behind, shrieking with rage. Then they fell silent, until—

"You think the river can save you?" one of them panted, letting out a laugh that raked along her bones. "You think if we get wet, we'll lose our form? I have worn the skins of fishes when mortals were scarce, female."

She had an image then, of the chaos waiting in that river—a flipping and near-drowning and dizziness—and something pulling her down, down, down to the still bottom.

"*Rowan*," she breathed, but he was already gone, his massive body hurtling straight off the cliff edge in a mighty leap.

There was no stopping the pursuit behind her. The skinwalkers were going to jump with them. And there would be nothing they could do to kill them, no mortal weapon they could use.

A well ripped open inside of her, vast and unyielding and horrible. Rowan had claimed no mortal weapon could kill them. But what of immortal ones?

Celaena broke through the line of trees, sprinting for the ledge that jutted out, bare granite beneath her as she threw her strength into her legs, her lungs, her arms, and *jumped*.

As she plummeted, she twisted to face the cliff, to face them. They were no more than three lean bodies leaping into the rainy night, shrieking with primal, triumphant, anticipated pleasure.

"*Shift*!" was the only warning she gave Rowan. There was a flash of light to tell her he'd obeyed.

Then she ripped everything from that well inside her, ripped it out with both hands and her entire raging, hopeless heart.

As she fell, hair whipping her face, Celaena thrust her hands toward the skinwalkers.

"Surprise," she hissed. The world erupted in blue wildfire.

Celaena shuddered on the riverbank, from cold and exhaustion and terror. Terror at the skinwalkers—and terror at what she had done.

His clothes dry thanks to shifting, Rowan stood a few feet away, monitoring the smoldering cliffs upriver. She'd incinerated the skinwalkers. They hadn't even had time to scream.

She hunched over her knees, arms wrapped around herself. The forest was burning on either side of the river—a radius that she didn't have the nerve to measure. It was a weapon, her power. A different sort of weapon than blades or arrows or her hands. A curse.

It took several attempts, but at last she spoke. "Can you put it out?"

"You could, if you tried." When she didn't respond, he said, "I'm almost done." In a moment the flames nearest the cliffs went out. How long had he been working to suffocate them? "We don't need something else attracted to your fires."

She might have bothered to respond to the jab, but she was too tired and cold. The rain filled the world, and for a while, silence reigned.

"Why is my shifting so vital?" she asked at last.

"Because it terrifies you," he said. "Mastering it is the first step toward learning to control your power. Without that control, with a blast like that, you could easily have burnt yourself out."

"What do you mean?"

Another stormy look. "When you access your power, what does it feel like?"

She considered. "A well," she said. "The magic feels like a well."

"Have you felt the bottom of it?"

"Is there a bottom?" She prayed there was.

"All magic has a bottom—a breaking point. For those with weaker gifts, it's easily depleted and easily refilled. They can access most of their power at once. But for those with stronger gifts, it can take hours to hit the bottom, to summon their powers at full strength."

"How long does it take you?"

"A full day." She jolted. "Before battle, we take the time, so that when we walk onto the killing field, we can be at our strongest. You can do other things at the same time, but some part of you is down in there, pulling up more and more, until you reach the bottom."

"And when you pull it all out, it just—releases in some giant wave?"

"If I want it to. I can release it in smaller bursts, and go on for a while. But it can be hard to hold it back. People sometimes can't tell friend from foe when they're handling that much magic."

When she'd drawn her power on the other side of the portal months ago, she'd felt that lack of control—known she was almost as likely to hurt Chaol as she was to hurt the demon he was facing. "How long does it take you to recover?"

"Days. A week, depending on how I used the power and whether I drained every last drop. Some make the mistake of trying to take more before they're ready, or holding on for too long, and they either burn out their minds or just burn up altogether. Your shaking isn't just from the river, you know. It's your body's way of telling you not to do that again."

"Because of the iron in our blood pushing against the magic?"

"That's how our enemies will sometimes try to fight against us if they don't have magic—iron everything." He must have seen her brows rise, because he added, "I was captured once. While on a campaign in the east, in a kingdom that doesn't exist anymore. They had me shackled head to toe in iron to keep me from choking the air out of their lungs."

She let out a low whistle. "Were you tortured?"

"Two weeks on their tables before my men rescued me." He unbuckled his vambrace and pushed back the sleeve of his right arm, revealing a thick, wicked scar curving around his forearm and elbow. "Cut me open bit by bit, then took the bones here and—"

"I can see very well what happened, and know exactly how it's done," she said, stomach tightening. Not at the injury, but—Sam. Sam had been strapped to a table, cut open and broken by one of the most sadistic killers she'd ever known.

"Was it you," Rowan said quietly, but not gently, "or someone else?"

"I was too late. He didn't survive." Again silence fell, and she cursed herself for a fool for telling him. But then she said hoarsely, "Thank you for saving me."

A slight shrug, barely a movement at all. As if her gratitude were harder to endure than her hatred and reticence. "I am bound by an unbreakable blood oath to my Queen, so I had no choice but to ensure you didn't die." A bit of that earlier heaviness settled in her veins again. "But," he went on, "I would not have left anyone to a fate at the hands of the skinwalkers."

"A warning would have been nice."

"I said they were on the loose—weeks ago. But even if I'd warned you today, you would not have listened."

It was true. She shivered again, this time so violently that her body shifted back, a flash of light and pain. If she'd thought she was cold in her Fae body, it was nothing compared to the cold of being human again.

"What was the trigger when you shifted earlier?" he asked, as if this moment were a reprieve from the real world, where the freezing storm and the surging river could muffle their words from the gods. She rubbed at her arms, desperate for any kind of warmth.

"It was nothing." His silence demanded information for information—a fair trade. She sighed. "Let's just say it was fear and necessity and impressively deep-rooted survival instincts."

"You didn't lose control immediately upon shifting. When you finally used your magic, your clothes didn't burn; neither did your hair. And the daggers didn't melt." As if just now remembering that she still had them, he swiped them from her.

He was right. The magic hadn't swarmed her the moment she'd shifted, and even in the explosion that had spread out in every direction, she'd had enough control to preserve herself. Not a single hair had burned.

"Why was it different this time?" he pressed.

"Because I didn't want you to die to save me," she admitted.

"Would you have shifted to save yourself?"

"Your opinion of me is pretty much identical to my own, so you know the answer."

He was quiet for long enough that she wondered if he was piecing the bits of her together. "You're not leaving," Rowan said at last, arms crossed. "I'm not letting you off double duty in the kitchens, but you're not leaving."

"Why?"

He unfastened his cloak. "Because I said so, that's why." And she might have told him it was the worst gods-damned reason she had ever heard, and that he was an arrogant prick, had he not tossed her his cloak—dry and warm. Then he dropped his jacket in her lap, too.

When he turned to go back to the fortress, she followed him.

23

For the past week, not much had changed for Manon and the Blackbeaks. They still flew daily to master the wyverns, and still managed to avoid outright war in the mess hall twice a day. The Yellowlegs heir tried to rile Manon whenever she could, but Manon paid her no more attention than she would a gnat buzzing about her head.

All that changed the day of the selection, when the heirs and their covens chose their mounts.

With three covens plus three Matrons, there were forty-two witches crowded around the training pit in the Northern Fang. Handlers rushed about below the viewing platform, readying themselves. The wyverns would be brought out one by one, and, using the bait beasts, would show off their qualities. Like the other witches, Manon had been sneaking by the cages every day. She still wanted Titus.

Wanted was a mortal word. Titus was *hers.* And if it came down to it, she'd disembowel any witch who challenged her. She'd sharpened her nails this morning in anticipation of it. All of the Thirteen had.

Claims would be settled in a civilized manner, however. The three Matrons would draw sticks if more than one claim was made on a mount. When it came to Titus, Manon knew precisely who would vie for him: Iskra and Petrah, the Yellowlegs and Blueblood heirs. She'd seen them both watching him with hungry eyes. Had Manon gotten her way, they would have fought for him in the sparring ring. She'd even suggested as much to her grandmother, but was told they didn't need to quarrel amongst themselves any more than necessary. It would be luck of the draw.

That didn't sit well with Manon, who stood along the open edge of the platform, Asterin flanking her. Her edginess only sharpened as the heavy grate lifted at the back of the pit. The bait beast was already chained to the bloodstained wall, a broken, scarred wyvern, half the size of the bulls, his wings tucked in tight. From the platform, she could see that the venomous spikes in his tail had been sawn off to keep him from defending himself against the invaluable mounts.

The bait beast lowered his head as the gate groaned open and the first wyvern was paraded in on tight chains held by very pale-faced men. They darted back as soon as the beast was through, dodging that deadly tail, and the grate shut behind them.

Manon loosed a breath. It wasn't Titus, but one of the medium-sized bulls.

Three sentinels stepped forward to claim him, but the Blueblood Matron, Cresseida, held up a hand. "Let us see him in action first."

One of the men whistled sharply. The wyvern turned on the bait beast.

Teeth and scales and claws, so fast and vicious that even Manon held her breath. Chained as he was, the bait beast didn't stand a chance and was pinned within a second, massive jaws holding down his neck. One command, one whistle, and the wyvern would snap it.

But the man let out a lower-note whistle, and the bull backed off. Another whistle and he sat on his haunches. Two more sentinels stepped forward. Five in the running. Cresseida held out a fistful of twigs to the contenders.

It went to the Blueblood sentinel, who grinned at the others, then down at her wyvern as it was led back into the tunnel. The bait beast, bleeding from his side, heaved himself into the shadows by the wall, waiting for the next assault.

One after another, the wyverns were brought out, attacking with swift, wicked force. And one by one, the sentinels claimed them. No Titus, not yet. She had a feeling the Matrons were drawing this out as some test—to see how well the heirs could control themselves while waiting for the best mounts, to see who would hold out longest. Manon kept one eye on the beasts and another on the other heirs, who watched her in turn as each wyvern was paraded.

Yet the first truly enormous female had Petrah, the Blueblood heir, stepping forward. The female was nearly Titus's size, and wound up taking a chunk out of the bait beast's flank before the trainers could get her to stop. Wild, unpredictable, lethal. Magnificent.

No one challenged the Blueblood heir. Petrah's mother only gave her a nod, as though they had already known what mount she desired.

Asterin took the fiercest stealth wyvern that came along, a cunning-eyed female. Her cousin had always been the best at scouting, and after a talk with Manon and the other sentinels that went long into the night, it had been decided that Asterin would continue that role in the Thirteen's new duties.

So when the pale blue female was presented, Asterin claimed her, her eyes promising such brutality to anyone who got in her way that they practically glowed. No one dared challenge her.

Manon was watching the tunnel entrance when she smelled the myrrh and rosemary scent of the Blueblood heir beside her. Asterin snarled a soft warning.

"Waiting for Titus, aren't you?" Petrah murmured, eyes also on the tunnel.

"And if I am?" Manon asked.

"I'd rather you have him than Iskra."

The witch's serene face was unreadable. "So would I." She wasn't sure what, exactly, but the conversation *meant* something.

Clearly, seeing them quietly talking meant something to everyone else, too. Especially Iskra, who sauntered over to Manon's other side. "Plotting already?"

The Blueblood heir lifted her chin. "I think Titus would make a good mount for Manon."

A line in the sand, Manon thought. What had the Blueblood Matron told Petrah about her? What schemes was she hatching?

Iskra's mouth twisted into a half grin. "We'll see what the Three-Faced Mother has to say."

Manon might have said something back, but then Titus thundered out.

As it had every other time, the breath went out of her at his sheer size and viciousness. The men had barely scrambled back through the gate before Titus whirled, snapping for them. They'd made only a few successful runs with him, she'd been told. Yet under the right rider, he'd fully break.

Titus didn't wait for the whistle before he wheeled on the bait beast, striking with his barbed tail. The chained beast ducked with surprising swiftness, as if he'd sensed the bull's attack, and Titus's tail imbedded itself in the stone.

Debris rained on the bait beast, and as he cringed back, Titus struck again. And again.

Chained to the wall, the bait beast could do nothing. The man whistled, but Titus kept at it. He moved with the fluid grace of untamed savagery.

The bait beast yelped, and Manon could have sworn the Blueblood heir flinched. She'd never heard a cry of pain from any of the wyverns, yet as Titus sank back on his haunches, she saw where he'd struck—right atop the earlier wound in the bait beast's flank.

As if Titus knew where to hit to inflict the most agony. She knew they were intelligent, but *how* intelligent? The man whistled again, and a whip sounded. Titus just kept pacing in front of the bait beast, contemplating how he would strike. Not out of strategy. No, he wanted to savor it. To taunt.

A shiver of delight went down Manon's spine. Riding a beast like Titus, ripping apart her enemies with him . . .

"If you want him so badly," Iskra whispered, and Manon realized she was still standing beside her, now only a step away, "why don't you go get him?"

And before Manon could move—before anyone could, because they were all enthralled by that glorious beast—iron claws shoved into her back.

Asterin's shout echoed, but Manon was falling, plunging the forty feet right into the stone pit. She twisted, colliding with a small, crumbling ledge jutting from the wall. It slowed her fall and saved her life, but she kept going until—

She slammed into the ground, her ankle wrenching. Cries came from above, but Manon didn't look up. If she had, she might have seen Asterin tackle Iskra, claws and teeth out. She might have seen her grandmother give the order that no one was to jump into the pit.

But Manon wasn't looking at them.

Titus turned toward her.

The wyvern stood between her and the gate, where the men were rushing to and fro, as if trying to decide whether they should risk saving her or wait until she was carrion.

Titus's tail lashed back and forth, his dark eyes pinned on her. Manon drew Wind-Cleaver. It was a dagger compared to the mass of him. She had to get to that gate.

She stared him down. Titus settled onto his haunches, preparing to attack. He knew where the gate was, too, and what it meant for her. His prey.

Not rider or mistress, but *prey*.

The witches had gone silent. The men at the gate and upper platforms had gone silent.

Manon rotated her sword. Titus lunged.

She had to roll to avoid his mouth, and was up in a second, sprinting like hell for that gate. Her ankle throbbed, and she limped, swallowing her scream of pain. Titus turned, fast as a spring stream down a mountainside, and as she hurtled for the gate, he struck with his tail.

Manon had enough sense to whirl to avoid the venomous barbs, but she caught an upper edge of the tail in the side and went flying, Wind-Cleaver wrenching from her grip. She hit the dirt near the opposite wall and slid, face scraping on the rocks. Her ribs bleated in agony as she scrambled into a sitting position and gauged the distance between herself and the sword and Titus.

But Titus was hesitating, his eyes lifted behind her, above her, to—

Darkness embrace her. She'd forgotten about the bait beast. The creature chained behind her, so close she could smell the carrion on his breath.

Titus's stare was a command for the bait beast to stand down. To let him eat Manon.

Manon dared a glance over her shoulder, to the sword in the shadows, so close to the chained anchor of the bait beast. She might have risked it if the beast wasn't there, if he wasn't looking dead at her, looking at her like she was—

Not prey.

Titus growled a territorial warning at the bait beast again, so loud she could feel it in every bone. Instead, the bait beast, small as he was, was gazing at her with something like rage and determination. Emotion, she might have called it. Hunger, but not for her.

No, she realized as the beast lifted its black gaze to Titus, letting out a low snarl in response. Not submissive in the least, that sound. A threat—a promise. The bait beast wanted a shot at Titus.

Allies. If only for this moment.

Again, Manon felt that ebb and flow in the world, that invisible current that some called Fate and some called the loom of the Three-Faced Goddess. Titus roared his final threat.

Manon twisted to her feet and ran.

Every step made stars flash, and the ground shook as Titus barreled after her, willing to tear through the bait beast to kill her if necessary.

Manon scooped up her sword and whirled, bringing it down upon the thick, rusted chain with every bit of strength left in her.

Wind-Cleaver, they called her blade. Now they would call it Iron-Cleaver. The chain snapped free as Titus leapt for her.

Titus didn't see it coming, and there was something like shock in his eyes as the bait beast tackled him and they rolled.

Titus was twice its size and uninjured, and Manon didn't wait to see the outcome before she took off for the tunnel, where the men were frantically lifting the grate.

But then a *boom* and a shocked murmur sounded, and Manon dared one look in time to see the wyverns leap apart and the bait beast strike again.

The blow from that scarred, useless tail was so strong Titus's head slammed into the dirt.

As Titus surged to his legs, the bait beast feinted with its tail and made a swipe with jagged claws that had Titus roaring in pain.

Manon froze, barely fifteen feet from the gate.

The wyverns circled each other, wings scraping against the ground. It should have been a joke. And yet the bait beast wouldn't stand down, despite the limp, despite the scars and the blood.

Titus went right for the throat with no warning growl.

The bait beast's tail connected with Titus's head. Titus reeled back but then lunged, jaws and tail snapping. Once those barbs got into the flesh of the bait beast, it would be done. The bait beast dodged the tail by slamming its own down atop it, but couldn't escape the jaws that latched on to its neck.

Over. It should be over.

The bait beast thrashed, but couldn't get free. Manon knew she should run. Others were shouting. She had been born without sympathy or mercy or kindness. She didn't care which one of them lived or died, so long as she escaped. But that current was still flowing, flowing toward the fight, not away from it. And she owed the bait beast a life debt.

So Manon did the most foolish thing she'd ever done in her long, wicked life.

She ran for Titus and brought Wind-Cleaver down upon his tail. She severed clean through flesh and bone, and Titus roared, releasing his prey. The stump of his tail lashed at her, and Manon took it right in the stomach, the air knocked out of her before she even hit the ground. When she raised herself, she saw the final lunge that ended it.

Throat exposed by his bellow of pain, Titus didn't stand a chance as the bait beast pounced and closed its jaws around that mighty neck.

Titus had one last thrash, one final attempt to pry himself free. The bait beast held firm, as though he'd been waiting for weeks or months or years. He clamped down and wrenched his head away, taking Titus's throat with him.

Silence fell. As if the world itself stopped when Titus's body crashed to the ground, black blood spilling everywhere.

Manon stood absolutely still. Slowly, the bait beast lifted its head from the carcass, Titus's blood dripping from his maw. Their eyes met.

People were shouting at her to run, and the gate groaned open, but Manon stared into those black eyes, one of them horribly scarred but intact. He took a step, then another toward her.

Manon held her ground. It was impossible. *Impossible.* Titus was twice his size, twice his weight, and had years of training.

The bait beast had trounced him—not because he was bigger or stronger, but because he wanted it more. Titus had been a brute and a killer, yet this wyvern before her . . . he was a *warrior.*

Men were rushing in with spears and swords and whips, and the bait beast growled.

Manon held up a hand. And again, the world stopped.

Manon, eyes still upon the beast, said, "He's mine."

He had saved her life. Not by coincidence, but by choice. He'd felt the current running between them, too. "What?" her grandmother barked from above.

Manon found herself walking toward the wyvern, and stopped with not five feet between them. "He's mine," Manon said, taking in the scars, the limp, the burning life in those eyes.

The witch and the wyvern looked at each other for a moment that lasted for a heartbeat, that lasted for eternity. "You're mine," Manon said to him.

The wyvern blinked at her, Titus's blood still dripping from his cracked and broken teeth, and Manon had the feeling that he had come to the same decision. Perhaps he had known long before tonight, and his fight with Titus hadn't been so much about survival as it had been a challenge to claim her.

As his rider. As his mistress. As *his.*

Manon named her wyvern Abraxos, after the ancient serpent who held the world between his coils at the behest of the Three-Faced Goddess. And that was about the only pleasant thing that happened that night.

When she'd returned to the others, Abraxos taken away for cleaning and mending and Titus's carcass hauled off by thirty men, Manon had stared down each and every witch who dared meet her eyes.

The Yellowlegs heir was being held by Asterin in front of the Matrons. Manon gazed at Iskra for a long moment before she simply said, "Looks like I lost my footing."

Iskra steamed at the ears, but Manon shrugged, wiping the dirt and blood from her face before limping back to the Omega. She wouldn't give Iskra the satisfaction of claiming she'd almost killed her. And Manon was in no shape to settle this in a proper fight.

Attack or clumsiness, Asterin was punished by Mother Blackbeak that night for letting the heir fall into the pit. Manon had asked to be the one to dispense the whipping, but her grandmother ignored her. Instead, she had the Yellowlegs heir do it. As Asterin's failure had occurred in plain sight of the other Matrons and their heirs, so would her punishment.

Standing in the mess hall, Manon watched each brutal lash, all ten of them at full strength, as Iskra sported a bruise on her jaw courtesy of Asterin.

To her everlasting credit, Asterin didn't scream. Not once. It still took all of Manon's self-restraint to keep from grabbing the whip and using it to strangle Iskra.

Then came the conversation with her grandmother. It wasn't so much a conversation as it was a slap in the face, then a verbal beating that—a day later—still made Manon's ears ring.

She'd humiliated her grandmother and every Blackbeak in history by picking that "runty scrap of meat," regardless of his victory. It was a fluke that he'd killed Titus, her grandmother ranted. Abraxos was the smallest of any of the mounts, and on top of that, because of his size, he had never flown a day in his life. They had never let him out of the warrens.

They didn't even know if he *could* fly after his wings had taken a beating for so long, and the handlers were of the opinion that should Abraxos attempt the Crossing, he'd splatter himself and Manon on the Gap floor. They claimed no other wyverns would ever accept his dominance, not as a Wing Leader. Manon had ruined all of her grandmother's plans.

All these facts were shouted at her again and again. She knew that if she even *wanted* to change mounts, her grandmother would force her to keep Abraxos, just to humiliate her when she failed. Even if it got her killed in the process.

Her grandmother hadn't been in the pit, though. She hadn't looked into Abraxos's eyes and seen the warrior's heart beating in him. She hadn't noticed that he'd fought with more cunning and ferocity than any of the others. So Manon held firm and took the slap to the face, and the lecture, and then the second slap that left her cheek throbbing.

Manon's face was still aching when she reached the pen in which Abraxos now made his home. He was curled by the far wall, silent and still when so many of the creatures were pacing or shrieking or growling.

Her escort, the overseer, peered through the bars. Asterin lurked in the shadows. After the whipping last night, her Second wasn't going to let her out of her sight anytime soon.

Manon hadn't apologized for the whipping. The rules were the rules, and her cousin had failed. Asterin deserved the lashing, just as Manon deserved the bruise on her cheek.

"Why's he curled up like that?" Manon asked the man.

"Suspect it's 'cause he's never had a pen to himself. Not this big, anyway."

Manon studied the penned-in cavern. "Where did they keep him before?"

The man pointed at the floor. "With the other baiters in the sty. He's the oldest of the baiters, you know. Survived the pits and the stys. But that doesn't mean he's suitable for you."

"If I wanted your opinion on his suitability, I'd ask for it," Manon said, eyes still on Abraxos as she approached the bars. "How long to get him in the skies?"

The man rubbed his head. "Could be days or weeks or months. Could be never."

"We begin training with our mounts this afternoon."

"Not going to happen." Manon raised her brows. "This one needs to be trained alone first. I'll get our best trainers on it, and you can use another wyvern in the meantime to—"

"First of all, human," Manon interrupted, "don't give me orders." Her iron teeth snapped out, and he flinched. "Second, I won't be training with another wyvern. I'll train with him."

The man was pale as death as he said, "All your sentinels' mounts will attack him. And the first flight will spook him so bad that he'll fight back. So unless you want your soldiers and their mounts to tear each other apart, I suggest you train alone." He trembled and added, "Milady."

The wyvern was watching them. Waiting. "Can they understand us?"

"No. Some spoken commands and whistles, but no more than a dog."

Manon didn't believe that for one moment. It wasn't that he was lying to her. He just didn't know any better. Or maybe Abraxos was different.

She'd use every moment until the War Games to train him. When she and her Thirteen were crowned victors, she'd make each and every one of the witches who doubted her, her grandmother included, curse themselves for fools. Because she was Manon Blackbeak, and she'd never failed at anything. And there would be nothing better than watching Abraxos bite off Iskra's head on the battlefield.

24

It was far too easy to lie to his men about the bruises and cuts on his face when Chaol returned to the castle—an unfortunate incident with a drunk vagrant in Rifthold. Enduring the lies and the injuries was better than being carrion. Chaol's bargain with Aedion and the rebels had been simple: information for information.

He'd promised more information about their queen, as well as about the king's black rings, in exchange for what they knew regarding the king's power. It had kept him alive that night, and every night afterward, when he'd waited for them to change their minds. But they never came for him, and tonight, he and Aedion waited until well past twelve before slipping into Celaena's old rooms.

It was the first time he'd dared return to the tomb since that night with Celaena and Dorian, and the skull-shaped bronze knocker, Mort, didn't move or speak at all. Even though Chaol wore the Eye of Elena at his throat, the knocker remained frozen. Perhaps Mort only answered to those with Brannon Galathynius's blood in their veins.

So he and Aedion combed through the tomb, the dusty halls, scouring every inch for signs of spies or ways to be discovered. When they were at last satisfied that no one could overhear them, Aedion said, "Tell me what I'm doing down here, Captain."

The general had shown no awe or surprise as Chaol had led him into Elena and Gavin's resting place, though his eyes had widened slightly at Damaris. But whether or not Aedion knew what it was, he'd said nothing. For all his brashness and arrogance, Chaol had a feeling the man had many, many secrets—and was damn good at concealing them.

It was the other reason why he'd offered the bargain to Aedion and his companions: if the prince's gifts were discovered, Dorian would need somewhere to hide, and someone to get him to safety if Chaol were incapacitated. Chaol said, "Are you prepared to share whatever information you've gathered from your allies?"

Aedion gave him a lazy grin. "So long as you share yours."

Chaol prayed to any god that would listen that he wasn't making the wrong move as he pulled the Eye of Elena from his tunic. "Your Queen gave this necklace to me when she left for Wendlyn. It belonged to her ancestor—who summoned her here, to give it to her." Aedion's eyes narrowed as he took in the amulet, the blue stone shimmering in the moonlight. "What I am about to tell you," Chaol said, "changes everything."

Dorian stood in the shadows of the stairwell, listening. Listening, and not quite wanting to accept that Chaol was in the tomb with Aedion Ashryver.

That had been the first shock. For the past week, he'd been creeping down here to hunt for answers after his explosion with Sorscha. Especially now that she had lied through her teeth and risked everything to keep his secret—and to help him find a way to control it.

Tonight he'd been horrified to find the secret door left slightly ajar. He shouldn't have come, but he'd done it anyway, making up an easy list of lies to tell should he find an unfriendly face down here. Then he'd gotten close enough to hear the two male voices and almost fled . . . Almost, until he'd realized who was talking.

It was impossible, because they hated each other. Yet there they were, in Elena's tomb. Allies. It was enough, too much. But then he'd heard it—heard what Chaol said to the general, so quietly it was barely audible. "Your Queen gave this necklace to me when she left for Wendlyn."

It was a mistake. It had to be a mistake, because . . . His chest had become too tight, too small.

You will always be my enemy. That's what Celaena had screamed at Chaol the night Nehemia died. And she'd said—said that she'd lost people ten years ago, but . . .

But.

Dorian couldn't move as Chaol launched into another story, another truth. About Dorian's own father. About the power the king wielded. Celaena had discovered it. Celaena was trying to find a way to destroy it.

His father had made that thing they'd fought in the library catacombs—that monstrous thing that had seemed human. Wyrdkeys. Wyrdgates. Wyrd-stone.

They had lied to him, too. They had decided he wasn't to be trusted. Celaena and Chaol—they'd decided against him. Chaol had known who and what Celaena truly was.

It was why he'd sent her to Wendlyn—why he'd gotten her out of the castle. Dorian was still frozen on the stairs when Aedion slipped out of the tomb, sword out and looking ready to attack whatever enemy he'd detected.

Spotting him, Aedion swore, low and viciously, his eyes bright in the glow of his torch.

Celaena's eyes. Aelin Ashryver—*Ashryver*—Galathynius's eyes.

Aedion was her cousin. And he was still loyal to her—lying through his teeth, through every action, about where his allegiance lay.

Chaol rushed into the hall, a hand lifted beseechingly. "Dorian."

For a moment, he could only stare at his friend. Then he managed to say, "Why?"

Chaol loosed a breath. "Because the fewer people who know, the safer—for her, for everyone. For you. They have information that might help you."

"You think I'd run to my father?" The words were barely more than a strangled whisper as the temperature plummeted.

Chaol stepped forward, putting himself between Aedion and Dorian, his palms exposed. Placating. "I can't afford to guess—to hope. Even with you."

"How long?" Ice coated his teeth, his tongue.

"She told me about your father before she left. I figured out who she is soon afterward."

"And you're working with *him* now."

The captain's breath clouded in front of him. "If we can find a way to free magic, it could save you. They think they might have some answers about what happened, and how to reverse it. But if Aedion and his allies are caught, if she is caught . . . they will die. Your father will put them all down, starting with her. And right now, Dorian, we need them."

Dorian turned to Aedion. "Are you going to kill my father?"

"Does he not deserve to die?" was the general's reply.

Dorian could see the captain wincing—not at the general's words, but at the cold. "Did you tell him—about me?" Dorian ground out.

"No," Aedion answered for Chaol. "Though if you don't learn to control yourself, there soon won't be a soul in the realm who doesn't know you have magic." Aedion slid those heirloom eyes to the captain.

"So that's why you were so desperate to trade secrets—you wanted the information for his sake." A nod from Chaol. Aedion smirked at Dorian, and ice coated the stairwell. "Does your magic manifest in ice and snow, then, princeling?" the general asked.

"Come closer and find out," Dorian said with a faint smile. Perhaps he could throw Aedion across the hall, just as he had with that creature.

"Aedion can be trusted, Dorian," Chaol said.

"He's as two-faced as they come. I don't believe for one heartbeat that he wouldn't sell us out if it meant furthering his own cause."

"He won't," Chaol snapped, cutting off Aedion's reply. Chaol's lips went blue from the cold.

Dorian knew he was hurting him—knew it, and didn't quite care. "Because you want to be Aedion's king someday?"

Chaol's face drained of color, from the cold or from fear, and Aedion barked a laugh. "My queen will die heirless sooner than marry a man from Adarlan."

Chaol tried to hide his flicker of pain, but Dorian knew his friend well enough to spot it. For a second he wondered what Celaena would think about Aedion's claim. Celaena, who had lied—Celaena, who was *Aelin*, whom he had met ten years ago, whom he had played with in her beautiful castle. And that day in Endovier—that first day, he had felt as if there were something familiar about her . . . Oh gods.

Celaena was Aelin Galathynius. He had danced with her, kissed her, slept beside her, his mortal enemy. *I'll come back for you*, she'd said her final day here. Even then, he'd known there was something else behind it. She would come back, but perhaps not as Celaena. Would it be to help him, or to kill him? Aelin Galathynius knew about his magic—and wanted to destroy his father, his kingdom. Everything she had ever said or done . . . He'd once thought it had been a charade to win favor as his Champion, but what if it had been because she was the heir of Terrasen? Was that why she was friends with Nehemia? What if, after a year in Endovier . . .

Aelin Galathynius had spent a year in that labor camp. A queen of their continent had been a slave, and would bear the scars of it forever. Perhaps that entitled her, and Aedion, and even Chaol who loved her, to conspire to deceive and betray his father.

"Dorian, please," Chaol said. "I'm doing this for you—I swear it."

"I don't care," Dorian said, staring them down as he walked out. "I will carry your secrets to the grave—but I want no part of them."

He ripped his cold magic from the air and turned it inward, wrapping it around his heart.

Aedion took the secret subterranean exit out of the castle. He'd told Chaol it was to avoid any suspicion, to lose anyone *else* trailing them as they went back to their rooms. One look from the captain told him he knew precisely where Aedion was headed.

Aedion contemplated what the captain had told him—and though any other man would be horrified, though Aedion *should* be horrified . . . he wasn't surprised. He'd suspected the king was wielding some sort of deadly power from the moment he'd given him that ring all those years ago, and it seemed in line with information his spies had long been gathering.

The Yellowlegs Matron had been here for a reason. Aedion was willing to bet good money that whatever monstrosities or weapons the king was creating, they would see them soon enough, perhaps with the witches in tow. Men didn't build more armies and forge more weapons without having plans to use them. And they certainly didn't hand out bits of mind-controlling jewelry unless they wanted absolute dominion. But he would face what was coming just as he had every other trial in his life: precisely, unyieldingly, and with lethal efficiency.

He spotted the two figures waiting in the shadows of a ramshackle building by the docks, the fog off the Avery making them little more than wisps of darkness.

"Well?" Ren demanded as Aedion leaned against a damp brick wall. Ren's twin swords were out. Good Adarlanian steel, nicked and scratched enough to show they'd been used, and well-oiled enough to show Ren knew how to care for them. They seemed to be the only things Ren cared about—his hair was shaggy, and his clothes looked a bit worse for wear.

"I already told you: we can trust the captain." Aedion looked at Murtaugh. "Hello, old man."

He couldn't see Murtaugh's face beneath the shadows of his hood, but his voice was too soft as he said, "I hope the information is worth the risks you are taking."

Aedion snarled. He wouldn't tell them the truth about Aelin, not until she was back at his side and could tell them herself.

Ren took a step closer. He moved with the self-assurance of someone who was used to fighting. And winning. Still, Aedion had at least three inches and twenty pounds of muscle on him. Should Ren attack, he'd find himself on his ass in a heartbeat. "I don't know what game you're playing, Aedion," Ren said, "but if you don't tell us where she is, how can we can trust you? And how does the captain know? Does the king have her?"

"No," Aedion said. It wasn't a lie, but it felt like one. As Celaena, she'd signed her soul to him. "The way I see it, Ren, you and your grandfather have little to offer me—or Aelin. You don't have a war band, you don't have lands, and the captain told me all about your affiliation with that piece of shit Archer Finn. Do I need to remind you what happened to Nehemia Ytger on your watch? So I'm not going to tell you; you'll receive information on a need-to-know basis."

Ren started. Murtaugh put an arm between them. "It's better we don't know, just in case."

Ren wouldn't back down, and Aedion's blood raced at the challenge. "What are we going to tell the court, then?" Ren demanded. "That she's not some imposter as we were led to believe, but actually alive—yet you won't tell us where?"

"Yes," Aedion breathed, wondering just how badly he could bloody up Ren without hurting Murtaugh in the process. "That's exactly what you'll tell them. If you can even find the court."

Silence. Murtaugh said, "We know Ravi and Sol are still alive and in Suria."

Aedion knew the story. Their family's trade business had been too important to the king to warrant executing both their parents. So their father had chosen the execution block, and their mother had been left to keep Suria running as a vital trade port. The two Surian boys would be twenty and twenty-two by now, and since his mother's death, Sol had become Lord of Suria. In his years leading the Bane, Aedion had never set foot in the coastal city. He didn't want to know if they'd damn him. Adarlan's Whore.

"Will they fight," Aedion said, "or will they decide they like their gold too much?"

Murtaugh sighed. "I've heard Ravi is the wilder one—he might be the one to convince."

"I don't want anyone that we have to *convince* to join us," Aedion said.

"You'll want people who aren't afraid of Aelin—or *you*," Murtaugh snapped. "You'll want levelheaded people who won't hesitate to ask the hard questions. Loyalty is earned, not given."

"She doesn't have to do a damn thing to earn our loyalty."

Murtaugh shook his head, his cowl swaying. "For some of us, yes. But others might not be so easily convinced. She has ten years to account for—and a kingdom in ruin."

"She was a *child.*"

"She is a woman now, and has been for a few years. Perhaps she will offer an explanation. But until then, Aedion, you *must* understand that others might not share your fervor. And others might take a good amount of convincing about you as well—about where your true loyalties lie and how you have demonstrated them over the years."

He wanted to bash Murtaugh's teeth down his throat, if only because he was right. "Who else of Orlon's inner circle is still alive?"

Murtaugh named four. Ren quickly added, "We heard they were in hiding for years—always moving around, like us. They might not be easy to find."

Four. Aedion's stomach dropped. "That's it?" He'd been in Terrasen, but he'd never looked for an exact body count, never wanted to know who made it through the bloodshed and slaughter, or who had sacrificed everything to get a child, a friend, a family member out. Of course he'd known deep down, but there had always been some fool's hope that most were still alive, still waiting to return.

"I'm sorry, Aedion," Murtaugh said softly. "Some minor lords escaped, and even managed to hold onto their lands and keep them thriving." Aedion knew and hated most of them—self-serving pigs. Murtaugh went on. "Vernon Lochan survived, but only because he was already the king's puppet, and after Cal was executed, Vernon seized his brother's mantle as Lord of Perranth. You know what happened to Lady Marion. But we never learned what happened to Elide." Elide—Lord Cal and Lady Marion's daughter and heir, almost a year younger than Aelin. If she were alive, she would be at least seventeen by now. "Lots of children vanished in the initial weeks," Murtaugh finished. Aedion didn't want to think about those too-small graves.

He had to look away for a moment, and even Ren stayed quiet. At last, Aedion said, "Send out feelers to Ravi and Sol, but hold off on the others. Ignore the minor lords for now. Small steps."

To his surprise, Ren said, "Agreed." For a heartbeat, their eyes met, and he knew that Ren felt what he often did—what he tried to keep buried. They had survived, when so many had not. And no one else could understand what it was like to bear it, unless they had lost as much.

Ren had escaped at the cost of his parents' lives—and had lost his home, his title, his friends, and his kingdom. He had hidden and trained and never lost sight of his cause.

They were not friends now; they never really had been. Ren's father hadn't particularly liked that Aedion, not Ren, was favored to take the blood oath to Aelin. The oath of pure submission—the oath that would have sealed Aedion as her lifelong protector, the one person in whom she could have absolute trust. Everything he possessed, everything he was, should have belonged to her.

Yet the prize now was not just a blood oath but a kingdom—a shot at vengeance and rebuilding their world. Aedion made to walk away, but looked back. Just two cloaked figures, one hunched, the other tall and armed. The first shred of Aelin's court. The court he'd raise for her to shatter Adarlan's chains. He could keep playing the game—for a little longer.

"When she returns," Aedion said quietly, "what she will do to the King of Adarlan will make the slaughtering ten years ago look merciful." And in his heart, Aedion hoped he spoke true.

25

A week passed without any further attempts to skin Celaena alive, so even though she made absolutely no progress with Rowan, she considered it to be a success. Rowan lived up to his word about her pulling double duty in the kitchens—the only upside of which was that she was so exhausted when she tumbled into bed that she did not remember dreaming. Another benefit, she supposed, was that while she was scrubbing the evening dishes, she could listen to Emrys's stories—which Luca begged for every night, regardless of rain.

Despite what had happened with the skinwalkers, Celaena was no closer to mastering her shift. Even though Rowan had offered his cloak that night beside the river, the next morning had brought them back to their usual vitriolic dislike. *Hatred* felt like a strong word, as she couldn't quite hate someone who had saved her, but *dislike* fit pretty damn well. She didn't particularly care what side of the hatred-dislike line Rowan was on. But gaining his approval to enter Doranelle was undoubtedly a long, long way off.

Every day, he brought her to the temple ruins—far enough away that if she did manage to shift and lost control of her magic in the process, she wouldn't incinerate anyone. Everything—*everything*—depended on that command: shift. But the memory of what the magic had felt like as it seared out of her, when it threatened to swallow her and the whole world, plagued her, waking and asleep. It was almost as bad as the endless sitting.

Now, after two miserable hours of it, she groaned and stood, stalking around the ruins. It was unusually sunny that day, making the pale stones seem to glow. In fact, she could have sworn that the whispered prayers of long-gone worshippers still resonated. Her magic had been flickering oddly in response—strange, in her human form, where it was normally so bolted down.

As she studied the ruins, she braced her hands on her hips: anything to keep from ripping out her hair. "What was this place, anyway?" Only slabs of broken stone remained to show where the temple had stood. A few oblong stones—pillars—were tossed about as if a hand had scattered them, and several stones grouped together indicated what had once been a road.

Rowan dogged her steps, a thundercloud closing in around her as she examined a cluster of white stones. "The Sun Goddess's temple."

Mala, Lady of Light, Learning, and Fire. "You've been bringing me here because you think it might help with mastering my powers—my shifting?"

A vague nod. She put a hand on one of the massive stones. If she felt like admitting it, she could almost sense the echoes of the power that had dwelled here long ago, a delicious heat kissing its way up her neck, down her spine, as if some piece of that goddess were still curled up in the corner. It explained why today, in the sun, the temple felt different. Why her magic was jumpy. Mala, Sun Goddess and Light-Bringer, was sister and eternal rival to Deanna, Keeper of the Moon.

"Mab was immortalized into godhood thanks to Maeve," Celaena mused as she ran a hand down the jagged block. "But that was over five hundred years ago. Mala had a sister in the moon long before Mab took her place."

"Deanna *was* the original sister's name. But you humans gave her some of Mab's traits. The hunting, the hounds."

"Perhaps Deanna and Mala weren't always rivals."

"What are you getting at?"

She shrugged and kept running her hands along the stone, feeling, breathing, smelling. "Did you ever know Mab?"

Rowan was quiet for a long moment—contemplating the usefulness of telling her, no doubt. "No," he said at last. "I am old, but not that old."

Fine—if he didn't want to give her an actual number . . . "Do you *feel* old?"

He gazed into the distance. "I am still considered young by the standards of my kind."

It wasn't an answer. "You said that you once campaigned in a kingdom that no longer exists. You've been off to war several times, it seems, and seen the world. That would leave its mark. Age you on the inside."

"Do *you* feel old?" His gaze was unflinching. A child—a girl, he'd called her.

She was a girl to him. Even when she became an old woman—if she lived that long—she'd still be a child in comparison to his life span. Her mission depended upon his seeing her otherwise, but she still said, "These days, I am very glad to be a mortal, and to only have to endure this life once. These days, I don't envy you at all."

"And before?"

It was her turn to stare toward the horizon. "I used to wish I had a chance to see it all—and hated that I never would."

She could feel him forming a question, but she started moving again, examining the stones. As she dusted the block off, an image emerged of a stag with a glowing star between its antlers, so like the one in Terrasen. She'd heard Emrys tell the story of the sun stags, who held an immortal flame between their massive antlers and who had once been stolen from a temple in this land . . . "Is this where the stags were kept—before this place was destroyed?"

"I don't know. This temple wasn't destroyed; it was abandoned when the Fae moved to Doranelle, and then ruined by time and weather."

"Emrys's stories said destroyed, not abandoned."

"Again, what are you getting at?"

But she didn't know, not yet, so she just shook her head and said, "The Fae on my continent—in Terrasen . . . they weren't like you. At least, I don't remember them being that way. There weren't many, but . . ." She swallowed hard. "The King of Adarlan hunted and killed them, so easily. Yet when I look at you, I don't understand how he did it." Even with the Wyrdkeys, the Fae had been stronger, faster. More should have survived, even if some had been trapped in their animal forms when magic vanished.

She looked over her shoulder at him, one hand still pressed against the warm carving. A muscle flickered in Rowan's jaw before he said, "I've never been to your continent, but I heard that the Fae there were gentler—less aggressive, very few trained in combat—and they relied heavily on magic. Once magic was gone from your lands, many of them might not have known what to do against trained soldiers."

"And yet Maeve wouldn't send aid."

"The Fae of your continent long ago severed ties with Maeve." He paused again. "But there were some in Doranelle who argued in favor of helping. My queen wound up offering sanctuary to any who could make it here."

She didn't want to know more—didn't want to know how many had made it, and whether he had been one of the few who argued to save their western brethren. So she moved away from the carving of the mythical stag, instantly cold as she severed contact with the delightful heat living within the stone. Part of her could have sworn that ancient, strange power was sad to see her go.

The next day, Celaena finished her breakfast shift in the kitchens achy and more drained than usual, as Luca hadn't been there to help, which meant she'd spent the morning chopping, washing, and then running the food upstairs.

Celaena passed a sentry she'd marked as Luca's friend and a frequent listener to Emrys's stories—young, leanly muscled, with no evidence of Fae ears or grace. Bas, the leader of the fortress scouts. Luca prattled about him endlessly. Celaena gave him a small smile and nod. Bas blinked a few times, gave a tentative smile back, and sauntered on, probably to his watch on the wall. She frowned. She'd said a civilized hello to plenty of them by now, but . . . She was still puzzling over his reaction when she reached her room and shrugged on her jacket.

"You're already late," Rowan said from the doorway.

"There were extra dishes this morning," she said, rebraiding her hair as she turned to where he lounged in the doorway. "Can I expect to do something useful with you today, or will it be more sitting and growling and glaring? Or will I just wind up chopping wood for hours on end?"

He merely started into the hall and she followed, still braiding her hair. They passed another two sentries. This time, she looked them both in the eye and smiled her greeting. Again, that blink, and a shared look between them, and a returned grin. Had she really become so unpleasant that a mere smile was surprising? Gods—when *had* she smiled last, at anyone or anything?

They were well away from the fortress, headed south and up into the mountains, when Rowan said, "They've all been keeping their distance because of the scent you put out."

"Excuse me?" She didn't want to know how he'd read her thoughts.

Rowan stalked through the trees, not even out of breath as he said, "There are more males than females here—and they're fairly isolated from the world. Haven't you wondered why they haven't approached you?"

"They stayed away because I . . . smell?" She didn't think she would have cared enough to be embarrassed, but her face was burning.

"Your scent says that you don't want to be approached. The males smell it more than the females, and have been staying the hell away. They don't want their faces clawed off."

She had forgotten how primal the Fae were, with their scents and mating and territorial nature. Such a strange contrast to the civilized world beyond the wall of the mountains. "Good," she wound up saying, though the idea of her having her emotions so easily identifiable was unsettling. It made lying and pretending almost worthless. "I'm not interested in men . . . males."

His tattoo was vivid in the dappled sunlight that streamed through the canopy as he stared pointedly at her ring. "What happens if you become queen? Will you refuse a potential alliance through marriage?"

An invisible hand seemed to wrap around her throat. She had not let herself consider that possibility, because the weight of a crown and a throne were enough to make her feel like she was in a coffin. The thought of marrying like that, of someone else's body on hers, someone who was *not* Chaol . . . She shoved the thought away.

Rowan was baiting her, as he always did. And she still had no plans to take up her uncle's throne. Her only plan was to do what she'd promised Nehemia. "Nice try," she said.

His canines gleamed as he smirked. "You're learning."

"You get baited by me every now and then, too, you know."

He gave her a look that said, *I let you bait me, in case you haven't noticed. I'm not some mortal fool.*

She wanted to ask why, but being cordial with him—with

anyone—was already odd enough. "Where the hell are we going today? We never head west."

The smirk vanished. "You want to do something useful. So here's your chance."

With Celaena in her human form, the bells of some nearby town were heralding three o'clock by the time they reached the pine wood.

She didn't ask what they were doing here. He'd tell her if he wanted to. Slowing to a prowl, Rowan tracked markers left on trees and stones, and she quietly trailed him, thirsty and hungry and a bit light-headed.

The terrain had shifted: pine needles crunched beneath her boots, and gulls, not songbirds, cried overhead. The sea had to be close. Celaena groaned as a cool breeze kissed her sweaty face, scented with salt and fish and sun-warmed rock. It wasn't until Rowan halted by a stream that she noticed the reek—and the silence.

The ground had been churned up across the stream, the brush broken and trampled. But Rowan's attention was fixed on the stream itself, on what had been wedged between the rocks.

Celaena swore. A body. A woman, by the shape of what was left of her, and—

A husk.

As if she had been drained of life, of substance. No wounds, no lacerations or signs of harm, save for a trickle of dried blood from her nose and ears. Her skin was leached of color, withered and dried, her hollowed-out face still stuck in an expression of horror—and sorrow. And the smell—not just the rotting body, but around it . . . the smell . . .

"What did this?" she asked, studying the disturbed forest beyond the stream. Rowan knelt as he examined the remains. "Why not just dump her in the sea? Leaving her in a stream seems idiotic. They left tracks, too—unless those are from whoever found her."

"Malakai gave me the report this morning—and he and his men are trained not to leave tracks. But this scent . . . I'll admit it's different." Rowan walked into the water. She wanted to tell him to stop, but he kept studying the remains from above, then below, circling. His eyes flashed to hers. They were furious. "So you tell me, assassin. You wanted to be useful."

She bristled at the tone, but—that was a woman lying there, broken like a doll.

Celaena didn't particularly want to smell *anything* on the remains, but she sniffed. And wished she hadn't. It was a smell she'd scented twice now—once in that bloody chamber a decade ago, and then recently . . . "You claimed you didn't know what that thing in the barrow field was," she managed to say. The woman's mouth was open in a scream, her teeth brown and cracked below the dried nosebleed. Celaena touched her own nose and winced. "I think this is what it does."

Rowan braced his hands on his hips, sniffing again, turning in the stream. He scanned Celaena, then the body. "You came out of that darkness looking as if someone had sucked the life from you. Your skin was a shade paler, your freckles gone."

"It forced me to go through . . . memories. The worst kind." The woman's horrified, sorrowful face gaped up at the canopy. "Have you ever heard of a creature that can feed on such things? When I glimpsed it, I saw a man—a beautiful man, pale and dark-haired, with eyes of full black. He wasn't human. I mean, he looked it, but his eyes—they weren't human at all."

Her parents had been assassinated. She'd seen the wounds. But the smell in their room had been so similar . . . She shook her head as if to clear it, to shake the creeping feeling moving up her spine.

"Even my queen doesn't know every foul creature roaming these lands. If the skinwalkers are venturing down from the mountains, perhaps other things are, too."

"The townspeople might know something. Maybe they've seen it or heard rumors."

Rowan seemed to be thinking the same thing, because he shook his head in disgust—and sorrow, to her surprise. "We don't have the time; you wasted daylight by coming here in your human form." They hadn't brought any overnight supplies, either. "We have an hour before we head back. Make the most of it."

The path led absolutely nowhere. It ran into a sea cliff with no way to the narrow strip of beach below, no sign of anyone living nearby. Rowan stood at the cliff's edge, arms crossed as he stared out at the jade sea. "It doesn't make sense," he said, more to himself than to her. "This is the fourth body in the last few weeks—none of them reported missing." He squatted on the sandy ground and drew a rough line in the dirt with a tattooed finger. The shape of Wendlyn's coastline. "They've been found here." Little dots, seemingly random save for being close to the water. "We're here," he said, making another dot. He sat back on his heels as Celaena peered at the crude map. "And yet you and I encountered the creature lurking amongst the barrow-wights here," he added, and drew an X where she assumed the mounds were, deep inland. "I haven't seen any further signs of it remaining by the barrows, and the wights have returned to their usual habits."

"Were the other bodies the same?"

"All were drained like this, with expressions of terror on their faces—not a hint of a wound, beyond dried blood at the nose and ears." From the way his tan skin paled beneath his tattoo, the way he gritted his teeth, she knew that it rankled his immortal pride not to know what this thing was.

"All dumped in the forest, not the sea?" A nod. "But all within walking distance of the water." Another nod. "If it were a skilled, sentient killer, it would hide the bodies better. Or, again, use the sea." She gazed to the blinding water, the sun starting its afternoon descent. "Or maybe it doesn't care. Maybe it wants us to know what it's doing. There were—there were times when I left bodies so that they'd be found by a certain person, or to send a type of message." Grave being the latest of them. "What do the victims have in common?"

"I don't know," he admitted. "We don't even know their names or where they came from." He rose and dusted his hands off. "We need to return to the fortress."

She grabbed his elbow. "Wait. Have you seen enough of the body?"

A slow nod. Good. So had she—and she'd had enough of the smell, too. She'd committed it to memory, noting everything that she could. "Then we've got to bury her."

"The ground's too hard here."

She stalked through the trees, leaving him behind. "Then we'll do it the ancient way," she called. She'd be damned if she left that woman's body decomposing in a stream, damned if she left her there for all eternity, wet and cold.

Celaena pulled the too-light body out of the stream, laying it on the brown pine needles. Rowan didn't say anything as she gathered kindling and branches and then knelt, trying not to look at the shriveled skin or the expression of lingering horror.

Neither did he mock her for the few times it took to get the fire started by hand, or make any snide comments once the pine needles finally crinkled and smoked, ancient incense for a rudimentary pyre. Instead, as she stepped from the rising flames, she felt him come to tower behind her, felt the surety and half wildness of him wrap around her like a phantom body. A warm breeze licked at her hair, her face. Air to help the fire; wind that helped consume the corpse.

The loathing she felt had nothing to do with her vow, or Nehemia. Celaena reached into the ageless pit inside her—just once—to see if she could pull up whatever trigger it was that caused the shift, so she could help her sad little fire burn more evenly, more proudly.

Yet Celaena remained stale and empty, stranded in her mortal body.

Still, Rowan didn't say anything about it, and his wind fed the flames enough to make quick work of the body, burning far faster than a mortal pyre. They watched in silence, until there was nothing but ashes—until even those were carried up and away, over the trees, and toward the open sea.

26

Chaol hadn't seen or heard from the general or the prince since that night in the tomb. According to his men, the prince was spending his time in the healers' catacombs, courting one of the young women down there. He hated himself, but some part of him was relieved to hear it; at least Dorian was talking to *someone*.

The rift with Dorian was worth it. For Dorian, even if his friend never forgave him; for Celaena, even if she never came back; even if he wished she were still Celaena and not Aelin . . . it was worth it.

It was a week before he had time to meet with Aedion again—to get the information that he hadn't received thanks to Dorian interrupting them. If Dorian had snuck up on them so easily, then the tomb wasn't the best place to meet. There was one place, however, where they could gather with minimal risk. Celaena had left it to him in her will, along with the address.

The secret apartment above the warehouse was untouched, though someone had taken the time to cover the ornate furniture. Pulling the sheets off one by one was like uncovering a bit more of who Celaena had been before Endovier—proof that her lavish tastes ran deep. She'd bought this place, she'd once told him, to have somewhere to call her own, a place outside the Assassins' Keep where she'd been raised. She'd dropped almost every copper she had into it—but it had been necessary, she said, for the bit of freedom it had granted her. He could have left the sheets on, probably should have, but . . . he was curious.

The apartment consisted of two bedrooms with their own bathing rooms, a kitchen, and a great room in which a deep-cushioned couch sprawled before a carved marble fireplace, accented by two oversized velvet armchairs. The other half of the room was occupied by an oak dining table capable of seating eight, its place settings still laid out: plates of porcelain and silver, flatware that had long since gone dull. It was the only evidence that this apartment had been untouched since whoever—Arobynn Hamel, probably—had ordered the place sealed up.

Arobynn Hamel, the King of the Assassins. Chaol gritted his teeth as he finished stuffing the last of the white sheets into the hallway closet. He'd been thinking a good deal about Celaena's old master in the past few days. Arobynn was smart enough to have put things together when he found a washed-up orphan right after the Princess of Terrasen went missing, her body vanished into the half-frozen Florine River.

If Arobynn had known, and done those things to her . . . The scar on Celaena's wrist flashed before him. He'd made her break her own hand. There must have been countless other brutalities that Celaena didn't even tell him about. And the worst of them, the absolute worst . . .

He'd never asked Celaena why, when she was appointed Champion, her first priority wasn't hunting down her master and cutting him into pieces for what he'd done to her lover, Sam Cortland. Arobynn had ordered Sam tortured and killed, and then devised a trap for Celaena that got her hauled off to Endovier. Arobynn must have expected to retrieve her someday, if he'd left this apartment untouched. He must have wanted to let her rot in Endovier—until he decided to free her and she crawled back to him, his eternally loyal servant.

It was her right, Chaol told himself. Her right to decide when and how to kill Arobynn. It was Aedion's right, too. Even the two lords of Terrasen had more of a claim on Arobynn's head than he did. But if Chaol ever saw him, he wasn't sure he would be able to restrain himself.

The rickety wooden staircase beyond the front door groaned, and Chaol had his sword drawn in a heartbeat. Then there was a low, two-note whistle and he relaxed, just slightly, and whistled back. He kept his sword drawn until Aedion strode through the door, sword out.

"I was wondering whether you'd be here alone, or with a gaggle of men waiting in the shadows," Aedion said by way of greeting, sheathing his sword.

Chaol glared at him. "Likewise."

Aedion moved farther into the apartment, the fierceness on his face shifting among wariness, wonder, and sorrow. And it occurred to Chaol that this apartment was the first time Aedion was seeing a piece of his lost cousin. These were her things. She had selected everything, from the figurines atop the mantel to the green napkins to the old farm table in the kitchen, flecked and marred by what seemed like countless knives.

Aedion paused in the center of the room, scanning everything. Perhaps to see if there were indeed any hidden forces lying in wait, but . . . Chaol muttered something about using the bathing room and gave Aedion the privacy he needed.

This was her apartment. Whether she accepted or hated her past, she'd decorated the dining table in Terrasen's royal colors—green and silver.

The table and the stag figurine atop the mantel were the only shreds of proof that she might remember. Might care.

Everything else was comfortable, tasteful, as if the apartment were for lounging and nights by the fire. And there were so many books—on shelves, on the tables by the couch, stacked beside the large armchair before the curtained floor-to-ceiling window spanning the entire length of the great room.

Smart. Educated. Cultured, if the knickknacks were any indication. There were things from across the kingdoms, as if she'd picked up something everywhere she went. The room was a map of her adventures, a map of a whole different person. Aelin had lived. She'd lived, and seen and done things.

The kitchen was small but cozy—and . . . Gods. She had a cooling box. The captain had mentioned her being notorious as an assassin, but he hadn't mentioned that she was rich. All that blood money—all these things just proof of what she'd lost. What he'd failed to protect.

She'd become a killer. A damn good one, if this apartment was any indication. Her bedroom was even more outrageous. It had a massive four-poster bed with a mattress that looked like a cloud, and an attached marble-tiled bathing room that possessed its own plumbing system.

Well, her closet hadn't changed. His cousin had always loved pretty clothes. Aedion pulled out a deep blue tunic, gold embroidery around the lapels and buttons glimmering in the light from the sconces. These were clothes for a woman's body. And the scent still clinging to the entire apartment belonged to a woman—so similar to what he remembered from childhood, but wrapped in mystery and secret smiles. It was impossible for his Fae senses not to notice, to react.

Aedion leaned against the wall of the dressing room, staring at the gowns and the displays of jewelry, now coated in dust. He didn't let himself care about what had been done to him in the past, the people he'd ruined, the battlefields he'd walked off covered in blood and gore that wasn't his own. As far as he was concerned, he'd lost everything the day Aelin died. He had deserved the punishment for how badly he'd failed. But Aelin . . .

Aedion ran his hands through his hair before stepping into the great room. Aelin would come back from Wendlyn, no matter what the captain believed. Aelin would come back, and when she did . . . With every breath, Aedion felt that lingering scent wrapping tighter around his heart and soul. When she came back, he was never letting her go.

Aedion sank onto one of the armchairs before the fire as Chaol said, "Well, I think I've waited long enough to hear what you have to say about magic. I hope it's worthwhile."

"Regardless of what I know, magic shouldn't be your main plan of defense—or action."

"I saw your queen cleave the earth in two with her power," Chaol said. "Tell me that wouldn't turn the tide on a battlefield—tell me that you wouldn't need that, and others like her."

"She won't be anywhere near those battlefields," Aedion snarled softly.

Chaol highly doubted that was true, but wished it was. Aedion would probably have to bind Celaena to her throne to keep her from fighting on the front lines with her people. "Just tell me."

Aedion sighed and gazed at the fire, as if beholding a distant horizon. "The burnings and executions had already started by the time magic disappeared, so the day it happened, I thought the birds were just fleeing the soldiers, or looking for carrion. I was locked in one of the tower rooms by the king's orders. Most days I didn't dare look out the window because I didn't want to see what was happening in the city below, but there was such noise from the birds that day that I looked. And . . ." Aedion shook his head. "Something sent them all flying up in one direction, then another. And then the screaming started. I heard some people just died right on the spot, as if an artery had been cut."

Aedion spread out a map on the low table between them and put a callused finger on Orynth. "There were two waves of birds. The first went north-northwest." He traced a vague line. "From the tower, I could see far enough that I knew many of them had come from the south—most of the birds near us didn't move much. But then the second wave shoved all of them to the north and east, like something from the center of the land threw them that way."

Chaol pointed to Perranth, the second-largest city in Terrasen. "From here?"

"Farther south." Aedion knocked Chaol's hand out of the way. "Endovier or even lower."

"You couldn't have seen that far."

"No, but the warrior-lords of my court made me memorize the birds in Oakwald and all their calls for hunting—and fighting. And there were birds flying up toward us that were only found in your country. I was counting them to distract myself while—" Another pause, as if Aedion hadn't meant to say that. "I don't remember hearing any birds from the three southern kingdoms."

Chaol made a rough line, starting in Rifthold and going out toward the mountains, toward the Ferian Gap. "Like something shot out in this direction."

"It wasn't until the second wave that magic stopped." Aedion raised a brow. "Don't *you* remember that day?"

"I was here; if anyone felt pain, they hid it. Magic's been illegal in Adarlan for decades. So where does all this get us, Aedion?"

"Well, Murtaugh and Ren had similar experiences." So then the general launched into another tale: like Aedion, Ren and Murtaugh had experienced a frenzy of local animals and twin waves of *something* the day magic had disappeared. But they'd been in the southern part of their continent, having just arrived in Skull's Bay.

It wasn't until six months ago, when they'd been lured into the city by Archer Finn's lies about Aelin's reemergence, that they'd started considering magic—contemplating ways to break the king's power for their queen. After comparing notes with the other rebels in Rifthold, they realized that others had experienced similar phenomena. Wanting to get a full account, they'd found a merchant from the Deserted Peninsula who was willing to talk—a man from Xandria who was surprisingly honest, despite the business he'd built on contraband items.

I stole an Asterion mare from the Lord of Xandria.

Of course Celaena had been to the Deserted Peninsula. And sought out trouble. Despite the ache in his chest, Chaol smiled at the memory as Aedion recalled Murtaugh's report of the merchant's account.

Not two waves when magic vanished in the desert, but three.

The first swept down from the north. The merchant had been with the Lord of Xandria in his fortress high above the city and had seen a faint tremor that made the red sand dance. The second came from the southwest, barreling right toward them like a sandstorm. The final pulse came from the same inland source Aedion remembered. Seconds later, magic was gone, and people were screaming in the streets, and the Lord of Xandria got the order, a week later, to put down all the known or registered magic-wielders in his city. Then the screaming had become different.

Aedion gave him a sly grin as he finished. "But Murtaugh figured out more. We're meeting in three days. He can tell you his theories then."

Chaol started from his chair. "That's it? That's all you know—what you've been lording over me these past few weeks?"

"There's still more for you to tell me, so why should I tell you everything?"

"I've told you vital, world-changing information," Chaol said through his teeth. "You've just told me stories."

Aedion's eyes took on a lethal glint. "You'll want to hear what Ren and Murtaugh have to say." Chaol didn't feel like waiting so long to hear it, but there were two state lunches and one formal dinner before then, and he was expected to attend all of them. And present the king with his defense plans for all the events as well.

After a moment, Aedion said, "How do you stand working for him? How do you pretend you don't know what that bastard is doing, what he's done to innocent people, to the woman you claim to love?"

"I'm doing what I have to do." He didn't think Aedion would understand, anyway.

"Tell me why the Captain of the Guard, a Lord of Adarlan, is helping his enemy. That's all the information I want from you today."

Chaol wanted to say that, given how much he'd already told him, he didn't have to offer a damn thing. Instead he said, "I grew up being told we were bringing peace and civilization to the continent. What I've seen recently has made me realize how much of it is a lie."

"You knew about the labor camps, though. About the massacres."

"It is easy to be lied to when you do not know any of those people firsthand." But Celaena with her scars, and Nehemia with her people butchered . . . "It's easy to believe when your king tells you that the people in Endovier deserve to be there because they're criminals or rebels who tried to slaughter innocent Adarlanian families."

"And how many of your countrymen would stand against your king if they, too, learned the truth? If they stopped to consider what it would be like if it were their family, their village, being enslaved or murdered? How many would stand if they knew what power their prince possessed—if their prince rose up to fight with us?"

Chaol didn't know, and he wasn't sure he wanted to. As for Dorian . . . he could not ask that of his friend. Could not expect it. His goal was keeping Dorian safe. Even if it would cost him their friendship, he didn't want Dorian involved. Ever.

The past week had been terrifying and wonderful for Dorian.

Terrifying because two more people knew his secret, and because he walked such a fine line when it came to controlling his magic, which seemed more volatile with each passing day.

Wonderful because every afternoon, he visited the forgotten workroom Sorscha had discovered tucked in a lower level of the catacombs where no one would find them. She brought books from the gods knew where, herbs and plants and salts and powders, and every day, they researched and trained and pondered.

There weren't many books about dampening a power like his—many had been burned, she'd told him. But she looked at the magic like a disease: if she could find the right channels to block, she could keep it contained. And if not, she always said, they could resort to drugging him, just enough to even out his moods. She didn't like the idea of it, and neither did he, though it was a comfort to know the option was there.

An hour each day was all they could manage together. For that hour, regardless of the laws they were breaking, Dorian felt like himself again. Not twisted and reeling and stumbling through the dark, but grounded. Calm. No matter what he told Sorscha, she never judged or betrayed him. Chaol had been that person once. Yet now, when it came to his magic, he could still see fear and a hint of disgust in Chaol's eyes.

"Did you know," Sorscha said from her spot across the worktable, "that before magic vanished, they had to find special ways of subduing gifted prisoners?"

Dorian looked up from his book, a useless tome on garden

remedies. Before magic vanished . . . at the hand of his father and his Wyrdkeys. His stomach turned. "Because they'd use their magic to break out of prison?"

Sorscha studied the book again. "That's why a lot of the old prisons use solid iron—it's immune to magic."

"I know," he said, and she raised a brow. She was slowly starting to come alive around him—though he'd also learned to read her subtle expressions better. "Back when my power first appeared, I tried using it on an iron door, and . . . it didn't go well."

"Hmm." Sorscha chewed on her lip. It was surprisingly distracting. "But iron's in your blood, so how does *that* work?"

"I think it was the gods' way of keeping us from growing too powerful: if we keep contact with the magic, if it's flowing through us for too long, we faint. Or worse."

"I wonder what would happen if we increased the iron in your diet, perhaps adding a large amount of treacle to your food. We give it to anemic patients, but if we gave you a highly concentrated dose . . . it would taste awful, and could be dangerous, but—"

"But perhaps if it's in my body, then when the magic rises up . . ." He grimaced. He might have balked at the memory of the agony when he'd tried to seal that iron door, but . . . He couldn't bring himself to say no to her. "Do you have any here? Just something to add to a drink?"

She didn't, but she got some. And within a quarter of an hour, Dorian said a prayer to Silba and swallowed it, cringing at the obscene sweetness. Nothing.

Sorscha's eyes darted from his own to the pocket watch in her hand. Counting. Waiting to see if there was an adverse reaction. A minute passed. And then ten. Dorian had to go soon, and so did she, but after a while, Sorscha quietly said, "Try it. Try summoning it. The iron should be in your blood now." He shut his eyes, and she added, "It reacts when you're upset—angry or scared or sad. Think about something that makes you feel that way."

She was risking her position, her life, everything for this. For him, the son of the man who had ordered his army to destroy her village, then slaughter her family with the other unwanted immigrants squatting in Rifthold. He didn't deserve it.

He breathed in. Out. She also didn't deserve the world of trouble he was bringing down upon her—or would continue to bring to her door every time he came here. He knew when women liked him, and he'd known from the first moment he'd seen her that she found him attractive. He'd hoped that opinion hadn't changed for the worse, but now . . . *Think of what upsets you.*

Everything upset him. It upset him that she was risking her life, that he had no choice but to endanger her. Even if he took that final step toward her, even if he took her into his bed like he so badly wanted to, he was still . . . the Crown Prince. *You will always be my enemy*, Celaena had once said.

There was no escaping his crown. Or his father, who would behead Sorscha, burn her, and scatter her ashes to the wind if he found out she'd helped him. His father, whom his friends were now working to destroy. They had lied to him and ignored him for that cause. Because he *was* a danger, to them, to Sorscha, and—

Roaring pain surged from his core and up his throat, and he gagged. There was another wave, and a cool breeze tried to kiss his face, but it vanished like mist under the sun as the pain trembled through him. He leaned forward, squeezing his eyes shut as the agony and then the nausea went through him again. And again.

But then it was quiet. Dorian opened his eyes to find Sorscha, clever, steady, wonderful Sorscha, standing there, biting her lip. She took one step—toward him, not away, for once. "Did it—"

Dorian was on his feet so fast the chair rocked behind him, and had her face between his hands a heartbeat after that. "*Yes*," he breathed, and kissed her. It was fast—but her face was flushed, and her eyes wide as he pulled back. His own eyes were wide, gods be damned, and he was still rubbing his thumb against her soft cheek. Still contemplating going back for more, because that hadn't been nearly enough.

But she pulled away, returning to her work. As if—as if it hadn't been anything, other than an embarrassment. "Tomorrow?" she murmured. She wouldn't look at him.

He could hardly muster the words to tell her yes as he staggered out. She'd looked so surprised, and if he didn't get out, he was likely to kiss her again.

But maybe she didn't want to be kissed.

27

Standing atop a viewing platform on the side of the Omega, Manon watched the first Yellowlegs coven of the day take the Crossing. The plunge down followed by the violent sweep up was stunning, even when it was the Yellowlegs riders astride the wind.

Leading them along the sheer face of the Northern Fang was Iskra. Her bull, a massive beast named Fendir, was a force of nature in himself. Though smaller than Titus, he was twice as nasty.

"They suit each other," Asterin said from beside Manon. The rest of the Thirteen were in the sparring room, instructing the other covens in hand-to-hand combat. Faline and Fallon, the green-eyed demon-twins, were undoubtedly taking some pleasure from torturing the newest sentinels. They thrived on that sort of thing.

Iskra and Fendir swept over the uppermost peak of the Northern Fang and vanished into the clouds, the other twelve riders trailing in tight formation. The cold wind whipped at Manon's face, beckoning to her. She was on her way to the caverns to see Abraxos, but she'd wanted to monitor the Yellowlegs Crossing first. Just to make sure they were truly gone for the next three hours.

She looked across the span of the bridge to the Fang and its giant entryway. Screeching and roaring echoed from it, reverberating across the mountains. "I want you to keep the Thirteen occupied for the rest of the day," Manon said.

As Second, Asterin was the only one of the Thirteen with any sort of right to question her, and even then, it was only in very limited circumstances. "You're going to train with him?" Manon nodded. "Your grandmother said she'd gut me if I let you out of my sight again." Golden hair twining about her in the wind, Asterin's face, with its now-crooked nose, was wary.

"You're going to have to decide," Manon said, not bothering to bare her iron teeth. "Are you her spy or my Second?"

No hint of pain or fear or betrayal. Just a slight narrowing of her eyes. "I serve you."

"She's your Matron."

"I serve you."

For a heartbeat, Manon wondered when she'd ever earned that kind of loyalty. They weren't friends—at least, not in the way that humans seemed to be friends. Every Blackbeak already owed her their loyalty and obedience as the heir. But this . . .

Manon had never explained herself, her plans, or her intentions to anyone except her grandmother. But she found herself saying to her Second, "I'm still going to be Wing Leader."

Asterin smiled, her iron teeth like quicksilver in the morning sun. "We know."

Manon lifted her chin. "I want the Thirteen adding tumbling to their hand-to-hand training. And when you can handle your wyvern on your own, I want you in the skies when the Yellowlegs are aloft. I want to know where they fly, how they fly, and what they do."

Asterin nodded. "I already have the Shadows watching the Yellowlegs in the halls," she said, a glimmer of rage and bloodthirst in those gold-flecked black eyes. When Manon raised a brow, Asterin said, "You didn't think I'd let Iskra off so easily, did you?"

Manon could still feel the iron-tipped fingers digging into her back, shoving her into the pit. Her ankle was sore and stiff from the fall, her ribs bruised from the beating she'd taken from Titus's tail. "Keep them in line. Unless you want your nose broken a second time."

Asterin flashed a grin. "We don't move without your command, Lady."

Manon didn't want the overseer in the pen. Or his three handlers, all bearing spears and whips. She didn't want any of them for three reasons.

The first was that she wanted to be alone with Abraxos, who was crouched against the back wall, waiting and watching.

The second was that the human smell of them, the beckoning warmth of the blood pulsing in their necks, was distracting. The stench of their fear was distracting. She'd debated for a good minute whether it would be worth it to gut one of them just to see what the others would do. Already, men were going missing from the Fang—men who were rumored to have crossed the bridge to the Omega and never returned. Manon hadn't killed any of the men here yet, but every minute alone with them tempted her to play.

And the third reason she resented their presence was that Abraxos loathed them, with their whips and spears and chains and their hulking presence. The wyvern wouldn't move from his spot against the wall no matter how viciously they cracked their whips. He hated whips—not just feared, but actually hated. The sound alone made him cringe and bare his teeth.

They'd been in the pen for ten minutes, attempting to get close enough to get him chained down and saddled. If it didn't happen soon, she'd have to go back to the Omega before the Yellowlegs returned.

"He's never taken a saddle," the overseer said to her. "Probably won't." She heard the unspoken words. *I'm not going to risk my men getting it on him. You're just being proud. Pick another mount like a good girl.*

Manon flashed her iron teeth at the overseer, her upper lip pulling back just enough to warn him. He backed up a step, whip drooping. Abraxos's mutilated tail slashed across the ground, his eyes never leaving the three men trying to force him into submission.

One of them cracked the whip, so close to Abraxos that he flinched away. Another snapped it near his tail—twice. Then Abraxos lunged, with both neck and tail. The three handlers scrambled, barely out of reach of his snapping teeth. Enough.

"Your men have cowards' hearts," she said, giving the overseer a withering look as she stalked across the dirt floor.

The overseer grabbed for her, but she slashed with iron-tipped fingers and sliced his hand open. He cursed, but Manon kept walking, licking his blood off her nails. She almost spat it out.

Vile. The blood tasted rotten, as if it had curdled or festered inside a corpse for days. She glanced at the blood on the rest of her hand. It was too dark for human blood. If witches had indeed been killing these men, why had no one reported this? She bit down the questions. She would think about it another time. Maybe drag the overseer into a forgotten corner and open him up to see what was decaying inside him.

But right now . . . The men had gone quiet. Each step brought her closer to Abraxos. A line had been marked in the dirt where the safety of the chains ended. Manon took three steps beyond it, one for each face of their Goddess: Maiden. Mother. Crone.

Abraxos crouched, the powerful muscles of his body tense, ready to spring.

"You know who I am," Manon said, gazing into those endless black eyes, not giving one inch to fear or doubt. "I am Manon Blackbeak, heir to the Blackbeak Clan, and you are *mine*. Do you understand?"

One of the men snorted, and Manon might have whirled to tear out his tongue right there, but Abraxos . . . Abraxos lowered his head ever so slightly. As if he understood.

"You are Abraxos," Manon said to him, a chill slithering down her neck. "I gave you that name because he is the Great Beast, the serpent who wrapped the world in his coils, and who will devour it at the very end when the Three-Faced Goddess bids him to. You are Abraxos," she repeated, "and you are *mine*."

A blink, then another. Abraxos took a step toward her. Leather groaned as someone tightened their grip on a coiled whip. But Manon held fast, lifting one hand toward her wyvern. "Abraxos."

The mighty head came toward her, those eyes pools of liquid night meeting her own. Her hand was still extended, tipped in iron and stained with blood. He pressed his snout into her palm and huffed.

His gray hide was warm and surprisingly soft—thick but supple, like worn leather. Up close, the variation in coloring was striking—not just gray, but dark green, brown, black. It was marred all over by thick scars, so many that they could have been the stripes of a jungle cat. Abraxos's teeth, yellow and cracked, gleamed in the torchlight. Some were missing, but those that remained were as long as a finger and twice as thick. His hot breath reeked, either from his diet or rotting teeth.

Each of the scars, the chipped teeth and broken claws, the mutilated tail—they weren't the markings of a victim. Oh, no. They were the trophies of a survivor. Abraxos was a warrior who'd had all the odds stacked against him and survived. Learned from it. Triumphed.

Manon didn't bother to look at the men behind her as she said, "Get out." She kept staring into those dark eyes. "Leave the saddle and get out. If you bring a whip in here again, I'll use it on you myself."

"But—"

"Now."

Muttering and clicking their tongues, the handlers shuffled out and shut the gate. When they were alone, Manon stroked the massive snout.

However the king had bred these beasts, Abraxos had somehow been born different. Smaller, but smarter. Or perhaps the others didn't ever need to think. Cared for and trained, they did what they were told. But Abraxos had learned to survive, and perhaps that had opened his mind. He could understand her words—her expressions.

And if he could comprehend those things . . . he could possibly teach the other mounts of the Thirteen. It was a small edge, but an edge that could make them Wing Leader—and make them invincible against the king's enemies.

"I am going to put this saddle on you," she said, still cupping that snout. He shifted, but Manon grabbed on tight, forcing him to look at her. "You want out of this shithole? Then you'll let me put this saddle on you to check the fit. And when we're done, you're going to let me look at your tail. Those human bastards cut off your spikes, so I'm going to build some for you. Iron ones. Like mine," she said, and flashed her iron nails for him to see. "And fangs, too," she added, baring her iron teeth. "It's going to hurt, and you're going to want to kill the men who put them in, but you're going to let them do it, because if you don't, then you will rot down here for the rest of your life. Understand?"

A long, hot huff of air into her hands.

"Once all that is done," she said, smiling faintly at her wyvern, "you and I are going to learn how to fly. And then we'll stain this kingdom red."

Abraxos did everything she asked, though he growled at the handlers who inspected and poked and prodded, and nearly bit off the arm of the physician who had to dig out his rotted teeth to make way for the iron fangs. It took five days to do it all.

He almost took out a wall when they welded the iron spikes onto his tail, but Manon stood with him the entire time, talking to him about what it was like to ride with the Thirteen on their ironwood brooms and hunt down the Crochan witches. She told the stories as much to distract him as she did to remind the men that if they made a mistake, if they hurt him, her retribution would be a long, bloody process. Not one of them made an error.

During the five days they worked on him, she missed her riding lessons with the Thirteen. And with each passing day, the window for getting Abraxos airborne became smaller and smaller.

Manon stood with Asterin and Sorrel in the training hall, watching the tail end of the day's sparring session. Sorrel had been working with the youngest coven of Blackbeaks—all of them under seventy, and few of them experienced.

"How bad?" Manon asked, crossing her arms.

Sorrel, small and dark-haired, crossed her arms as well. "Not as bad as we feared. But they're still sorting out coven dynamics—and their leader is . . ." Sorrel frowned at a mousy-looking witch who had just been thrown to the ground by an inferior. "I'd suggest either having her coven decide what to do with her or picking a new leader. One weak coven in the wing and we could lose the War Games."

The coven leader was panting on the hard stone floor, nose dripping blue blood. Manon ground her teeth. "Give her two days—let's see if she sorts herself out." No need to have word of unstable covens get around. "But have Vesta take her out tonight," Manon added, glancing to the red-haired beauty leading another coven in archery drills. "To wherever she's been going to torment the men in the Northern Fang."

Sorrel raised her thick brows innocently, and Manon rolled her eyes. "You're a worse liar than Vesta. You think I haven't noticed those men grinning at her at all hours of the day? Or the bite marks on them? Just keep the death toll down. We have enough to worry about as it is—we don't need a mutiny from the mortals."

Asterin snorted, but when Manon gave her a sidelong look, the witch kept her gaze ahead, face all too innocent. Of course, if Vesta had been bedding and bleeding the men, then Asterin had been right there with her. Neither of them had reported anything about the men tasting strange.

"As you will it, Lady," Sorrel said, a faint hint of color on her tan cheeks. If Manon was ice and Asterin was fire, then Sorrel was rock. Her grandmother had told her on occasion to make Sorrel her Second, as ice and stone were sometimes too similar. But without Asterin's flame, without her Second being able to rile up a host or rip out the throat of any challenger to Manon's dominance, Manon would not have led the Thirteen so successfully. Sorrel was grounded enough to even them both out. The perfect Third.

"The only ones having fun right now," Asterin said, "are the green-eyed demon-twins."

Indeed, the midnight-haired Faline and Fallon were grinning with maniacal glee as they led three covens in knife-throwing exercises, using their inferiors as target practice. Manon just shook her head. Whatever worked; whatever shook the dust off these Blackbeak warriors.

"And my Shadows?" Manon asked Asterin. "How are they doing?"

Edda and Briar, two cousins that were as close as sisters, had been trained since infancy to blend into any sliver of darkness and listen—and they were nowhere to be seen in this hall. Just as Manon had ordered.

"They'll have a report for you tonight," Asterin said. Distant cousins to Manon, the Shadows bore the same moon-white hair. Or they had, until they'd discovered eighty years ago that the silver hair was as good as a beacon and dyed it solid black. They rarely spoke, never laughed, and sometimes even Asterin herself couldn't detect them until they were at her throat. It was their sole source of amusement: sneaking up on people, though they'd never dared do it to Manon. It was no surprise they'd taken two onyx wyverns.

Manon eyed her Second and Third. "I want you both in my room for their report, too."

"I'll have Lin and Vesta stand watch," Asterin said. They were Manon's fallback sentries—Vesta for the disarming smiles, and Lin because if anyone ever called her by her full name, Linnea—the name her softhearted mother had given her before Lin's grandmother tore out her heart—that person wound up with missing teeth at best. A missing face at worst.

Manon was about to turn away when she caught her Second and Third watching her. She knew the question they didn't dare ask, and said, "I'll be airborne with Abraxos in a week, and then we'll be flying as one."

It was a lie, but they believed her anyway.

28

Days passed, and not all of them were awful. Out of nowhere, Rowan decided to take Celaena to the commune of healers fifteen miles away, where the finest healers in the world learned, taught, and worked. Situated on the border between the Fae and mortal world, they were accessible to anyone who could reach them. It was one of the few *good* things Maeve had done.

As a child, Celaena had begged her mother to bring her. But the answer had always been no, accompanied by a vague promise that they would someday take a trip to the Torre Cesme in the southern continent, where many of the teachers had been taught by the Fae. Her mother had done everything she could to keep her from Maeve's clutches. The irony of it wasn't wasted on her.

So Rowan took her. She could have spent all day—all month—wandering the grounds under the clever, kind eyes of the Head Healer. But her time there was halved thanks to the distance and her inability to shift, and Rowan wanted to be home before nightfall. Honestly, while she'd actually enjoyed herself at the peaceful riverside compound, she wondered whether Rowan had just brought her there to make her feel bad about the life she'd fallen into. It had made her quiet on the long hike back.

And he didn't give her a moment's rest: they were to set out the following dawn on an overnight trip, but he wouldn't say where. Fantastic.

Already making the day's bread, Emrys only looked faintly amused as Celaena hurried in, stuffed her face with food and guzzled down tea, and hurried back out.

Rowan was waiting by her rooms, a small pack dangling from his hands. He held it open for her. "Clothes," he said, and she stuffed the extra shirt and underclothes she'd laid out into the bag. He shouldered it—which she supposed meant he was in a good mood, as she'd fully expected to play pack mule on their way to wherever they were going. He didn't say anything until they were in the mist-shrouded trees, again heading west. When the fortress walls had vanished behind them, the ward-stones zinging against her skin as they passed through, he stopped at last, throwing back the heavy hood of his jacket. She did the same, the cool air biting her warm cheeks.

"Shift, and let's go," he said. His second words to her this morning.

"And here I was, thinking we'd become friends."

He raised his brows and gestured with a hand for her to shift. "It's twenty miles," he said by way of encouragement, and gave her a wicked grin. "We're running. Each way."

Her knees trembled at the thought of it. Of course he'd make this into some sort of torture session. Of course. "And *where* are we going?"

He clenched his jaw, the tattoo stretching. "There was another body—a demi-Fae from a neighboring fortress. Dumped in the same area, same patterns. I want to go to the nearby town to question the citizens, but . . ." His mouth twisted to the side, then he shook his head at some silent conversation with himself. "But I need your help. It'll be easier for the mortals to talk to you."

"Is that a compliment?" He rolled his eyes.

Perhaps yesterday's outing to the healers' compound hadn't been out of spite. Maybe he'd . . . been trying to do something nice for her. "Shift, or it'll take us twice as long."

"I *can't*. You know it doesn't work like that."

"Don't you want to see how fast you can run?"

"I can't use my other form in Adarlan anyway, so what's the point?" Which was the start of a whole massive issue she hadn't yet let herself contemplate.

"The point is that you're here now, and you haven't properly tested your limits." It was true. She hadn't really seen what she was capable of. "The point is, another husk of a body was found, and I consider that to be unacceptable."

Another body—from that creature. A horrible, wretched death. It *was* unacceptable.

He gave her braid a sharp, painful tug. "Unless you're still frightened."

Her nostrils flared. "The only thing that frightens me is how *very much* I want to throttle you." More than that, she wanted to find the creature and destroy it, for those it had murdered and for what it had made *her* walk through. She would kill it—slowly. A miserable sort of pressure and heat began building under her skin.

Rowan murmured, "Hone it—the anger."

Was that why he'd told her about the body? Bastard—bastard for manipulating her, for making her pull double duty in the kitchen. But his face was unreadable as he said, "Let it be a blade, Aelin. If you cannot find the peace, then at least hone the anger that guides you to the shift. Embrace and control it—it is not your enemy."

Arobynn had done everything he could to make her hate her heritage, to fear it. What he'd done to her, what she'd allowed herself to become . . . "This will not end well," she breathed.

He didn't back down. "See what you want, Aelin, and seize it. Don't ask for it; don't wish for it. *Take it*."

"I'm certain the average magic instructor would not recommend this to most people."

"You are not most people, and I think you like it that way. If it's a darker set of emotions that will help you shift on command, then that's what we'll use. There might come a day when you find that anger doesn't work, or when it is a crutch, but for now . . ." A contemplative look. "It was the common denominator those times you shifted—anger of varying kinds. So own it."

He was right—and she didn't want to think on it any more than that, or let herself get that enraged, not when she had been so angry for so long. For now . . .

Celaena took a long breath. Then another. She let the anger anchor her, a knife slicing past the usual hesitation and doubt and emptiness.

She brushed up against that familiar inner wall—no, a veil, shimmering with a soft light. All this time, she thought she'd been reaching *down* for the power, but this was more of a reach *in*. Not a wish, but a command. She *would* shift—because there was a creature prowling these lands, and it deserved to pay. With a silent growl, she punched herself through the veil, pain shooting along every inch and pore as she shifted.

A fierce, challenging grin, and Rowan *moved*, so fast she could hardly follow as he appeared on her other side and yanked on her braid again. When she whirled, he was already gone, and— She yelped as he pinched her side. "*Stop—*"

He was standing in front of her now, a wild invitation in his eyes. She'd been studying the way he moved, his tricks and tells, the way he assumed she'd react. So when she crossed her arms, feigning the tantrum he expected, she waited. Waited, and then—

He shot left to pinch or poke or hit her, and she whirled, slamming down his arm with an elbow and whacking him upside the head with her other hand. He stopped dead and blinked a few times. She smirked at him.

He bared his teeth in a feral, petrifying grin. "Oh, you'd *better* run now."

When he lunged, she shot through the trees.

She had a suspicion that Rowan was letting her get ahead for the first few minutes, because though she moved faster, she could barely adjust enough to her altered body to leap over rocks and fallen trees. He'd said they were going southwest, and that was where she went, dodging between the trees, the anger simmering away, shifting into something else entirely.

Rowan was a silver and white streak beside and behind her, and every time he got too close, she veered the other way, testing out the senses that told her where the trees were without seeing them—the smell of oak and moss and living things, the open coolness of the mist passing between them like a path that she followed.

They hit a plateau, the ground easy beneath her boots. Faster—she wanted to see if she could go *faster*, if she could outrun the wind itself.

Rowan appeared at her left, and she pumped her arms, her legs, savoring the breath in her lungs—smooth and calm, ready to see what she would do next. More—this body wanted *more*.

She wanted more.

And then she was going swifter than she ever had in her life, the trees a blur, her immortal body singing as she let its rhythms fall into place. Her powerful lungs gobbled down the misty air and filled with the smell and taste of the world, only instinct and reflex guiding her, telling her she could go faster still, feet eating up the loamy earth step by step by step.

Gods. *Oh, gods.*

She could have flown, could have soared for the sudden surge of ecstasy in her blood, the sheer freedom granted by the marvel of creation that was her body.

Rowan shot at her from the right, but she dodged a tree with such ease she let out a whoop, then threw herself between two long-hanging branches, mere hurdles that she landed with feline skill.

Rowan was at her side again, lunging with a snap of his teeth, but she whirled and leapt over a rock, letting the moves she'd honed as an assassin blend into the instincts of her Fae body.

She could die for love of this speed, this surety in her bones. How had she been afraid of this body for so long? Even her soul felt looser. As if it had been locked up and buried and was only now starting to shake free. Not joy, perhaps not ever, but a glimmer of what she had been before grief had decimated her so thoroughly.

Rowan raced beside her, but made no move to grab her. No, Rowan was . . . playing.

He threw a glance at her, breathing hard but evenly. And it might have been the sun through the canopy, but she could have sworn that she saw his eyes alight with a glimmer of that same, feral contentment. She could have sworn he was smiling.

It was the fastest twenty miles of her life. Granted, the last five were slower, and by the time Rowan brought them to a halt, they were both gulping down air. It was only then, as they stared at each other between the trees, that she realized the magic hadn't once flared—hadn't once tried to overpower or erupt. She could feel it waiting down in her gut, warm but calm. Slumbering.

She wiped the sweat from her brow, her neck, her face. Though she was panting, she still could have run for miles more. Gods, if she had been this fast the night Nehemia had—

It wouldn't have made a difference. Nehemia had orchestrated every step in her own destruction, and would have found another way. And she had only done it because Celaena refused to help—refused to act. Having this glorious Fae body changed nothing.

She blinked, realizing she'd been staring at Rowan, and that whatever satisfaction she'd seen on his face had again turned to ice. He tossed something at her—the shirt he'd carried with him. "Change." He turned and stripped off his own shirt. His back was just as tan and scarred as the rest of him. But seeing those markings didn't make her want to show him what her own ruined back looked like, so she moved between the trees until she was sure he couldn't see her, and swapped her shirt. When she returned to where he'd dumped the pack, he tossed her a skein of water, which she gulped down. It tasted . . . She could taste each layer of minerals in the water, and the musk of the skein itself.

By the time they strode into the red-roofed little town, Celaena could breathe again.

They quickly learned that it was almost impossible to get *anyone* to talk, especially to two Fae visitors. Celaena debated returning to her human form, but with her accent and ever-worsening mood, she was fairly certain a woman from Adarlan wouldn't be much better received than a Fae. Windows were shuttered as they passed, probably because of Rowan, who looked like nothing short of death incarnate. But he was surprisingly calm with the villagers they approached. He didn't raise his voice, didn't snarl, didn't threaten. He didn't smile, but for Rowan, he was downright cheerful.

Still, it got them nowhere. No, they had not heard of a missing demi-Fae, or any other bodies. No, they had not seen any strange people lurking about. No, livestock were not disappearing, though there *was* a chicken thief a few towns away. No, they were perfectly safe and protected in Wendlyn, and didn't appreciate Fae and demi-Fae poking into their business, either.

Celaena had given up on flirting with a pock-faced stable boy at the inn, who had just gawked at her ears and canines as though she were one heartbeat away from eating him alive.

She stalked down the pleasant main street, hungry and tired and annoyed that they were indeed going to need their bedrolls because the innkeeper had already informed them he had no vacancies. Rowan fell into step beside her, the storm clouds in his eyes saying enough about how his conversation with the taproom maid had gone.

"I could believe it was a half-wild creature if at least some of them knew these people had vanished," she mused. "But consistently selecting someone who wouldn't be missed or noticed? It must be sentient enough to know who to target. The demi-Fae has to be a message—but what? To stay away? Then why leave bodies in the first place?" She tugged at the end of her braid, stopping in front of a clothier's window. Simple, well-cut dresses stood on display, not at all like the elegant, intricate fashions in Rifthold.

She noticed the wide-eyed, pale shopkeeper a heartbeat before the woman slashed the curtains shut. Well, then.

Rowan snorted, and Celaena turned to him. "You're used to this, I assume?"

"A lot of the Fae who venture into mortal lands have earned themselves a reputation for . . . taking what they want. It went unchecked for too many years, but even though our laws are stricter now, the fear remains." A criticism of Maeve?

"Who enforces these laws?"

A dark smile. "I do. When I'm not off campaigning, my aunt has me hunt down the rogues."

"And kill them?"

The smile remained. "If the situation calls for it. Or I just haul them back to Doranelle and let Maeve decide what to do with them."

"I think I'd prefer death at your hands to death at Maeve's."

"That might be the first wise thing you've said to me."

"The demi-Fae said you have five other warrior friends. Do they hunt with you? How often do you see them?"

"I see them whenever the situation calls for it. Maeve has them serve her as she sees fit, as she does with me." Every word was clipped. "It is an honor to be a warrior serving in her inner circle." Celaena hadn't suggested otherwise, but she wondered why he felt the need to add it.

The street around them was empty; even food carts had been abandoned. She took a long breath, sniffing, and—was that chocolate? "Did you bring any money?"

A hesitant lift of his brow. "Yes. They won't take your bribes, though."

"Good. More for me, then." She pointed out the pretty sign swaying in the sea breeze. *Confectionery*. "If we can't win them with charm, we might as well win them with our business."

"Did you somehow *not* hear what I just—" But she had already reached the shop, which smelled divine and was stocked with chocolates and candies and *oh gods*, hazelnut truffles. Even though the confectioner blanched as the two of them overpowered the space, Celaena gave the woman her best smile.

Over her rotting corpse was she letting these people get away with shutting curtains in her face—or letting them think that she was here to plunder. Nehemia had never once let the preening, bigoted idiots in Rifthold shut her out of any store, dining room, or household.

And she had the sense that her friend might have been proud of the way she went from shop to shop that afternoon, head held high, and charmed the ever-loving hell out of those villagers.

Once word spread that the two Fae strangers were spending silver on chocolates, then a few books, then some fresh bread and meat, the streets filled again. Vendors bearing everything from apples to spices to pocket watches were suddenly eager to chat, so long as they sold something.

When Celaena popped in to the cramped messenger's guild to mail a letter, she managed to ask a few novices if they'd been hired by anyone of interest. They hadn't, but she still tipped them handsomely.

Rowan dutifully carried every bag and box Celaena bought save the chocolates, which she ate as she strolled around, one after another after another. When she offered one to him, he claimed he didn't eat sweets. *Ever.* Not surprising.

The villagers wound up not knowing anything, which she supposed was good, because it meant that they hadn't been lying, but the crab-monger *did* say he'd found a few discarded knives—small, sharp-as-death knives—in his nets recently. He tossed them all back into the water as gifts for the Sea God. The creature had sucked these people dry, not cut them up. So it was likely that Wendlynite soldiers had somehow lost a trunk of their blades in some storm.

At sunset, the innkeeper even approached them about a suddenly vacant suite. The very best suite in town, he claimed, but Celaena was starting to wonder whether they might attract the wrong sort of attention, and she wasn't particularly in the mood to see Rowan disembowel a would-be thief. So she politely refused, and they set out down the street, the light turning thick and golden as they entered the forest once more.

Not a bad day, she realized as she nodded off under the forest canopy. Not bad at all.

Her mother had called her Fireheart.

But to her court, to her people, she would one day be Queen. To them, she was the heir to two mighty bloodlines, and to a tremendous power that would keep them safe and raise their kingdom to even greater heights. A power that was a gift—or a weapon.

That had been the near-constant debate for the first eight years of her life. As she grew older and it became apparent that while she'd inherited most of her mother's looks, she'd received her father's volatile temper and wildness, the wary questions became more frequent, asked by rulers in kingdoms far from their own.

And on days like this, she knew that everyone would hear of the event, for better or worse.

She was supposed to be asleep, and was wearing her favorite silk nightgown, her parents having tucked her in minutes ago. Though they had told her they weren't, she knew they were exhausted, and frustrated. She'd seen the way the court was acting, and how her uncle had put a gentle hand on her father's shoulder and told him to take her up to bed.

But she couldn't sleep, not when her door was cracked open, and she could hear her parents from their bedroom in the suite they shared in the upper levels of the white castle. They thought they were speaking quietly, but it was with an immortal's ears that she listened in the near-dark.

"I don't know what you expect me to do, Evalin," her father said. She could almost hear him prowling before the giant bed on which she had been born. "What's done is done."

"Tell them it was exaggerated, tell them the librarians were making a fuss over nothing," her mother hissed. "Start a rumor that someone else did it, trying to pin the blame on her—"

"This is all because of Maeve?"

"This is because she is going to be hunted, *Rhoe. For her whole life, Maeve and others will hunt her for this power—"*

"And you think agreeing to let those little bastards ban her from the library will prevent that? Tell me: why does our daughter love reading so much?"

"That has nothing to do with it."

"Tell me." *When her mother didn't respond, her father growled. "She is eight—and she has told me that her dearest friends are characters in books."*

"She has Aedion."

"She has Aedion because he is the only child in this castle who isn't petrified of her—who hasn't been kept away because we have been lax with her

training. She needs training, Ev—training, and friends. If she doesn't have either, that's *when she'll turn into what they're afraid of."*

Silence, and then—a huff from beside her bed.

"I'm not a child," Aedion hissed from where he sat in a chair, arms crossed. He'd slipped in here after her parents had left—to talk quietly to her, as he often did when she was upset. "And I don't see why it's a bad thing if I'm your only friend."

"Quiet," she hissed back. Though Aedion couldn't shift, his mixed blood allowed him to hear with uncanny range and accuracy, better even than hers. And though he was five years older, he was *her only friend. She loved her court, yes—loved the adults who pampered and coddled her. But the few children who lived in the castle kept away, despite their parents' urging. Like dogs, she'd sometimes thought. The others could smell her differences.*

"She needs friends her age," her father went on. "Maybe we should send her to school. Cal and Marion have been talking about sending Elide next year—"

"No schools. And certainly not that so-called magic school, when it's so close to the border and we don't know what Adarlan is planning."

Aedion loosed a breath, his legs propped on the mattress. His tan face was angled toward the cracked door, his golden hair shining faintly, but there was a crease between his brows. Neither of them took well to being separated, and the last time one of the castle boys had teased him for it, Aedion had spent a month shoveling horse dung for beating the boy into a pulp.

Her father sighed. "Ev, don't kill me for this, but—you're not making this easy. For us, or for her." Her mother was quiet, and she heard a rustle of clothing and a murmur of, "I know, I know," before her parents started speaking too quietly for even her Fae ears.

Aedion growled again, his eyes—their matching eyes—gleaming in the dark. "I don't see what all the fuss is about. So what if you burned a few books? Those librarians deserve it. When we're older, maybe we'll burn it to the ground together."

She knew he meant it. He'd burn the library, the city, or the whole world to ashes if she asked him. It was their bond, marked by blood and scent and something else she couldn't place. A tether as strong as the one that bound her to her parents. Stronger, in some ways.

She didn't answer him, not because she didn't have a reply but because the door groaned, and before Aedion could hide, her bedroom flooded with light from the foyer.

Her mother crossed her arms. Her father, however, let out a soft laugh, his brown hair illuminated by the hall light, his face in shadow. "Typical," he said, stepping aside to clear a space for Aedion to leave. "Don't you have to be up at dawn to train with Quinn? You were five minutes late this morning. Two days in a row will earn you a week on stable duty. Again."

In a flash, Aedion was on his feet and gone. Alone with her parents, she wished she could pretend to sleep, but she said, "I don't want to go away to school."

Her father walked to her bed, every inch the warrior Aedion aspired to be. A warrior-prince, she heard people call him—who would one day make a mighty king. She sometimes thought her father had no interest in being king, especially on days when he took her up into the Staghorns and let her wander through Oakwald in search of the Lord of the Forest. He never seemed happier than at those times, and always seemed a little sad to go back to Orynth.

"You're not going away to school," he said, looking over his broad shoulder at her mother, who lingered by the doorway, her face still in shadow. "But do you understand why the librarians acted the way they did today?"

Of course she did. She felt horrible for burning the books. It had been an accident, and she knew her father believed her. She nodded and said, "I'm sorry."

"You have nothing *to be sorry for," her father said, a growl in his voice.*

"I wish I was like the others," she said.

Her mother remained silent, unmoving, but her father gripped her hand. "I know, love. But even if you were not gifted, you would still be our daughter—you would still be a Galathynius, and their queen one day."

"I don't want to be queen."

Her father sighed. This *was a conversation they'd had before. He stroked her hair. "I know," he said again. "Sleep now—we'll talk about it in the morning."*

They wouldn't, though. She knew they wouldn't, because she knew there was no escaping her fate, even though she sometimes prayed to the gods that she could. She lay down again nonetheless, letting him kiss her head and murmur good night.

Her mother still said nothing, but as her father walked out, Evalin remained, watching her for a long while. Just as she was drifting off, her mother left—and as she turned, she could have sworn that tears gleamed on her pale face.

Celaena jolted awake, hardly able to move, to think. It had to be the smell—the smell of that gods-damned body yesterday that had triggered the dream. It was agony seeing her parents' faces, seeing Aedion. She blinked, focusing on her breathing, until she was no longer in that beautiful, jewel box–like room, until the scent of the pine and snow on the northern wind had vanished and she could see the morning mist weaving through the canopy of leaves above her. The cold, damp moss seeped through her clothes; the brine of the nearby sea hung thick in the air. She lifted her hand to examine the long scar carved on her palm.

"Do you want breakfast?" Rowan asked from where he crouched over unlit logs—the first fire she'd seen him assemble. She nodded, then rubbed her eyes with the heels of her palms. "Then start the fire," he said.

"You can't be serious." He didn't deign to respond. Groaning, she rotated on her sleeping roll until she sat cross-legged facing the logs. She held a hand toward the wood.

"Pointing is a crutch. Your mind can direct the flames just fine."

"Perhaps I like the dramatics."

He gave her a look she interpreted to mean *Light the fire. Now.*

She rubbed her eyes again and concentrated on the logs.

"Easy," Rowan said, and she wondered if that was approval in his voice as the wood began to smoke. "A knife, remember. You are in control."

A knife, carving out a small bit of magic. She could master this. Light one single fire.

Gods, she was so heavy again. That stupid dream—memory, whatever it was. Today would be an effort.

A pit yawned open inside her, the magic rupturing out before she could shout a warning.

She incinerated the entire surrounding area.

When the smoke and flames cleared thanks to Rowan's wind, he merely sighed. "At least you didn't panic and shift back into your human form."

She supposed that was a compliment. The magic had felt like a release—a thrown punch. The pressure under her skin had lessened.

So Celaena just nodded. But shifting, it seemed, was to be the least of her problems.

29

It had just been a kiss, Sorscha told herself every day afterward. A quick, breathless kiss that made the world spin. The iron in the treacle had worked, though it bothered Dorian enough that they started to toy with the dosage . . . and ways to mask it. If he were caught ingesting powders at all hours of the day, it would lead to questions.

So it became a daily contraceptive tonic. Because no one would bat an eye at that—not with his reputation. Sorscha was still reassuring herself that the kiss had meant nothing more than a thank-you as she reached the door to Dorian's tower room, his daily dose in hand.

She knocked, and the prince called her inside. The assassin's hound was sprawled on his bed, and the prince himself was lounging on his shabby couch. He sat up, however, and smiled at her in that way of his.

"I think I found a better combination—the mint might go down better than the sage," she said, holding up the glass of reddish liquid. He came toward her, but there was something in his gait—a kind of prowl—that made her straighten. Especially as he set down the glass and stared at her, long and deep. "What?" she breathed, backing up a step.

He gripped her hand—not hard enough to hurt, but enough to stop her retreat. "You understand the risks, and yet you're still helping me," he said. "Why?"

"It's the right thing."

"My father's laws say otherwise."

Her face heated. "I don't know what you want me to say."

His hands were cool as he brushed her cheeks, his calluses scraping gently. "I just want to thank you," he murmured, leaning in. "For seeing me and not running."

"I—" She was burning up from the inside out, and she pulled back, hard enough that he let go. Amithy was right, even if she was vicious. There *were* plenty of beautiful women here, and anything more than a flirtation would end poorly. He was Crown Prince, and she was nobody. She gestured to the goblet. "If it's not too much trouble, Your Highness"—he cringed at the title—"send word about how this one works for you."

She didn't dare a by-your-leave or farewell or anything that would keep her in that room a moment longer. And he didn't try to stop her as she walked out and shut the door behind her.

She leaned against the stone wall of the narrow landing, a hand on her thundering heart. It was the smart thing to do, the right thing to do. She had survived this long, and would only survive the road ahead if she continued to be unnoticed, reliable, quiet.

But she didn't want to be unnoticed—not with him, not forever.

He made her want to laugh and sing and shake the world with her voice.

The door swung open, and she found him standing in the doorway, solemn and wary.

Maybe there could be no future, no hope of anything more, but just looking at him standing there, in this moment, she wanted to be selfish and stupid and wild.

It could all go to hell tomorrow, but she had to know what it was like, just for a little while, to belong to someone, to be wanted and cherished.

He did not move, didn't do anything but stare—seeing her exactly how she saw him—as she grabbed the lapels of his tunic, pulled his face down to hers, and kissed him fiercely.

Chaol had been barely able to concentrate for the past few days thanks to the meeting he was moments away from having. It had taken longer than he had anticipated before Ren and Murtaugh were finally ready to meet him—their first encounter since that night in the slums. Chaol had to wait for his next night off, Aedion had to find a secure location, and then they had to coordinate with the two lords from Terrasen. He and the general had left the castle separately, and Chaol had hated himself when he lied to his men about where he was going—hated that they wished him fun, hated that they trusted him, the man who was meeting with their mortal enemies.

Chaol shoved those thoughts aside as he approached the dim alley a few blocks from the decrepit boarding house where they were to meet. Under his heavy-hooded cloak he was armed more heavily than he usually bothered. Every breath he took felt too shallow. A two-note whistle sounded down the alley, and he echoed it. Aedion stalked through the low-lying mist coming off the Avery, his face concealed in the cowl of his own cloak.

He wasn't wearing the Sword of Orynth. Instead, an assortment of blades and fighting knives were strapped to the general—a man able to walk into hell itself and come out grinning.

"Where are the others?" Chaol said softly. The slums were quiet tonight—too quiet for his liking. Dressed as he was, few would dare approach him, but the walk through the crooked and dark streets had been harrowing. Such poverty and despair—and desperation. It made people dangerous, willing to risk anything to scratch out another day of living.

Aedion leaned against the crumbling brick wall behind them. "Don't get your undergarments in a twist. They'll be here soon."

"I've waited long enough for this information."

"What's the rush?" Aedion drawled, scanning the alley.

"I'm leaving Rifthold in a few weeks to return to Anielle." Aedion didn't look directly at him, but he could feel the general staring at him from beneath his dark hood.

"So get out of it—tell them you're busy."

"I made a promise," Chaol said. "I've already bargained for time, but I want to have . . . *done* something for the prince before I leave."

The general turned to him then. "I'd heard you were estranged from your father; why the sudden change?"

It would have been easier to lie, but Chaol said, "My father is a powerful man—he has the ear of many influential members at court and is on the king's council."

Aedion let out a low laugh. "I've butted heads with him in more than a few war councils."

That Chaol would have paid good money to see, but he wasn't smiling as he said, "It was the only way I could get her sent to Wendlyn." He quickly explained the bargain he'd made, and when he was finished, Aedion loosed a long breath.

"Damn," the general said, then shook his head. "I didn't think that kind of honor still existed in Adarlan."

He supposed it was a compliment—and a high one, coming from Aedion. "And what of your father?" Chaol said, if only to shift conversation away from the hole in his chest. "I know your mother was kin to—to *her*, but what of your father's line?"

"My mother never admitted who my father was, even when she was wasting away on her sickbed," Aedion said flatly. "I don't know if it was from shame, or because she couldn't even remember, or to protect me somehow. Once I was brought over here, I didn't really care. But I'd rather have no father than your father."

Chaol chuckled and might have asked another question had boots not scraped on stone at the other end of the alley, followed by a rasping breath.

That fast, Aedion had palmed two fighting knives, and Chaol drew his own sword—a bland, nondescript blade he'd swiped from the barracks—as a man staggered into view.

He had an arm wrapped around his middle, the other bracing himself against the brick wall of an abandoned building. Aedion was instantly moving, knives sheathed again. It wasn't until Chaol heard him say, "Ren?" that he also hurried toward the young man.

In the moonlight, the blood on Ren's tunic was a shining, deep stain.

"Where is Murtaugh?" Aedion demanded, slinging an arm under Ren's shoulders.

"Safe." Ren panted, his face dealthy pale. Chaol scanned either end of the alley. "We were—followed. So we tried losing them." He heard, more than saw, Ren's wince. "They cornered me."

"How many?" Aedion said softly, though Chaol could almost feel the violence simmering off the general.

"Eight," Ren said, and hissed in pain. "Killed two, then got free. They're following me."

Leaving six. If they were unharmed, they were probably close behind. Chaol examined the stones beyond Ren. The wound to his abdomen couldn't be deep, if he'd managed to keep the blood flow from leaving a trail. But it still had to be agonizing—potentially fatal, if it had pierced the wrong spot.

Aedion went rigid, hearing something that Chaol couldn't. He quietly, gently passed the sagging Ren into Chaol's arms. "There are three barrels ten paces away," the general said with lethal calm as he faced the alley entrance. "Hide behind them and keep your mouths shut."

That was all Chaol needed to hear as he took Ren's weight and hauled him to the large barrels, then eased him onto the ground. Ren stifled a groan of pain, but kept still. There was a small crack between two of the barrels where Chaol could see the alley, and the six men who stalked into it almost shoulder-to-shoulder. He couldn't make out much more than dark tunics and cloaks.

The men paused when they beheld Aedion standing before them, still hooded. The general drew his fighting knives and purred, "None of you are leaving this alley alive."

They didn't.

Chaol marveled at Aedion's skill—the speed and swiftness and utter confidence that made it like watching a brutal, unforgiving dance.

It was over before it really started. The six assailants seemed at ease with weapons, but against a man with Fae blood surging in his veins, they were useless.

No wonder Aedion had risen to such high ranking so quickly. He'd never seen another man fight like that. Only—only Celaena had come close. He couldn't tell which of them would win if they were ever matched against each other, but together . . . Chaol's heart went cold at the thought. Six men dead in a matter of moments—six.

Aedion wasn't smiling as he came back over to Chaol and dropped a scrap of fabric on the ground before them. Even Ren, panting through clenched teeth, looked.

It was a black, heavy material—and emblazoned on it in dark thread, nearly invisible save for the glint of the moonlight, was a wyvern. The royal sigil.

"I don't know these men," Chaol said, more to himself than to protest his innocence. "I've never seen that uniform."

"From the sound of it," Aedion said, that rage still simmering in his voice as he cocked his head toward noises that Chaol could not hear with his human ears, "there are more of them out there, and they're combing the slums door-to-door for Ren. We need a place to hide."

Ren held on to consciousness long enough to say, "I know where."

30

Chaol held his breath for the entire walk as he and Aedion gripped the half-conscious Ren between them, the three of them swaying and staggering, looking for all the world like drunkards out for a night of thrills in the slums. The streets were still teeming despite the hour, and one of the women they passed slouched over and gripped Aedion's tunic, spewing a slur of sultry words. But the general used a gentle hand to disengage her and said, "I don't pay for what I can get for free."

Somehow, it felt like a lie, since Chaol hadn't seen or heard of Aedion sharing anyone's bed all these weeks. But perhaps knowing that Aelin was alive changed his priorities.

They reached the opium den Ren had named in between spurts of unconsciousness just as the shouts of soldiers storming into boarding-houses, inns, and taverns echoed from down the street. Chaol didn't wait to see who they were and shoved through the carved wooden door. The reek of unwashed bodies, waste, and sweet smoke clotted in

Chaol's nostrils. Even Aedion coughed and gave Ren, who was almost a dead weight in their arms, a disapproving stare.

But the aging madam swept forward to greet them, her long tunic and over-robe flowing on some phantom wind, and ushered them down the wood-paneled hallway, her feet soft on the worn, colorful rugs. She began prattling off prices and the night's specials, but Chaol took one look in her green, cunning eyes and knew she was familiar with Ren—someone who had probably built herself her own empire here in Rifthold.

She set them up in a veiled-off alcove littered with worn silk cushions that stank of sweet smoke and sweat, and after she lifted her brows at Chaol, he handed over three gold pieces. Ren groaned from where he was sprawled on the cushions between Aedion and Chaol, but before Chaol could so much as say a word, the madam returned with a bundle in her arms. "They are next door," she said, her accent lovely and strange. "Hurry."

She'd brought a tunic. Aedion made quick work of stripping Ren, whose face was deathly pale, lips bloodless. The general swore as they beheld the wound—a slice low in his belly. "Any deeper and his damn intestines would be hanging out," Aedion said. He took a strip of clean fabric from the madam and wrapped it around the young lord's muscled abdomen. There were scars all over Ren already. If he survived, this probably would not be the worst of them.

The madam knelt before Chaol and opened the box in her hands. Three pipes now lay on the low-lying table before them. "You need to play the part," she breathed, glancing over her shoulder through the thick black veil, no doubt calculating how much time they had left.

Chaol didn't even try to object as she used rouge to redden the skin around his eyes, applied some paste and powder to leech the color from his face, shook free a few buttons on his tunic, and mussed his hair. "Lay back, limp and loose, and keep the pipe in your hand.

Smoke it if you need to take the edge off." That was all she told him before she got to work on Aedion, who had finished stuffing Ren into his clean clothes. In moments, the three of them were reclined on the reeking cushions, and the madam had bustled off with Ren's bloody tunic.

The lord's breathing was labored and uneven, and Chaol fought the shaking in his own hands as the front door banged open. The soft feet of the madam hurried past to greet the men. Though Chaol strained to hear, Aedion seemed to be listening without a problem.

"Five of you, then?" the madam chirped loudly enough for them to hear.

"We're looking for a fugitive," was the growled response. "Clear out of the way."

"Surely you would like to rest—we have private rooms for groups, and you are all such big men." Each word was purred, a sensual feast. "It is extra for bringing in swords and daggers—a liability, you see, when the drug takes you—"

"Woman, *enough*," the man barked. Fabric ripped as each veiled alcove was inspected. Chaol's heart thundered, but he kept his body limp, even as he itched to reach for his blade.

"Then I shall leave you to your work," she said demurely.

Between them, Ren was so dazed that he truly could have been drugged out of his mind. Chaol just hoped his own performance was convincing as the curtain ripped back.

"Is that the wine?" Aedion slurred, squinting at the men, his face wan and his lips set in a loose grin. He was hardly recognizable. "We've been waiting twenty minutes, you know."

Chaol smiled blearily up at the six men peering into the room. All in those dark uniforms, all unfamiliar. Who the hell were they? Why had Ren been targeted?

"Wine," Aedion snapped, a spoiled son of a merchant, perhaps. "Now."

The men just swore at them and continued on. Five minutes later, they were gone.

The den must have been a meeting point, because Murtaugh found them there an hour later. The madam had brought them to her private office, and they'd been forced to pin Ren to the worn couch as she—with surprising adeptness—disinfected, stitched, and bound up his nasty wound. He would survive, she said, but the blood loss and injury would keep him incapacitated for a while. Murtaugh paced the entire time, until Ren collapsed into a deep sleep, courtesy of some tonic the woman made him choke down.

Chaol and Aedion sat at the small table crammed in amongst the crates upon crates of opium stacked against the walls. He didn't want to know what was in the tonic Ren had ingested.

Aedion was watching the locked door, head cocked as if listening to the sounds of the den, as he said to Murtaugh, "Why were you being followed, and who were those men?"

The old man kept pacing. "I don't know. But they knew where Ren and I would be. Ren has a network of informants throughout the city. Any one of them could have betrayed us."

Aedion's attention remained on the door, a hand on one of his fighting knives. "They wore uniforms with the royal sigil—even the captain didn't recognize them. You need to lay low for a while."

Murtaugh's silence was too heavy. Chaol asked quietly, "Where do we bring him when he can be moved?"

Murtaugh paused his pacing, his eyes full of grief. "There is no place. We have no home."

Aedion looked sharply at him. "Where the hell have you been staying all this time?"

"Here and there, squatting in abandoned buildings. When we are able to take work, we stay in boardinghouses, but these days . . ."

They would not have access to the Allsbrook coffers, Chaol realized. Not if they had been in hiding for so many years. But to be homeless . . .

Aedion's face was a mask of disinterest. "And you have no place in Rifthold safe enough to hold him—to see to his mending." Not a question, but Murtaugh nodded all the same. Aedion examined Ren, sprawled on the dark sofa against the far wall. His throat bobbed once, but then he said, "Tell the captain your theory about magic."

In the long hours that passed as Ren regained his strength enough to be moved, Murtaugh explained everything he knew. His entire story came out, the old man almost whispering at times—of the horrors they'd fled, and how Ren had gotten each and every scar. Chaol understood why the young man had been so close-lipped until now. Secrecy had kept them alive.

All together, Murtaugh and Ren had learned, the various waves the day magic had vanished formed a rough triangle across the continent. The first line went right from Rifthold to the Frozen Wastes. The second went down from the Frozen Wastes to the edge of the Deserted Peninsula. The third line went from there back to Rifthold. A spell, they believed, had been the cause of it.

Standing around the map Aedion had produced, the general traced a finger over the lines again and again, as if sorting out a battle strategy. "A spell sent from specific points, like a beacon."

Chaol thumped his knuckles on the table. "Is there some way of undoing it?"

Murtaugh sighed. "Our work was interrupted by the disturbance with Archer, and our sources vanished from the city for fear of their lives. But there has to be a way."

"So where do we start looking?" Aedion asked. "There's no chance in hell the king would leave clues lying around."

Murtaugh nodded. "We need eyewitnesses to confirm what we suspect, but the places we think the spell originated are occupied by the king's forces. We've been waiting for an in."

Aedion gave him a lazy grin. "No wonder you kept telling Ren to be nice to me."

As if in response, Ren groaned, struggling to rise to consciousness. Had the young lord ever felt safe or at peace at any point in the past ten years? It would explain that anger—the reckless anger that coursed through all the young, shattered hearts of Terrasen, including Celaena's.

Chaol said, "There is an apartment hidden in a warehouse in the slums. It's secure, and has all the amenities you need. You're welcome to stay there for however long you require."

He felt Aedion watching him carefully. But Murtaugh frowned. "However generous, I cannot accept the offer to stay in your house."

"It's not my house," Chaol said. "And believe me, the owner won't mind one bit."

31

"Eat it," Manon said, holding out the raw leg of mutton to Abraxos. The day was bright, but the wind off the snowy peaks of the Fangs still carried a brutal chill. They'd been going outside the mountain for little spurts to stretch his legs, using the back door that opened onto a narrow road leading into the mountains. She'd guided him by the giant chain—as if it would do anything to stop him from taking off—up a sharp incline, and then onto the meadow atop a plateau.

"Eat it," she said, shaking the freezing meat at Abraxos, who was now lying on his belly in the meadow, huffing at the first grasses and flowers to poke through the melting ice. "It's your reward," she said through her teeth. "You earned it."

Abraxos sniffed at a cluster of purple flowers, then flicked his eyes to her. *No meat*, he seemed to say.

"It's good for you," she said, and he went right back to sniffing the violets or whatever they were. If a plant wasn't good for poisoning or healing or keeping her alive if she were starving, she'd never bothered to learn its name—especially not wildflowers.

She tossed the leg right in front of his massive mouth and tucked her hands into the folds of her red cloak. He snuffed at it, his new iron teeth glinting in the radiant light, then stretched out one massive, claw-tipped wing and—

Shoved it aside.

Manon rubbed her eyes. "Is it not fresh enough?"

He moved to sniff some white-and-yellow flowers.

A nightmare. This was a nightmare. "You can't really like flowers."

Again those dark eyes shifted to her. Blinked once. *I most certainly do*, he seemed to say.

She splayed her arms. "You never even smelled a flower until yesterday. What's wrong with the meat now?" He needed to eat tons and tons of meat to put on the muscle he was lacking.

When he went back to sniffing the flowers rather delicately—the insufferable, useless worm—she stalked to the leg of mutton and hauled it up. "If you won't eat it," she snarled at him, hoisting it up with both hands to her mouth and popping her iron teeth down, "then I will."

Abraxos watched her with those bemused dark eyes as she bit into the icy, raw meat. And spat it everywhere.

"What in the Mother's dark shadow—" She sniffed at the meat. It wasn't rancid, but like the men here, it tasted off. The sheep were raised inside the mountain, so maybe it was something in the water. As soon as she got back, she'd give the Thirteen the order not to touch the men—not until she knew what in hell was making them taste and smell that way.

Regardless, Abraxos had to eat, because he had to get strong—so she could be Wing Leader, so she could see the look on Iskra's face when she ripped her apart at the War Games. And if this was the only way to get the worm to eat . . .

"Fine," she said, chucking the leg away. "You want fresh meat?" She scanned the mountains towering around them, eyeing the gray stones. "Then we're going to have to hunt."

"You smell like shit and blood." Her grandmother didn't turn from her desk, and Manon didn't flinch at the insult. She was covered in both, actually.

It was thanks to Abraxos, the flower-loving worm, who had just watched while she scaled one of the nearby cliffs and brought down a braying mountain goat for him. "Brought down" was a more elegant phrase than what had actually happened: she half froze to death as she waited for some goats to pass on their treacherous climb, and then, when she'd finally ambushed one, she'd not only rolled in its dung as she'd grappled with it but it had also dumped a fresh load on her, right before it went tumbling out of her arms and broke its skull on the rocks below.

It had nearly taken her with it, but she'd managed to grab on to a dead root. Abraxos was still lying on his belly, sniffing the wildflowers, when she returned with the dead goat in her arms, its blood now iced on her cloak and tunic.

He'd devoured the goat in two bites, then gone back to enjoying the wildflowers. At least he'd eaten. Getting him back to the Northern Fang, however, was a trial in itself. He hadn't hurt her, hadn't fled, but he'd pulled on the chains, shaking his head again and again as they neared the cavernous back door where the sounds of the wyverns and men reached them. But he'd gone in—though he'd snapped and growled at the handlers who rushed out to retrieve him. For some reason, she hadn't been able to stop thinking about his reluctance—the way he'd looked at her with a mute plea. She didn't pity him, because she pitied nothing, but she couldn't stop thinking about it.

"You summoned me," said Manon, head high. "I did not want to keep you waiting."

"You *are* keeping me waiting, Manon." The witch turned, eyes full of death and promises of endless pain. "It has been weeks now, and you are not airborne with your Thirteen. The Yellowlegs have been flying as a host for three days. Three days, Manon. And you're coddling your beast."

Manon didn't show one flicker of feeling. Apologizing would make it worse, as would excuses. "Give me orders, and they will be done."

"I want you airborne by tomorrow evening. Don't bother coming back if you aren't."

"I hate you," Manon panted through her iron teeth as she and Abraxos finished their grueling trek to the top of the mountain peak. It had taken half a day to get here—and if this didn't work, it would take until evening to get back to the Omega. To pack her belongings.

Abraxos was curled up like a cat on the narrow stretch of flat rock atop the mountain. "Willful, lazy worm." He didn't even blink at her.

Take the eastern side, the overseer had said as he'd helped her saddle up and set out from the back door of the Northern Fang before dawn. They used this peak to train the hatchling wyverns—and reluctant fliers. The eastern side, Manon saw as she peered over the lip she'd just climbed, was a smooth incline after a twenty-foot drop. Abraxos could take a running start off the edge, try to glide, and if he fell . . . Well, it would only be twenty feet and then wind-smooth rock to slide down for a ways. Slim possibility for death.

No, death lay on the western side. Frowning at Abraxos, who was licking his new iron claws, Manon crossed the plateau and, despite herself, winced at the blistering wind that shot up.

To the west was an endless plunge through nothing until the spiked, unforgiving rocks below. It would take a crew of men to scrape off her remains. Eastern side it was.

She checked her tight braid and flicked her clear inner lid into place. "Let's go."

Abraxos lifted his massive head as if to say, *We just got here.*

She pointed to the eastern edge. "Flying. Now."

He huffed, curling his back to her, the leather saddle gleaming. "Oh, I don't think so," she snapped, stalking around to get in his face. She pointed to the edge again. "We're flying, you rutting coward."

He tucked his head toward his belly, his tail wrapping around him. He was pretending he couldn't hear her.

She knew it might cost her life, but she gripped his nostrils—hard enough to make his eyes fly open. "Your wings are functional. The humans said they were. So you can fly, and you are *going* to fly, because I say so. I've been fetching your useless carcass mountain goats by the herd, and if you humiliate me, I'll use your hide for a new leather coat." She rustled her torn and stained crimson cloak. "This is ruined, thanks to your goats."

He shifted his head away, and she let go—because it was either let go or be tossed into the air. He set down his head and closed his eyes.

This was punishment, somehow. For what, she didn't know. Perhaps her own stupidity in picking a bait beast for a mount.

She hissed to herself, eyeing the saddle on his back. Even with a running jump she couldn't make it. But she needed to be in that saddle and airborne, or else . . . Or else the Thirteen would be broken apart by her grandmother.

Abraxos continued to lie in the sun, vain and indulgent as a cat. "Warrior heart indeed."

She eyed the eastern edge, the saddle, the dangling reins. He'd bucked and thrashed the first time they'd shoved the bit into his mouth, but he'd gotten used to it now—at least, enough so that he'd tried to take off the head of only one handler today.

The sun was still rising high, but soon it would start its descent, and then she'd be completely and perfectly ruined. Like hell she would be.

"You had this coming" was all the warning she gave him before she took a running leap, landing on his haunch and then scrambling, so fast he had barely lifted his head by the time she scuttled across his scaly back and into the saddle.

He jerked upright, stiff as a board as she shoved her booted feet into the stirrups and gripped the reins. "We're flying—*now*." She dug her heels into his sides.

Perhaps the spurs hurt or surprised him, because Abraxos bucked—bucked and roared. She yanked on the reins as hard as she could. "*Enough*," she barked, hauling with one arm to guide him over the eastern edge. "Enough, Abraxos."

He was still thrashing, and she clenched her thighs as hard as she could to stay in the saddle, leaning into each movement. When the bucking didn't dislodge her, he lifted his wings, as if he would fling her off. "Don't you dare," she growled, but he was still twisting and bellowing.

"*Stop it.*" Her brain rattled in her skull and her teeth clacked together so hard she had to retract her fangs so they didn't punch right through her skin.

But Abraxos kept bucking, wild and frantic. Not toward the eastern edge, but away—toward the lip of the western plunge.

"Abraxos, *stop*." He was going to go right over. And then they'd splatter on the stones.

He was so panicked, so enraged that her voice was no more than a crackling leaf on the wind. The western drop loomed to her right, then her left, flashing beneath the leathery, mottled wings as they flapped and snapped. Under Abraxos's massive talons, stones hissed and crumbled as he neared the edge.

"*Abraxos—*" But then his leg slid off the cliff, and Manon's world tilted down—down, down, as he lost his grip and they plummeted into open air.

32

Manon didn't have time to contemplate her oncoming death.

She was too busy holding on to the saddle, the world flipping and spinning, the wind shrieking, or perhaps that was Abraxos, as they plunged down the cliff face.

Her muscles locked and trembled, but she kept her arms laced through the straps, the only thing keeping her from death, even as it swiftly approached with every rotation of Abraxos's ruined body.

The trees below took shape, as did the spiked, wind-carved rocks between them. Faster and faster, the cliff wall a blur of gray and white.

Maybe his body would take the impact and she could walk away.

Maybe all those rocks would go right through them both.

Maybe he'd flip and she would land on the rocks first.

She hoped it would happen too quickly for her to recognize just how she was dying, to know what part of her broke first. They hurtled down. There was a little river running through the spiked rocks.

Wind slammed into them from below, a draft that rocked Abraxos upright, but they were still rotating, still plunging.

"Open your wings!" she screamed over the wind, over her thundering heart. They stayed shut.

"Open them and pull up!" she bellowed, just as the rapids on the stream began to appear, just as she understood that she hated the oncoming embrace of the Darkness, and that there was nothing to do to stop this splattering, this doom from—

She could see the pine cones on the trees. *"Open them!"* A last, rallying war cry against the Darkness.

A war cry that was answered with a piercing shriek as Abraxos flung open his wings, caught the updraft, and sent them soaring away from the ground.

Manon's stomach went from her throat right out her ass, but they were swooping upward, and his wings were pumping, each boom the most beautiful sound she had ever heard in her long, miserable life.

Higher he flapped, legs tucked beneath him. Manon crouched in her saddle, clinging to his warm hide as he took them up the face of the neighboring mountain. Its peaks rose to meet them like lifted hands, but he wobbled past, beating hard. Manon lifted and fell with him, not taking one breath as they cleared the highest snow-capped peak and Abraxos, in joy or rage or for the hell of it, gripped clawfuls of snow and ice and set them scattering behind, the sun lighting them up like a trail of stars.

The sun was blinding as they hit the open sky, and there was nothing around them but clouds as massive as the mountains far below, castles and temples of white and purple and blue.

And the cry that Abraxos let out as they entered that hall of clouds, as he leveled out and caught a lightning-fast current carving a pathway through it . . .

She had not understood what it had been like for him to live his entire life underground, chained and beaten and crippled—until then. Until she heard that noise of undiluted, unyielding joy.

Until she echoed it, tipping her head back to the clouds around them.

They sailed over a sea of clouds, and Abraxos dipped his claws in them before tilting to race up a wind-carved column of cloud. Higher and higher, until they reached its peak and he flung out his wings in the freezing, thin sky, stopping the world entirely for a heartbeat.

And Manon, because no one was watching, because she did not care, flung out her arms as well and savored the freefall, the wind now a song in her ears, in her shriveled heart.

The gray skies were just filling with light as the sun slipped over the horizon at their backs. Bundled in her red cloak, Manon sat atop Abraxos, her vision slightly cloudy from the inner lid she'd already blinked into place. Still, she surveyed her Thirteen, astride their wyverns at the mouth of the canyon run.

They'd assembled in two rows of six, Asterin and her pale blue mount directly behind Manon, leading the first row, Sorrel claiming center in the second. They were all awake and alert—and slightly befuddled. Abraxos's damaged wings weren't ready to make the narrow Crossing, not yet. So they'd met at the back door, where they'd walked their wyverns the two miles to the first canyon run—walked like a proper unit, in rank and quietly.

The mouth of the canyon was wide enough for Abraxos to leap into an easy glide. Takeoffs were a problem thanks to the shredded muscle and weak spots in his wings—areas that had taken too many beatings and might never be at their full strength.

But she did not explain that to her Thirteen, because it was none of their damn business and it did not impact them.

"Every morning, from today until the War Games," Manon said, staring into the labyrinth of ravines and archways that made up the wind-carved canyon, "we will meet here, and until breakfast, we are going to train. Then we'll have our afternoon training with the other covens. Tell no one." She'd just have to leave early so she could get Abraxos airborne while the others made the Crossing.

"I want us in close quarters. I don't care what the men say about keeping the mounts separate. Let the wyverns sort out their dominance, let them squabble, but they are going to fly, tight as armor. There will be no gaps and no room for attitude or territorial horseshit. We fly this canyon together, or we don't fly at all."

She looked each of the witches and their mounts in the eye. Abraxos, to her surprise, did the same. What he lacked in size he made up for in sheer will, speed, and dexterity. He sensed currents even before Manon did. "When we are done, if we survive, we'll meet on the other side and do it again. Until it's perfect. Your beasts will learn to trust each other and follow orders." The wind kissed her cheeks. "Don't fall behind," she said, and Abraxos plunged into the canyon.

33

In the week that followed, there were no more bodies, and certainly no hint of the creature that had drained those people, though Celaena often found herself thinking over the details as Rowan made her light candle after candle at the ruins of the Sun Goddess's temple. Now that she could shift on command, this was her new task: to light a candle without destroying everything in sight. She failed every time, singeing her cloak, cracking the ruins, incinerating trees as her magic tore out of her. But Rowan had a bottomless supply of candles, so she spent her days staring at them until her eyes crossed. She could sweat for hours and focus on honing her anger and all that nonsense but not get as much as a tendril of smoke. The only thing that came of it was an unending appetite: Celaena ate whatever and whenever she could, thanks to her magic gobbling so much of her energy.

The rain returned, and with it, the crowd for Emrys's stories. Celaena always listened while she washed the night's dishes, to tales of shield maidens and enchanted animals and cunning sorcerers, all the legends of Wendlyn. Rowan still appeared in his hawk form—and there were some nights when she even sat beside the back door, and Rowan sidled a bit closer, too.

Celaena was standing at the sink, back throbbing and hunger gnawing at her belly as she scrubbed the last of the copper pots while Emrys finished narrating the story of a clever wolf and a magical firebird. There was a pause, and then came the usual requests for the same old stories. Celaena didn't acknowledge the heads that turned in her direction as she asked from the sink, "Do you know any stories about Queen Maeve?"

Dead. Silence. Emrys's eyes widened before he smiled faintly and said, "Lots. Which one would you like to hear?"

"The earliest ones that you know. All of them." If she was going to face her aunt again, perhaps she should start learning as much as she could. Emrys might know stories that hadn't reached the shores of her own lands. If the stories about the skinwalkers had been true, if the immortal stags were real . . . perhaps she could glean something vital here.

There were some nervous glances, but at last Emrys said, "Then I shall start at the beginning."

Celaena nodded and moved to sit in her usual chair, propped against the back door near the sharp-eyed hawk. Rowan clicked his beak, but she didn't dare look over her shoulder at him. Instead, she dug into an entire loaf of bread.

"Long ago, when there was no mortal king on Wendlyn's throne, the faeries still walked among us. Some were good and fair, some were prone to little mischiefs, and some were fouler and darker than the blackest night. But they were all of them ruled by Maeve and her two sisters, whom they called Mora and Mab. Cunning Mora, who bore the shape of a great hawk"—that was Rowan's mighty bloodline—"Fair Mab, who bore the shape of a swan. And the dark Maeve, whose wildness could not be contained by any single form."

Emrys recited the history, much of which Celaena knew: Mora and Mab had fallen in love with human men, and yielded their immortality. Some said Maeve forced them to give up their gift of eternal life as punishment. Some said they wanted to, if only to escape their sister.

And when Celaena asked, the room falling deathly silent again, if Maeve herself had ever mated, Emrys told her no—though she had come close, at the dawn of time. A warrior, rumor claimed, had stolen her heart with his clever mind and pure soul. But he had died in some long-ago war and lost the ring he'd intended for her, and since then, Maeve had cherished her warriors above all others. They loved her for it—made her a mighty queen whom no one dared challenge. Celaena expected Rowan to puff his feathers at that, but he remained still and quiet on his perch.

Emrys told stories about the Fae Queen well into the night, painting a portrait of a ruthless, cunning ruler who could conquer the world if she wished, but instead kept to her forest realm of Doranelle, planting her stone city in the heart of a massive river basin.

Celaena picked through the details and committed them to memory, trying not to think about the prince perched a few feet above her who had willingly sworn a blood oath to the immortal monster who dwelled beyond the mountains. She was about to ask for another story when she caught the motion in the trees.

She choked on the piece of blackberry pie she was in the middle of devouring as the massive mountain cat trotted from the forest and across the rain-drenched grass, heading right for their door. The rain had darkened its golden fur, and its eyes gleamed in the torches. Did the guards not see it? Malakai was listening to his mate with rapt attention. She opened her mouth to shout a warning when she paused.

The guards saw everything. And weren't shooting. Because it wasn't a mountain cat, but—

In a flash that could have been distant lightning, the mountain cat became a tall, broad-shouldered male walking toward the open door. Rowan surged into flight, then shifted, seamlessly landing midstride as he walked into the rain.

The two males clasped forearms and clapped each other on the back—a quick, efficient greeting. With the rain and Emrys's narrating it was hard to hear, and she silently cursed her mortal ears as she strained to listen.

"I've been looking for you for six weeks," the golden-haired stranger said, his voice sharp but hollow. Not urgent, but tired and frustrated. "Vaughan said you were at the eastern border, but Lorcan said you were on the coast, inspecting the fleet. Then the twins told me that the queen had been all the way out here with you and returned alone, so I came on a hunch . . ." He was babbling, his lack of control at odds with his hard muscles and the weapons strapped to him. A warrior, like Rowan—though his surprisingly lovely face had none of the prince's severity.

Rowan put a hand on the male's shoulder. "I heard what happened, Gavriel." Was this one of Rowan's mysterious friends? She wished Emrys were free to identify him. Rowan had told her so little about his five companions, but it was clear that Rowan and Gavriel were more than acquaintances. She sometimes forgot that Rowan had a life beyond this fortress. It hadn't bothered her before, and she wasn't sure why remembering it now suddenly settled in her stomach like a dead weight, or why it suddenly mattered that Rowan at least acknowledge that she was there. That she existed.

Gavriel scrubbed at his face, his heavily muscled back expanding as he took a breath. "I know you probably don't want to—"

"Just tell me what you want and it will be done."

Gavriel seemed to deflate, and Rowan guided him toward another door. They both moved with unearthly, powerful grace—as if the rain itself parted to let them through. Rowan didn't even look back at her before he disappeared.

Rowan didn't come back for the rest of the night, and curiosity, not kindness, made her realize his friend probably hadn't had dinner. At least, no one had brought anything out of the kitchen, and Rowan hadn't called for food. So why not bring up a tray of stew and bread?

Balancing the heavy tray on her hip, she knocked on his door. The murmuring within went silent, and for a second, she had the mortifying thought that perhaps the male was here for a far more intimate reason. Then someone snapped, "What?" and she eased open the door wide enough to glance in. "I thought you might want some stew and—"

Well, the stranger *was* half-naked. And lying on his back atop Rowan's worktable. But Rowan was fully clothed, seated before him, and looking pissed as hell. Yes, she had certainly walked in on something private.

It took a heartbeat to note the flattened needles, the small cauldron-shaped vat of dark pigment, the rag soaked with ink and blood, and the tracings of a tattoo snaking from the stranger's left pectoral down his ribs and right to his hip bone.

"Get out," Rowan said flatly, lowering the needle. Gavriel lifted his head, the bright candles showing tawny eyes glazed with pain—and not necessarily from the markings being etched over his heart and rib cage. Words in the Old Language, just like Rowan's. There were already so many—most of them aged and interrupted by various scars.

"Do you want the stew?" she asked, still staring at the tattoo, the blood, the little iron pot of ink, and the way Rowan seemed as much at ease with the tools in his hands as he did with his weapons. Had he made his own tattoo?

"Leave it," he said, and she knew—just knew—that he would bite her head off later. Schooling her features into neutrality, she set the tray on the bed and walked back to the door.

"Sorry to interrupt." Whatever the tattoos were for, however they knew each other, she had no right to be in here. The pain in the stranger's eyes told her enough. She'd seen it in her own reflection plenty. Gavriel's attention darted between her and Rowan, his nostrils flaring—he was smelling her.

It was definitely time to get the hell out. "Sorry," she said again, and shut the door behind her.

She made it two steps down the hall before she had to stop and lean against the stone wall, rubbing at her face. Stupid. Stupid to even care what he did outside of training, to think he might consider sharing personal information with her, even if it was only that he was retiring to his rooms early. It hurt, though—more than she wanted to admit.

She was about to drag herself to her room when the door flung open down the hall and Rowan stormed out, practically glowing with ire. But just seeing the lividness written all over him had her riding that reckless, stupid edge again, and clinging to the anger was easier than embracing the quiet darkness that wanted to pull her down, down, down. Before he could start shouting, she asked, "Do you do it for money?"

A flicker of teeth. "One, it's none of your business. And two, I would never stoop so low." The look he gave her told her exactly what he thought of *her* profession.

"You know, it might be better if you just slapped me instead."

"Instead of what?"

"Instead of reminding me again and again how rutting worthless and awful and cowardly I am. Believe me, I can do the job well enough on my own. So just hit me, because I'm damned tired of trading insults. And you know what? You didn't even bother to tell me you'd be unavailable. If you'd said something, I never would have come. I'm sorry I did. But you just *left* me downstairs."

Saying those last words made a sharp, quick panic rise up in her, an aching pain that had her throat closing. "You left me," she repeated. Maybe it was only out of blind terror at the abyss opening up again around her, but she whispered, "I have no one left. No one."

She hadn't realized how much she meant it, how much she needed it not to be true, until now.

His features remained impassive, turning vicious, even, as he said, "There is nothing that I can give you. Nothing I *want* to give you. You are not owed an explanation for what I do outside of training. I don't care what you have been through or what you want to do with your life. The sooner you can sort out your whining and self-pity, the sooner I can be rid of you. You are nothing to me, and I *do not care*."

There was a faint ringing in her ears that turned into a roar. And beneath it, a sudden wave of numbness, a too-familiar lack of sight or sound or feeling. She didn't know why it happened, because she had been so dead set on hating him, but . . . it would have been nice, she supposed. It would have been nice to have one person who knew the absolute truth about her—and didn't hate her for it.

It would have been really, really nice.

She walked away without another word. With each step she took back to her room, that flickering light inside of her guttered.

And went out.

34

Celaena did not remember curling up in her bed, boots still on. She did not remember her dreams, or feel the pangs of hunger or thirst when she awoke, and she could barely respond to anyone as she trudged down to the kitchen and set about helping with breakfast. Everything swirled past in dull colors and whispers of sound. But she was still. A bit of rock in a stream.

Breakfast passed, and when it was done, in the quiet of the kitchen, the sounds sorted out into voices. A murmur—Malakai. A laugh—Emrys.

"Look," Emrys said, coming up to where Celaena stood at the kitchen sink, still staring out at the field. "Look what Malakai bought me."

She caught the flash of the golden hilt before she understood Emrys was holding out a new knife. It was a joke. The gods had to be playing a joke. Or they just truly, truly hated her.

The hilt was engraved with lotus blossoms, a ripple of lapis lazuli edging the bottom like a river wave. Emrys was smiling, eyes bright. But that knife, the gold polished and bright . . .

"I got it from a merchant from the southern continent," Malakai said from the table, his satisfied tone enough to tell her that he was beaming. "It came all the way from Eyllwe."

The numbness snapped.

Snapped with such a violent crack that she was surprised they didn't hear it.

And in its place was a screaming, high-pitched and keening, loud as a teakettle, loud as a storm wind, loud as the sound the maid had emitted the morning she'd walked into Celaena's parents' bedroom and seen the child lying between their corpses.

It was so loud that she could hardly hear herself as she said, "I do not care." She couldn't hear anything over that silent screaming, so she raised her own voice, breath coming fast, too fast, as she repeated, "I. Do. Not. Care."

Silence. Then Luca warily said from across the room, "Elentiya, don't be rude."

Elentiya. Elentiya. *Spirit that cannot be broken*.

Lies, lies, *lies*. Nehemia had lied about everything. About her stupid name, about her plans, about *every damn thing*. And she was *gone*. All that Celaena would have left of her were reminders like this—weapons similar to the ones the princess had worn with such pride. Nehemia was gone, and she had nothing left.

Trembling so hard she thought her body would fall apart at the seams, she turned. "I do not care about you," she hissed to Emrys and Malakai and Luca. "I do not care about your knife. I do not care about your stories or your little kingdom." She pinned Emrys with a stare. Luca and Malakai were across the room in an instant, stepping in front of the old man—teeth bared. Good. They should feel threatened. "So leave me alone. Keep your gods-damned lives to yourselves and *leave me alone*."

She was shouting now, but she couldn't stop hearing the screaming, couldn't hone the anger into anything, couldn't tell which way was up or down, only that Nehemia had lied about everything, and her friend once had sworn an oath not to—sworn an oath and broken it, just as she'd broken Celaena's own heart the day she let herself die.

She saw the tears in Emrys's eyes then. Sorrow or pity or anger, she didn't care. Luca and Malakai were still between them, growling softly. A family—they were a family, and they stuck together. They would rip her apart if she hurt one of them.

Celaena let out a low, joyless laugh as she took in the three of them. Emrys opened his mouth to say whatever it was he thought would help.

But Celaena let out another dead laugh and walked out the door.

After an entire night of tattooing the names of the fallen onto Gavriel's flesh and listening to the warrior talk about the men he'd lost, Rowan sent him on his way and headed for the kitchen. He found it empty save for the ancient male, who sat at the empty worktable, hands wrapped around a mug. Emrys looked up, his eyes bright and . . . grieving.

The girl was nowhere to be seen, and for a heartbeat, he hoped she'd left again, if only so he didn't have to face what he'd said yesterday. The door to the outside was open—as if someone had thrown it wide. She'd probably gone that way.

Rowan took a step toward it, nodding his greeting, but the old male looked him up and down and quietly said, "What are you doing?"

"What?"

Emrys didn't raise his voice as he said, "To that girl. What are you doing that makes her come in here with such emptiness in her eyes?"

"That's none of your concern."

Emrys pressed his lips into a tight line. "What do you see when you look at her, Prince?"

He didn't know. These days, he didn't know a damn thing. "That's none of your concern, either."

Emrys ran a hand over his weathered face. "I see her slipping away, bit by bit, because you shove her down when she so desperately needs someone to help her back up."

"I don't see why I would be of any use to—"

"Did you know that Evalin Ashryver was my friend? She spent almost a year working in this kitchen—living here with us, fighting to convince your queen that demi-Fae have a place in your realm. She fought for our rights until the very day she departed this kingdom—and the many years after, until she was murdered by those monsters across the sea. So I knew. I knew who her daughter was the moment you brought her into this kitchen. All of us who were here twenty-five years ago recognized her for what she is."

It wasn't often that he was surprised, but . . . Rowan just stared.

"She has no hope, Prince. She has no hope left in her heart. Help her. If not for her sake, then at least for what she represents—what she could offer all of us, you included."

"And what is that?" he dared ask.

Emrys met his gaze unflinchingly as he whispered, "A better world."

Celaena walked and walked, until she found herself by the tree-lined shore of a lake, glaringly bright in the midday sun. She figured it was as good a spot as any as she crumpled to the mossy bank, as her arms wrapped tight around herself and she bowed over her knees.

There was nothing that could be done to fix her. And she was . . . she was . . .

A whimpering noise came out of her, lips trembling so hard she had to clamp down to keep the sound inside.

But the sound was in her throat and her lungs and her mouth, and when she took a breath, it cracked out. Once she heard it, everything came spilling into the world, until her body ached with the force of it.

She vaguely felt the light shifting on the lake. Vaguely felt the sighing wind, warm as it brushed against her damp cheeks. And heard, so soft it was as if she dreamed it, a woman's voice whispering, *Why are you crying, Fireheart?*

It had been ten years—ten long years since she had heard her mother's voice. But she heard it then over the force of her weeping, as clear as if she knelt beside her. *Fireheart—why do you cry?*

"Because I am lost," she whispered onto the earth. "And I do not know the way."

It was what she had never been able to tell Nehemia—that for ten years, she had been unsure how to find the way home, because there was no home left.

Storm winds and ice crackled against her skin before she registered Rowan sitting down beside her, legs out, palms braced behind him in the moss. She raised her head, but didn't bother to wipe her face as she stared across the glittering lake.

"You want to talk about it?" he asked.

"No." Swallowing a few times, she yanked a handkerchief from her pocket and blew her nose, her head clearing with each breath.

They sat in silence, no sound but the quiet lapping of the lake on the mossy bank and the wind in the leaves. Then— "Good. Because we're going."

Bastard. She called him as much, and then asked, "Going *where*?"

He smiled grimly. "I think I've started to figure you out, Aelin Galathynius."

"What in every burning ring of hell," Celaena panted, gazing at the cave mouth nestled into the base of the craggy mountain, "are we doing here?"

It had been a five-mile hike. Uphill. With hardly anything in her stomach.

The trees butted against the gray stones, flowing up the slope for a ways and then fading into lichen-covered rock that eventually turned into the snow-capped peak that marked the barrier between Wendlyn and Doranelle beyond. For some reason, this hulking giant made the hair on her neck stand up. And it had nothing to do with the frozen wind.

Rowan strode into the gaping maw of the cave mouth, his pale-gray cloak flapping behind him. "Hurry up."

Pulling her own cloak tighter around her, she staggered after him. This was a bad sign. A horrible sign, actually, because whatever was in that cave . . .

She walked into the dark, following Rowan by the light on his hair, letting her eyes adjust. The ground was rocky, the stones small and worn smooth. And littered with rusted weapons, armor, and—clothes. No skeletons. Gods, it was so cold that she could see her breath, see—

"Tell me I'm hallucinating."

Rowan had stopped at the edge of an enormous frozen lake, stretching into the gloom. Sitting on a blanket in its center, the chains around his wrists anchored under the ice, was Luca.

Luca's chains clanked as he raised a hand in greeting. "I thought you'd never show. I'm *freezing*," he called, and tucked his hands back under his arms. The sound echoed throughout the chamber.

The thick sheet of ice covering the lake was so clear that she could see the water beneath—pale stones on the bottom, what looked to be old roots from trees long dead, and no sign of life whatsoever. An occasional sword or dagger or lance poked up from the stones. "What is this place?"

"Go get him," was Rowan's answer.

"Are you out of your mind?"

Rowan gave her a smile that suggested he was, in fact, insane. She stepped toward the ice, but he blocked her path with a muscled arm. "In your other form."

Luca's head was angled, as if trying to hear. "He doesn't know what I am," she murmured.

"You've been living in a fortress of demi-Fae, you know. He won't care."

That was the least of her concerns, anyway. "How dare you drag him into this?"

"You dragged him in yourself when you insulted him—and Emrys. The least you can do is retrieve him." He blew out a breath toward the lake, and the ice thawed by the shore, then hardened. Holy gods. He'd frozen the whole damn lake. He was *that* powerful?

"I hope you brought snacks!" Luca said. "I'm starving. Hurry up, Elentiya. Rowan said you had to do this as part of your training, and . . ." He prattled on and on.

"What is the gods-damned point of this? Just punishment for acting like an ass?"

"You can control your power in human form—keep it dormant. But the moment you switch, the moment you get agitated or angry or afraid, the moment you remember how much your power scares you, your magic rises up to protect you. It doesn't understand that *you* are the source of those feelings, not some external threat. When there *is* an outside threat, when you forget to fear your power long enough, you have control. Or *some* control." He pointed again to the sheet of ice between her and Luca. "So free him."

If she lost control, if her fire got out of her . . . well, fire and ice certainly went well together, didn't they? "What happens to Luca if I fail?"

"He'll be very cold and very wet. And possibly die." From the smile on his face, she knew he was enough of a sadist to let the boy go under with her.

"Were the chains really necessary? He'll go right to the bottom." A stupid, bleating kind of panic was starting to fill her veins.

When she held out her hand for the key to Luca's chains, Rowan shook his head. "Control is your key. And focus. Cross the lake, then figure out how to free him without drowning the both of you."

"Don't give me a lesson like you're some mystical-nonsense master! This is the *stupidest* thing I have ever had to—"

"Hurry," Rowan said with a wolfish grin, and the ice gave a collective groan. As if it was melting. Though some small voice in her head told her he wouldn't let the boy drown, she couldn't trust him, not after last night.

She took one step closer to the ice. "You are a *bastard*." When Luca was safely home, she would start finding ways to make Rowan's life a living hell. She punched through her inner veil, the pain barely registering as her features shifted.

"I was waiting to see your Fae form!" Luca said. "We were all taking bets on when—" And on and on.

She scowled at Rowan, his tattoo even more detailed now that she was seeing it with Fae eyes. "It gives me comfort to know that people like you have a special place in hell waiting for them."

"Tell me something I don't already know."

She gave him a particularly vulgar gesture as she stepped onto the ice.

As she took each tentative step—small ones at first—she could see the lake bottom sloping away into darkness, swallowing the spread of lost weapons. Luca had finally shut up.

It was only when she stepped past the visible edge of the rocky shelf and hovered over the dark depths that her breath hitched. She slid her foot, and the ice groaned.

Groaned, and *cracked*, spiderwebbing under her foot. She froze, gaping like a fool as the cracks spread wider and wider, and then—she kept moving. There was another crack beneath her boots. Did the ice move? "*Stop it*," she hissed at Rowan, but didn't dare look behind her.

Her magic shuddered awake, and she went still as death. *No.*

But there it was, filling up the spaces in her.

The ice emitted a deep groan that could only mean something cold and wet was coming her way really damn soon, and she took another step, if only because the way back seemed like it would shatter. She was sweating now—the magic, the fire was warming her from the inside out.

"Elentiya?" Luca asked, and she held out a hand toward him—a silent gesture to shut his stupid mouth as she closed her eyes and *breathed*, imagining the cold air around them filling her lungs, freezing over the well of power. Magic—it was *magic*. In Adarlan it was a death trap.

She clenched her hands into fists. Here it was *not* a death trap. In this land, she could have it, could wear whatever form she wished.

The ice stopped groaning, but it had clouded and thinned around her. She started sliding her feet, keeping as balanced and fluid as she could, humming a melody—a bit of a symphony that used to calm her. She let the beat anchor her, dull the edge of her panic.

The magic simmered to embers, pulsing with each breath. *I am safe*, she told it. *Relatively safe*. If Rowan was right, and it was just a reaction to protect her from some enemy . . .

Fire was the reason she'd been banned from the Library of Orynth when she was eight, after accidentally incinerating an entire bookcase of ancient manuscripts when she grew irritated with the Master Scholar lecturing her about decorum. It had been a beautiful, horrible relief to wake up one day not too many months after that and know magic was gone. That she could hold a book—hold what she adored most—and not worry about turning it to ash if she became upset or tired or excited.

Celaena Sardothien, gloriously mortal Celaena, never had to worry about accidentally scorching a playmate, or having a nightmare that might incinerate her bedroom. Or burning all of Orynth to the ground. Celaena had been everything Aelin wasn't. She had embraced that life, even if Celaena's accomplishments were death and torture and pain.

"Elentiya?" She'd been staring at the ice. Her magic flickered again.

Burning a city to the ground. That was the fear she overheard Melisande's emissary hiss at her parents and uncle. She'd been told he had come to see about an alliance, but she later understood he'd really come to gather information on *her*. Melisande had a young queen on its throne, and she wanted to assess the threat she might face from the heir of Terrasen one day. Wanted to know if Aelin Galathynius would become a weapon of war.

The ice fogged over, and a *crack* splintered through the air. The magic was pulsing its way out of her, snapping its jaws at every breath she took.

"*You* are in control now," Rowan said from the shore. "*You* are its master."

She was halfway there. She took one more step toward Luca, and the ice cracked further. His chains rustled—impatience, or fear?

She had never been in control. Even as Celaena, control had been an illusion. Other masters had held her reins.

"You are the keeper of your own fate," Rowan said softly from the shore, as if he knew exactly what was flowing through her head.

She hummed some more, the music wending its way from her memory. And somehow . . . somehow the flame grew quiet. Celaena took a step forward, then another. The power smoldering in her veins would never go away; she was far more likely to hurt someone if she didn't master it.

She scowled over her shoulder at Rowan, who was now striding along the shore, examining some of the fallen blades. There was a hint of triumph in his usually hollow eyes, but he turned away and approached a small crevice in the cave wall, feeling for something inside. She kept walking, the watery abyss deepening. She had mastered her mortal body as an assassin. Mastering her immortal power was just another task.

Luca's eyes were wide as she came at last within touching distance. "You have nothing to hide, you know. We all knew you could shift, anyway," he said. "And if it makes you feel any better, Sten's animal form is a pig. He won't even shift for shame."

She would have laughed—actually felt her insides tighten to bark out the sound that had been buried for months, but then she remembered the chains around his wrists. The magic had quieted down, but now . . . melt through them, or melt the ice where they were anchored and let him drag the chains back? If she went for the ice, she could easily send them right to the bottom of this ancient lake. And if she went for the chains . . . Well, she could lose control and send them to the bottom, but she could also wind up burning him. At best, branding him where the manacles were. At worst, melting his bones. Better to risk the ice.

"Erm," Luca said. "I'll forgive every awful thing you said earlier if we can go eat something right now. It smells awful in here." His senses had to be sharper than hers—the cave had only a faint hint of rust, mold, and rotting things.

"Just hold still and stop talking," she said, more sharply than she'd intended. But he shut up as she eased to the spot where Rowan had frozen the chains. As carefully as she could, she knelt, spreading her weight out evenly.

She slid one palm against the ice, eyeing the chain's path to the hanging length swaying in the water beneath.

Swaying—there must be a current. Which meant Rowan had to be constantly sealing the ice . . . The cold bit into her palm, and she eyed Luca on the fur blanket before she turned back to the anchor. If the ice broke, she'd have to grab him. Rowan was out of his damned mind.

She took several long breaths, letting the magic calm and cool and gutter. Then, hand pressed flat against the ice, she crooked an inner finger at her power and pulled out a tiny, burning thread. It flowed down her arm, snaked around her wrist, and then settled in her palm, her skin warming, the ice . . . *glowing* a bright red. Luca yelped as the ice splintered around them.

"*Control*," Rowan barked from the shore, pulling free a discarded sword from where it had been knocked into the little crevice in the wall, its golden hilt glinting. Celaena clamped on the magic so hard it suffocated. A small hole had melted where her palm had been—but not all the way through. Not big enough to free the chain.

She could master this. She could master herself again. The well inside of her filled up and she pushed back, willing only that thread to squeeze free and into the ice, burrowing like a worm, gnawing away at the cold . . . There was a clank of metal, and a hiss, and then— "Oh, thank the gods," Luca moaned, hauling the length of chain out of the hole.

She spooled the thread of power back into herself, into that well, and was suddenly cold.

"Please tell me you brought food," Luca said again.

"Is that why you came? Rowan promised you snacks?"

"I'm a growing boy." He winced when he looked at Rowan. "And you don't say no to him."

No, indeed, no one ever said no to him, and that was probably why Rowan thought a scheme like this was acceptable. Celaena sighed through her nose and looked at the small hole she'd made. A feat—a miracle. As she was about to stand and help Luca navigate the way back to shore, she glanced at the ice once more. No, not the ice—the water beneath.

Where a giant red eye was staring right at her.

35

The next four words that came out of Celaena's mouth were so vulgar that Luca choked. But Celaena didn't move as a massive, jagged, white line gleamed unnervingly far from that red eye.

"Get off the ice *now*," she breathed to Luca.

Because that jagged white line—those were teeth. Big, rip-your-arm-off-in-one-bite teeth. And they were floating up from the depths, toward the hole she'd made. That was why there were no skeletons—only the weapons that had failed the fools who'd wandered into this cave.

"Holy gods," Luca said, peering from behind her. "What *is* that?"

"Shut up and go," she hissed. On the shore, Rowan's eyes were wide, his face strained beneath his tattoo. He hadn't realized this lake wasn't empty.

"Now, Luca," Rowan growled, his sword out, the blade he'd swiped from the ground still sheathed in his other hand.

It was swimming toward them, lazily. Curious. As it neared, she could make out a snaking body as pale as the stones on the bottom of the lake. She'd never seen anything so huge, so ancient, and—and there was only a thin layer of ice keeping her separated from it.

When Luca started trembling, his tan skin going pale, Celaena surged to her feet, the ice groaning. "Don't look down," she said, gripping his elbow. A patch of thicker ice hardened under their feet and spread—a path for the shore. "*Go*," she told the boy, giving him a light shove. He started into a swift shuffle-slide. She let him get ahead, giving him time so she could guard his back, and glanced down again.

She swallowed her shout as a scaled, massive head stared up at her. Not a dragon or a wyvern, not a serpent or a fish, but something in between. It was missing an eye, the flesh scarred around the empty socket. What in hell had done that? Was there something *worse* down there, swimming at the belly of the mountain? Of course—of course she'd be left unarmed in the center of a lake lined with weapons.

"*Faster*," Rowan barked. Luca was already halfway to the shore.

Celaena broke into Luca's same shuffle-slide, not trusting herself to stay upright if she ran. Just as she took her third step, a flash of bone-white snapped up through the depths, twisting like a striking asp.

The long tail whipped against the ice and the world *bounced*.

She went up, legs buckling as the ice lifted from the blow, and then slammed onto her hands and knees. Celaena shoved down the magic that arose to protect and burn and maim. She scrambled and veered aside as the scaly, horned head hurtled toward the ice near her feet.

The surface jolted. Farther out, but getting closer, the ice was breaking. As if all of Rowan's concentration was now spent on keeping a thin bridge of ice frozen between her and the shore. "Weapon," she gasped out, not daring to take her attention off the creature.

"*Hurry*," Rowan barked, and Celaena lifted her head long enough to see him slide the blade he'd found across the ice, a brisk wind spinning it toward her. Luca abandoned the blanket, shuffle-running, and Celaena scooped up the golden-hilted sword as she followed him. A ruby the size of a chicken egg was embedded in the hilt, and despite the age of the scabbard, the blade shone when she whipped it free, as if it had been freshly polished. Something clattered from the scabbard onto the ice—a plain golden ring. She grabbed it, shoving it into her pocket, and ran faster, as—

The ice lifted again, the *boom* of that mighty tail as horrific as the moving surface beneath her. Celaena stayed up this time, sinking onto her haunches as she clutched the sword, part of her marveling at the balance and beauty if it; but Luca, slipping and sliding, went down. She reached him in a few heartbeats, hauling him up by the back of his tunic and gripping him tight as the ice lifted again and again and again.

They got past the drop-off, and she almost groaned with relief at the sight of the pale stone shelf beneath their feet. The ice behind them exploded up, freezing water showering them, and then—

She didn't stop as those nostrils huffed. Didn't stop hauling Luca toward Rowan, whose brow gleamed with sweat as massive talons scraped over the ice, gouging four deep lines.

She dragged the boy the last ten yards, then five, then they were on the shore and to Rowan, who let out a shuddering breath. Celaena turned in time to see something out of a nightmare trying to crawl onto the ice, its one red eye wild with hunger, its massive teeth promising a brutal and cold kind of death. As Rowan's sigh finished sounding, the ice melted, and the creature plunged below.

Back on solid ground, suddenly aware that the ice had also been a barrier, Celaena again grabbed Luca, who was looking ready to vomit, and bolted from the cave. There was nothing keeping that creature from climbing out of the water, and the sword was about as useful as a toothpick against it. Who knew how fast it could move on land?

Luca was chanting a steady stream of prayers to various gods as

Celaena yanked him down the rocky path and into the glaring afternoon sun, stumbling near-blind until they hit the murky woods, dodging trees mostly by luck, faster and faster downhill, and then—

A roar that shook the stones and sent the birds scattering into the air, the leaves rustling. But a roar of rage and hunger—not of triumph. As if the creature had reached the edge of the cave and, after millennia in the watery dark, could not withstand the sunshine. She didn't want to consider, as they kept running from the echoing roar, what might have happened if it had been night. What still might happen at nightfall.

After a while, she sensed Rowan behind them. Yet she cared only for her young charge, who panted and cursed all the way back to the fortress.

When Mistward was in sight, she told Luca only one thing before she sent him ahead: keep his mouth shut about what had happened in the cave. The moment the sounds of him crashing through the brush had faded, she turned.

Rowan was standing there, panting as well, his sword now sheathed. She plunged her new blade into the earth, the ruby in the hilt glowing in a patch of sunlight.

"I will *kill* you," she snarled. And launched herself at him.

Even in her Fae form, he still was faster than her, stronger, and dodged her with fluid ease. Slamming face-first into the tree was better than colliding with the stone walls of the fortress, though not by much. Her teeth sang, but she whirled and lunged for Rowan again, now standing so close, his teeth bared. He couldn't dodge her as she grabbed him by the front of his jacket and connected.

Oh, hitting him in the face felt *good*, even as her knuckles split and throbbed.

He snarled and threw her to the ground. The air whooshed out of her chest, and the blood trickling out of her nose shot back down her throat. Before he could sit on her, she got her legs around him and shoved with every ounce of that immortal strength. And just like that, he was pinned, his eyes wide with what could only be fury and surprise.

She hit him again, her knuckles barking in agony. "If you *ever* again bring someone else into this," she panted, hitting him on his tattoo—on that gods-damned tattoo. "If you ever endanger *anyone* else the way you did today . . ." The blood on her nose splattered on his face, mingling, she noted with some satisfaction, with blood from the blows she'd given him. "I will kill you." Another strike, a backhanded blow, and it vaguely occurred to her that he had gone still and was taking it. "I will rip out your rutting throat." She bared her canines. "You understand?"

He turned his head to the side to spit blood.

Her blood was pounding, so wild that every little restraint she'd locked into place shattered. She shoved back against it, and the distraction cost her. Rowan moved, and then she was under him again. She'd mangled his face, but he didn't seem to care as he growled, "I will do whatever I please."

"You will keep other people out of it!" she screamed, so loudly that the birds stopped chattering. She thrashed against him, gripping his wrists. "No one else!"

"Tell me why, Aelin."

That gods-damned name . . . She dug her nails into his wrists. "Because I am *sick* of it!" She was gulping down air, each breath shuddering as the horrific realization she'd been holding at bay since Nehemia's death came loose. "I told her I would not help, so she orchestrated her own death. Because she thought . . ." She laughed—a horrible, wild sound. "She thought that her death would spur me into action. She thought I could somehow do more than her—that she was worth more dead. And she lied—about *everything*. She lied to me because I was a coward, and I hate her for it. I hate her for leaving me."

Rowan still pinned her, his warm blood dripping onto her face.

She had said it. Said the words she'd been choking on for weeks and weeks. The rage seeped from her like a wave pulling away from shore, and she let go of his wrists. "Please," she panted, not caring that she was begging, "please don't bring anyone else into it. I will do anything you ask of me. But that is my line. Anything else but that."

His eyes were veiled as he finally let go of her arms. She gazed up at the canopy. She would not cry in front of him, not again.

He peeled back, the space between them now a tangible thing. "How did she die?"

She let the moisture against her back seep into her, cool her bones. "She manipulated a mutual acquaintance into thinking he needed to kill her in order to further his agenda. He hired an assassin, made sure I wasn't around, and had her murdered."

Oh, Nehemia. She had done it all out of a fool's hope, not realizing what a waste it was. She could have allied with flawless Galan Ashryver and saved the world—found a truly useful heir to the throne.

"What happened to the two men?" A cold question.

"The assassin I hunted down and left in pieces in an alleyway. And the man who hired him . . ." Blood on her hands, on her clothes, in her hair, Chaol's horrified stare. "I gutted him and dumped his body in a sewer."

They were two of the worst things she'd done, out of pure hatred and vengeance and rage. She waited for the lecture. But Rowan merely said, "Good."

She was so surprised that she looked at him—and saw what she had done. Not his already bruised and bleeding face, or his ripped jacket and shirt, now muddy. But right where she'd gripped his forearms, the clothes were burned through, the skin beneath covered in angry red welts.

Handprints. She'd burned right through the tattoo on his left arm. She was on her feet in an instant, wondering if she should be on her knees begging for forgiveness instead.

It must have hurt like hell. Yet he had taken it—the beating, the burning—while she let out those words that had clouded her senses for so many weeks now. "I am . . . so sorry," she started, but he held up a hand.

"You do not apologize," he said, "for defending the people you care about."

She supposed it was as much of an apology as she would ever get from him. She nodded, and he took that as answer enough. "I'm keeping the sword," she said, yanking it free of the earth. She'd be hard-pressed to find a better one anywhere in the world.

"You haven't earned it." He fell silent, then added, "But consider this a favor. Leave it in your rooms when we're training."

She would have debated, but this was a compromise, too. She wondered if he'd made a compromise any time in the last century. "What if that thing tracks us to the fortress once darkness falls?"

"Even if it does, it can't get past the wards." When she raised her brows, he said, "The stones around the fortress have a spell woven between them to keep out enemies. Even magic bounces off it."

"Oh." Well, that explained why they called it Mistward. A calm, if not pleasant, silence fell between them while they walked. "You know," she said slyly, "that's twice now you've made a mess of my training with your tasks. I'm fairly sure that makes you the worst instructor I've ever had."

He gave her a sidelong look. "I'm surprised it took you this long to call attention to it."

She snorted, and as they approached the fortress, the torches and candles ignited as if to welcome them home.

"I've never seen such a sorry sight," Emrys hissed as Rowan and Celaena trudged into the kitchen. "Blood and dirt and leaves over every inch of you both."

Indeed, they were something to behold, both of their faces swollen and lacerated, covered in each other's blood, hair a mess, and Celaena limping slightly. The knuckles of two of her fingers were split, and her knee throbbed from an injury she did not recall getting.

"No better than alley cats, brawling at all hours of the day and night," Emrys said, slamming two bowls of stew onto the worktable. "Eat, both of you. And then get cleaned up. Elentiya, you're off kitchen duty tonight and tomorrow." Celaena opened her mouth to object, but the old man held up a hand. "I don't want you bleeding on everything. You'll be more trouble than you're worth." Wincing, Celaena slumped next to Rowan on the bench, and swore viciously at the pain in her leg, her face, her arms. Swore at the pain in the ass sitting right next to her. "Clean out your mouth, too, while you're at it," Emrys snapped.

Luca was huddled by the fire, wide-eyed and making a sharp, cutting gesture across his neck, as if to warn Celaena about something. Even Malakai, seated at the other end of the table with two weathered sentries, was watching her with raised brows.

Rowan was already hunched over the table, digging into his stew. She glanced again at Luca, who frantically tapped his ears.

She hadn't shifted back. And—well, now they'd all noticed, even with the blood and dirt and leaves. Malakai met her stare, and she dared him—just *dared* the old man to say anything. But he shrugged and went back to his meal. So it really wasn't a surprise after all. She took a bite of her stew and had to bite back her moan. Was it her Fae senses, or was it even more delicious tonight?

Emrys was watching from the hearth, and Celaena gave him that challenging look, too. She punched back through the veil, aching as she shifted into her mortal form. But the old man brought her and

Rowan a loaf of bread and said, "Makes no difference to me whether your ears are pointy or round, or what your teeth look like. But," he added, looking at Rowan, "I can't deny I'm glad to see you got in a few punches this time."

Rowan's head snapped up from his bowl, and Emrys pointed a spoon at him. "Don't you think you've had enough of beating each other into a pulp?" Malakai stiffened, but Emrys went on, "What good does it accomplish, other than providing me with a scullery maid whose face scares the wits out of our sentries? You think any of us like to hear you two cursing and screaming every afternoon? The language you use is enough to curdle all the milk in Wendlyn."

Rowan lowered his head and mumbled something into his stew.

For the first time in a long, long while, Celaena felt the corners of her lips tug up.

And that was when Celaena walked to the old man—and got onto her knees. She apologized, profusely. To Emrys, to Luca, to Malakai. Apologized because they deserved it. They accepted, but Emrys still looked wary. Hurt, even. The shame of what she'd said to that man, to all of them, would cling to her for a while.

Though it made her stomach twist and palms sweat, though they didn't mention names, she wasn't all that surprised when Emrys told her that he and the other old Fae knew who she was, and that her mother had worked to help them. But she *was* surprised when Rowan took a spot at the sink and helped clean up after the evening meal.

They worked in an easy silence. There were still truths she hadn't confessed to, stains on her soul she couldn't yet explore or express. But maybe—maybe he wouldn't walk away whenever she did find the courage to tell him.

At the table, Luca was grinning with delight. Just seeing that smile—that bit of proof that today's events hadn't scarred him completely—made Celaena look at Emrys and say, "We had an adventure today."

Malakai set down his spoon and said, "Let me guess: it had something to do with that roar that sent the livestock into pandemonium."

Though Celaena didn't smile, her eyes crinkled. "What do you know of a creature that dwells in the lake under . . ." She glanced at Rowan to finish.

"Bald Mountain. And he can't know that story," Rowan said. "No one does."

"I am a Story Keeper," Emrys said, staring down at him with all the wrath of one of the iron figurines on the mantel. "And that means that the tales I collect might not come from Fae or human mouths, but I hear them anyway." He sat down at the table, folding his hands in front of him. "I heard one story, years ago, from a fool who thought he could cross the Cambrian Mountains and enter Maeve's realm without invitation. He was on his way back, barely clinging to life thanks to Maeve's wild wolves in the passes, so we brought him here while we sent for the healers."

Malakai murmured, "So that's why you wouldn't give him a moment's peace." A twinkle in those old eyes, and Emrys gave his mate a wry smile.

"He had a fierce infection, so at the time I thought it might have been a fever dream, but he told me he found a cave at the base of the Bald Mountain. He camped there, because it was raining and cold and he planned to be off at first light. Still, he felt like something was watching him from the lake. He drifted off, and awoke only because the ripples were lapping against the shore—ripples from the center of the lake. And just beyond the light of his fire, out in the deep, he spied something swimming. Bigger than a tree or any beast he'd ever seen."

"Oh, it was horrific," Luca cut in.

"You said you were out with Bas and the other scouts on border patrol today!" Emrys barked, then gave Rowan a look that suggested he'd better test his next meal for poison.

Emrys cleared his throat and was soon staring at the table again, lost in thought. "What the fool learned that night was this: the creature was almost as old as the mountain itself. It claimed to have been born in another world, but had slipped into this one when the gods were looking elsewhere. It had preyed upon Fae and humans until a mighty Fae warrior challenged it. And before the warrior was through, he carved one of the creature's eyes out—for spite or sport—and cursed the beast, so that as long as that mountain stood, the creature would be forced to live beneath it."

A monster from another realm. Had it been let in during the Valg wars, when demons had opened and closed portals to another world at will? How many of the horrific creatures that dwelled in this land were only here because of those long-ago battles over the Wyrdkeys?

"So it has dwelled in the labyrinth of underwater caves under the mountain. It has no name—for it forgot what it was called long ago, and those who meet it do not return home."

Celaena rubbed her arms, wincing as the split skin of her knuckles stretched with the movement. Rowan was staring directly at Emrys, his head cocked ever so slightly to the side. Rowan glanced at her, as if to make sure she was listening, and asked, "Who was the warrior who carved out its eye?"

"The fool didn't know, and neither did the beast. But the language it spoke was Fae—an archaic form of the Old Language, almost indecipherable. It could remember the gold ring he bore, but not what he looked like."

It took every ounce of effort not to grab for her pocket and the ring she'd put in there, or to examine the sword she'd left by the door, and the ruby that might not be a ruby after all. But it was impossible—too much of a coincidence.

She might have given in to the urge to look had Rowan not reached for his glass of water. He hid it well, and she didn't think anyone else noticed, but as the sleeve of his jacket shifted, he winced, ever so slightly. From the burns she'd given him. They'd been blistering earlier—they must be screaming in agony now.

Emrys pinned the prince with a stare. "No more adventures."

Rowan glanced at Luca, who seemed about to explode with indignation. "Agreed."

Emrys didn't back down. "And no more brawling."

Rowan met Celaena's stare over the table. His expression yielded nothing. "We'll try."

Even Emrys deemed that an acceptable answer.

Despite the exhaustion that slammed into her like a wall, Celaena couldn't sleep. She kept thinking of the creature, of the sword and the ring she'd examined for an hour without learning anything, and the control, however shaky, she'd managed to have on the ice. Yet she kept circling back to what she'd done to Rowan—how badly she'd burned him.

His pain tolerance must be tremendous, she thought as she twisted on her cot, huddled against the cold in the room. She eyed her tin of salve. *He should have gone to a healer for those burns.* She tossed and turned for another five minutes before she yanked on her boots, grabbed the tin, and left. She'd probably get her head bitten off again, but she wouldn't get a wink of sleep if she were too busy feeling guilty. Gods, she felt *guilty*.

She knocked softly on his door, half hoping he wasn't there. But he snapped "*What*?" and she winced and went in.

His room was toasty and warm, if not a little old and shabby, especially the worn rugs thrown over much of the gray stone floor. A large four-poster bed occupied much of the space, a bed that was still made—and empty. Rowan was seated at the worktable in front of the carved fireplace, shirtless and examining what looked to be a map marked with the locations of those bodies.

His eyes flashed with annoyance, but she ignored him as she studied the massive tattoo that went from his face down his neck and shoulders and covered the entirety of his left arm, straight to his fingertips. She hadn't really looked that day in the woods, but now she marveled at its beautiful, unbroken lines—save for the manacle-like burn around his wrist. Both wrists.

"What do you want?"

She hadn't inspected his body too closely before, either. His chest—tan enough to suggest he spent a good amount of time without a shirt—was sculpted with muscle and covered in thick scars. From fights or battles or the gods knew what. A warrior's body that he'd had centuries to hone.

She tossed the salve to him. "I thought you might want this."

He caught it with one hand, but his eyes remained on her. "I deserved it."

"Doesn't mean I can't feel bad."

He turned the tin over and over between his fingers. There was a particularly long and nasty scar down his right pectoral—where had it come from? "Is this a bribe?"

"Give it back, if you're going to be a pain in my ass." She held out her hand.

But he closed his fingers around the tin, then set it on his worktable. He said, "You could heal yourself, you know. Heal me, too. Nothing major, but you have that gift."

She knew—sort of. Her magic had sometimes healed her injuries without conscious thought. "It's—it's the drop of water affinity I inherited from Mab's line." The fire had been the gift of her father's bloodline. "My mother"—the words made her sick, but she said them for some reason—"told me that the drop of water in my magic was my salvation—and sense of self-preservation." A nod from him, and she admitted, "I wanted to learn to use it like the other healers—long ago, I mean. But never was allowed to. They said . . . well, it wouldn't be all that useful, since I didn't have much of it, and Queens don't become healers." She should stop talking.

For some reason, her stomach dropped as he said, "Go to bed. Since you're banned from the kitchen tomorrow, we're training at dawn." Well, she certainly deserved the dismissal after burning him like that. So she turned, and maybe she looked as pathetic as she felt, because he suddenly said, "Wait. Shut the door."

She obeyed. He didn't give her leave to sit, so she leaned against the wooden door and waited. He kept his back to her, and she watched the powerful muscles expand and contract as he took a deep breath. Then another. Then—

"When my mate died, it took me a very, very long time to come back."

It took her a moment to think of what to say. "How long ago?"

"Two hundred three years, twenty-seven days ago." He gestured to the tattoo on his face, neck, arms. "This tells the story of how it happened. Of the shame I'll carry until my last breath."

The warrior who had come the other day had such hollow eyes . . . "Others come to you to have their own grief and shame tattooed on them."

"Gavriel lost three of his soldiers in an ambush in the southern mountains. They were slaughtered. He survived. For as long as he's been a warrior, he's tattooed himself with the names of those under his command who have fallen. But where the blame lies has little to do with the point of the markings."

"Were you to blame?"

Slowly, he turned—not quite all the way, but enough to give her a sidelong glance. "Yes. When I was young, I was . . . ferocious in my efforts to win valor for myself and my bloodline. Wherever Maeve sent me on campaigns, I went. Along the way, I mated a female of our race. Lyria," he said, almost reverently. "She sold flowers in the market in Doranelle. Maeve disapproved, but . . . when you meet your mate, there is nothing you can do to alter it. She was mine, and no one could tell me otherwise. Mating her cost me Maeve's favor, and I still yearned so badly to prove myself. So when war came calling and Maeve offered me a chance to redeem myself, I took it. Lyria begged me not to go. But I was so arrogant, so misguided, that I left her at our mountain home and went off to war. I left her alone," he said, and again looked at Celaena.

You left me, she had said to him. That was when he'd snapped—the wounds of centuries ago rising up to swallow him as viciously as her own past consumed her.

"I was gone for months, winning all that glory I so foolishly sought. And then we got word that our enemies had been secretly trying to gain entrance to Doranelle through the mountain passes." Her stomach dropped to her feet. Rowan ran a hand through his hair, scratched at his face. "I flew home. As fast as I'd ever flown. When I got there, I found that . . . found she had been with child. And they had slaughtered her anyway, and burnt our house to cinders.

"When you lose a mate, you don't . . ." A shake of the head. "I lost all sense of self, of time and place. I hunted them down, all the males who hurt her. I took a long while killing them. She was pregnant—had been pregnant since I'd left her. But I'd been so enamored with my own foolish agenda that I hadn't scented it on her. I left my pregnant mate alone."

Her voice broke, but she managed to say, "What did you do after you killed them?"

His face was stark and his eyes focused on some far-off sight. "For ten years, I did nothing. I vanished. I went mad. Beyond mad. I felt nothing at all. I just . . . left. I wandered the world, in and out of my forms, hardly marking the seasons, eating only when my hawk told me it needed to feed or it would die. I *would* have let myself die—except I . . . couldn't bring myself . . ." He trailed off and cleared his throat. "I might have stayed that way forever, but Maeve tracked me down. She said it was enough time spent in mourning, and that I was to serve her as prince and commander—to work with a handful of other warriors to protect the realm. It was the first time I had spoken to anyone since that day I found Lyria. The first time I'd heard my name—or remembered it."

"So you went with her?"

"I had nothing. No one. At that point, I hoped serving her might get me killed, and then I could see Lyria again. So when I returned to Doranelle, I wrote the story of my shame on my flesh. And then I bound myself to Maeve with the blood oath, and have served her since."

"How—how did you come back from that kind of loss?"

"I didn't. For a long while I couldn't. I think I'm still . . . not back. I might never be."

She nodded, lips pressed tight, and glanced toward the window.

"But maybe," he said, quietly enough that she looked at him again. He didn't smile, but his eyes were inquisitive. "Maybe we could find the way back together."

He would not apologize for today, or yesterday, or for any of it. And she would not ask him to, not now that she understood that in the weeks she had been looking at him it had been like gazing at a reflection. No wonder she had loathed him.

"I think," she said, barely more than a whisper, "I would like that very much."

He held out a hand. "Together, then."

She studied the scarred, callused palm, then the tattooed face, full of a grim sort of hope. Someone who might—who *did* understand what it was like to be crippled at your very core, someone who was still climbing inch by inch out of that abyss.

Perhaps they would never get out of it, perhaps they would never be whole again, but . . . "Together," she said, and took his outstretched hand.

And somewhere far and deep inside her, an ember began to glow.

PART TWO

HEIR OF FIRE

36

"Things are ready for your meeting tonight with Captain Westfall?" Aedion could have sworn Ren Allsbrook bristled as he bit out the name.

Seated beside the young lord on the ledge of the roof of the warehouse apartment, Aedion considered Ren's tone, decided it wasn't enough of a challenge to warrant a verbal slap, and gave a nod as he went back to cleaning his nails with one of his fighting knives.

Ren had been recovering for days now, after the captain had set him up in the guest room of the apartment. The old man had refused to take the main bedroom, saying he'd prefer the couch, but Aedion wondered what exactly Murtaugh had observed when they arrived in the apartment. If he suspected who the owner was—Celaena or Aelin or both—he revealed nothing.

Aedion hadn't seen Ren since the opium den, and didn't really know why he'd bothered to come tonight. He said, "You've managed to build yourself a network of lowlifes here. That's a far cry from the lofty towers of Allsbrook Castle."

Ren's jaw tightened. "You're a far cry from the white towers of Orynth, too. We all are." A breeze ruffled Ren's shaggy hair. "Thank you. For—helping that night."

"It was nothing," Aedion said coolly, giving him a lazy smile.

"You killed for me, then hid me. That isn't nothing. I owe you."

Aedion was plenty used to accepting gratitude from other men, from his men, but this . . . "You should have told me," he said, dropping the grin as he watched the golden lights twinkling across the city, "that you and your grandfather had no home." Or money. No wonder Ren's clothes were so shabby. The shame Aedion had felt that night had almost overwhelmed him—and had haunted him for the past few days, honing his temper to a near-lethal edge. He'd tried working it off with the castle guards, but sparring with the men who protected the king had only sharpened it.

"I don't see how it's relevant to anything," Ren said tightly. Aedion could understand pride. The kind Ren had went deep, and admitting this vulnerability was as hard for him as it was for Aedion to accept Ren's gratitude. Ren said, "If you find out how to break the spell on magic, you're going to do it, right?"

"Yes. It could make a difference in whatever battles lie ahead."

"It didn't make a difference ten years ago." Ren's face was a mask of ice, and then Aedion remembered. Ren hardly had a drop of magic. But Ren's two elder sisters . . . The girls had been away at their mountain school when everything went to hell. A school for magic.

As if reading his thoughts, as if this were a reprieve from the city below them, Ren said, "When the soldiers dragged us to the butchering blocks, that was what they mocked my parents about. Because even with their magic, my sisters' school was defenseless—they could do nothing against ten thousand soldiers."

"I'm sorry," Aedion said. That was all he could offer for the time being, until Aelin returned.

Ren looked right at him. "Going back to Terrasen will be . . . hard. For me, and for my grandfather." He seemed to struggle with the words, or just with the idea of telling anyone anything, but Aedion gave him the time he needed. At last Ren said, "I'm not sure I'm civilized enough anymore. I don't know if . . . if I could be a lord, even. If my people would *want* me as lord. My grandfather is better suited, but he's an Allsbrook by marriage and he says he doesn't want to rule."

Ah. Aedion found himself actually pausing—contemplating. The wrong word, the wrong reaction, could make Ren shut up forever. It shouldn't matter, but it did. So he said, "My life has been war and death for the past ten years. It will probably be war and death for the next few as well. But if there's ever a day when we find peace . . ." Gods, that word, that beautiful word. "It'll be a strange transition for all of us. For whatever it's worth, I don't see how the people of Allsbrook wouldn't embrace a lord who spent years trying to break Adarlan's rule—or a lord who spent years in poverty for that dream."

"I've . . . done things," Ren said. "Bad things." Aedion had suspected as much from the moment Ren gave them the address of the opium den.

"So have we all," Aedion said. *So has Aelin*. He wanted to say it, but he still didn't want Ren or Murtaugh or anyone knowing a damn thing about her. It was her story to tell.

Aedion knew the conversation was about to take a turn for the ugly when Ren tensed and asked too quietly, "What do you plan to do about Captain Westfall?"

"Right now, Captain Westfall is useful to me, and useful to our queen."

"So as soon as he's outlived his usefulness . . ."

"I'll decide that when the time comes—if it's safe to leave him alive." Ren opened his mouth, but Aedion added, "This is the way it has to be. The way I operate." Even if he'd helped save Ren's life and given him a place to stay.

"I wonder what our queen will think of the way you operate."

Aedion flashed him a glare that had sent men running. But he knew Ren wasn't particularly scared of him, not with what he had seen and endured. Not after Aedion had killed for him.

Aedion said, "If she's smart, then she'll let me do what needs to be done. She'll use me as the weapon I am."

"What if she wishes to be your friend? Would you deny her that, too?"

"I will deny her nothing."

"And if she asks you to be her king?"

Aedion bared his teeth. "Enough."

"Do you want to be king?"

Aedion swung his legs back onto the roof and stood. "All I want," he snarled, "is for my people to be free and my queen restored to her throne."

"They burned the antler throne, Aedion. There is no throne for her."

"Then I'll build one myself from the bones of our enemies."

Ren winced as he stood as well, his injuries no doubt bothering him, and kept his distance. He might not be afraid, but he wasn't stupid. "Answer the question. Do you want to be king?"

"If she asked me, I would not refuse her." It was the truth.

"That's not an answer."

He knew why Ren had asked. Even Aedion was aware that he *could* be king—with his legion and ties to the Ashrvyers, he'd be an advantageous match. A warrior-king would make any foes think twice. Even before their kingdom shattered, he'd heard the rumors . . .

"My only wish," Aedion said, growling in Ren's face, "is to see her again. Just once, if that's all the gods will allow me. If they grant me more time than that, then I'll thank them every damn day of my life.

But for now, all I'm working for is to see her, to know for certain that she's real—that she survived. The rest is none of your concern."

He felt Ren's eyes on him as he vanished through the door to the apartment below.

The tavern was packed with soldiers on rotation home to Adarlan, the heat and reek of bodies making Chaol wish Aedion had done this alone. There was no hiding now that he and Aedion were *drinking friends*, as the general trumpeted for everyone to hear while the soldiers cheered.

"Better to hide it right under everyone's noses than pretend, eh?" Aedion murmured to Chaol as yet another free drink was slapped down on their stained, sodden table, courtesy of a soldier who had bowed—actually *bowed*—to Aedion. "For the Wolf," said the scarred and tan-skinned soldier, before returning to his packed table of comrades.

Aedion saluted the man with the mug, getting a cheer in response, and there was nothing faked about his feral grin. It hadn't taken Aedion long to find the soldiers Murtaugh thought they should question—soldiers who had been stationed at one of the suspected spell origin points. While Aedion had been searching for the right group of men, Chaol had taken the time to go about his own duties—which now included considering a candidate to replace him—and packing for his return to Anielle. He'd come into Rifthold today with the excuse of finding a company to ship his first trunk of belongings, a task he'd actually accomplished. He didn't want to think of what his mother would do when the trunk of books arrived at the Keep.

Chaol didn't bother looking pleasant as he said, "Get on with it."

Aedion stood, hoisting his mug. As though they'd all been watching him, the room quieted.

"Soldiers," he said, loud and soft at once, grave and reverent. He turned in place, mug still upheld. "For your blood, for your scars, for every dent in your shield and nick in your sword, for every friend and foe dead before you . . ." The mug raised higher, and Aedion bowed his head, golden hair gleaming in the light. "For what you have given, and have yet to give, I salute you."

For a heartbeat, as the room thundered with roars and cries, Chaol beheld what truly made Aedion a threat—what made him a god to these men, and why the king tolerated his insolence, ring or no ring.

Aedion was not a noble in a castle, sipping wine. He was metal and sweat, sitting in this filthy tavern, drinking their ale. Whether it was real or not, they believed he cared about them, listened to them. They preened when he remembered their names, their wives' and sisters' names, and slept assured that he saw them as his brothers. Aedion made sure that they believed he would fight and die for them. Thus they would fight and die for him.

And Chaol was afraid, but not for himself.

He was afraid of what would come when Aedion and Aelin were reunited. For he'd seen in her that same glittering ember that made people look and listen. Had seen her stalk into a council meeting with Councilor Mullison's head and smile at the King of Adarlan, every man in that room enthralled and petrified by the dark whirlwind of her spirit. The two of them together, both of them lethal, working to build an army, to ignite their people . . . He was afraid of what they would do to his kingdom.

Because this was still his kingdom. He was working for Dorian, not Aelin—not Aedion. And he didn't know where all of this put him.

"A contest!" Aedion called, standing on the bench. Chaol hadn't moved during the long, long hour Aedion had been saluted and toasted by half the men in this room, each one getting a turn to stand and tell his story to the general.

When Aedion had enough of being serenaded by his own enemy, his Ashryver eyes brilliant with a rush that Chaol knew was precisely because he hated each and every one of them and they were eating out of his palm like rabbits, the general roared for the contest.

There were a few shouted suggestions for drinking games, but Aedion hoisted his mug again, and silence fell. "Farthest to travel drinks for free."

There were cries of Banjali, Orynth, Melisande, Anielle, Endovier, but then . . . "Quiet, all of you!" An older, gray-haired soldier stood. "I got you all beat." He lifted his glass to the general, and pulled a scroll from his vest. Release papers. "I just spent five years at Noll."

Bulls-eye. Aedion thumped the empty seat at the table. "Then you drink with us, my friend." The room cheered again.

Noll. It was a speck on the map at the farthest end of the Deserted Peninsula.

The man sat down, and before Aedion could raise a finger to the barkeep, a fresh pint was before the stranger. "Noll, eh?" Aedion said.

"Commander Jensen, of the twenty-fourth legion, sir."

"How many men were under you, commander?"

"Two thousand—all of us sent back here last month." Jensen took a long drink. "Five years, and we're done just like that." He snapped his scarred, thick fingers.

"I take it His Majesty didn't give you any warning?"

"With all due respect, general . . . he didn't tell us shit. I got the word that we were to move out because new forces were coming in, and we weren't needed anymore."

Chaol kept his mouth shut, listening, as Aedion had told him to do.

"What for? Is he sending you to join another legion?"

"No word yet. Didn't even tell us who was taking our place."

Aedion grinned. "At least you're not in Noll anymore."

Jensen looked into his drink, but not before Chaol caught the shadow in the man's eyes.

"What was it like? Off the record, of course," Aedion said.

Jensen's smile had faded, and when he looked up, there was no light in his eyes. "The volcanoes are active, so it's always dark, you see, because the ash covers everything. And because of the fumes, we always had headaches—sometimes men went mad from them. Sometimes we got nosebleeds from them, too. We got our food once a month, occasionally less than that depending on the season and when the ships could bring in supplies. The locals wouldn't make the trek across the sands, no matter how much we threatened and bribed them."

"Why? Laziness?"

"Noll isn't much—just the tower and town we built around it. But the volcanoes were sacred, and ten years ago, maybe a bit longer, apparently we . . . not my men, because I wasn't there, but rumor says the king took a legion into those volcanoes and sacked the temple." Jensen shook his head. "The locals spit on us, even the men who weren't there, for that. The tower of Noll was built afterward, and then the locals cursed it, too. So it was always just us."

"A tower?" Chaol said quietly, and Aedion frowned at him.

Jensen drank deeply. "Not that we were ever allowed in."

"The men who went mad," Aedion said, a half smile on his face. "What did they do, exactly?"

The shadows were back and Jensen glanced around him, not to see who was listening, but almost as if he wanted to find a way out of this conversation. But then he looked at the general and said, "Our reports say, general, that we killed them—arrows to the throat. Quick and clean. But . . ."

Aedion leaned closer. "Not a word leaves this table."

A vague nod. "The truth was, by the time we got our archers ready, the men who went mad had already bashed their own skulls in. Every time, as if they couldn't get the pain out."

Celaena claimed Kaltain and Roland had complained about headaches. As a result of the king's magic being used on them, his horrible power. And she had told him she got a pounding headache when she uncovered those secret dungeons beneath the castle. Dungeons that led to . . .

"The tower—you were never allowed in?" Chaol ignored Aedion's warning glare.

"There was no door. Always seemed more decorative than anything. But I hated it—we all did. It was just this awful black stone."

Just like the clock tower in the glass castle. Built around the same time, if not a few years before. "Why bother?" Aedion drawled. "A waste of resources, if you ask me."

There were still so many shadows in the man's eyes, full of stories that Chaol didn't dare ask about. The commander drained his glass and stood. "I don't know why they bothered—with Noll, or Amaroth. We'd sometimes send men up and down the Western Sea with messages between the towers, so we knew they had a similar one. We didn't even really know what the hell we were all doing out there, anyway. There was no one to fight."

Amaroth. The other outpost, and Murtaugh's other possible origin point for their spell. Due north from Noll. Both the same distance from Rifthold. Three towers of black stone, all three points making an equilateral triangle. It had to be part of the spell, then.

Chaol traced the rim of his glass. He had sworn to keep Dorian out of it, to leave him alone . . .

He had no way of testing out any theory, and didn't want to get within ten feet of that clock tower. But perhaps the theory could be tested on a small scale. Just to see if they were right about what the king had done. Which meant . . .

He needed Dorian.

37

It was two weeks of training for Manon and her Thirteen. Two weeks of waking up before the sun to fly each canyon run, to master it as one unit. Two weeks of scratches and sprained limbs, of near deaths from falls or the wyverns squabbling or just stupid miscalculation.

But slowly, they developed instincts—not just as a fighting unit, but as individual riders and mounts. Manon didn't like the thought of the mounts eating the foul-tasting meat raised within the mountain, so twice a day they hunted the mountain goats, swooping to pluck them off the mountainsides. It wasn't long before the witches started eating the goats themselves, building hasty fires in the mountain passes to cook their breakfast and evening meals. Manon didn't want any of them—mounts or riders—taking another bite of the food given to them by the king's men, or tasting the men themselves. If it smelled and tasted strange, odds were something was wrong with it.

She didn't know if it was the fresh meat or the extra lessons, but the Thirteen were starting to outpace every coven. To the point where Manon ordered the Thirteen to hold back whenever the Yellowlegs gathered to watch their lessons.

Abraxos was still a problem. She hadn't dared take the Crossing with him, as his wings, while slightly stronger, weren't better by much—at least not enough to brave the sheer plunge through the narrow pass. Manon had been chewing it over every night when the Thirteen gathered in her room to compare notes about flying, their iron nails glinting as they used their hands to demonstrate the ways they'd taught their wyverns to bank, to take off, to do some fancy maneuver.

For all the excitement, they were exhausted. Even the lofty-headed Bluebloods had their tempers on tight leashes, and Manon had been called in a dozen times now to break apart brawls.

Manon used her downtime to see Abraxos—to check on his iron claws and teeth, to take him out for extra rides when everyone else had passed out in their cots. He needed as much training as he could get, and she liked the quiet and stillness of the night, with the silvered mountain peaks and the river of stars above, even if it made waking up the next day difficult.

So after braving the wrath of her grandmother, Manon won two days off for the Blackbeaks, convincing her that if they didn't rest, there would be outright war in the middle of the mess hall and the king wouldn't have an aerial cavalry left to ride his wyverns into battle.

They got two days to sleep and eat and see to whatever needs only the men across the mountain could provide. That was something a good number of the Thirteen were doing, as she'd seen Vesta, Lin, Asterin, and the demon twins stalking across the bridge.

No sleeping for Manon today or tomorrow. No eating. Or bedding men.

No, she was taking Abraxos out into the Ruhnns.

He was already saddled, and Manon ensured Wind-Cleaver was tightly strapped to her back as she mounted him. The saddlebags were an unexpected weight behind her, and she made a note to start training the Thirteen and the rest of the covens with them. If they were to be an army, then they'd carry their supplies, as most soldiers did. And training with weights would make them faster when it came time to fly without them.

"You sure I can't convince you not to go?" the overseer said as she paused at the back gates. "You know the stories as well as I do—this won't come without a cost."

"His wings are weak, and so far everything else we've tried to reinforce them has failed," she said. "It might be the only material that could patch up his wings and withstand the winds. As I don't see any markets nearby, I suppose I'll have to go directly to the source."

The overseer frowned at the gray sky beyond. "Bad day for flying—storm's coming."

"It's the only day I have." Even as she said it, she wished that she could take the Thirteen into the skies when the storm hit—to train them in that, too.

"Be careful, and think through any bargain they offer you."

"If I wanted your advice, I'd ask for it, mortal," she said, but he was right.

Still, Manon led Abraxos out through the gates and to their usual takeoff spot. They had a long way to fly today and tomorrow—all the way to the edge of the Ruhnn Mountains.

To find spidersilk. And the legendary Stygian spiders, large as horses and deadlier than poison, who wove it.

The storm hit right as Manon and Abraxos circled the westernmost outcropping of the Ruhnns. Through the icy rain lashing her face and soaking right through her layers of clothes, she could see that the mist hung low over the mountains, veiling much of the ash-gray, jagged labyrinth below.

With the rising winds and lightning thrashing around them, Manon grounded Abraxos on the only open bit of land she could spot. She'd wait until the storm had passed, and then they would take to the skies and scan the area until they found the spiders. Or at least clues about their whereabouts—mostly in the form of bones, she expected.

But the storm continued, and though she and Abraxos pressed themselves into the side of a little cliff, it did nothing to shield them. She would have preferred snow over this freezing rain, which came with so much wind that she couldn't light a fire.

Night fell swiftly thanks to the storm, and Manon had to put her iron teeth away to keep them from chattering right through her lip. Her hood was useless, soaked and dripping in her eyes, and even Abraxos had curled into as tight a ball as he could against the storm.

Stupid, horrible idea. She pulled a goat leg from a saddle bag and tossed it to Abraxos, who uncurled himself long enough to chomp it down, and then went right back to shielding himself against the storm. She cursed herself for a fool as she choked down her own meal of soggy bread and a freezing apple, then gnawed on a bit of cheese.

It was worth it. To secure victory for the Thirteen, to be Wing Leader, one night in a storm was nothing. She'd been through worse, trapped in snowy mountain passes with fewer layers of clothes, no way out, and no food. She'd survived storms some witches didn't awaken from the next morning. But she still would have preferred snow.

Manon studied the labyrinth of rock around them. She could feel eyes out there—observing. Yet nothing came closer, nothing dared. So after a while, she curled on her side, just like Abraxos, her head and chest angled toward the cliff face, and tucked her arms across herself, holding tight.

Mercifully, it stopped raining in the night, or at least the angle of the wind shifted to stop pounding on them. She slept better after that, but she still shook from cold—though it felt slightly warmer. Those small hints of warmth and dryness were probably what kept her from shaking to death or getting ill, she realized as she dozed off, awakening at the gray light of dawn.

When she opened her eyes, she was in shadow—shadow, but dry and warm, thanks to the massive wing shielding her from the elements and the heat of Abraxos's breath filling the space like a little furnace. He was still snoozing—a deep, heavy sleep.

She had to brush ice crystals off his outstretched wing before he came awake.

The storm had cleared and the skies were an untamed blue—clear enough that they only needed to circle the western outcropping of the Ruhnns once before Manon spotted what she'd been looking for. Not just bones, but trees shrouded in dusty gray webs like mourning widows.

It wasn't spidersilk, she saw as Abraxos swooped low, gliding over the trees. These were only ordinary webs.

If you could call an entire mountain wood shrouded in webs ordinary. Abraxos growled every so often at something below—shadows or whispers she couldn't see. But she did notice the crawling on the branches, spiders of every shape and size, as if they had all been summoned here to live under the protection of their massive brethren.

It took them half the morning to find the ashen mountain caves hovering above the veiled wood, where bare bones littered the ground. She circled a few times, then set Abraxos down on an outcropping of stone at one of the cave mouths, the cliff face behind them a sheer plunge to a dried-out ravine below.

Abraxos paced like a mountain cat, tail lashing this way and that as he watched the cave.

She pointed to the edge of the cliff. "Enough. Sit down and stop moving. You know why we're here. So don't ruin it."

He huffed but plopped down, shooting grayish dust into the air. He draped his long tail along the length of the cliff's edge, a physical barrier between Manon and the plunge. Manon stared him down for a moment before an otherworldly, feminine laugh flittered from the cave mouth. "Now that beast is one we have not seen for an age."

Manon kept her face blank. The light was bright enough to reveal several ancient, merciless eyes looming within the cave mouth—and three massive shadows lurking behind. The voice said, closer now, pincers clicking like an accompanying drum, "And it has been an age since we dealt with the Ironteeth."

Manon didn't dare touch Wind-Cleaver as she said, "The world is changing, sister."

"Sister," the spider mused. "I suppose we are sisters, you and I. Two faces of the same dark coin, from the same dark maker. Sisters in spirit, if not in flesh."

Then she emerged into the murky light, the mist sweeping past her like a pilgrimage of phantom souls. She was black and gray, and the sheer mass of her was enough to make Manon's mouth go dry. Despite the size, she was elegantly built, her legs long and smooth, her body streamlined and gleaming. Glorious.

Abraxos let out a soft growl, but Manon held out a hand to silence him.

"I see now," Manon said softly, "why my Blueblood sisters still worship you."

"Do they, now?" The spider remained motionless, but the three behind her crept closer, silent and observing with their many dark eyes. "We can hardly recall the last time the Blueblood priestesses brought their sacrifices to our foothills. We do miss them."

Manon smiled tightly. "I can think of a few I'd like to send your way."

A soft, wicked laugh. "A Blackbeak, no doubt." Those eight massive eyes took her in, swallowed her whole. "Your hair reminds me of our silk."

"I suppose I should be flattered."

"Tell me your name, Blackbeak."

"My name does not matter," Manon said. "I've come to bargain."

"What would a Blackbeak witch want with our precious silk?"

She turned to reveal the vigilant Abraxos, his focus pinned on the massive spider, tense from the tip of his nose to his iron-spiked tail. "His wings need reinforcement. I heard the legends and wondered if your silk might help."

"We have bartered our silk to merchants and thieves and kings, to be spun into dresses and veils and sails. But never for wings."

"I'll need ten yards of it—woven bolts, if you have them."

The spider seemed to still further. "Men have sacrificed their lives for a yard."

"Name your price."

"Ten yards . . ." She turned to the three waiting behind her—offspring or minions or guards, Manon didn't know. "Bring out the bolt. I shall inspect it before I name my price."

Good. This was going well. Silence fell as the three scuttled into the cave, and Manon tried not to kick any of the tiny spiders crawling across her boots. Or look for the eyes she felt watching from the nearby caves across the ravine.

"Tell me, Blackbeak," the spider said, "how did you come across your mount?"

"He was a gift from the King of Adarlan. We are to be a part of his host, and when we are done serving him, we will take them home—to the Wastes. To reclaim our kingdom."

"Ah. And is the curse broken?"

"Not yet. But when we find the Crochan who can undo it . . ." She would enjoy that bloodletting.

"Such a delightfully nasty curse. You won the land, only for the cunning Crochans to curse it beyond use. Have you seen the Wastes these days?"

"No," Manon said. "I have not yet been to our home."

"A merchant came by a few years ago—he told me there was a mortal High King who had set himself up there. But I heard a whisper on the wind recently that said he'd been deposed by a young woman with wine-red hair who now calls herself their High Queen."

Manon bristled. High Queen of the Wastes indeed. She would be the first Manon would kill when she returned to reclaim the land, when she finally saw it with her own eyes, breathed in its smells and beheld its untamable beauty.

"A strange place, the Wastes," the spider continued. "The merchant himself was from there—a former shape-shifter. Lost his gifts, just like all of you truly mortal things. He was stuck in a man's body, thankfully, but he did not realize that when he sold me twenty years of his life, some of his gifts passed to me. I can't use them, of course, but I wonder . . . I do wonder what it would be like. To see the world through your pretty eyes. To touch a human man."

The hair on Manon's neck rose. "Here we are," the spider said as the three approached, a bolt of silk flowing between them like a river of light and color. Manon's breath caught. "Isn't it magnificent? Some of the finest weaving I've ever done."

"Glorious," Manon admitted. "Your price?"

The spider stared at her for a long time. "What price could I ask of a long-lived witch? Twenty years off your lifespan is nothing to you, even with magic aging you like an ordinary woman. And your dreams . . . what dark, horrible dreams they must be, Blackbeak. I do not think I should like to eat them—not those dreams." The spider came closer. "But what of your face? What if I took your beauty?"

"I do not think I'd walk away if you took my face."

The spider laughed. "Oh, I don't mean your literal face. But the color of your skin, the hue of your burnt gold eyes. The way your hair catches the light, like moonlight on snow. Those things I could take. That beauty could win you a king. Perhaps if magic returns, I'll use it for my woman's body. Perhaps I'll win a king of my very own."

Manon didn't particularly care about her beauty, weapon though it was. But she wasn't about to say that, or to offer it without bargaining. "I'd like to inspect the silk first."

"Cut a swatch," the spider ordered the three, who gently set down the yards of silk while one sliced off a perfect square. Men had killed for smaller amounts—and here they were, cutting it as if it were ordinary wool. Manon tried not to think about the size of the pincer that extended it to her. She stalked to the cliff edge, stepping over Abraxos's tail as she held the silk to the light.

Darkness embrace her, it sparkled. She tugged it. Flexible, but strong as steel. Impossibly light. But—

"There's an imperfection here . . . Can I expect the rest of it to be similarly marred?" The spider hissed and the ground thudded as she neared. Abraxos stopped her with a warning growl that set the other three coming up behind her—guards, then. But Manon held up the swatch to the light. "Look," Manon said, pointing to a vein of color running through it.

"That's no imperfection," the spider snapped. Abraxos's tail curled around Manon, a shield between her and the spiders, bringing her closer to the wall of his body.

Manon held it higher, angling it toward the sun. "Look in the better light. You think I'm going to give away my beauty for second-rate weaving?"

"Second rate!" the spider seethed. Abraxos's tail curled tighter.

"No—it appears I'm mistaken." Manon lowered her arms, smiling. "It seems I'm not in the bargaining mood today."

The spiders, now standing along the cliff's edge, didn't even have time to move as Abraxos's tail unwound like a whip and slammed into them.

They went flying into the ravine, shrieking. Manon didn't waste a second as she stuffed the remaining yards of silk into the empty saddlebags. She mounted Abraxos and they leapt into the air, the cliff the perfect takeoff spot, just as she'd planned.

The perfect trap for those foolish, ancient monsters.

38

Manon gave a foot of spidersilk to the overseer after he carefully grafted it onto Abraxos's wings. She'd gotten extra—lots of it, in case it ever wore down—and it was now locked in the false bottom of a trunk. She told no one where she had been, or why Abraxos's wings now shimmered in a certain light. Asterin would have murdered her for the risk, and her grandmother would have butchered Asterin for not being there. Manon was in no mood to replace her Second and find a new member for the Thirteen.

Once Abraxos had healed, Manon brought him to the mouth of the Northern Fang to try the Crossing. Before, his wings had been too weak to attempt the plunge—but with the silk reinforcements, he'd stand a far greater chance.

But the risk remained, which was why Asterin and Sorrel waited behind her, already on their mounts. If things went wrong, if Abraxos couldn't pull up or the silk failed, she was to jump—jump away from him. Let him die, while one of them caught her in the claws of their wyverns.

Manon wasn't too keen on that plan, but it was the only way Asterin and Sorrel would agree to let her do it. Though Manon was the Blackbeak heir, they would have locked her in a wyvern pen rather than let her make the Crossing without the proper precautions. She might have called them softhearted and given them the beatings they deserved, but it was smart. Tensions were worse than ever, and she wouldn't put it past the Yellowlegs heir to spook Abraxos during the Crossing.

Manon nodded her readiness to her Second and Third before approaching her beast. Not many had gathered, but Iskra was on the viewing platform, smiling faintly. Manon checked the stirrups, the saddle, and the reins one more time, Abraxos tense and snarling.

"Let's go," she said to him, pulling the reins to lead him a bit farther ahead so she could mount him. He still had plenty of space to get a running start—and with his new wings, she knew he would be fine. They'd done steep plunges and hard upswings before. But Abraxos wouldn't move.

"Now," she snapped at him, tugging hard.

Abraxos turned an eye to her and growled. She lightly smacked his leathery cheek. *"Now."*

Those hind legs dug in, and he tucked his wings in tight. *"Abraxos."*

He was looking at the Crossing, then back at her. Wide-eyed. Petrified—utterly petrified. Useless, stupid, cowardly beast.

"Stop it," she said, moving to climb into the saddle instead. "Your wings are fine now." She reached for his haunch but he reared away, the ground shaking as he slammed down. Behind her, Asterin and Sorrel murmured to their mounts, who had skittered back and snapped at Abraxos, and at each other.

There was a soft laugh from the viewing platform, and Manon's teeth popped down.

"Abraxos. *Now.*" She reached for the saddle again.

He bucked away, slamming into the wall and shrinking back.

One of the men brought out a whip, but she held out a hand. "Don't take another step," she snapped, iron nails out. Whips only made Abraxos more uncontrollable. She turned to her mount. "You rutting coward," she hissed at the beast, pointing to the Crossing. "Get back in line." Abraxos met her stare, refusing to back down. "Get in line, Abraxos!"

"He can't understand you," Asterin said quietly.

"Yes, he—" Manon shut her mouth. She hadn't told them that theory, not yet. She turned back to the wyvern. "If you don't let me into that saddle and make that jump, I'm going to have you confined to the darkest, smallest pit in this bloody mountain."

He bared his teeth. She bared hers.

The staring contest lasted for a full minute. One humiliating, enraging minute.

"Fine," she spat, turning from the beast. He was a waste of her time. "Have him locked up wherever he'll be the most miserable," she said to the overseer. "He's not coming out until he's willing to make the Crossing."

The overseer gaped, and Manon snapped her fingers at Asterin and Sorrel to signal them to dismount. She'd never hear the end of this—not from her grandmother, or from the Yellowlegs witches, or from Iskra, who was already making her way across the floor of the pit.

"Why don't you stay, Manon?" Iskra called. "I could show your wyvern how it's done."

"Keep walking," Sorrel murmured to Manon, but she didn't need a reminder.

"They say it's not the beasts who are the problem, but the riders," Iskra went on, loud enough for everyone to hear. Manon didn't turn.

She didn't want to see them take Abraxos back to the gate, to whatever hole they'd lock him in. Stupid, useless beast.

"Though," Iskra said thoughtfully, "perhaps your mount needs a bit of discipline."

"Let's go," Sorrel coaxed, pressing in tight to Manon's side. Asterin walked a step behind, guarding Manon's back.

"Give that to me," Iskra barked at someone. "He just needs the right encouragement."

A whip snapped behind them, and there was a roar—of pain and fear.

Manon stopped dead.

Abraxos was huddling against the wall.

Iskra stood before him, whip bloody from the line she'd sliced down his face, narrowly missing his eye. Her iron teeth shining bright, Iskra smiled at Manon as she raised the whip again and struck. Abraxos yelped.

Asterin and Sorrel weren't fast enough to stop Manon as she hurtled past and tackled Iskra.

Teeth and nails out, they rolled across the dirt floor, flipping and shredding and biting. Manon thought she might be roaring, roaring so loud the hall shook. Feet slammed into her stomach, and the air shot out of her as Iskra kicked her off.

Manon hit the earth, spat out a mouthful of blue blood, and was up in a heartbeat. The Yellowlegs heir slashed with an iron-tipped hand, a blow that could have severed through bone and flesh. Manon ducked past her guard and threw Iskra onto the unforgiving stone.

Iskra groaned above the shouts of the swarming witches, and Manon brought her fist down onto her face.

Her knuckles howled in pain, but all she could see was that whip, the pain in Abraxos's eyes, the fear. Struggling against Manon's weight, Iskra swiped at her face. Manon reeled back, the blow cutting down her neck. She didn't quite feel the stinging, or the warm trickle of blood. She just drew back her fist, knee digging harder into Iskra's chest, and struck. Again. And again.

She lifted her aching fist once more, but there were hands at her wrist, under her arms, hauling her off. Manon thrashed against them, still screaming, the sound wordless and endless.

"*Manon*!" Sorrel roared in her ear, and nails cut into her shoulder—not hard enough to damage but to make her pause, to realize there were witches everywhere, in the pit and in the viewing platform, gaping. Sword raised, Asterin was standing between her and—

And Iskra, on the ground, face bloodied and swollen, her own Second's sword out and poised to meet Asterin's.

"He is fine," Sorrel said, squeezing her tighter. "Abraxos is fine, Manon. Look at him. *Look* at him and see that he's fine." Breathing through her mouth thanks to her blood-clogged nose, Manon obeyed, and found him crouching, eyes wide and on her. His wound had already clotted.

Iskra hadn't moved an inch from where Manon had thrown her onto the floor. But Asterin and the other Second were growling, ready to launch into another fight that might very well rip this mountain apart.

Enough.

Manon shook off Sorrel's firm grip. Everyone went dead silent as Manon wiped her bloody nose and mouth on the back of her wrist. Iskra snarled at her from the floor, blood from her broken nose leaking onto her cut lip.

"You touch him again," Manon said, "and I'll drink the marrow from your bones."

The Yellowlegs heir got a second beating that night from her mother in the mess hall—plus two lashes of the whip for the blows she'd given

Abraxos. She'd offered them to Manon, but Manon refused under the guise of indifference.

Her arm was actually too stiff and aching to use the whip with any efficiency.

Manon had just entered Abraxos's cage the next day, Asterin on her heels, when the Blueblood heir appeared at the stairway entrance, her red-haired Second close behind. Manon, her face still swollen and eye beautifully black, gave the witch a tight nod. There were other pens down here, though she rarely ran into anyone else, especially not the two heirs.

But Petrah paused at the bars, and it was then that Manon noticed the goat's leg in her Second's arms. "I heard the fight was something to behold," Petrah said, keeping a respectful distance from Manon and the open door to the pen. Petrah smiled faintly. "Iskra looks worse."

Manon flicked her brows up, though the motion made her face throb.

Petrah held out a hand to her Second, and the witch passed her the leg of meat. "I also heard that your Thirteen and your mounts only eat the meat they catch. My Keelie caught this on our morning flight. She wanted to share with Abraxos."

"I don't accept meat from rival clans."

"Are we rivals?" Petrah asked. "I thought the King of Adarlan had convinced us to fly under one banner again."

Manon took a long breath. "What do you want? I have training in ten minutes."

Petrah's Second bristled, but the heir smiled. "I told you—my Keelie wanted to give this to him."

"Oh? She told you?" Manon sneered.

Petrah cocked her head. "Doesn't your wyvern talk to you?"

Abraxos was watching with as much awareness as the other witches. "They don't talk."

Petrah shrugged, tapping a hand casually over her heart. "Don't they?"

She left the goat leg before walking off into the raucous gloom of the pens.

Manon threw the meat away.

39

"Tell me about how you learned to tattoo."

"No."

Hunched over the wooden table in Rowan's room a night after their encounter with the creature in the lake, Celaena looked up from where she held the bone-handled needle over his wrist. "If you don't answer my questions, I might very well make a mistake, and . . ." She lowered the tattooing needle to his tan, muscled arm for emphasis. Rowan, to her surprise, let out a huff that might have been a laugh. She figured it was a good sign that he'd asked her to help shade in the parts of his arm he couldn't reach himself; the tattoo around his wrist needed to be re-inked now that the wounds from her burning him had faded. "Did you learn from someone? Master and apprentice and all that?"

He gave her a rather incredulous look. "Yes, master and apprentice and all that. In the war camps, we had a commander who used to tattoo the number of enemies he'd killed on his flesh—sometimes he'd write the whole story of a battle. All the young soldiers were enamored of it, and I convinced him to teach me."

"With that legendary charm of yours, I suppose."

That earned her a half smile at least. "Just fill in the spots where I—" A hiss as she took the needle and little mallet and made another dark, bloody mark in him. "Good. That's the right depth." With his immortal, fast-healing body, Rowan's ink was mixed with salt and powdered iron to keep the magic in his blood from wiping away any trace of the tattoo.

She'd awoken that morning feeling . . . clear. The grief and pain were still there, writhing inside her, but for the first time in a long while, she felt as though she could see. As though she could breathe.

Focusing on keeping her hand steady, she made another little mark, then another. "Tell me about your family."

"Tell me about yours and I'll tell you about mine," he said through gritted teeth as she kept going. He'd instructed her thoroughly before he had let her take the needles to his skin.

"Fine. Are your parents alive?" A stupid, dangerous question to ask, given what had happened with his mate, but there was no grief in his face as he shook his head.

"My parents were very old when they conceived me." Not old in the human sense, she knew. "I was their only child in the millennia they'd been mated. They faded into the Afterworld before I reached my second decade."

Before she could think more on that interesting, different way of describing death, Rowan said, "You had no siblings."

She focused on her work as she let out the thinnest tendril of memory. "My mother, thanks to her Fae heritage, had a difficult time with the pregnancy. She stopped breathing during labor. They said it was my father's will that kept her tethered to this world. I don't know if she even *could* have conceived again after that. So, no siblings. But—" Gods, she should shut her mouth. "But I had a cousin. He was five years older than me, and we fought and loved each other like siblings."

Aedion. She hadn't spoken that name aloud in ten years. But she'd heard it, and seen it in papers. She had to set down the needle and mallet and flex her fingers. "I don't know what happened, but they started saying his name—as a skilled general in the king's army."

She had failed Aedion so unforgivably that she couldn't bring herself to blame or detest him for what he'd become. She'd avoided learning any details about what, exactly, he'd done in the north all these years. Aedion had been fiercely, wildly loyal to Terrasen as a child. She didn't want to know what he'd been forced to do, what had happened to him, to change that. It was by luck or fate or something else entirely that he had never been in the castle when she was there. Because not only would he have recognized her, but if he knew what she had done with her life . . . his hatred would make Rowan's look pleasant, probably.

Rowan's features were set in a mask of contemplation as she said, "I think facing my cousin after everything would be the worst of it—worse than facing the king." There was nothing she could say or do to atone for what she'd become while their kingdom fell into ruin and their people were slaughtered or enslaved.

"Keep working," Rowan said, jerking his chin at the tools sitting in her lap. She obeyed, and he hissed again at the first prick. "Do you think," he said after a moment, "your cousin would kill you or help you? An army like his could change the tide of any war."

A chill went down her spine at that word—*war.* "I don't know what he would think of me, or where his loyalties lie. And I'd rather not know. Ever."

Though their eyes were identical, their bloodlines were distant enough that she'd heard servants and courtiers alike pondering the usefulness of a Galathynius-Ashryver union someday. The idea was as laughable now as it had been ten years ago.

"Do *you* have cousins?" she asked.

"Too many. Mora's line was always the most widespread, and my meddlesome, gossiping cousins make my visits to Doranelle . . . irksome." She smiled a little at the thought. "You'd probably get along with my cousins," he said. "Especially with the snooping."

She paused her inking and squeezed his hand hard enough to hurt anyone but an immortal. "You're one to talk, *Prince*. I've never been asked so many questions in my life."

Not quite true, but not quite an exaggeration, either. No one had ever asked her *these* questions. And she'd never told anyone the answers.

He bared his teeth, though she knew he didn't mean it, and glanced meaningfully at his wrist. "Hurry up, *Princess*. I want to go to bed at some point before dawn."

She used her free hand to make a particularly vulgar gesture, and he caught it with his own, teeth still out. "*That* is not very queenly."

"Then it's good I'm not a queen, isn't it?"

But he wouldn't let go of her hand. "You have sworn to free your friend's kingdom and save the world—but will not even consider your own lands. What scares you about seizing your birthright? The king? Facing what remains of your court?" He kept his face so close to hers that she could see the flecks of brown in his green eyes. "Give me one good reason why you won't take back your throne. One good reason, and I'll keep my mouth shut about it."

She weighed the earnestness in his gaze, his breathing, and then said, "Because if I free Eyllwe and destroy the king as Celaena, I can go anywhere after that. The crown . . . my crown is just another set of shackles."

It was selfish and horrible, but it was true. Nehemia, long ago, had once said as much—it was her most ardent and selfish wish to be ordinary, without the weight of her crown. Had her friend known how deeply those words had echoed in her?

She waited for the scolding, saw it simmering in Rowan's eyes. But then he quietly said, "What do you mean, *another* set of shackles?"

He loosened his grip to reveal the two thin bands of scars that wrapped around her wrist. His mouth tightened, and she yanked her wrist back hard enough that he let go.

"Nothing," she said. "Arobynn, my master, liked to use them for training every now and then." Arobynn *had* chained her to make her learn how to get free. But the shackles at Endovier had been crafted with people like her in mind. It wasn't until Chaol had removed them that she'd gotten out.

She didn't want Rowan knowing that—any of it. Anger and hatred she could handle, but pity . . . And she couldn't talk about Chaol, couldn't explain just how much he had rebuilt and then shattered her heart, not without explaining Endovier. Not without explaining how one day, she didn't know how distant, she was going back to Endovier and freeing them all. Each and every slave, even if she had to unshackle them all herself.

Celaena went back to her work, and Rowan's face remained tight—as if he could smell her half truth. "Why did you stay with Arobynn?"

"I knew I wanted two things: First, to disappear from the world and from my enemies, but . . . ah." It was hard to look him in the eye. "I wanted to hide from myself, mostly. I convinced myself I should disappear, because the second thing I wanted, even then, was to be able to someday . . . hurt people the way I had been hurt. And it turned out that I was very, very good at it.

"If he had tossed me away, I would either have died or wound up with the rebels. If I had grown up with them, I probably would have been found by the king and slaughtered. Or I would have grown up so hateful that I would have been killing Adarlanian soldiers from a young age." His brows rose, and she clicked her tongue. "You thought I was just going to spread my whole history at your feet the moment I met you? I'm sure you have even more stories than I do, so stop looking so surprised. Maybe we should just go back to beating each other into a pulp."

His eyes gleamed with near-predatory intent. "Oh, not a chance, Princess. You can tell me what you want, when you want, but there's no going back now."

She lifted her tools again. "I'm sure your other friends just adore having you around."

A feral smile, and he grabbed her by the chin—not hard enough to hurt, but to get her to look at him. "First thing," he breathed, "we're not friends. I'm still training you, and that means you're still under my command." The flicker of hurt must have shown, because he leaned closer, his grip tightening on her jaw. "Second—whatever we are, whatever this is? I'm still figuring it out, too. So if I'm going to give you the space you deserve to sort yourself out, then you can damn well give it to me."

She studied him for a moment, their breath mingling.

"Deal," she said.

40

"Tell me your greatest wish," Dorian murmured into Sorscha's hair as he entwined their fingers, marveling at the smoothness of her tan skin against the calluses of his. Such pretty hands, like mourning doves.

She smiled onto his chest. "I don't have a greatest wish."

"Liar." He kissed her hair. "You're the world's worst liar."

She turned toward the window of his bedroom, the morning light making her dark hair glow. It had been two weeks since that night she'd kissed him, two weeks since she'd started creeping up here after the castle had gone to sleep. They'd been sharing a bed, though not in the manner he still yearned to. And he detested the sneaking and the hiding.

But she'd lose her position if they were found out. With him being who he was . . . he could bring down a world of trouble on her just for being associated with him. His mother alone could find ways to get her shipped off somewhere.

"Tell me," he said again, bending to snatch a kiss. "Tell me, and I'll make it happen."

He'd always been generous with his lovers. Usually he gave them gifts to keep them from complaining when he lost interest, but this time he genuinely *wanted* to give her things. He had tried giving her jewelry and clothes, and she had refused it all. So he'd taken to giving her hard-to-come-by herbs and books and special tools for her workroom. She'd tried to refuse those, but he'd worn her down quickly—mostly by kissing away her protests.

"And if I asked for the moon on a string?"

"Then I would start praying to Deanna."

She smiled, but Dorian's own grin faded. Deanna, Lady of the Hunt. He usually tried not to think about Celaena, Aelin—whoever she was. Tried not to think about Chaol and his lying, or Aedion and his treason. He wanted nothing to do with them, not now that Sorscha was with him. He'd been a fool once, swearing he would tear the world apart for Celaena. A boy in love with a wildfire—or believing he was in love with one.

"Dorian?" Sorscha pulled back to study his face. She looked at him the way he'd once caught Celaena looking at Chaol.

He kissed her again, soft and lingering, and her body melted into his. He savored the silkiness of her skin as he ran a hand down her arm. She yanked back. "I have to go. I'm late."

He groaned. It was indeed almost breakfast—and she would be noticed if she didn't leave. She shimmied out of his embrace and into her dress, and he helped tie the stays in the back. Always hiding—was that to be his life? Not just the women he loved, but his magic, his true thoughts . . .

Sorscha kissed him and was at the door, a hand on the knob. "My greatest wish," she said with a little smile, "is for a morning when I don't have to run out the door at first light."

Before he could say anything, she was gone.

But he didn't know what he could say, or do, to make it happen. Because Sorscha had her obligations, and he had his.

If he left to be with her, if he turned on his father, or if his magic was discovered, then his brother would become heir. And the thought of Hollin as king one day . . . What he would do to their world, especially with their father's power . . . No, Dorian could not have the luxury of choosing, because there was no option. He was bound to his crown, and would be until the day he died.

There was a knock on his door, and Dorian smiled, wondering if Sorscha had come back. The grin vanished as the door opened.

"We need to talk," Chaol said from the threshold. Dorian hadn't seen him in weeks, and yet—his friend looked older. Exhausted.

"Not going to bother with flattery?" Dorian said, plopping onto the couch.

"You would see through it anyway." Chaol shut the door behind him and leaned against it.

"Humor me."

"I am sorry, Dorian," Chaol said softly. "More than you know."

"Sorry because lying cost you me—and her? Would you be sorry if you hadn't been caught?"

Chaol's jaw tightened. And perhaps Dorian was being unfair, but he didn't care.

"I am sorry for all of it," Chaol said. "But I—I've been working to fix it."

"And what about Celaena? Is working with Aedion actually to help me, or her?"

"Both of you."

"Do you still love her?" He didn't know why he cared, why it was important.

Chaol closed his eyes for a moment. "A part of me will always love her. But I had to get her out of this castle. Because it was too dangerous, and she was . . . what she was becoming . . ."

"She was not becoming anything different from what she always was and always had the capacity to be. You just finally saw everything. And once you saw that other part of her . . . ," Dorian said quietly. It had taken him until now, until Sorscha, to understand what that meant. "You cannot pick and choose what parts of her to love." He pitied Chaol, he realized. His heart hurt for his friend, for all that Chaol had surely been realizing these past few months. "Just as you cannot pick which parts of me you accept."

"I don't—"

"You do. But what's done is done, Chaol. And there is no going back, no matter how hard you try to change things. Like it or not, you played a role in getting us all to this point, too. You set her down that path, to revealing what and who she is, to whatever she decides to do now."

"You think I wanted any of this to happen?" Chaol splayed his arms. "If I could, I would put it all back to the way it was. If I could, she wouldn't be queen, and you wouldn't have magic."

"Of course—of course you still see the magic as a problem. And of course you wish she wasn't who she is. Because you're not really scared of those things, are you? No—it's what they represent. The change. But let me tell you," Dorian breathed, his magic flickering and then subsiding in a flash of pain, "things have already changed. And changed because of *you*. I have magic—there is no undoing that, no getting rid of it. And as for Celaena . . ." He clamped down on the power that surged as he imagined—for the first time, he realized—what it was to be her. "As for Celaena," he said again, "you do not have the right to wish she were not what she is. The only thing you have a right to do is decide whether you are her enemy or her friend."

He did not know all of her story, did not know what had been truth and what had been lies, or what it had been like in Endovier to slave beside her countrymen, or to bow to the man who had murdered her family. But he had seen her—seen glimpses of the person beneath, regardless of name or title.

And he knew, deep down, that she had not blinked at his magic but rather understood that burden, and that fear. She had not walked away or wished him to be anything but what he was. *I'll come back for you.*

So he stared down his friend, even though he knew Chaol was hurting and adrift, and said, "I've already made my decision about her. And when the time comes, regardless of whether you are here or in Anielle, I hope your choice is the same as mine."

Aedion hated to admit it, but the captain's self-control was impressive as they waited in the hidden apartment for Murtaugh to arrive. Ren, who couldn't keep his ass planted in a chair for more than a moment even with his still-healing wounds, paced around the great room. But Chaol sat beside the fire, saying little but always watching, always listening.

Tonight the captain seemed different. Warier, but tighter. Thanks to all those meetings where he'd carefully watched the captain's movements, every breath and blink, Aedion instantly noted the difference. Had there been some news, some development?

Murtaugh was to return tonight, after a few weeks near Skull's Bay. He had refused Ren's offer to go with him and told his grandson to rest. Which, though Ren tried to hide it, left the young lord anxious, ungrounded, and aggressive. Aedion was honestly surprised the apartment hadn't been torn to shreds. In his war camp, Aedion might have taken Ren into the sparring ring and let him fight it out. Or sent him on some mission of his own. Or at least made him chop wood for hours.

"So we're just going to wait all night," Ren said at last, pausing before the dining table and looking at them both.

The captain yielded nothing more than a vague nod, but Aedion crossed his arms and gave him a lazy grin. "You have something better to do, Ren? Are we interfering with a visit to one of your opium dens?" A low blow, but nothing that the captain hadn't already guessed about Ren. And if Ren showed any indication of that sort of habit, Aedion wouldn't let him within a hundred miles of Aelin.

Ren shook his head and said, "We're always waiting these days. Waiting for Aelin to send some sign, waiting for nothing. I bet my grandfather will have nothing, too. I'm surprised we're not all dead by now—that those men didn't track me down." He stared into the fire, the light making his scar look even deeper. "I have someone who . . ." Ren trailed off, glancing at Chaol. "They could find out more about the king."

"I don't trust your sources one bit—especially not after those men found you," Chaol said. It had been one of Ren's informants—caught and tortured—who had given his location away. And even though the information had been yielded under duress, it still didn't sit well with Aedion. He said as much, and Ren tensed, opening his mouth to snap something undoubtedly stupid and brash, but a three-note whistle interrupted.

The captain whistled back, and Ren was at the door, opening it to find his grandfather there. Even with his back to them, Aedion could see the relief flooding Ren's body as they clasped forearms, weeks of waiting without word finally over. Murtaugh wasn't young by any means—and as he threw back his hood, his face was pale and grim.

"There's brandy on the buffet table," Chaol said, and Aedion, yet again, had to admire the captain's keen eyes—even if he would never tell him. The old man nodded his thanks, and didn't bother to remove his cloak as he knocked back a glass of it. "Grandfather." Ren lingered by the door.

Murtaugh turned to Aedion. "Answer me truthfully, boy: do you know who General Narrok is?"

Aedion rose to his feet in a smooth movement. Ren took a few steps toward them, but Murtaugh held his ground as Aedion stalked to the buffet table and slowly, with deliberate care, poured himself a glass of brandy. "Call me boy again," Aedion said with lethal calm, holding the old man's stare, "and you'll find yourself back squatting in shanties and sewers."

The old man threw up his hands. "When you're my age, Aedion—"

"Don't waste your breath," Aedion said, returning to his chair. "Narrok's been in the south—last I heard, he was bringing the armada to the Dead Islands." Pirate territory. "But that was months ago. We're kept on a need-to-know basis. I learned about the Dead Islands because some of the Pirate Lord's ships sailed north looking for trouble, and they informed us that they'd come to avoid Narrok's fleet."

The pirates had scattered, actually. The Pirate Lord Rolfe had taken half of them south; some had gone east; and some had made the fatal mistake of sailing to Terrasen's north coast.

Murtaugh sagged against the buffet table. "Captain?"

"I'm afraid I know even less than Aedion," Chaol said.

Murtaugh rubbed his eyes, and Ren pulled out a chair at the table for his grandfather. The old man slid into it with a small groan. It was a miracle the bag of bones was still breathing. Aedion shoved down a flicker of regret. He'd been raised better than that—he knew better than to act like an arrogant, hotheaded prick. Rhoe would have been ashamed of him for speaking to an elder in that manner. But Rhoe was dead—all the warriors he'd loved and worshipped were ten years dead, and the world was worse for it. Aedion was worse for it.

Murtaugh sighed. "I fled here as quickly as I could. I have not rested for more than a few hours this past week. Narrok's fleet is gone. Captain

Rolfe is again Pirate Lord of Skull's Bay, though not more than that. His men do not venture into the eastern Dead Islands."

Despite the hint of shame, Aedion ground his teeth when Murtaugh didn't immediately get to the point. "Why?" he demanded.

The lines of Murtaugh's face deepened in the light of the fire. "Because the men who go into the eastern islands do not come back. And on windy nights, even Rolfe swears he can hear . . . roaring, roaring from the islands; human, but not quite.

"The crew that hid in the islands during Narrok's occupation claim it's quieted down, as if he took the source of the sound with him. And Rolfe . . ." Murtaugh rubbed the bridge of his nose. "He told me that on the night they sailed back into the islands, they saw something standing on an outcropping of rocks, just on the border of the eastern islands. Looked like a pale man, but . . . not. Rolfe might be in love with himself, but he's not a liar. He said whatever—whoever—it was felt *wrong*. Like there was a hole of silence around it, at odds with the roaring they usually hear. And that it just watched them sail past. The next day, when they returned to the same spot, it was gone."

"There have always been legends of strange creatures in the seas," the captain said.

"Rolfe and his men swore that this was nothing from legend. It was *made*, they said."

"How did they know?" Aedion asked, eyeing the captain, whose face was still bone-white.

"It bore a black collar—like a pet. It took a step toward them, as if to go into the sea and hunt them down, but it was yanked back by some invisible hand—some hidden leash."

Ren raised his scarred brow. "The Pirate Lord thinks there are *monsters* in the Dead Islands?"

"He thinks, and I also believe, that they were being made there. And Narrok took some of them with him."

It was Chaol who asked, "Where did Narrok go?"

"To Wendlyn," Murtaugh said. Aedion's heart, damn him, stopped. "Narrok took the fleet to Wendlyn—to launch a surprise attack."

"That's impossible," the captain said, shooting to his feet. "Why? Why now?"

"Because *someone*," the old man said, sharper than Aedion had ever heard him, "convinced the king to send his Champion there to kill the royal family. What better time to try out these alleged monsters than when the country is in chaos?"

Chaol gripped the back of a chair. "She's not actually going to kill them—she would never. It—it was all a ruse," he said. Aedion supposed that was all he would tell the Allsbrook men, and all they really needed to know right now. He ignored the wary glance Ren tossed him, no doubt to see how he would react to news of his Ashryver kin having targets on their backs. But they'd been dead to him for ten years already, from the moment they refused to send aid to Terrasen. Gods help them if he ever set foot in their kingdom. He wondered what Aelin thought of them—if she thought Wendlyn might be convinced of an alliance now, especially with Adarlan launching a larger-scale assault on their borders. Perhaps she would be content to let them all burn, as the people of Terrasen had burned. He wouldn't mind either way.

"It doesn't matter if they are assassinated or not," Murtaugh said. "When these things arrive, I think the world will soon learn what our queen is up against."

"Can we send a warning?" Ren demanded. "Can Rolfe get word to Wendlyn?"

"Rolfe will not get involved. I offered him promises of gold, of land when our queen returns . . . nothing can sway him. He has his territory back, and he will not risk his men again."

"Then there has to be some blockade runner, some message we can smuggle," Ren went on. Aedion debated informing Ren that Wendlyn hadn't bothered to help Terrasen, but decided he didn't particularly feel like getting into an ethical debate.

"I have sent a few that way," Murtaugh said, "but I do not have much faith in them. And by the time they arrive, it may be too late."

"So what do we do?" Ren pushed.

Murtaugh sipped his brandy. "We keep looking for ways to help here. Because I do not believe for one moment that His Majesty's newest surprises were located only in the Dead Islands."

That was an interesting point. Aedion took a sip from the brandy, but set it down. Alcohol wouldn't help him sort through the jumble of forming plans. So Aedion half listened to the others as he slipped into the steady rhythm, the beat to which he calculated all his battles and campaigns.

Chaol watched Aedion pace in the apartment, Murtagh and Ren having left to see to their own agendas. Aedion said, "You want to tell me why you look like you're going to vomit?"

"You know everything I know, so it's easy to guess why," Chaol said from his armchair, his jaw clenched. His fight with Dorian had left him in no hurry to get back to the castle, even if he needed the prince to test out his theories on that spell. Dorian had been right about Celaena—about Chaol resenting her darkness and abilities and true identity, but . . . it hadn't changed how he felt.

"I still don't quite grasp your role in things, Captain," Aedion said. "You're not fighting for Aelin or for Terrasen; for what, then? The greater good? Your prince? Whose side does that put you on? Are you a traitor—a rebel?"

"No." Chaol's blood chilled at the thought. "I'm on neither side. I only wish to help my friend before I leave for Anielle."

Aedion's lip pulled back in a snarl. "Perhaps that's your problem.

Perhaps not picking a side is what costs you. Perhaps you need to tell your father you're breaking your promise."

"I will not turn my back on my kingdom or my prince," Chaol snapped. "I will not fight in your army and slaughter my people. And I will not break my vow to my father." His honor might very well be all he would have left at the end of this.

"What if your prince sides with us?"

"Then I will fight alongside him, however I am able, even if it's from Anielle."

"So you will fight alongside him, but not for what is right. Have you no free will, no wants of your own?"

"My wants are none of your concern." And those wants . . . "Regardless of what Dorian decides, he would never sanction the killing of innocents."

A sneer. "No taste for blood?"

Chaol wouldn't give him the satisfaction of rising to meet his temper. Instead he went for the throat and said, "I think your queen would condemn you if you spilled one drop of innocent blood. She would spit in your face. There are good people in this kingdom, and they deserve to be considered in any course of action your side takes."

Aedion's eyes flicked to the scar on Chaol's cheek. "Just like how she condemned you for the death of her friend?" Aedion gave him a slow, vicious smile, and then, almost too fast to register, the general was in his face, arms braced on the wings of the chair.

Chaol wondered if Aedion would strike him, or kill him, as the general's features turned more lupine than he'd ever seen them, nose crinkled, teeth exposed. Aedion said, "When your men have died around you, when you have seen your women unforgivably hurt, when you have watched droves of orphaned children starve to death in the streets of your city, *then* you can talk to me about sparing innocent lives. Until then, the fact remains, Captain, that you have not picked a side because you are still a boy, and you are still afraid. Not of losing innocent lives, but of losing whatever dream it is you're clinging to. Your prince has moved on, my queen has moved on. But *you* have not. And it will cost you in the end."

Chaol had nothing to say after that and quickly left the apartment. He hardly slept that night, hardly did anything but stare at his sword, discarded on his desk. When the sun rose, he went to the king and told him of his plans to return to Anielle.

41

The next two weeks fell into a pattern—enough that Celaena started to find comfort in it. There were no unexpected stumbles or turns or pitfalls, no deaths or betrayals or nightmares made flesh. In the mornings and evenings, she played scullery maid. Late morning until dinner she spent with Rowan, slowly, painfully exploring the well of magic inside her—a well that, to her horror, had no bottom in sight.

The small things—lighting candles, putting out hearth fires, weaving a ribbon of flame through her fingers—were still the hardest. But Rowan pushed, dragging her from ruin to ruin, the only safe places for her to lose control. At least he brought food with him now, as she was constantly starving and could hardly go an hour without eating something. Magic gobbled up energy, and she was eating double or triple what she used to.

Sometimes they would talk. Well, she would make him talk, because after telling him about Aedion and her own selfish wish for freedom, she decided that talking was . . . good. Even if she wasn't able to open up about some things, she liked hearing Rowan speak. She managed to get him to tell her about his various campaigns and adventures, each more brutal and harrowing than the next. There was a whole giant world to the south and east of Wendlyn, kingdoms and empires she'd heard of in passing but had never known much about. Rowan was a true warrior, who had walked on and off of killing fields, led men through hell, sailed on raging seas and seen distant, strange shores.

Though she envied his long life—and the gift of seeing the world that went along with it—she could still feel the undercurrent of rage and grief beneath each tale, the loss of his mate that haunted him no matter how far he rode or sailed or flew. He spoke very little of his friends, who sometimes accompanied him on his journeys. She did not envy him the battles he had fought, the wars in far-off lands, or the bloody years spent laying siege to cities of sand and stone.

She did not tell him that, of course. She only listened as he narrated while instructing her. And as she listened, she began to hate Maeve—truly hate her aunt in her core. That rage drove her to request legends about her aunt from Emrys every night. Rowan never reprimanded her when she asked for those stories, never showed any alarm.

It came as some surprise when Emrys announced one day that Beltane was two days off and they would begin preparations for their feasting and dancing and celebrating. Already Beltane, and according to Rowan, she was still far from ready to go to Doranelle, despite mastering the shift. Spring would now be in full bloom on her own continent. Maypoles would be raised, hawthorn bushes decorated—that was about as much as the king would allow. There would be no small gifts left at crossroads for the Little Folk. The king permitted the bare bones only, with the focus squarely on the gods and planting for the harvest. Not a hint or whisper of magic.

Bonfires would be ignited and a few brave souls would jump across for luck, to ward off evil, to ensure a good crop—whatever they hoped would come of it. As a child, she had run rampant through the field before the gates of Orynth, the thousand bonfires burning like the lights of the invading army that would too soon be encamped around the white city. It was *her* night, her mother had said—a night when a fire-bearing girl had nothing to fear, no powers to hide. *Aelin Fireheart*, people had whispered as she bounded past, embers streaming from her like ribbons, Aedion and a few of her more lethal court members trailing as indulgent guards. *Aelin of the Wildfire.*

After days of helping Emrys with the food (and devouring it when the cook wasn't looking), she was hoping for a chance to relax on Beltane, but Rowan hauled her to a field atop the mountain plateau. Celaena bit into an apple she'd pulled from her pocket and raised her brows at Rowan, who was standing in front of a massive pile of wood for the bonfire, flanked by two small unlit fires on either side.

Around them, some of the demi-Fae were still hauling in more wood and kindling, others setting up tables to serve the food that Emrys had been laboring over without rest.

Dozens of other demi-Fae had arrived from their various outposts, with little fanfare and much embracing and good-natured teasing. Between helping Emrys and training with Rowan, Celaena hardly had time to inspect them—though a wretched part of her was somewhat pleased by the few admiring glances she caught being thrown in her direction by the visiting males.

She didn't fail to notice how quickly they looked away when they beheld Rowan at her side. Though she *did* catch a few females looking at him with far warmer interest. She wanted to claw their faces off for it.

She munched on the apple as she studied him now, in his usual pale-gray tunic and wide belt, hood thrown back and leather vambraces gleaming in the late afternoon sunlight. Gods, she had no interest in him like that, and she was certain he had no inclination to take her to his bed, either. Maybe it was just from spending so much time in her Fae body that she felt . . . territorial. Territorial and grumpy and mean. Last night, she had *growled* at a female in the kitchen who would *not* stop staring at him and had actually taken a step toward him as if to say hello.

Celaena shook her head to clear away the instincts that were starting to make her see fire at all hours of the day. "I assume you brought me here so I could practice?" She chucked the apple core across the field and rubbed at her shoulder. She'd been feverish the night before thanks to Rowan making her practice all afternoon, and had awoken exhausted this morning.

"Ignite them, and keep the fires controlled and even all night."

"All three." Not a question.

"Keep the end ones low for the jumpers. The middle one should be scorching the clouds."

She wished she hadn't eaten the apple. "This could easily turn lethal."

He lifted a hand and wind stirred around her. "I'll be here," he said simply, eyes shining with an arrogance he'd more than earned in his centuries of living.

"And if I somehow still manage to turn someone into a living torch?"

"Then it's a good thing the healers are also here to celebrate."

She gave him a dirty look and rolled her shoulders. "When do you want to start?"

Her stomach clenched as he said, "Now."

She was burning, but remaining steady, even as the sun set and the field became packed with revelers. Musicians took up places by the forest edge and the world filled with their violins and fiddles and flutes and drums, such beautiful, ancient music that her flames moved with it, turning into rubies and citrines and tigereyes and deepest sapphires. Her magic didn't manifest in only blue wildfire anymore; it had been slowly changing, growing, these past few weeks. No one really noticed her, standing on the outskirts of the fire's light, though a few marveled at the flames that burned but did not consume the wood.

Sweat ran down every part of her—mostly thanks to the terror of people jumping over the lower-burning bonfires. Yet Rowan remained beside her, murmuring as if she were a nervous horse. She wanted to tell him to go away, to maybe indulge one of those doe-eyed females who kept silently inviting him to dance. But she focused on the flames and on maintaining that shred of control, even though her blood was starting to boil. A knot tightened in her lower back, and she shifted. Gods, she was soaked—every damn crevice was damp.

"Easy," Rowan said as the flames danced a little higher.

"I know," she gritted out. The music was already so inviting, the dancing around the fire so joyous, the food on the tables smelling so delicious . . . and here she was, far from it all, just burning. Her stomach grumbled. "When can I stop?" She shifted on her feet again, and the largest bonfire twisted, the flame slithering with her body. No one noticed.

"When I say so," he said. She knew he was using the people around them, her fear for their safety, to get her to master her control, but . . .

"I'm sweating to death, I'm starving, and I want a break."

"Resorting to whining?" But a cool breeze licked up her neck, and she closed her eyes, moaning. She could feel him watching her, and after a moment he said, "Just a little while longer."

She almost sagged with relief, but opened her eyes to focus. She could hold out for a bit, then go eat and eat and eat. Maybe dance.

She hadn't danced in so long. Maybe she would try it out, here in the shadows. See if her body could find room for joy, even though it was currently so hot and aching that she would bet good money that the moment she stopped, she would fall asleep.

But the music was entrancing, the dancers mere shadows swirling around. Unlike in Adarlan, there were no guards monitoring the festivities, no villagers lurking to see who might cross the line into treason and earn a pretty coin for whoever they turned in. There was just the music and the dancing and the food and the fire—her fire.

She tapped a foot, bobbing her head, eyes on the three smokeless fires and the silhouettes dancing around them. She *did* want to dance. Not from joy, but because she felt her fire and the music meld and pulse against her bones. The music was a tapestry woven of light and dark and color, building delicate links in a chain that latched on to her heart and spread out into the world, binding her to it, connecting everything.

She understood then. The Wyrdmarks were—were a way of harnessing those threads, of weaving and binding the essence of things. Magic could do the same, and from her power, from her imagination and will and core, she could create and shape.

"Easy," Rowan said, then added with a hint of surprise, "Music. That day on the ice, you were humming." She registered another cool wind on her neck, but her skin was already pulsing in time with the drums. "Let the music steady you."

Gods, to be free like this . . . The flames roiled and undulated with the melody.

"Easy." She could barely hear him above the wave of sound filling her up, making her feel each tether binding her to the earth, each infinite thread. For a breath she wished for a shape-shifter's heart so she could shed her skin and weave herself into something else, the music or the wind, and blow across the world. Her eyes were stinging, almost blurry from staring so long at the flames, and a muscle in her back twinged.

"Steady." She didn't know what he was talking about—the flames were calm, lovely. What would happen if she walked through them? The pulsing in her head seemed to say *do it, do it, do it*.

"That's enough for now." Rowan grabbed her arm, but hissed and let go. "That is *enough*."

Slowly, too slowly, she looked at him. His eyes were wide, the light of the fire making them almost blaze. Fire—*her* fire. She returned to the flame, submitted to it. The music and the dancing continued, bright and merry.

"Look at me," Rowan said, but didn't touch her. *"Look at me."*

She could hardly hear him, as if she were underwater. There was a pounding in her now—edged with pain. It was a knife that sliced into her mind and her body with each pulse. She couldn't look at him—didn't dare take her attention from the fire.

"Let the fires burn on their own," Rowan ordered. She could have sworn she heard something like fear in his voice. It was an effort of will, and pain spiked down the tendons in her neck, but she looked at him. His nostrils flared. "Aelin, stop right now."

She tried to speak, but her throat was raw, burning. She couldn't move her body.

"Let go." She tried to tell him she couldn't, but it hurt. She was an anvil and the pain was a hammer, striking again and again. "If you don't let go, you are going to burn out completely."

Was this the end of her magic, then? A few hours tending fires? Such a relief—such a blessed relief, if it were true.

"You are on the verge of roasting yourself from the inside out," Rowan snarled.

She blinked, and her eyes ached as if she had sand in them. Agony lashed down her spine, so hard she fell to the grass. Light flared—not from her or Rowan, but from the fires surging. People yelled, the music faltered. The grass hissed beneath her hands, smoking. She groaned, fumbling inside for the three tethers to the fires. But she was a maze, a labyrinth, the strings all tangled, and—

"I'm sorry," Rowan hissed, swearing again, and the air vanished.

She tried to groan, to move, but she had no air. No air for that inner fire. Blackness swept in.

Oblivion.

Then she was gasping, arcing off the grass, the fires now crackling naturally and Rowan hovering over her. "Breathe. Breathe."

Though he'd snapped her tethers to the fires, she was still burning.

Not burning on the outside, where even the grass had stopped smoldering.

She was burning up from within. Each breath sent fire down her lungs, her veins. She could not speak or move.

She had shoved herself over some boundary—hadn't heard the warning signs to turn back—and she was burning alive beneath her skin.

She shook with tearless, panicked sobs. It hurt—it was endless and eternal and there was no dark part of her where she could flee to escape the flames. Death would be a mercy, a cold, black haven.

She didn't know Rowan had left until he came sprinting back, two females in tow. One of them said, "Can you stand to carry her? There aren't any water-wielders here, and we need to get her into cold water. *Now.*"

She didn't hear what else was said, heard nothing but the pounding-pounding of that forge under her skin. There was a grunt and a hiss, and then she was in Rowan's arms, bouncing against his chest as he hurtled through the woods. Every step sent splinters of red-hot pain through her. Though his arms were ice cold, a frigid wind pressing on her, she was adrift in a sea of fire.

Hell—this was what the dark god's underworld felt like. This was what awaited her when she took her last breath.

It was the horror of that thought that made her focus on what she could grasp—namely the pine-and-snow smell of Rowan. She pulled that smell into her lungs, pulled it down deep and clung to it as though it were a lifeline tossed into a stormy sea. She didn't know how long it took, but her grasp on him was weakening, each pulse of fiery pain fraying it.

But then it was darker than the woods, and the sounds echoed louder, and they took stairs, and then—"Get her into the water."

She was lowered into the water in the sunken stone tub, then steam brushed her face. Someone swore. "Freeze it, Prince," the second voice commanded. "Now."

There was a moment of blissful cold, but then the fire surged, and—

"Get her out!" Strong hands yanked at her, and she had the vague sense of hearing bubbling.

She had boiled the water in that tub. Almost boiled herself. She was in another tub a moment later, the ice forming again—then melting. Melting, and— "*Breathe*," Rowan said by her ear, kneeling at the head of the tub. "Let it go—let it get out of you."

Steam rose, but she took a breath. "Good," Rowan panted. Ice formed again. Melted.

She was sweating, heat pulsing against her skin like a drum. She did not want to die like this. She took another breath.

Like the ebb and flow of the tide, the bath froze, then melted, froze, then melted, slower each time. And each time, the cold soaked into her a bit more, numbing her, urging her body to relax.

Ice and fire. Frost and embers. Locked in a battle, pushing and pulling. Beneath it, she could almost taste Rowan's steel will slamming against her magic—a will that refused to let the fire burn her into nothing.

Her body ached, but now the pain was mortal. Her cheeks were still aflame, but the water went cold, then lukewarm, then warm and—stayed that way. Warm, not hot.

"We need to get those clothes off her," one of the females said. Celaena lost track of time as two small sets of hands eased up her head and then stripped off her sodden clothes. Without them, she was almost weightless in the water. She didn't care if Rowan saw—didn't think there was an inch of a woman's body he hadn't already explored anyway. She lay there, eyes shut, face tilted toward the ceiling.

After a while, Rowan said, "Just answer yes or no. That's all you have to do." She managed a slight nod, though she winced as pain shot down her neck and shoulders. "Are you in danger of flaring up again?"

She was breathing as evenly as she could, the heat pounding in her cheeks, her legs, her core, but it was steadily diminishing. "No," she whispered, a brush of hot air from her tongue.

"Are you in pain?" Not a sympathetic question, but a commander assessing his soldier's condition to sort out the best course of action.

"Yes." A hiss of steam.

A woman said, "We will prepare a tonic. Just keep her cool." Soft feet padded on the stone floors on their way out, then came the snick of the door to the baths closing. There was a slosh of water in a bucket, then—

Celaena sighed, or tried to, as an ice-cold cloth was laid on her forehead. More sloshing, then another cloth dripped freezing water onto her hair, her neck.

"The burnout," Rowan said quietly. "You should have told me you were at your limit."

Speaking was too hard, but she opened her eyes to find him kneeling at the head of the bath, a bucket of water beside him and a cloth in his hands. He wrung it again over her brow, the water so wonderful she would have moaned. The bath cooled further, but was still warm—too warm.

"If you'd gone on any longer, the burnout would have destroyed you. You *must* learn to recognize the signs—and how to pull back before it's too late." Not a statement, but a command. "It will rip you apart inside. Make this . . ." He shook his head again. "Make this look like nothing. You don't *touch* your magic until you've rested for a while. Understand?"

She tilted her head up, beckoning for more cold water on her face, but he refused to wring the cloth until she nodded her agreement. He cooled her off for another few moments, then slung the cloth over the side of the bucket and stood. "I'm going to check on the tonic. I'll be back soon." He left once she'd nodded again. If she hadn't known better, she might have thought he was fussing. Worried, even.

She hadn't been old enough in Terrasen to have anyone teach her about the deadly side to her power—and no one had explained, since her lessons had been so limited. She hadn't *felt* like she was burning out. It had come on so quickly. Maybe that was all there was to her magic. Maybe her well didn't go as deep as everyone had thought. It would be a relief if that were true.

She lifted her legs, groaning at the aches along her muscles, and leaned forward far enough to hug her knees. Above the lip of the sunken tub, there were a few candles burning on the stones, and she glared at the flames. *Hated* the flames. Though she supposed they needed light in here.

She rested her forehead on her scarred knees, her skin nearly scorching. She shut her eyes, piecing her splintered consciousness together.

The door opened. Rowan. She kept herself in that cool darkness, savoring the growing chill in the water, the quieting pulse under her skin. He sounded about halfway across the room when his footsteps halted.

His breath caught, harsh enough that she looked over her shoulder.

But his eyes weren't on her face. Or the water. They were on her bare back.

Curled as she was against her knees, he could see the whole expanse of ruined flesh, each scar from the lashings. "Who did that do you?"

It would have been easy to lie, but she was so tired, and he had saved her useless hide. So she said, "A lot of people. I spent some time in the Salt Mines of Endovier."

He was so still that she wondered if he'd stopped breathing. "How long?" he asked after a moment. She braced herself for the pity, but his face was so carefully blank—no, not blank. Calm with lethal rage.

"A year. I was there a year before . . . it's a long story." She was too exhausted, her throat too raw, to say the rest of it. She noticed then that his arms were bandaged, and more bandages across his broad chest peeked up from beneath his shirt. She'd burned him again. And yet he had held on to her—had run all the way here and not let go once.

"You were a slave."

She gave him a slow nod. He opened his mouth, but shut it and swallowed, that lethal rage winking out. As if he remembered who he was talking to and that it was the least punishment she deserved.

He turned on his heel and shut the door behind him. She wished he'd slammed it—wished he'd shattered it. But he closed it with barely more than a click and did not return.

42

Her back.

Rowan soared over the trees, riding and shaping the winds to push him onward, faster, their roar negligible to the bellowing in his head. He took in the passing world out of instinct rather than interest, his eyes turned inward—toward that slab of ruined flesh glistening in the candlelight.

The gods knew he'd seen plenty of harrowing injuries. He'd bestowed plenty of them on his enemies and friends alike. In the grand sense of things, her back wasn't even close to some of those wounds. Yet when he'd seen it, his heart had clean stopped—and for a moment, there had been an overwhelming silence in his mind.

He felt his magic and his warrior's instincts honing into a lethal combination the longer he stared—howling to rip apart the people who had done that with his bare hands. Then he'd just left, hardly making it out of the baths before he shifted and soared into the night.

Maeve had lied. Or lied by omission. But she knew. She knew what the girl had gone through—knew she'd been a slave. That day—that day early on, he'd threatened to *whip* the girl, gods above. And she had lost it. He'd been such a proud fool that he'd assumed she'd lashed out because she was nothing more than a child. He should have known better—should have known that when she *did* react to something like that, it meant the scars went deep. And then there were the other things he'd said . . .

He was almost to the towering line of the Cambrian Mountains. She had barely been grown into her woman's body when they hurt her like that. Why hadn't she told him? Why hadn't Maeve told him? His hawk loosed a piercing cry that echoed on the dark gray stones of the mountain wall before him. A chorus of unearthly howls rose in response—Maeve's wild wolves, guarding the passes. Even if he flew all the way to Doranelle, he'd reach his queen and demand answers and . . . she would not give them to him. With the blood oath, she could command he not go back to Mistward.

He gripped the winds with his magic, choking off their current. Aelin . . . Aelin had not trusted him—had not wanted him to know.

And she'd almost burned out completely, gods be damned, leaving her currently defenseless. Primal anger sharpened in his gut, brimming with a territorial, possessive need. Not a need for her, but a need to protect—a male's duty and honor. He had not handled the news as he should have.

If she hadn't wanted to tell him about being a slave, then she probably had done so assuming the worst about him—just as she was probably assuming the worst about his leaving. The thought didn't sit well.

So he veered back to the north and reined his magic to pull the winds with him, easing his flight back to the fortress.

He would get answers from his queen soon enough.

The healers gave her a tonic, and when Celaena reassured them that she wasn't going to incinerate herself, she stayed in the bath until her teeth were chattering. It took three times as long as usual to get back to her rooms, and she was so frozen and drained that she didn't change into clothes before she dropped into bed.

She didn't want to think about what it meant that Rowan had left like that, but she did, aching and cramping from the magic. She drifted into a jerking, fitful sleep, the cold so fierce she couldn't tell whether it was from the temperature or the aftermath of the magic. At some point, she was awoken by the laughing and singing of the returning revelers. After a while, even the drunkest found their bed or someone else's. She was almost asleep again, teeth still chattering, when her window groaned open in the breeze. She was too cold and sore to get up. There was a flutter of wings and a flash of light, and before she could roll over, he'd scooped her up, blanket and all.

If she'd had any energy, she might have objected. But he carried her up the two flights of stairs, down the hall, and then—

A roaring fire, warm sheets, and a soft mattress. And a heavy quilt that was tucked in with surprising gentleness. The fire dimmed on a phantom wind, and then the mattress shifted.

In the flickering dark, he said roughly, "You're staying with me from now on." She found him lying as far away from her as he could get without falling off the mattress. "The bed is for tonight. Tomorrow, you'll get a cot. You'll clean up after yourself or you'll be back in that room."

She nestled into her pillow. "Very well." The fire dimmed, yet the room remained toasty. It was the first warm bed she'd had in months. But she said, "I don't want your pity."

"This is not pity. Maeve decided not to tell me what happened to you. You have to know that I—I wasn't aware you had—"

She slid an arm across the bed to grasp his hand. She knew that if she wanted to, she could strike him a wound so deep it would fracture him. "I knew. At first, I was afraid you'd mock me if I told you, and I would kill you for it. Then I didn't want you to pity me. And more than any of that, I didn't want you to think it was ever an excuse."

"Like a good soldier," he said. She had to look away for a moment to keep from letting him see just what that meant to her. He took a long breath that made his broad chest expand. "Tell me how you were sent there—and how you got out."

She was tired in her bones, but she rallied her energy one last time and told him of the years in Rifthold, of stealing Asterion horses and racing across the desert, of dancing until dawn with courtesans and thieves and all the beautiful, wicked creatures in the world. And then she told him about losing Sam, and of that first whipping in Endovier, when she'd spat blood in the Chief Overseer's face, and what she had seen and endured in the following year. She spoke of the day she had snapped and sprinted for her own death. Her heart grew heavy when at last she got to the evening when the Captain of the Royal Guard prowled into her life, and a tyrant's son had offered her a shot at freedom. She told him what she could about the competition and how she'd won it, until her words slurred and her eyelids drooped.

There would be more time to tell him of what happened next—of the Wyrdkeys and Elena and Nehemia and how she had become so broken and useless. She yawned, and Rowan rubbed his eyes, his other hand still in hers. But he didn't let go. And when she awoke before dawn, warm and safe and rested, Rowan was still holding her hand, clasped to his chest.

Something molten rushed through her, pouring over every crack and fracture still left gaping and open. Not to hurt or mar—but to weld.

To forge.

43

Rowan didn't let her get out of bed that day. He brought trays of food, going so far as to make sure she consumed every last drop of beef stew, half a loaf of crusty bread, a bowl of the first spring berries, and a mug of ginger tea. He hardly needed to offer any encouragement to eat; she was starving. But if she didn't know better, she'd say he was fussing.

Emrys and Luca visited once to see if she was alive, took one look at Rowan's stone-cold face, heard the ripple of a growl, and took off, saying she was in more than competent hands and promising to come back when she was feeling better.

"You know," Celaena said, propped in bed with her fourth mug of tea of the day, "I highly doubt anyone is going to attack me *now*, if they've already put up with my nonsense for this long."

Rowan, who was yet again poring over the map of the location of the bodies, didn't even look up from his seat at his worktable. "This isn't negotiable."

She might have laughed had her body not given a burst of twisting, blinding pain. She bore down on it, clenching her mug, focusing on her breathing. *That* was why she'd allowed him to fuss. Thanks to her magical meltdown last night, every damn part of her was sore. The constant throb and stinging and twisting, the headache between her brows, the fuzziness on the edge of her vision . . . even sliding her gaze across the room sent sparks of pain through her head.

"So you mean to tell me that whenever someone comes close to burnout, she not only goes through all this misery, but if she's female, the males around her go this berserk?"

He set down his pen and twisted to examine her. "*This* is hardly berserk. At least you can defend yourself by physical means when your magic is useless. For other Fae, even if they've had weapons and defense training, if they can't touch their magic, they're vulnerable, especially when they're drained and in pain. That makes people—usually males, yes—somewhat edgy. Others have been known to kill without thought any perceived threat, real or otherwise."

"What sort of threat? Maeve's lands are peaceful." She leaned over to set down her tea, but he was already moving, so swift that he intercepted her mug before it could hit the table. He took it from her with surprising gentleness, saw that she'd drained it, and poured another cup.

"Threats from anywhere—males, females, creatures . . . You can't reason against it. Even if it wasn't in our culture, there would still be an instinct to protect the defenseless, regardless of whether they're female or male, young or old." He reached for a slice of bread and a bowl of beef broth. "Eat this."

"It pains me to say this, but one more bite and I'll be sick all over the place." Oh, he was definitely fussing, and though it warmed her miserable heart, it was becoming rather irritating.

The bastard just dipped the bread into the broth and held them out to her. "You need to keep up your energy. You probably came so close to burnout because you didn't have enough food in your stomach."

Fine; it smelled too good to resist, anyway. She took the bread and the broth. While she ate, he made sure the room passed inspection: the fire was still high (suffocatingly hot, as it had been since morning, thanks to the chills that had racked her), only one window was cracked (to allow in the slightest of breezes when she had hot flashes), the door was shut (and locked), and yet another pot of tea was waiting (currently steeping on his worktable). When he was done ensuring all was accounted for and no threats lurked in the shadows, he looked her over with the same scrutiny: skin (wan and gleaming from the remnants of those hot flashes), lips (pale and cracked), posture (limp and useless), eyes (pain-dimmed and increasingly full of irritation). Rowan frowned again.

After handing the empty bowl to him, she rubbed her thumb and forefinger against the persistent headache between her eyebrows. "So when the magic runs out," she said, "that's it—either you stop or you burn out?"

Rowan leaned back in his chair. "Well, there's the *carranam*." The Old Language word was beautiful on his tongue—and if she'd had a death wish, she might have begged him to speak only in the ancient language, just to savor the exquisite sounds.

"It's hard to explain," Rowan went on. "I've only ever seen it used a handful of times on killing fields. When you're drained, your *carranam* can yield their power to you, as long as you're compatible and actively sharing a blood connection."

She tilted her head to the side. "If we were *carranam*, and I gave you my power, would you still only be using wind and ice—not my fire?" He nodded gravely. "How do you know if you're compatible with someone?"

"There's no way of telling until you try. And the bond is so rare that the majority of Fae never meet someone who is compatible, or whom they trust enough to test it out. There's always a threat that they could take too much—and if they're unskilled, they could shatter your mind. Or you could both burn out completely."

Interesting. "Could you ever just steal magic from someone?"

"Less savory Fae once attempted to do so—to win battles and add to their own power—but it never worked. And if it did, it was because the person they held hostage was coincidentally compatible. Maeve outlawed any forced bonds long before I was born, but . . . I've been sent a few times to hunt down corrupt Fae who keep their *carranam* as slaves. Usually, the slaves are so broken there's no way to rehabilitate them. Putting them down is the only mercy I can offer."

His face and voice didn't change, but she said softly, "Doing that must be harder than all the wars and sieges you've ever waged."

A shadow darted across his harsh face. "Immortality is not as much of a gift as mortals would believe. It can breed monsters that even you would be sick to learn about. Imagine the sadists you've encountered—and then imagine them with millennia to hone their craft and warped desires."

Celaena shuddered. "This conversation's become too awful to have after eating," she said, slumping against the pillows. "Tell me which one of your little cadre is the handsomest, and if he would fancy me."

Rowan choked. "The thought of you with any of my companions makes my blood run cold."

"They're that awful? Your kitty-cat friend looked decent enough."

Rowan's brows rose high. "I don't think my *kitty-cat* friend would know what to do with you—nor would any of the others. It would likely end in bloodshed." She kept grinning, and he crossed his arms. "They would likely have very little interest in you, as you'll be old and decrepit soon enough and thus not worth the effort it would take to win you."

She rolled her eyes. "Killjoy."

Silence fell, and he looked her over again (lucid, if drained and moody), and she wasn't that surprised when he glanced at her bare wrists—one of the few bits of skin showing thanks to all the blankets he'd piled on top of her. They hadn't discussed it last night, but she knew he'd been working up to it.

There was no judgment in his eyes as he said, "A skilled healer could probably get rid of those scars—definitely the ones on your wrist, and most on your back."

She clenched her jaw, but after a moment loosed a long breath. Even though she knew he would understand without much explanation, she said, "There were cells in the bowels of the mines that they used to punish slaves. Cells so dark you would wake up in them and think you'd been blinded. They locked me in there sometimes—once for three weeks straight. And the only thing that got me through it was reminding myself of my name, over and over and over—*I am Celaena Sardothien*."

Rowan's face was drawn, but she went on. "When they would let me out, so much of my mind had shut down in the darkness that the only thing I could remember was that my name was Celaena. Celaena Sardothien, arrogant and brave and skilled, Celaena who did not know fear or despair, Celaena who was a weapon honed by Death." She ran a shaking hand through her hair. "I don't usually let myself think about that part of Endovier," she admitted. "After I got out, there were nights when I would wake up and think I was back in those cells, and I would have to light every candle in my room to prove I wasn't. They don't just kill you in the mines—they break you.

"There are thousands of slaves in Endovier, and a good number are from Terrasen. Regardless of what I do with my birthright, I'm going to find a way to free them someday. I *will* free them. Them, and all the slaves in Calaculla, too. So my scars serve as a reminder of that."

She'd never said it, but there it was. Once she dealt with the King of Adarlan, if destroying him somehow didn't put an end to the labor camps, she would. Stone by stone, if necessary.

Rowan asked, "What happened ten years ago, Aelin?"

"I'm not going to talk about that."

"If you took up your crown, you could free Endovier far more easily than—"

"I *can't* talk about it."

"Why?"

There was a pit in the memory—a pit she couldn't climb out of if she ever fell in. It wasn't her parents' deaths. She had been able to tell others in vague terms about their murders. That pain was still staggering, still haunted her. But waking up between their corpses wasn't the moment that had shattered everything Aelin Galathynius was and might have been. In the back of her mind, she heard another woman's voice, lovely and frantic, another woman who—

She rubbed her brows again. "There is this . . . rage," she said hoarsely. "This despair and hatred and *rage* that lives and breathes inside me. There is no sanity to it, no gentleness. It is a monster dwelling under my skin. For the past ten years, I have worked every day, every hour, to keep that monster locked up. And the moment I talk about those two days, and what happened before and after, that monster is going to break loose, and there will be no accounting for what I do.

"That is how I was able to stand before the King of Adarlan, how I was able to befriend his son and his captain, how I was able to live in that palace. Because I did not give that rage, those memories, one inch. And right now I am looking for the tools that might destroy my enemy, and I cannot let out the monster, because it will make me use those tools against the king, not put them back as I should—and I might very well destroy the world for spite. So *that* is why I must be Celaena, not Aelin—because being Aelin means facing those things, and unleashing that monster. Do you understand?"

"For whatever it's worth, I don't think you would destroy the world from spite." His voice turned hard. "But I also think you like to suffer. You collect scars because you want proof that you are paying for whatever sins you've committed. And I know this because I've been doing the same damn thing for two hundred years. Tell me, do you think you will go to some blessed Afterworld, or do you expect a burning hell? You're hoping for hell—because how could you face them in the Afterworld? Better to suffer, to be damned for eternity and—"

"That's enough," she whispered. She must have sounded as miserable and small as she felt, because he turned back to the worktable. She shut her eyes, but her heart was thundering.

She didn't know how much time passed. After a while, the mattress shifted and groaned, and a warm body pressed against hers. Not holding her, just lying beside her. She didn't open her eyes, but she breathed in the smell of him, the pine and snow, and her pain settled a bit.

"At least if you're going to hell," he said, the vibrations in his chest rumbling against her, "then we'll be there together."

"I feel bad for the dark god already." He brushed a large hand down her hair, and she almost purred. She hadn't realized just how much she missed being touched—by anyone, friend or lover. "When I'm back to normal, can I assume you're going to yell at me about almost burning out?"

He let out a soft laugh but continued stroking her hair. "You have no idea."

She smiled against the pillow, and his hand stilled for a moment—then started again.

After a long while he murmured, "I have no doubt that you'll be able to free the slaves from the labor camps some day. No matter what name you use."

Her eyes burned behind their lids, but she leaned into his touch some more, even going so far as to put a hand on his broad chest, savoring the steady, assured heartbeat pounding beneath.

"Thank you for looking after me," she said. He grunted—acceptance or dismissal, she didn't know. Sleep tugged at her, and she followed it into oblivion.

Rowan kept her cooped up in his room for a few more days, and even once she told him she was feeling fine, he made her spend an extra half day in bed. She supposed it was nice, having someone, even an overbearing, snarling Fae warrior, bothering to care whether she lived or died.

Her birthday arrived—nineteen somehow felt rather dull—and her sole present was that Rowan left her alone for a few hours. He came back with the news of another demi-Fae corpse found near the coast. She asked him to let her see it, but he flat-out refused (barked at her was more like it) and said he'd already gone to see it himself. It was the same pattern: a dried nosebleed, a body drained until only a husk remained, and then a careless dumping. He'd also gone back to that town—where they had been more than happy to see him, since he'd brought gold and silver.

And he'd returned to Celaena with chocolates, since he claimed to be insulted that she considered his absence a proper birthday present. She tried to embrace him, but he would have none of that, and told her as much. Still, the next time she used the bathing room, she'd snuck behind his chair at the worktable and planted a great, smacking kiss on his cheek. He'd waved her off and wiped his face with a snarl, but she had the suspicion that he'd let her get past his defenses.

It was a mistake to think that finally going back outdoors would be delightful.

Celaena was standing across a mossy clearing from Rowan, her knees slightly bent, hands in loose fists. Rowan hadn't told her to, but she'd gotten into a defensive position upon seeing the faint gleam in his eyes.

Rowan only looked like this when he was about to make her life a living hell. And since they hadn't gone to the temple ruins, she assumed he thought she'd at least mastered one element of her power, despite the events of Beltane. Which meant they were on to mastering the next.

"Your magic lacks shape," Rowan said at last, standing so still that she envied him for it. "And because it has no shape, you have little control. As a form of attack, a fireball or wave of flame is useful, yes. But if you are engaging a skilled combatant—if you want to be able to *use* your power—then you have to learn to fight with it." She groaned. "But," he added sharply, "you have one advantage that many magic-wielders do not: you already know how to fight with weapons."

"First chocolates on my birthday, now an actual compliment?"

His eyes narrowed, and they had yet another of their wordless conversations. *The more you talk, the more I'm going to make you pay in a moment.*

She smiled slightly. *Apologies, master. I am yours to instruct.*

Brat. He jerked his chin at her. "Your fire can take whatever form you wish—the only limit being your imagination. And considering your upbringing, should you go on the offensive—"

"You want me to make a sword out of fire?"

"Arrows, daggers—you direct the power. Visualize it, and use it as you would a mortal weapon."

She swallowed.

He smirked. *Afraid to play with fire, Princess?*

You won't be happy if I singe your eyebrows off.

Try me. "When you trained as an assassin, what was the first thing you learned?"

"How to defend myself."

She understood why he'd looked so amused for the past few minutes when he said, "Good."

Not surprisingly, having ice daggers thrown at her was miserable.

Rowan hurled dagger after magical dagger at her—and every damn time, the shield of fire that she tried (and failed) to imagine did nothing. If it appeared at all, it always manifested too far to the left or right.

Rowan didn't want a wall of flame. No—he wanted a small, controlled shield. And it didn't matter how many times he nicked her hands or arms or face, it didn't matter that dried blood was now itching down her cheeks. One shield—that was all she had to craft and he would stop.

Sweating and panting, Celaena was beginning to wonder if she should step directly into the path of his next dagger and put herself out of her suffering when Rowan growled. "Try harder."

"I am trying," she snapped, rolling aside as he sent two gleaming ice daggers at her head.

"You're acting like you're on the verge of a burnout."

"Maybe I am."

"If you believe for one moment that you're close to a burnout after an hour of practicing—"

"It happened that quickly on Beltane."

"That was *not* the end of your power." His next ice dagger hovered in the air beside his head. "You fell into the lure of the magic and let it do what it wanted—let it consume you. Had you kept your head, you could have had those fires burning for weeks—months."

"No." She didn't have any better answer than that.

His nostrils flared slightly. "I knew it. You wanted your power to be insignificant—you were relieved when you thought that was all you had."

Without warning, he sent the dagger, then the next, then the next at her. She raised her left arm as she would raise a shield, picturing the flame surrounding her arm, blocking those daggers, obliterating them, but—

She cursed so loudly that the birds stopped their chatter. She clutched her forearm as blood welled and soaked into her tunic. "Stop *hitting* me! I get the point!"

But another dagger came. And another.

Ducking and dodging, raising her bloodied arm again and again, she gritted her teeth and swore at him. He sent a dagger twirling with deadly efficiency—and she couldn't move fast enough to avoid the thin scratch along her cheekbone. She hissed.

He was right—he was always right, and she *hated* that. Almost as much as she hated the power that flooded her and did what it wanted. It was *hers* to command—not the other way around. She was not its slave. She was no one's slave anymore. And if Rowan threw one more damned dagger at her *face*—

He did.

The ice crystal didn't make it past her upraised forearm before it vanished in a hiss of steam.

Celaena gazed over the flickering edge of the compact red-burning flame before her arm. Shaped like—a shield.

Rowan smiled slowly. "We're done for today. Go eat something."

The circular shield did not burn her, though its flames swirled and sizzled. As she'd commanded. It had . . . worked.

So she raised her eyes to Rowan. "No. *Again*."

After a week of making shields of various sizes and temperatures, Celaena could have multiple defenses burning at once, and encircle the entire glen with half a thought to protect it from outside assault. And when she awoke one morning before dawn, she couldn't say why she did it, but she slipped from the room she shared with Rowan and went down to the ward-stones.

She shivered from more than the early morning cold as the power of the curving gate-stones zinged against her skin when she passed through. But none of the sentries on the battlements ordered her to stop as she walked along the line of towering, carved rocks until she found a bit of even ground and began to practice.

44

As one the Thirteen flew; as one the Thirteen led the other Blackbeak covens in the skies. Drill after drill, through rain and sun and wind, until they were all tanned and freckled. Even though Abraxos had yet to make the Crossing, the Spidersilk patching on his wings improved his flying significantly.

It was all going beautifully. Abraxos had gotten into a brawl for dominance with Lin's bull and emerged victorious, and after that, none in her coven or any other challenged him. The War Games were fast approaching, and though Iskra hadn't been any trouble since the night Manon had half killed her, they watched their backs: in the baths, around every dark corner, double-checking every rein and strap before they mounted their wyverns.

Yes, it was all going beautifully, until Manon was summoned to her grandmother's room.

"Why is it," her grandmother said by way of greeting, pacing the room, teeth always out, "that I have to hear from gods-damned

Cresseida that your runty, useless wyvern hasn't made the Crossing? Why is it that I am in the middle of a meeting, planning these War Games so *you* can win, and the other Matrons tell me that *you* aren't allowed to participate because your mount will not make the Crossing and therefore isn't allowed to fly in the host?"

Manon glimpsed the flash of nails before they raked down her cheek. Not hard enough to scar, but enough to bleed.

"You and that beast are an embarrassment," her grandmother hissed, teeth snapping in her face. "All I want is for you to win these Games—so we can take our rightful place as queens, not High Witches. *Queens* of the Waste, Manon. And you are doing your best to *ruin* it." Manon kept her eyes on the ground. Her grandmother dug a nail into her chest, cutting through her red cloak, piercing the flesh right above her heart. "Has your heart melted?"

"No."

"No," her grandmother sneered. "No, it cannot melt, because you *do not have a heart*, Manon. We are not born with them, and we are glad of it." She pointed to the stone floor. "Why is it that I am informed *today* that Iskra caught a gods-damned Crochan spying on us? Why am I the last to know that she is in our dungeons and that they have been interrogating her for *two days*?"

Manon blinked, but that was all the surprise she let show. If Crochans were spying on them . . . Another slice to the face, marring the other cheek.

"You will make the Crossing tomorrow, Manon. Tomorrow, and I don't care if you splatter yourself on the rocks. If you live, you had better pray to the Darkness that you win those Games. Because if you don't . . ." Her grandmother sliced a nail across Manon's throat. A scratch to set the blood running.

And a promise.

Everyone came this time to watch the Crossing. Abraxos was saddled, focus pinned on the cave mouth open to the night beyond. Asterin and Sorrel were behind her—but beside their mounts, not astride them. Her grandmother had gotten wind of how they planned to save her and forbidden it. It was Manon's own stupidity and pride that had to pay, she'd said.

Witches lined the viewing platform, and from high above, the High Witches and their heirs watched from a small balcony. The noise was near deafening. Manon glanced at Asterin and Sorrel and found them looking stone-cold fierce, but tense.

"Keep to the walls so he doesn't spook your wyverns," she told them. They nodded grimly.

Since grafting the Spidersilk onto Abraxos's wings, Manon had been careful not to push him too hard until the healing was absolutely complete. But the Crossing, with its plunge and winds . . . his wings could be shredded in a matter of seconds if the silk didn't hold.

"We're waiting, Manon," her grandmother barked from above. She waved a hand toward the cave mouth. "But by all means, take your time."

Laughter—from the Yellowlegs, Blackbeaks . . . everyone. Yet Petrah wasn't smiling. And none of the Thirteen, gathered closest along the viewing platform, were smiling, either.

Manon turned to Abraxos, looking into those eyes. "Let's go." She tugged on the reins.

But he refused to move—not from fear or terror. He slowly lifted his head—looking to where her grandmother stood—and let out a low, warning growl. A threat.

Manon knew she should reprimand him for the disrespect, but the fact that he could grasp what was occurring in this hall . . . it should have been impossible.

"The night is waning," her grandmother called, heedless of the beast that stared at her with such rage in his eyes.

Sorrel and Asterin exchanged glances, and she could have sworn her Second's hand twitched toward the hilt of her sword. Not to hurt Abraxos, but . . . Every single one of the Thirteen was casually reaching for their weapons. To fight their way out—in case her grandmother gave the order to have Manon and Abraxos put down. They'd heard the challenge in Abraxos's growl—understood that the beast had drawn a line in the sand.

They were not born with hearts, her grandmother said. They had all been told that. Obedience, discipline, brutality. Those were the things they were supposed to cherish.

Asterin's eyes were bright—stunningly bright—and she nodded once at Manon.

It was that same feeling she'd gotten when Iskra whipped Abraxos—that thing she couldn't describe, but it blinded her.

Manon gripped Abraxos's snout, forcing his gaze away from her grandmother. "Just once," she whispered. "All you have to do is make this jump just *once*, Abraxos, and then you can *shut them up forever.*"

Then, rising up from the deep, there came a steady two-note beat. The beat of the chained bait beasts, who hauled the massive machines around. Like a thudding heart. Or beating wings.

Louder the beat sounded, as if the wyverns down in the pits knew what was happening. It grew and grew, until it reached the cavern—until Asterin reached for her shield and joined in. Until each one of the Thirteen took up the beat. "You hear that? *That* is for you."

For a moment, as the beat pulsed around them, phantom wings from the mountain itself, Manon thought that it would not be so bad to die—if it was with him, if she was not alone.

"You are one of the Thirteen," she said to him. "From now until the Darkness cleaves us apart. You are mine, and I am yours. Let's show them why."

He huffed into her palms as if to say he already knew all that and that she was just wasting time. She smiled faintly, even as Abraxos cast another challenging glare in her grandmother's direction. The wyvern lowered himself to the ground for Manon to climb into the saddle.

The distance to the entrance seemed so much shorter in the saddle than on foot, but she did not let herself doubt him as she blinked her inner lid into place and retracted her teeth. The Spidersilk would hold—she would consider no other alternative. "Fly, Abraxos," she told him, and dug her spurs into his sides.

Like a roaring star, he thundered down the long shoot, and Manon moved with him, meeting each gallop of his powerful body, each step in time with the beat of the wyverns locked in the belly of the mountain. Abraxos flapped his wings open, pounding them once, twice, gathering speed, fearless, unrelenting, ready.

Still, the beat did not stop, not from the wyverns or from the Thirteen or from the Blackbeak covens, who picked it up, stomping their feet or clapping their hands. Not from the Blueblood heir, who clapped her sword against her dagger, or the Blueblood witches who followed her lead. The entire mountain shook with the sound.

Faster and faster, Abraxos raced for the drop, and Manon held on tight. The cave mouth opened wide. Abraxos tucked in his wings, using the movement to give his body one last shove over the lip as he took Manon with him and plunged.

Fast as lightning arcing across the sky, he plummeted toward the Gap floor.

Manon rose up into the saddle, clinging as her braid ripped free from her cloak, then came loose from its bonds, pulling painfully behind her, making her eyes water despite the lids. Down and down he fell, wings tucked in tight, tail straight and balanced.

Down into hell, into eternity, into that world where, for a moment, she could have sworn that something tightened in her chest.

She did not shut her eyes, not as the moon-illuminated stones of the Gap became closer, clearer. She did not need to.

Like the sails of a mighty ship, Abraxos's wings unfurled, snapping tight. He tilted them upward, pulling against the death trying to drag them down.

And it was those wings, covered in glimmering patches of Spider-silk, that stayed strong and sturdy, sending them soaring clean up the side of the Omega and into the starry sky beyond.

45

To their credit, the sentries didn't jump when Rowan shifted beside them atop the battlement wall. They had eyes keen enough to have detected his arrival as he swooped in. A slight tang of fear leaked from them, but that was to be expected, even if it troubled him more than it had in the past. But they did stir slightly when he spoke. "How long has she been down there?"

"An hour, Prince," one said, watching the flashing flames below.

"For how many mornings in a row?"

"This is the fourth, Prince," the same sentry replied.

The first three days she'd slipped from bed before dawn, he'd assumed she'd been helping in the kitchens. But when they'd trained yesterday she'd . . . *improved* at a rate she shouldn't have, as if overnight. He had to give her credit for resourcefulness.

The girl stood outside the ward-stones, fighting with herself.

A dagger of flame flew from her hand toward the invisible barrier between two stones, then another, as if racing for the head of an opponent. It hit the magic wall with a flash of light and bounced back, reflected off the protective spell encircling the fortress. And when it reached her, she shielded—swift, strong, sure. A warrior on a battlefield.

"I've never seen anyone . . . fight like that," the sentry said.

It was a question, but Rowan didn't bother to answer. It wasn't their business, and he wasn't entirely certain if his queen would be pleased with the demi-Fae learning to use their powers in such a way. Though he fully planned to tell Lorcan, his commander and the only male who outranked him in Doranelle, just to see whether they could use it in their training.

The girl moved from throwing weapons to hand-to-hand combat: a punch of power, a sweeping kick of flame. Her flames had become gloriously varied—golds and reds and oranges. And her technique—not the magic, but the way she moved . . . Her master had been a monster, there was no doubt of that. But he had trained her thoroughly. She ducked and flipped and twisted, relentless, raging, and—

She swore with her usual color as the wall sent the punch of ruby flame back at her. She managed to shield, but still got knocked on her ass. Yet none of the sentries laughed. Rowan didn't know if it was because of his presence or because of her.

He got his answer a heartbeat later, as he waited for her to shout or shriek or walk away. But the princess just slowly got to her feet, not bothering to brush off the dirt and leaves, and kept practicing.

The next corpse appeared a week later, setting a rather wretched tone for the crisp spring morning as Celaena and Rowan ran for the site.

They'd spent the past week fighting and defending and manipulating her magic, interrupted only by a rather miserable visit from some

Fae nobility traveling through the area—which left Celaena in no hurry to set foot in Doranelle. Thankfully, the guests stayed for one night, hardly disrupting her lessons.

They worked only with fire, ignoring the drop of water affinity that she'd been given. She tried again and again to summon the water, when she was drinking, while in the bath, when it rained, but to no avail. Fire it was, then. And while she knew Rowan was aware of her early morning practicing, he never lightened her training, though she could have sworn she occasionally felt their magic . . . playing together, her flame taunting his ice, his wind dancing amongst her embers. But each morning brought something new, something harder and different and miserable. Gods, he was brilliant. Cunning and wicked and brilliant.

Even when he beat the hell out of her. Every. Damn. Day.

Not from malice, not like it had been before, but to prove his point—her enemies would give no quarter. If she needed to pause, if her power faltered, she died.

So he knocked her into the mud or the stream or the grass with a blast of wind or ice. So she rose, shooting arrows of flame, her shield now her strongest ally. Again and again, hungry and exhausted and soaking with rain and mist and sweat. Until shielding was an instinct, until she could hurl arrows and daggers of flame together, until she knocked *him* on his ass. There was always more to learn; she lived and breathed and dreamt of fire.

Sometimes, though, her dreams were of a brown-eyed man in an empire across the sea. Sometimes she'd awaken and reach for the warm, male body beside hers, only to realize it was not the captain—that she would never again lie next to Chaol, not after what had happened. And when she remembered that, it sometimes hurt to breathe.

There was nothing romantic about sharing a bed with Rowan, and they kept to their own sides. There certainly was nothing romantic about it when they reached the site of the corpse and she peeled off her shirt to cool down. In nothing but her underclothes, Celaena's skin was bitten by the sea air with a delightful chill, and even Rowan unbuttoned his heavy jacket as they carefully approached the coordinates.

"Well, I can certainly smell him this time," Celaena said between panting breaths. They'd reached the site in little less than three hours, guessing by the sun. That was faster and longer than she'd ever run, thanks to the Fae form she'd been training in.

"This body has been rotting here longer than the demi-Fae from three days ago."

She bit back her retort. There had been another demi-Fae body found, and he hadn't let her go see it, instead forcing her to practice all day while he flew to the site. But this morning, he'd taken one look at the fire smoldering in her eyes and relented.

Celaena stepped carefully on the pine carpet, scanning for any signs of a fight or of the attacker. The ground was churned up, and despite the rushing stream, the flies were buzzing near what appeared to be a heap of clothing peeking from behind a small boulder.

Rowan swore, low and viciously, even lifting his forearm to cover his nose and mouth as he examined the husk that remained, the demi-Fae male's face twisted in horror. Celaena might done the same, except . . . except—

That second smell was here, too. Not as strong as it had been at the first site, but it lingered. She shoved back against the memory that wanted to rise in response to the smell, the memory that had overwhelmed her that day in the barrow-field.

"It has our attention and it knows it," she said. "It's targeting demi-Fae—either to send a message, or because they . . . taste good. But—" She pictured the map Rowan kept in his room, detailing the wide area where the corpses had been found, and winced. "What if there's more than one?" Rowan looked back at her, brows high. She didn't say anything else until she had moved to where he stood by the body, careful not to disturb any clues. Her stomach lurched and bile stung the back of her throat, but she clamped down on the horror with a wall of ice that even her fire could not melt. "You're old as hell," she said. "You must have considered that we're dealing with a few of them, given how vast the territory is. What if the one we saw in the barrows wasn't even the creature responsible for these bodies?"

He narrowed his eyes, but conceded a nod. She studied the hollowed-out face, the torn clothes.

Torn clothes, what looked like small cuts along the palms—as if he'd dug in his fingernails. The others had barely been touched, but this . . .

"Rowan." She waved away flies. "Rowan, tell me you see what I'm seeing."

Another vicious curse. He crouched, using the tip of a dagger to push back a bit of clothing torn at the collar. "This male—"

"Fought. He fought back against it. None of the others did, according to the reports."

The stench of the corpse was nearly enough to bring her to her knees. But she squatted by the decaying hand and forearm, shriveled and wasted from the inside out. She held out a hand for Rowan's dagger, still possessing none of her own. He hesitated as she looked up at him.

Only for the afternoon, he seemed to growl as he pressed the hilt into her open palm.

She yanked down the dagger. *I know, I know. I haven't earned my weapons back yet. Don't get your feathers ruffled.*

She turned back to the husk, cutting off their wordless conversation and getting a snarl in response. Butting heads with Rowan was the least of her concerns, even if it had become one of her favorite activities.

There was something so familiar about doing this, she thought as she carefully, as gently and respectfully as she could, ran the tip of the dagger under the male's cracked and filthy nails, then smeared the contents on the back of her own hand. Dirt and black . . . black . . .

"What the hell is that?" Rowan demanded, kneeling beside her, sniffing her outstretched hand. He jerked back, snarling. "That's not dirt."

No, it wasn't. It was blacker than night, and reeked just as badly as it had the first time she'd smelled it, in the catacombs beneath the library, an obsidian, oily pool of blood. Slightly different from that other, horrific smell that loitered around this place, but similar. So similar to—

"This isn't possible," she said, jolting to her feet. "This—this—this—" She paced, if only to keep from shaking. "I'm wrong. I have to be wrong."

There had been so many cells in that forgotten dungeon beneath the library, beneath the king's Wyrdstone clock tower. The creature she'd encountered there had possessed a human heart. It had been left, she'd suspected, because of some defect. What if . . . what if the perfected ones had been moved elsewhere? What if they were now . . . ready?

"Tell me," Rowan growled, the words barely understandable as he seemed to struggle to rein in the killing edge he rode in response to the threat lurking somewhere in these woods.

She lifted her hand to rub her eyes, but realized what was on her fingers and went to wipe them on her shirt. Only to recall that she was wearing nothing but the soft white band around her breasts, and that she was cold to her very bones. She rushed to the nearby stream to scrub off the dried black blood, hating even that the trace of it would be in the water, in the world, and quickly, quietly told Rowan of the creature in the library, the Wyrdkeys, and the information Maeve held hostage regarding how to destroy that power. Power that was being used by the king to *make* things—and targeting people with magic in their blood to be their hosts.

A warm breeze wrapped around her, heating her bones and blood, steadying her. "How did it get here?" Rowan asked, his features now set with icy calm.

"I don't know. I hope I'm wrong. But that *smell*—I'll never forget that smell as long as I live. Like it had rotted from the inside out, its very essence ruined."

"But it retained some cognitive abilities. And whatever this is, it must have them, too, if it's dumping the bodies."

She tried to swallow—twice—but her mouth was dry. "Demi-Fae . . . they would make perfect hosts, with so many of them able to use magic and no one in Wendlyn or Doranelle caring if they live or die. But these corpses—if he wanted to kidnap them, why kill them?"

"Unless they weren't compatible," Rowan said. "And if they weren't compatible, then what better use for them than to drain them dry?"

"But what's the point of leaving the bodies where we can find them? To drum up fear?"

Rowan ground his jaw and stalked through the area, examining the ground, the trees, the rocks. "Burn the body, Aelin." He removed the sheath and belt that had housed the dagger still dangling from her hand and tossed them to her. She caught them with her free hand. "We're going hunting."

They found nothing, even when Rowan shifted into his other form and circled high above. As the light grew dim, they climbed into the biggest, densest tree in the area. They squeezed onto a massive branch, huddling together, as he would not let her summon even a flicker of flame.

When she complained about the conditions, Rowan pointed out that there was no moon that night, and worse things than the skinwalkers prowled the woods. That shut her up until he asked her to tell him more about the creature in the library, to explain every detail and weakness and strength.

After she finished, he took out one of his long knives—a fraction of the marvelous assortment he carried—and began cleaning it. With her heightened senses, she could see enough in the starlight to make out the steel, his hands, and the shifting muscles in his shoulders as he wiped the blade. He himself was a beautiful weapon, forged by centuries of ruthless training and warring.

"Do you think I was mistaken?" she said as he put away the knife and reached for the ones hidden beneath his clothes. Like the first, none of them were dirty, but she didn't point it out. "About the creature, I mean."

Rowan slung his shirt over his head to get at the weapons strapped beneath, revealing his broad back, muscled and scarred and glorious. Fine—some very feminine, innate part of her appreciated *that*. And she didn't mind his half-nakedness. He'd seen every inch of her now. She supposed there was no part of him that would be much of a surprise, either, thanks to Chaol. But—no, she wouldn't think about Chaol. Not when she was feeling balanced and clear-headed and *good*.

"We're dealing with a cunning, lethal predator, regardless of where it originated and how many there are," he said, cleaning a small dagger that had been strapped across his pectoral muscle. She followed the path of his tattoo down his face, neck, shoulders, and arm. Such a stark, brutal marking. Had the scars on Chaol's face healed, or would they be a permanent reminder of what she'd done to him? "If you were mistaken, I'd consider it a blessing."

She slumped against the trunk. That was twice now she'd thought of Chaol. She must truly be exhausted, because the only other option was that she just wanted to make herself feel miserable.

She didn't want to know what Chaol had been doing these months, or what he now thought of her. If he'd sold the information about her past to the king, maybe the king had sent one of those things here, to hunt her. And Dorian—gods, she'd been so lost in her own misery that she'd hardly wondered about him, whether he'd managed to keep his magic secret. She prayed he was safe.

She suffered with her own thoughts until Rowan finished with his weapons, then took out their skin of water and rinsed his hands, neck, and chest. She watched him sidelong, the way the water gleamed on his skin in the starlight. It was a damn good thing Rowan had no interest in her, either, because she knew she was stupid and reckless enough to consider whether moving on in the physical sense might solve the problem of Chaol.

There was still such a mighty hole in her chest. A hole that grew bigger, not smaller, and that no one could fix, not even if she took Rowan to bed. There were some days when the amethyst ring was her most precious belonging—others when it was all she could do not to melt it down in a flame of her own making. Maybe she had been a fool to love a man who served the king, but Chaol had been what she needed after losing Sam, after surviving the mines.

But these days . . . she didn't know what she needed. What she wanted. If she felt like admitting it, she actually didn't have the faintest clue who the hell she was anymore. All she knew was that whatever and whoever climbed out of that abyss of despair and grief would not be the same person who had plummeted in. And maybe that was a good thing.

Rowan put his clothes back on and settled against the trunk, his body warm and solid against hers. They sat in the dark for a little until she said quietly, "You once told me that when you find your mate, you can't stomach the idea of hurting them physically. Once you're mated, you'd sooner harm yourself."

"Yes; why?"

"I tried to kill him. I mauled his face, then held a dagger over his heart because I thought he was responsible for Nehemia's death. I would have done it if someone hadn't stopped me. If Chaol—if he'd truly been my mate, I wouldn't have been able to do that, would I?"

He was silent for a long while. "You hadn't been in your Fae form for ten years, so perhaps your instincts weren't even able to take hold. Sometimes, mates can be together intimately before the actual bond snaps into place."

"It's a useless hope to cling to, anyway."

"Do you want the truth?"

She tucked her chin into her tunic and closed her eyes. "Not tonight."

46

Shielding her eyes from the glare, Celaena scanned the cliffs and the spit of beach far below. It was scorching, with hardly a breeze, but Rowan remained in his heavy pale-gray jacket and wide belt, vambraces strapped to his forearms. He'd deigned to give her a few of his weapons that morning—as a precaution.

They'd returned to the latest site at dawn to retrace their steps—and that was where Celaena had picked up a trail. Well, she'd spied a droplet of dark blood on a nearby rock, and then Rowan had followed the scent back toward the cliffs. She looked down the beach, at the natural-cut arches of the many caves along its curving length. But there was nothing here—and the trail, thanks to the sea and wind and elements, had gone cold. They'd been here for the past half hour, looking for any other signs, but there was nothing. Nothing, except—

There. A sagging curve in the cliff edge, as if many pairs of feet had worn the lip down as they slid carefully over the edge. Rowan gripped her arm as she leaned to view the crumbled, hidden stair. She glared at him, but he didn't let go. "I'm trying not to be insulted," she said. "Look."

They were hardly steps now—just lumps of rock and sand peppered with shrubs. The water beyond the beach was so clear and calm that a slight break could be seen in the barrier reef that guarded these shores. It was one of the few ways to make a safe landing here without shattering your boat, only wide enough for a small craft to pass through. No warships or merchant vessels would fit, undoubtedly one reason this area had never been developed. It was the perfect place, however, if you wanted to surreptitiously enter the country—and stay hidden.

She began sketching in the sandy earth, a long, hard line, then drew dot after dot after dot.

"The bodies were dumped in streams and rivers," she said.

"The sea was never far off," he said, kneeling beside her. "They could have dumped the bodies there. But—"

"But then those bodies probably would drift right back to shore, and prompt people to look along the beach. Look here," she said, pointing to the stretch of coastline she'd sketched—and where they were currently sitting, smack dab in the middle of it.

"There are countless caves along this section of the shore."

She indicated where the waves broke on the reef and the small, calm space between them. "It's an easy access point from—" She swore. She couldn't say it. There were no ships along here, but that didn't mean that one or two or more couldn't have come from Adarlan, sneaking in at night, and slipped in their violent, vicious cargo using smaller boats.

Rowan stood. "We're leaving. Now."

"Don't you think they would already have attacked if they'd seen us?"

Rowan pointed to the sun. If he was about to tell her it wasn't safe for a queen to be throwing herself into danger, then he could— "If we're going to explore, then we're going to do it under cover of darkness. So we're going back to the stream, and we're going to find something to eat. And then, Princess," he said with a wild grin, "we are going to have some fun."

Some god must have decided to take pity on them, because the rain started right after sunset, thundering clouds rolling in with a vengeance to conceal any sound they made as they returned to the beach and began a thorough search of the caves.

But that was about where their favor from the gods ended, because what they found, while lying on their bellies on a narrow cliff overhanging a barren beach, was worse than anything they'd anticipated. It wasn't only monsters of the king's making.

It was a host of soldiers.

A few men came out of the massive cave mouth, which was camouflaged among the rocks and sand. They might have missed them had it not been for Rowan's keen sense of smell. He did not have the words, he said, to describe what that smell was like. But she knew it.

Celaena's mouth had gone dry, her stomach a knot as the dark figures slipped in and out of the cave with disciplined, economic movements that suggested they were highly trained. They weren't rabid, half-feral monsters like the one in the library, or cold, flawless creatures like what she'd seen in the barrows, but mortal soldiers. All of them aware, disciplined, ruthless.

"The crab-monger," Celaena murmured to Rowan. "In the village. He said—he said he found weapons in his nets. They must be taking ships and then getting close enough to swim through the reef without attracting attention. We need to get a closer look." She raised her brows at Rowan, who gave her a hunter's smile. "I knew you'd be useful someday."

Rowan just snorted and shifted, a flicker of light that she hoped was gobbled up by the storm. He flapped over the cliff edge and glided across the water, nothing more than a predator looking for a meal, then circled back until he rested on a rock just beyond the breaking waves. She watched him hunt, moving toward the cave itself, an animal looking for shelter from the rain. And then, keeping close to the towering ceiling of the cave, he swept inside.

She didn't breathe the entire time he was out of her sight. She counted the gaps between the thunder and the lightning, her fingers itching to grab on to the hilt of her sword.

But at long last, Rowan swooped out of the cave in a leisurely flight. He made his way up to her, then flew past, heading into the woods. A message to follow. Carefully, she dragged herself through the dirt and mud and rocks until she was far enough away to slip between the trees. She followed Rowan for a ways, the forest growing denser, the rain masking all sounds.

She found him standing with crossed arms against a gnarled pine. "There are about two hundred mortal soldiers and three of those creatures in the caves. There's a hidden network of them all along the shore."

Her throat closed up. She made herself wait for him to go on.

"They are under the command of someone called General Narrok. The soldiers all look highly trained, but they keep well away from the three creatures." Rowan wiped at his nose, and in the flash of lightning, she beheld the blood. "You were right. The three creatures look like men, but aren't men. Whatever dwells inside their skin is . . . disgusting isn't the right word. It was as if my magic, my blood—my very essence was repelled by them." He examined the blood on his fingers. "All of them seem to be waiting."

Three of those things. Just one had nearly killed her. "Waiting for what?"

Rowan's animal eyes glowed as they fixed on her. "Why don't you tell me?"

"The king never said *anything* about this. He—he . . ." Had something gone wrong in Adarlan? Had Chaol somehow told the king who and what she was, and the king sent these men here to . . . No, it had to have taken weeks, months, to get these creatures smuggled here. "Send word for Wendlyn's forces—warn them right now."

"Even if I reached Varese tomorrow, it would take over a week to get here on foot. Most of the units have been deployed in the north all spring."

"We still need to warn them that they're at risk."

"Use your head. There are endless caves and places to hide along the western coastline. And yet they pick here, this access point."

She visualized the map of the area. "The mountain road will take them past the fortress." Her blood chilled, and even her magic, flickering in an attempt to soothe her, could not warm her as she said, "No—not past. *To* the fortress. They're going after the demi-Fae."

A slow, grave nod. "I think those bodies we found were experiments. To learn the weaknesses and strengths of the demi-Fae, to learn which ones were . . . compatible with whatever it is they do to warp beings. With these numbers, I'd suggest this unit was sent here to capture and retrieve the demi-Fae, or to wipe out a potential threat."

Because if they could not be converted and enslaved to Adarlan, then the demi-Fae could be convinced to potentially fight for Wendlyn in a war. They could be the strongest warriors in Wendlyn's forces—and cause more than a bit of trouble for Adarlan as a result.

She lifted her chin and said, "Then right now—right now, we'll go down to that beach and unleash our magic on them all. While they're sleeping." She turned, even as part of her soul started bucking and thrashing at the thought of it.

Rowan grabbed her elbow. "If I had thought there was a way to do it, I would have suffocated them all. But we can't—not without endangering our lives in the process."

"Believe me, I can and I will." They were Adarlan's soldiers—they had butchered and pillaged and done more evil than she could stomach. She could do it. She *would* do it.

"No. You physically cannot harm them, Aelin. Not right now. They know enough about those Wyrdmarks to have protected their whole rutting camp from our kind of magic. Wards—like the stones around the fortress, but different. They wear iron everywhere they can, in their weapons, in their armor. They know their enemy well. We might be good, but we can't take them on alone and walk out of those caves alive."

Celaena paced, running her hands through her rain-wet hair, and then realized he hadn't finished. "Say it," she demanded.

"Narrok is in the very back of the caves, in a private chamber. He is like them, a creature wearing the skin of a man. He sends out his three monsters to retrieve the demi-Fae, and they bring them back to the cave—for him to experiment on."

She knew, then, why Rowan had moved her into the trees, far from the beach. Not for safety, but because—because there was a demi-Fae in there right now.

"I tried to cut off her air—to make it easier for her," Rowan said. "But they have her in too much iron, and . . . she won't make it through the night, even if we go in there now. She is already a husk, barely able to breathe. There is no coming back from what they've done. They've fed on the very life of her, trapping her in her mind, making her relive whatever horrors and miseries she's already encountered."

Even the fire in her blood froze. "It truly fed on me that day in the barrows," she whispered. "If I hadn't managed to escape, it would have drained me like that." A low, confirming growl rippled out of Rowan.

Nauseated, Celaena scrubbed at her face—tipped her head back to the rain trickling in from the canopy above, then finally took a long breath and faced Rowan. "We cannot kill them with our magic while they are encamped. Wendlyn's forces are too far away, and Narrok is going after the demi-Fae with three of those monsters plus two hundred soldiers." She was thinking aloud, but Rowan nodded anyway. "How many of the sentries at Mistward have actually seen battle?"

"Thirty or less. And some, like Malakai, are too old, but will fight anyway—and die."

Rowan walked deeper into the woods. She followed him, if only because she knew if she took one step closer to the beach, she would go after that female. From the tension in Rowan's shoulders, she knew he felt the same.

The rain ceased, and Celaena pulled back her hood to let the misty air soak into her too-hot face. This area was full of shepherds and farmers and fishermen. Aside from the demi-Fae, there was no one else to fight the creatures. They had no advantage, save for knowing their territory better than their enemy. They would send word to Wendlyn, of course, and maybe, maybe help would arrive in the next week.

Rowan held up a fist, and she halted as he scanned the trees ahead and behind. With expert quietness, he unsheathed one of the blades in his vambraces. The smell hit her a second later—the stench of whatever those creatures were beneath the mortal meat.

"Only one." He was so quiet she could hardly hear even with her Fae ears.

"That's not reassuring," she said with equal softness, drawing her own dagger.

Rowan pointed. "He's coming dead at us. You head to the right for twenty yards, I'll go left. When he's between us, wait for my signal, then strike. No magic—it might attract too much attention if others are nearby. Keep it quick and quiet and fast."

"Rowan, this thing—"

"Quick and quiet and fast."

His green eyes flashed, but she held his stare. *It fed on me and would have turned me into a husk*, she silently said. *We could easily meet that fate right now.*

You were unprepared, he seemed to say. *And I was not with you.*

This is insane. I faced one of the defective ones, too, and it almost killed me.

Scared, Princess?

Yes, and wisely so.

But he was right. These were their woods, and they were warriors. This time, it would be different. So she nodded, a soldier accepting orders, and did not bother with farewells before she slipped into the trees. She made her footfalls light, counting the distance, listening to the forest around them, keeping her breathing steady.

She ducked behind a mossy tree and drew her other blade. The smell deepened into a steady reek that made her head pound. As the clouds overhead cleared further, the starlight faintly illuminated the low-lying mist on the loamy earth. Nothing.

She was starting to wonder whether Rowan had been mistaken when the creature appeared between the trees ahead—closer to her than she'd anticipated. Much, much closer.

She felt him first: the smudge of blackness, the silence that enveloped him like an extra cloak. Even the fog seemed to pull away from him.

Beneath his hood, she could only glimpse pale skin and sensual lips. He did not bother with weapons. But it was his nails that made her breath catch. Long, sharp nails that she remembered all too well—how they'd felt when they ripped into her in the library.

Unlike those nails, these were unbroken, the polished black curves gleaming. The skin on his fingers was bone-white and flawless, too smooth to be natural. Indeed, she could have sworn she saw dark, glittering veins, a mockery of the blood that had once flowed there.

Celaena didn't dare bat an eyelash as the thing turned his hooded head toward her. Rowan still didn't give the signal. Did he realize how close it was?

A wet trickle of warmth flowed onto her lips from one of her nostrils. She tensed, bracing herself, and wondered how fast he could move and how deeply she would have to slice with her long knives. The sword would be a last resort, as it was more cumbersome. Even if using the knives meant getting in close.

He scanned the trees, and Celaena pressed behind hers. The creature beneath the library had torn through metal doors as if they were curtains. And it knew how to use the Wyrdmarks—

She glanced out in time to see him step toward her tree, the movement deadly elegant and promising a long, painful end. He had not had his mind broken; he still retained the ability to think, to calculate. These things were so good at their work, it seemed that the king had thought only three were necessary here. How many others remained hidden on her continent?

The forest had fallen so still that she could hear a huffing sound. He was scenting her. Her magic flared, and she shoved it down. She didn't want her magic touching this thing, with or without Rowan's command. The creature sniffed again—and took another step in her direction. Just like that day at the barrows, the air began to hollow out, pulsing against her ears. Her other nostril began to bleed. *Shit.*

The thought hit her then, and the world stumbled. What if it had gotten to Rowan first? She dared another glance around the tree.

The creature was gone.

47

Celaena silently swore, scanning the trees. Where in hell had the creature gone? The rain began again, but the dead scent still clung to everything. She lifted her long dagger to angle it in Rowan's direction—to signal him to indicate whether he was breathing. He had to be; she would accept no other alternative. The blade was so clean she could see her face in it, see the trees and the sky and—

And the creature now standing behind her.

Celaena pivoted, swiping for its exposed side, one blade angled to sink straight into its ribs, the other slashing for the throat. A move she'd practiced for years and years, as easy as breathing.

But its black, depthless eyes met hers, and Celaena froze. In her body, her mind, her soul. Her magic sputtered and went out.

She scarcely heard the damp thud of her blades hitting the earth. The rain on her face dulled to a distant sensation.

The darkness around them spread, welcoming, embracing. Comforting. The creature pulled back the cowl of its cloak.

The face was young and male—unearthly perfection. Around his neck, a torque of dark stone—Wyrdstone, she vaguely recalled—gleamed in the rain. This was the god of death incarnate. It was not with any mortal man's expression or voice that he smiled and said, "You."

She couldn't look away. There were screams in the darkness—screams she had drowned out for so many years. But now they beckoned.

His smile widened, revealing too-white teeth, and he reached a hand for her throat.

So gentle, those icy fingers, as his thumb brushed her neck, as he tilted her face up to better stare into her eyes. "Your agony tasted like wine," he murmured, peering into the core of her.

Wind was tearing at her face, her arms, her stomach, roaring her name. But there was eternity and calm in his eyes, a promise of such sweet darkness, and she could not look away. It would be a blessed relief to let go. She need only surrender to the dark, just as he asked. *Take it*, she wanted to say, tried to say. *Take everything.*

A flash of silver and steel pierced the inky veil, and another creature—a monster made of fangs and rage and wind—was there, ripping her away. She clawed at him, but he was ice—he was . . . Rowan.

Rowan was hauling her away, shouting her name, but she couldn't reach him, couldn't stop that pull toward the other creature.

Teeth pierced the spot between her neck and shoulder, and she jerked, latching on to the pain as if it were a rope yanking her out of that sea of stupor, up, up, until—

Rowan crushed her against him with one arm, sword out, her blood dripping down his chin as he backed away from the creature that lingered by the tree. Pain—that was why the body that morning had been marred. The demi-Fae had tried to use physical pain to break free of these things, to remind the body of what was real and not real.

The creature huffed a laugh. Oh gods. It had placed her in its thrall.

That swiftly, that easily. She hadn't stood a chance, and Rowan wasn't attacking because—

Because in the dark, with limited weapons against an enemy who did not need blades to kill them, even Rowan was outmatched. A true warrior knew when to walk away from a fight. Rowan breathed, "We have to run."

There was another low laugh from the creature, who stepped closer. Rowan pulled them farther back. "You can try," it said in that voice that did not come from her world.

That was all Celaena needed to hear. She flung out her magic.

A wall of flame sprang up as she and Rowan sprinted away, a shield into which she poured every ounce of will and horror and shame, damning the consequences. The creature hissed, but she didn't know if it was due to the light stinging its eyes or merely frustration.

She didn't care. It bought them time, a whole minute hurtling uphill through the trees. Then crashing came from behind, that reeking stain of darkness spreading like a web.

Rowan knew the woods, knew how to hide their trail. It bought them more time and distance. The creature stalked them, even as Rowan used his wind to blow their scent away.

Mile after mile they ran, until her breath was like shards of glass in her lungs and even Rowan seemed to be tiring. They weren't going to the fortress—no, they wouldn't lead this thing within ten miles of there. Rather, they headed into the Cambrian Mountains, the air growing chilled, the hills steeper. Still the creature followed.

"He won't stop," Celaena panted as they hauled themselves up a harrowing incline, almost on all fours. She pushed against the urge to fall to her knees and vomit. "He's like a hound on a scent." *Her* scent. Far below, the thing prowled after them.

Rowan bared his teeth, rain sluicing down his face. "Then I'll run him down until he drops dead."

Lightning illuminated a deer path atop the hill. "Rowan," she panted. "Rowan, I have an idea."

Celaena wondered if she still had a death wish.

Or perhaps the god of death just liked to play with her too much.

It was another uphill trek to the trees whose bark had been skinned off. And then she made herself a merry fire and burned a torch beside a forgotten road, the light shining through those skinless trees.

Far below, she prayed that Rowan was keeping the creature occupied the way she'd told him to—leading it in circles with the scent on her tunic.

Screee went the whetting stone down her dagger as she perched atop a large rock. Despite her incessant trembling, she hummed as she sharpened, a symphony she'd gone to see performed in Rifthold every year until her enslavement. She controlled her breathing and focused on counting the minutes, wondering how long she could remain before she had to find another way. *Screee.*

A rotting scent stuffed itself up her nose, and the already quiet forest went still.

Screee. Not her own blade sharpening but another's, almost in answer to her own.

She sagged in relief and ran the whetting stone down her dagger one more time before standing, willing strength to her knees. She did not allow herself to flinch when she beheld the five of them standing beyond the skinned trees, tall and lean and bearing their wicked tools.

Run, her body screamed, but she held her ground. Lifted her chin and smiled into the dark. "I'm glad you received my invitation." Not a hint of sound or movement. "Your four friends decided to come uninvited to my last campfire—and it didn't end well for them. But I'm sure you know that already."

Another one sharpened his blades, firelight shivering on the jagged metal. "Fae bitch. We'll take our sweet time with you."

She sketched a bow, even though her stomach was heaving at the reek of carrion, and waved her torch as if it were a baton at what awaited below. "Oh, I certainly hope you do," she said.

Before they could surround her, she burst into a sprint.

Celaena knew they were near not because of the crashing brush or the whip of their blades through the air but from the stench that tore gnarled fingers through her senses. Clutching her torch in one hand, she used the other to keep herself aloft as she bounded down the steep road, dodging rocks and brambles and loose stones.

It was a mile down to where she'd told Rowan to lead the creature, a mad flight through the dark. Ankles and knees barking in protest, she leapt and ran, the skinwalkers closing in around her like wolves on a deer.

The key was not to panic—panic made you stupid. Panic got you killed. There was a piercing cry—a hawk's screech. Rowan was exactly where they'd planned, the king's creature perhaps a minute behind and slinking through the brush. Right by the creek, where she dumped her torch. Right where the road curved around a boulder.

The ancient road went one way, but she went another. A wind shoved past, going in the direction of the road. She threw herself behind a tree, a hand over her mouth to keep her jagged breaths contained as the wind pushed her scent away.

A heartbeat later, a hard body enveloped hers, shielding and sheltering. And then five pairs of bare feet slithered along the road, after the scent that now darted and hurtled down, down to the creature running right at them.

She pressed her face into Rowan's chest. His arms were solid as walls, his assortment of weapons just as reassuring.

At last, he tugged at her sleeve, nudging her upward—to climb. In a few deft movements, she hauled herself up the tree to a wide branch near its top. A moment later, Rowan was behind her, sitting against the trunk. He pulled her against him, her back to his chest as he folded his arms around her, hiding her scent from the monsters raging below.

A minute passed before the screaming began—bleating shrieks and shouts and roars of two different sets of monsters who knew death was upon them, and the face it bore was not kind.

For the better part of half an hour, the creatures fought in the rainy dark, until those wretched shrieks turned victorious, and the unearthly roars sounded no more.

Celaena and Rowan held tight to each other and did not dare close their eyes for the entirety of the night.

48

There was no uproar, no hysteria when they told the fortress what they'd discovered. Malakai immediately dispatched messengers to Wendlyn's king to beg for help; to the other demi-Fae settlements to order those who could not fight to flee; and to the healers' compound, to help every single patient who was not bed-bound evacuate.

Messengers returned from the king, promising as many men as could be spared. It was a relief, Celaena thought—but a bit of a terror, too. If Galan showed up, if any of her mother's kin arrived here . . . She wouldn't care, she told herself. There were bigger matters at hand. And so she prayed for their swift arrival, and prepared with the rest of the fortress's residents. They would face the threat head-on, starting by taking out the two hundred mortal soldiers that accompanied Narrok and his three creatures as soon as they left their protected caves.

Rowan seized control of the fortress with no fuss—only gratitude from the others, actually. Even Malakai thanked the prince as Rowan set about organizing rotations, delegating tasks, and planning their survival. They had a few days until reinforcements arrived and they could launch their assault, but should their enemy march sooner, Rowan wanted them slowed down and incapacitated as much as possible until help arrived. The demi-Fae were not an army and did not have the resources of a fully stocked fortress, so Rowan declared they'd make do with what they did possess: their wits, determination, and knowledge of the terrain. From the sound of it, somehow the skinwalkers had brought down one of the creatures, so they weren't truly invincible—but without a body the following morning, they hadn't learned how it had been killed.

Rowan and Celaena went out with the small groups that were preparing the forest for the attack. If Narrok's force was going to take the deer path to sack the fortress, then they'd find themselves taking it through pitfall-laden territory: through glens of venomous creatures, over concealed holes full of spikes, and into snares at every turn. It might not kill them, but it would slow them down enough to buy more time for aid to come. And should they wind up under siege, there was a secret tunnel leading out of the fortress itself, so ancient and neglected that most of the residents hadn't even known it existed until Malakai mentioned it. It was better than nothing.

A few days later, Rowan assembled a small group of captains around a table in the dining hall. "Bas's scouting team reported that the creatures look like they're readying to move in a few days," he said, pointing to a map. "Are the first and second miles of traps almost done?" The captains gave their confirmation. "Good. Tomorrow, I want your men preparing the next few miles, too."

Standing beside Rowan, Celaena watched as he led them through the meeting, keeping track of all the various legs and arms of their plan—not to mention remembering all the names of the captains, their soldiers, and what they were responsible for. He remained calm and steady—fierce, even—despite the hell that might soon be upon them.

Glancing at the demi-Fae assembled, their attention wholly on Rowan, she could see that they clung to that steadiness, that cold determination and clever mind—and centuries of experience. She envied him for it. And beneath that, with a growing heaviness she could not control, she wished that when she left this continent . . . she wouldn't go alone.

"Get some sleep. You're no use to me completely dazed."

She blinked. She'd been staring at him. The meeting was over, the captains already walking away to attend to their various tasks.

"Sorry." She rubbed her eyes. They'd been up since before dawn, readying the last few miles of path, checking that all the traps were secure. Working with him was so effortless. There was no judgment, no need to explain herself. She knew no one would ever replace Nehemia, and she never wanted anyone to, but Rowan made her feel . . . better. As if she could finally breathe after months of suffocating. Yet now . . .

He was still watching her, frowning. "Just say it."

She examined the map on the table between them. "We can handle the mortal soldiers, but those creatures and Narrok . . . if we had Fae warriors—like your companion who came to receive his tattoo"—she didn't think calling him Rowan's *kitty-cat friend* would help her case this time—"or all five of your cadre, even, it could turn the tide." She traced the line of mountains that separated these lands from the immortal ones beyond. "But you have not sent for them. Why?"

"You know why."

"Would Maeve order you home out of spite for the demi-Fae?"

His jaw tightened. "For a few reasons, I think."

"And this is the person you chose to serve."

"I knew what I was doing when I drank her blood to seal the oath."

"Then let's hope Wendlyn's reinforcements get here quickly." She pursed her lips and turned to go to their room. He gripped her wrist.

"Don't do that." A muscle feathered in his jaw. "Don't look at me like that."

"Like what?"

"With that . . . disgust."

"I'm not—" But he gave her a sharp look. She sighed. "This . . . all this, Rowan . . ." She waved a hand to the map, to the doors the demi-Fae had passed through, to the sounds of people readying their supplies and defenses in the courtyard. "For whatever it's worth, all of this just proves that she doesn't deserve you. I think you know that, too."

He looked away. "That isn't your concern."

"I know. But I thought you should still hear it."

He didn't respond, wouldn't even meet her eyes, so she walked away. She looked over her shoulder once, to find him still hunched over the table, hands braced on its surface, the powerful muscles of his back visible through his shirt. And she knew he wasn't looking at the map, not really.

But saying that she wished he could return with her to Adarlan, to Terrasen, was pointless. He had no way to break his oath to Maeve, and she had nothing to entice him with even if he could. She was not a queen. She had no plans to be one, and even if she had a kingdom to give him if he were free . . . Telling him all that was useless.

So she left Rowan in the hall. But it did not stop her from wishing she could keep him.

The next afternoon, after washing her face and bandaging a burn on her forearm in Rowan's room, Celaena was just coming down to help with the dinner preparations when she felt, rather than heard, the ripple of silence through the fortress, deeper and heavier than the nervous quiet that had hovered over the compound the last few days.

The fortress had not been this tense since that first night Maeve had been here.

It was too soon for her aunt to be checking on her. She had little to show so far other than a few somewhat useful tricks and her various shields.

She took the stairs two at a time until she reached the kitchen. If Maeve learned about the invasion and ordered Rowan to leave . . . Breathing, thinking—those were the key tools to enduring this encounter.

The heat and yeasty scent hit her as she bounded down the last steps, slowing her gait, lifting her chin, even though she doubted her aunt would condescend to meet in the kitchen. Unless she wanted her unbalanced. But—

But Maeve was not in the kitchen.

Rowan was, and his back was to her as he stood at the other end with Emrys, Malakai, and Luca, talking quietly. Celaena stopped dead as she beheld at Emrys's too pale face, the hand gripping Malakai's arm.

As Rowan turned to her, lips thin and eyes wide with—with shock and horror and grief—the world stopped dead, too.

Rowan's arms hung slack at his sides, his fingers clenching and unclenching. For a heartbeat, she wondered if she went back upstairs, whatever he had to say would not be true.

Rowan took a step toward her—one step, and that was all it took before she began shaking her head, before she lifted her hands in front of her as if to push him away. "Please," she said, and her voice broke. "Please."

Rowan kept approaching, the bearer of some inescapable doom. And she knew that she could not outrun it, and could not fall on her knees and beg for it to be undone.

Rowan stopped within reach but did not touch her, his features hardening again—not from cruelty. Because he knew, she realized, that one of them would have to hold it together. He needed to be calm—needed to keep his wits about him for this.

Rowan swallowed once. Twice. "There was . . . there was an uprising at the Calaculla labor camp," he said.

Her heart stumbled on a beat.

"After Princess Nehemia was assassinated, they say a slave girl killed her overseer and sparked an uprising. The slaves seized the camp." He took a shallow breath. "The King of Adarlan sent two legions to get the slaves under control. And they killed them all."

"The slaves killed his legions?" A push of breath. There were thousands of slaves in Calaculla—all of them together would be a mighty force, even for two of Adarlan's legions.

With horrific gentleness, Rowan grasped her hand. "No. The soldiers killed every slave in Calaculla."

A crack in the world, through which a keening wail pushed in like a wave. "There are thousands of people enslaved in Calaculla."

The resolve in Rowan's countenance splintered as he nodded. And when he opened and closed his mouth, she realized it was not over. The only word she could breathe was "Endovier?" It was a fool's plea.

Slowly, so slowly, Rowan shook his head. "Once he got word of the uprising in Eyllwe, the King of Adarlan sent two other legions north. None were spared in Endovier."

She did not see Rowan's face when he gripped her arms as if he could keep her from falling into the abyss. No, all she could see were the slaves she'd left behind, the ashy mountains and those mass graves they dug every day, the faces of her people, who had worked beside her—her people whom she had left behind. Whom she had let herself forget, had let suffer; who had prayed for salvation, holding out hope that someone, anyone would remember them.

She had abandoned them—and she had been too late.

Nehemia's people, the people of other kingdoms, and—and her people. The people of Terrasen. The people her father and mother and court had loved so fiercely. There had been rebels in Endovier—rebels who fought for her kingdom when she . . . when she had been . . .

There were children in Endovier. In Calaculla.

She had not protected them.

The kitchen walls and ceiling crushed her, the air too thin, too hot. Rowan's face swam as she panted, panted, faster and faster—

He murmured her name too softly for the others to hear.

And the sound of it, that name that had once been a promise to the world, the name she had spat on and defiled, the name she did not deserve . . .

She tore off his grip, and then she was walking out the kitchen door, across the courtyard, through the ward-stones, and along the invisible barrier—until she found a spot just out of sight of the fortress.

The world was full of screaming and wailing, so loud she drowned in it.

Celaena did not utter a sound as she unleashed her magic on the barrier, a blast that shook the trees and set the earth rumbling. She fed her power into the invisible wall, begging the ancient stones to take it, to use it. The wards, as if sensing her intent, devoured her power whole, absorbing every last ember until it flickered, hungry for more.

So she burned and burned and burned.

49

For weeks now, Chaol hadn't had any contact with any of his friends—allies, whatever they had been. So, one last time, Chaol slipped into the rhythm of his old duties. Though it was more difficult than ever to oversee the king's luncheons, though making his reports was an effort of will, he did it. He had heard nothing from Aedion or Ren, and still hadn't yet asked Dorian to use his magic to test out their theories about the spell. He was starting to wonder if he was done playing his part in Aelin's growing rebellion.

He'd gathered enough information, crossed enough lines. Perhaps it was time to learn what could be done from Anielle. He would be closer to Morath, and maybe he could uncover what the king was brewing down there. The king had accepted his plans to take up his mantle as heir to Anielle with hardly any objections. Soon, he was to present options for a replacement.

Chaol was currently standing guard at a state luncheon in the great hall, which Aedion and Dorian were both attending. The doors had been thrown open to welcome in the spring air, and Chaol's men were standing at each one, weapons at the ready.

Everything was normal, everything was going smoothly, until the king stood, his black ring seeming to gobble up the midday sun streaming in through the towering windows. He lifted a goblet, and the room fell silent. Not in the way it did when Aedion spoke. Chaol hadn't been able to stop thinking about what the general had said to him about choosing a side, or what Dorian had said about his refusal to accept Celaena and the prince for what they really were. Over and over again, he'd contemplated it.

But nothing could prepare Chaol, or anyone in that silent hall, as the king smiled to the tables below his dais and said, "Good news arrived this morning from Eyllwe and the north. The Calaculla slave rebellion has been dealt with."

They'd heard nothing of it, and Chaol wished he could cover his ears as the king said, "We'll have to work to replenish the mines, there and in Endovier, but the rebel taint has been purged."

Chaol was glad he was leaning against a pillar. It was Dorian who spoke, his face bone-white. "What are you talking about?"

His father smiled at him. "Forgive me. It seems the slaves in Calaculla got it into their heads to start an uprising after Princess Nehemia's unfortunate death. We got it into our heads not to allow it. Or any other potential uprisings. And as we didn't have the resources to devote to interrogating each and every slave to weed out the traitors . . ."

Chaol understood what strength it took for Dorian not to shake his head in horror as he did the calculations and understood just how many people had been slaughtered.

"General Ashryver," the king said. Aedion sat motionless. "You and your Bane will be pleased to know that since the purge in Endovier, many of the rebels in your territory have ceased their . . . antics. It seems they did not want a fate similar to that of their friends in the mines."

Chaol didn't know how Aedion found the courage and will, but the general smiled and bowed his head. "Thank you, Majesty."

Dorian burst into Sorscha's workroom. She jumped from her spot at the table, a hand on her chest. "Did you hear?" he asked, shutting the door behind him.

Her eyes were red enough to suggest that she had. He took her face in his hands, pressing his brow against hers, needing that cool strength. He didn't know how he'd kept from weeping or vomiting or killing his father on the spot. But looking at her, breathing in her rosemary-and-mint scent, he knew why.

"I want you out of this castle," he said. "I'll give you the funds, but I want you away from here as soon as you can find a way to go without raising suspicion."

She yanked out of his grasp. "Are you mad?"

No, he'd never seen anything more clearly. "If you stay, if we are caught . . . I will give you whatever money you need—"

"No money you could offer could convince me to leave."

"I'll tie you to a horse if I have to. I'm getting you out—"

"And who will look after you? Who will make your tonics? You're not even talking to the captain anymore. How could I leave now?"

He gripped her shoulders. She had to understand—he had to make her understand. Her loyalty was one of the things he loved, but now . . . it would only get her killed. "He murdered *thousands* of people in one sweep. Imagine what he'll do if he finds you've been helping me. There are worse things than death, Sorscha. Please—*please*, just go."

Her fingers found his, entwining tight. "Come with me."

"I can't. It will get worse if I leave, if my brother is made heir. And

I think . . . I know of some people who might be trying to stop him. If I am here, perhaps I can help them in some way."

Oh, Chaol. He understood completely now why he had sent Celaena to Wendlyn—understood that his return to Anielle . . . Chaol had sold himself to get Celaena to safety.

"If you stay, I stay," Sorscha said. "You cannot convince me otherwise."

"Please," he said, because he didn't have it in him to yell, not with the deaths of those people hanging over him. "Please . . ."

But she brushed her thumb across his cheek. "Together. We'll face this together."

And it was selfish and horrible of him, but he put up no further argument.

Chaol went to the tomb for privacy, to mourn, to scream. But he was not alone.

Aedion was sitting on the steps of the spiral stairwell, his forearms braced on his knees. He didn't turn as Chaol set down his candle and sat beside him.

"What do you suppose," Aedion breathed, staring into the darkness, "the people on other continents, across all those seas, think of us? Do you think they hate us or pity us for what we do to each other? Perhaps it's just as bad there. Perhaps it's worse. But to do what I have to do, to get through it . . . I have to believe it's better. Somewhere, it's better than this."

Chaol had no answer.

"I have . . ." Aedion's teeth gleamed in the light. "I have been forced to do many, many things. Depraved, despicable things. Yet nothing made me feel as filthy as I did today, thanking that man for murdering my people."

There was nothing he could say to console him, nothing he could promise. So Chaol left Aedion staring into the darkness.

There was not one empty seat in the Royal Theater that night. Every box and tier was crammed with nobility, merchants, whoever could afford the ticket. Jewels and silk gleamed in the light of the glass chandeliers, the riches of a conquering empire.

The news about the slave massacres had struck that afternoon, spreading through the city on a wave of murmuring, leaving only silence behind. The upper tiers of the theater were unusually still, as if the audience had come to be soothed, to let the music sweep away the stain of the news.

Only the boxes were full of chatter. About what this meant for the fortunes of those seated in the plush crimson velvet chairs, debates over where the new slaves would come from to ensure there was no pause in labor, and about how they should treat their own slaves afterward. Despite the chiming bells and the raising and dimming of the chandeliers, it took the boxes far longer to quiet than usual.

They were still talking when the red curtains pulled back to reveal the seated orchestra, and it was a miracle they bothered to applaud for the conductor as he hobbled across the stage.

That was when they noticed that every musician on the stage was wearing mourning black. That was when they shut up. And when the conductor raised his arms, it was not a symphony that filled the cavernous space.

It was the Song of Eyllwe.

Then the Song of Fenharrow. And Melisande. And Terrasen. Each nation that had people in those labor camps.

And finally, not for pomp or triumph, but to mourn what they had become, they played the Song of Adarlan.

When the final note finished, the conductor turned to the crowd, the musicians standing with him. As one, they looked to the boxes, to all those jewels bought with the blood of a continent. And without a word, without a bow or another gesture, they walked off the stage.

The next morning, by royal decree, the theater was shut down.

No one saw those musicians or their conductor again.

50

A cooling breeze kissed down Celaena's neck. The forest had gone silent, as if the birds and insects had been quieted by her assault on the invisible wall. The barrier had gobbled down every spark of magic she'd launched at it, and now seemed to hum with fresh power.

The scent of pine and snow wrapped around her, and she turned to find Rowan standing against a nearby tree. He'd been there for some time now, giving her space to work herself into exhaustion.

But she was not tired. And she was not done. There was still wildfire in her mind, writhing, endless, damning. She let it dim to embers, let the grief and horror die down, too.

Rowan said, "Word just arrived from Wendlyn. Reinforcements aren't coming."

"They didn't come ten years ago," she said, her throat raw though she had not spoken in hours. Cold, glittering calm was now flowing in her veins. "Why should they bother helping now?"

His eyes flickered. "Aelin." When she only gazed into the darkening forest, he suddenly said, "You do not have to stay—we can go to Doranelle tonight, and you can retrieve your knowledge from Maeve. You have my blessing."

"Do not insult me by asking me to leave. I am fighting. Nehemia would have stayed. My parents would have stayed."

"They also had the luxury of knowing that their bloodline did not end with them."

She gritted her teeth. "You have experience—*you* are needed here. You are the only person who can give the demi-Fae a chance of surviving; you are trusted and respected. So I am staying. Because you are needed, and because I will follow you to whatever end." And if the creatures devoured her body and soul, then she would not mind. She had earned that fate.

For a long moment, he said nothing. But his brows narrowed slightly. "To whatever end?"

She nodded. He had not needed to mention the massacres, had not needed to try to console her. He knew—he understood without her having to say a word—what it was like.

Her magic thrummed in her blood, wanting out, wanting *more*. But it would wait—it had to wait until it was time. Until she had Narrok and his creatures in her sight.

She realized that Rowan saw each of those thoughts and more as he reached into his tunic and pulled out a dagger. Her dagger. He extended it to her, its long blade gleaming as if he'd been secretly polishing and caring for it these months.

And when she grasped the dagger, its weight lighter than she remembered, Rowan looked into her eyes, into the very core of her, and said, "Fireheart."

Reinforcements from Wendlyn weren't coming—not out of spite but because a legion of Adarlan's men had attacked the northern border. Three thousand men in ships had launched a full-on assault. Wendlyn had sent every last soldier to the northern coast, and there they would remain. The demi-Fae were to face Narrok and his forces alone. Rowan calmly encouraged the nonfighters at the fortress to flee.

But no one fled. Even Emrys refused, and Malakai merely said that where his mate went, he went.

For hours, they adjusted their plans to accommodate the lack of reinforcements. In the end they didn't have to change much, thankfully. Celaena contributed what she could to the planning, letting Rowan order everyone about and adjust the masterful strategy in that brilliant head of his. She tried not to think about Endovier and Calaculla, but the knowledge of it still simmered in her, brewing during the long hours that they debated.

They planned until Emrys hauled up a pot from the kitchen and began whacking it with a spoon, ordering them out because dawn would come too soon.

Within a minute of returning to their room, Celaena was undressed and flopping into bed. Rowan took his time, however, peeling off his shirt and striding to the washbasin. "You did well helping me plan tonight."

She watched him wash his face, then his neck. "You sound surprised."

He wiped his face with a towel, then leaned against the dresser, bracing his hands against either end. The wood groaned, but his face remained still.

Fireheart, he had called her. Did he know what that name meant to her? She wanted to ask, still had so many questions for him, but right now, after all the news of the day, she needed to sleep.

"I sent word," Rowan said, letting go of the dresser and approaching the bed. She'd left the sword from the mountain cave on the bedpost, and its smoldering ruby now glinted in the dim light as he ran a finger down the golden hilt. "To my . . . *cadre*, as you like to call them."

She braced herself on her elbows. "When?"

"A few days ago. I don't know where they all are or whether they'll arrive in time. Maeve might not let them come—or some of them might not even ask her. They can be . . . unpredictable. And it may be that I just get the order to return to Doranelle, and—"

"You actually called for aid?"

His eyes narrowed. *I just said that I did.*

She stood, and he retreated a step. *What changed your mind?*

Some things are worth the risk.

He didn't back away again as she approached and said with every ember left in her shredded heart, "I claim you, Rowan Whitethorn. I don't care what you say and how much you protest. I claim you as my friend."

He just turned to the washbasin again, but she caught the unspoken words that he'd tried to keep her from reading on his face. *It doesn't matter. Even if we survive, when we go to Doranelle, you will walk out of Maeve's realm alone.*

Emrys joined them—along with all the demi-Fae at Mistward who had not been dispatched with messages—in traveling down to the healers' compound the next morning to help cart the patients to safety. Anyone who could not fight remained to help the sick and wounded, and Emrys declared he would stay there until the very end. So they left him, along with a small contingent of sentries in case things went very, very wrong. When Celaena headed off into the trees with Rowan, she did not bother with good-byes. Many of the others did not say farewell, either—it seemed like an invitation for death, and Celaena was fairly certain she wasn't on the good side of the gods.

She was awoken that night by a large, callused hand on her shoulder, shaking her awake. It seemed that death was already waiting for them.

51

"Get your sword and your weapons, and *hurry*," Rowan said to Celaena as she instantly came to her feet, reaching for the dagger beside the bed.

He was already halfway across the room, slinging on his clothes and weapons with lethal efficiency. She didn't bother with questions—he would tell her what was necessary. She hopped into her pants and boots.

"I think we've been betrayed," Rowan said, and her fingers caught on a buckle of her sword-belt as she turned to the open window. Quiet. Absolute quiet in the forest.

And along the horizon, a growing smear of blackness. "They're coming tonight," she breathed.

"I did a sweep of the perimeter." Rowan stuffed a knife into his boot. "It's as if someone told them where every trap, every warning bell is located. They'll be here within the hour."

"Are the ward-stones still working?" She finished braiding her hair and strapped her sword across her back.

"Yes—they're intact. I raised the alarm, and Malakai and the others are readying our defenses on the walls." A small part of her smiled at the thought of what it must have been like for Malakai to find a half-naked Rowan shouting orders in his room.

She asked, "Who would have betrayed us?"

"I don't know, and when I find them, I'll splatter them on the walls. But for now, we have bigger problems to worry about."

The darkness on the horizon had spread, devouring the stars, the trees, the light. "What *is* that?"

Rowan's mouth tightened into a thin line. "Bigger problems."

The ward-stones were the last line of defense before the fortress itself. If Narrok planned to lay siege to Mistward, they couldn't outlast him forever—but hopefully the barrier would wear down the creatures and their power a bit. On the battlements, in the courtyard and atop the towers, stood the demi-Fae. Archers would take down as many men as possible once the barrier fell, and they would use the oak doors of the fortress as a bottleneck into the courtyard.

But there were still the creatures and Narrok, along with the darkness that they carried with them. Birds and animals streamed past the fortress as they fled—an exodus of flapping wings, padding feet, claws clicking on stone. Herding the animals to safety were the Little Folk, hardly more than a gleam of night-seeing eyes. Whatever darkness Narrok and the creatures brought . . . once you went in, you did not come out.

She was standing with Rowan just beyond the gates of the courtyard, the grassy expanse of earth between the fortress and the ward-stones feeling far too small. The animals and Little Folk had stopped appearing moments before, and even the wind had died.

"As soon as the barrier falls, I want you to put arrows through their eyes," Rowan said to her, his bow slack in his hands. "Don't give them a chance to enthrall you—or anyone. Leave the soldiers to the others."

They hadn't heard or seen any of the two hundred men, but she nodded, gripping her own bow. "What about magic?"

"Use it sparingly, but if you think you can destroy them with it, don't hesitate. And don't get fancy. Take them down by any means possible." Such icy calculation. Purebred, undiluted warrior. She could almost feel the aggression pouring off him.

A reek was rising from beyond the barrier, and some of the sentries in the courtyard behind them began murmuring. A smell from another world, from whatever hellish creature lurked under mortal skin. Some straggling animals darted out of the trees, foaming at the mouth, the darkness behind them thickening. "Rowan," she said as she felt rather than saw them. "They're here."

At the edge of the trees, hardly five yards from the ward-stones, the creatures emerged.

Celaena started. Three.

Three, not two. "But the skinwalkers—" She couldn't finish the words as the three men surveyed the fortress. They were clad in deepest black, their tunics open to reveal the Wyrdstone torques at their throats. The skinwalkers hadn't killed it—no, because there was that same perfect male, looking straight at her. Smiling at her. As if he could already taste her.

A rabbit bolted out of the bushes, racing for the ward-stones. Like the paw of a massive beast, the darkness behind the creatures lashed out, sweeping over the fleeing animal.

The rabbit fell midleap, its fur turning dull and matted, bones pushing through as the life was sucked out of it. The sentries on the walls and towers stirred, some swearing. She had stood a chance of escaping the clutches of just one of those creatures. But all three together became something else, something infinitely powerful.

"The barrier cannot be allowed to fall," Rowan said to her. "That blackness will kill anything it touches." Even as he spoke, the darkness stretched around the fortress. Trapping them. The barrier hummed, and the reverberations zinged against the soles of her boots.

She shifted into her Fae form, wincing against the pain. She needed the sharper hearing, the strength and healing. Still, the three creatures remained on the forest edge, the darkness spreading. No sign of the two hundred soldiers.

As one, the three half turned to the shadows behind them and stepped aside, heads bowed. Then, stalking out of the trees, Narrok appeared.

Unlike the others, Narrok was not beautiful. He was scarred and powerfully built, and armed to the teeth. But he, too, had skin carved with those glittering black veins, and wore that torque of obsidian. Even from this distance, she could see the devouring emptiness in his eyes. It seeped toward them like blood in a river.

She waited for him to say something, to parlay and offer a choice between yielding to the king's power or death, to give some speech to break their morale. But Narrok looked upon Mistward with a slow, almost delighted sweep of the head, drew his iron blade, and pointed at the curving ward-stone gates.

There was nothing Celaena or Rowan could do as a whip of darkness snapped out and struck the invisible barrier. The air shuddered, and the stones whined.

Rowan was already moving toward the oak doors, shouting orders to the archers to ready themselves and use whatever magic they had to shield against the oncoming darkness. Celaena remained where she was. Another strike, and the barrier rippled.

"Aelin," Rowan snapped, and she looked over her shoulder at him. "Get inside the gates."

But she slung her bow across her back, and when she raised her hand, it was consumed with fire. "In the woods that night, it balked from the flame."

"To use it, you'll have to get outside the barrier, or it'll just rebound against the walls."

"I know," she said quietly.

"The last time, you took one look at that thing and fell under its spell."

The darkness lashed again.

"It won't be like last time," she said, eyes on Narrok, on his three creatures. Not when she had a score to settle. Her blood heated, but she said, "I don't know what else to do."

Because if that darkness reached them, then all the blades and arrows would be useless. They wouldn't have a chance to strike.

A cry sounded behind them, followed by a few more, then the clash of metal on metal. Someone shouted, "The tunnel! They've been let in through the tunnel!"

For a moment, Celaena just stood there, blinking. The escape tunnel. They *had* been betrayed. And now they knew where the soldiers were: creeping through the underground network, let in perhaps because the ward-stones, with that strange sentience, were too focused on the threat above to be able to contain the one below.

The shouting and fighting grew louder. Rowan had stationed their weaker fighters inside to keep them safe—right in the path of the tunnel entrance. It would be a slaughterhouse. "Rowan—"

Another blow to the barrier from the darkness, and another. She began walking toward the stones, and Rowan growled. "Do not take one more step—"

She kept going. Inside the fortress, screaming had begun—pain and death and terror. Each step away from it tore at her, but she headed to the stones, toward the megalith gates. Rowan grabbed her elbow. "That was an *order*."

She knocked his hand away. "You're needed inside. Leave the barrier to me."

"You don't know if it'll work—"

"It will work," she snarled. "I'm the expendable one, Rowan."

"You are heir to the throne of—"

"Right now, I am a woman who has a power that might save lives. Let me do this. Help the others."

Rowan looked at the ward-stones, at the fortress and the sentries scrambling to help below. Weighing, calculating. At last, Rowan said, "Do not engage them. You focus on that darkness and keeping it away from the barrier, and that's it. Hold the line, Aelin."

But she didn't want to hold the line—not when her enemy was so close. Not when the weight of those souls at Calaculla and Endovier pressed on her, screaming as loudly as the soldiers inside the fortress. She had failed all of them. She had been too late. And it was *enough.* But she nodded, like the good soldier Rowan believed she was, and said, "Understood."

"They will attack you the moment you set foot outside the barrier," he said, releasing her arm. Her magic began to boil in her veins. "Have a shield ready."

"I know" was her only answer as she neared the barrier and the swirling dark beyond. The curving stones of the gateway loomed, and she drew the sword from her back with her right hand, her left hand enveloped in flame.

Nehemia's people, butchered. Her own people, butchered. *Her* people.

Celaena stepped under the archway of stones, magic zinging and kissing her skin. Just a few steps would take her outside the barrier. She could feel Rowan lingering, waiting to see if she would survive the first moments. But she would—she was going to burn these things into ash and dust.

This was the least she owed those murdered in Endovier and Calaculla—the least she could do, after so long. A monster to destroy monsters.

The flames on her left hand burned brighter as Celaena stepped beyond the archway and into the beckoning abyss.

52

The darkness lashed at Celaena the moment she passed beyond the invisible barrier.

A wall of flame seared across the spear of blackness, and, just as she'd gambled, the blackness recoiled. Only to strike again, swift as an asp.

She met it blow for blow, willing the fire to spread, a wall of red and gold encasing the barrier behind her. She ignored the reek of the creatures, the hollowness of the air at her ears, the overwhelming throbbing in her head, so much worse beyond the protection of the wards, especially now that all three creatures were gathered. But she did not give them one inch, even as blood began trickling from her nose.

The darkness lunged for her, simultaneously assaulting the wall, punching holes through her flame. She patched them by reflex, allowing the power to do as it willed, but with the command to protect—to keep that barrier shielded. She took another step beyond the stone gateway.

Narrok was nowhere to be seen, but the three creatures were waiting for her.

Unlike the other night in the woods, they were armed with long, slender swords that they drew with their unearthly grace. And then they attacked.

Good.

She did not look them in the eyes, nor did she acknowledge the bleeding from her nose and the pressure in her ears. She merely called in a shield of fire around her left forearm and begin swinging that ancient sword.

Whether Rowan lingered to see her break his first order, then his next, then his next, she didn't know.

The three creatures kept coming at her, swift and controlled, as if they'd had eons to practice swordplay, as if they were all of one mind, one body. Where she deflected one, another was there; where she punched one with flame and steel, another was ducking beneath it to grab her. She could not let them touch her, could not let herself meet their gaze.

The shield around the barrier burned hot at her back, the darkness of the creatures stinging and biting at it, but she held firm. She had not lied to Rowan about that—about protecting the wall.

One of them swept its blade at her—not to kill. To incapacitate.

It was second nature, somehow, that flames leapt down her blade as she struck back, willing fire into the sword itself. When it met the black iron of the creature, blue sparks danced, so bright that she dared look into the creature's face to glimpse—surprise. Horror. Rage.

The hilt of the sword was warm—comforting—in her hand, and the red stone glowed as if with a fire of its own.

The three creatures stopped in unison, their sensual mouths pulling back from their too-white teeth in a snarl. The one in the center, the one who had tasted her before, hissed at the sword, "Goldryn."

The darkness paused, and she used its distraction to patch her shields, a chill snaking up her spine even as the flames warmed her. She lifted the sword higher and advanced another step.

"But you are not Athril, beloved of the dark queen," one of them said. Another said, "And you are not Brannon of the Wildfire."

"How do you—" But the words caught in her throat as a memory struck, from months ago—a lifetime ago. Of a realm that was in-between, of the thing that lived inside Cain speaking. To her, and—Elena. Elena, daughter of Brannon. *You were brought back*, it said. *All the players in the unfinished game*.

A game that had begun at the dawn of time, when a demon race had forged the Wyrdkeys and used them to break into this world, and Maeve had used their power to banish them. But some demons had remained trapped in Erilea and waged a second war centuries later, when Elena fought against them. What of the others, who had been sent back to their realm? What if the King of Adarlan, in learning of the keys, had also learned where to find them? Where to . . . harness them?

Oh gods. "You are the Valg," she breathed.

The three things inside those mortal bodies smiled. "We are princes of our realm."

"And what realm is that?" She poured her magic into the shield behind her.

The Valg prince in the center seemed to reach toward her without moving an inch. She sent a punch of flame at him, and he curled back. "A realm of eternal dark and ice and wind," he said. "And we have been waiting a very, very long time to taste your sunshine again."

The King of Adarlan was either more powerful than she could imagine, or the most foolish man to ever live if he thought he could control these demon princes.

Blood dripped onto her tunic from her nose. Their leader purred, "Once you let me in, girl, there shall be no more blood, or pain."

She sent another wall of flame searing at them. "Brannon and the others beat you into oblivion once," she said, though her lungs were burning. "We can do it again."

Low laughter. "We were not beaten. Only contained. Until a mortal man was foolish enough to invite us back in, to use these glorious bodies."

Were the men who had once occupied them still inside? If she cut off their heads—that torque of Wyrdstone—would the creatures vanish, or be unleashed in another form?

This was far, far worse than she had expected.

"Yes," the leader said, taking a step toward her and sniffing. "You should fear us. And embrace us."

"Embrace this," she snarled, and flung a hidden dagger from her vambrace at his head.

He was so swift that it scraped his cheek rather than wedging itself between its eyes. Black blood welled and flowed; he raised a moon-white hand to examine it. "I shall enjoy devouring you from the inside out," he said, and the darkness lunged for her again.

The battle was still raging inside the fortress, which was good, because it meant they hadn't all died yet. And Celaena was still swinging Goldryn against the three Valg princes—though it grew heavier by the moment, and the shield behind her was beginning to fray. She had not had time to tunnel down into her power, or to consider rationing it.

The darkness that the Valg brought with them continued to strike the wall, so Celaena threw up shield after shield, fire flaming through her blood, her breath, her mind. She gave her magic free rein, only asking it to keep the shield behind her alive. It did so, gobbling up her reserves.

Rowan had not come back to help. But she told herself he would come, and he would help, because it was not weakness to admit she needed him, needed his help and—

Her lower back cramped, and it was all she could do to keep her grip on the legendary blade as the leader of the Valg princes swiped for her neck. *No.*

A muscle twinged near her spine, twisting until she had to bite down a scream as she deflected the blow. It couldn't be a burnout. Not so soon, not after practicing so much, not—

A hole tore through the shield behind her, and the darkness slammed into the barrier, making the magic ripple and shriek. She flung a thought toward it, and as the flame patched it up, her blood began to pound.

The princes were closing in again. She growled, sending a wall of white-hot flame at them, pushing them back, back, back while she took a deep breath.

But blood came coughing out instead of air.

If she ran inside the gates, how long would the shield last before it fell to the princes and their ancient darkness? How long would any of those inside last? She didn't dare look behind to see who was winning. It didn't sound good. There were no cries of victory, only pain and fear.

Her knees quaked, but she swallowed the blood in her mouth and took another breath.

She had not imagined it would end like this. And maybe it was what she deserved, after turning her back on her kingdom.

One of the Valg princes ripped a hand through the wall of flame separating them, the darkness shielding his flesh from being melted off. She was about to send another blast at him when a movement from the trees caught her eye.

Far up the hill, as if they had come racing down from the mountains and had not stopped for food or water or sleep, were a towering man, a massive bird, and three of the largest predators she had ever seen.

Five in all.

Answering their friend's desperate call for aid.

They hurtled through the trees and over stones: two wolves, one black and one moon-white; the powerfully built male; the bird swooping low over them; and a familiar mountain cat racing behind. Heading for the darkness looming between them and the fortress.

The black wolf skidded to a halt as they neared the darkness, as if sensing what it could do. The screaming in the fortress rose. If the newcomers could destroy the soldiers, the survivors could take the tunnel and flee before the dark consumed everything.

Sweat stung Celaena's eyes, and pain sliced into her so deep that she wondered if it was permanent. But she had not lied to Rowan about saving lives.

So she did not stop to doubt or consider as she flung the remnants of her power toward Rowan's five friends, a bridge of flame through the darkness, cleaving it in two.

A path toward the gates behind her.

To their credit, Rowan's friends did not hesitate as they raced for it, the wolves leading the way, the bird—an osprey—close behind. She poured her power into the bridge, gritting her teeth against the agony as the five rushed past, not sparing her a glance. But the golden mountain cat slowed as he charged through the gates behind her, as her chest seized and she coughed, her blood bright on the grass.

"He's inside," she choked out. "Help him."

The great cat lingered, assessing her, and the wall, and the princes fighting against her flame. "*Go*," she wheezed. The bridge through the darkness collapsed, and she staggered back a step as that black power slammed into her, the shield, the world.

The blood was roaring so loudly in her ears that she could barely hear when the mountain cat raced for the fortress. Rowan's friends had come. Good. Good that he would not be alone, that he had people in the world.

She coughed blood again, splattering it on the ground—on the legs of the Valg prince.

She barely moved before he slammed her into her own flames, and she hit the magical wall beneath, as hard and unforgiving as if it were made of stone. The only way into the fortress was through the ward-gates. She swiped with Goldryn, but the blow was feeble. Against the Valg, against this horrible power that the King of Adarlan possessed, the army at his disposal . . . it was all useless. As useless as the vow she'd made to Nehemia's grave. As useless as an heir to a broken throne and a broken name.

The magic was boiling her blood. The darkness—it would be a relief compared to the hell smoldering in her veins. The Valg prince advanced, and part of her was screaming—screaming at herself to get up, to keep fighting, to rage and roar against this horrible end. But moving her limbs, even breathing, had become a monumental effort.

She was so tired.

The fortress was a hell of yelling and fighting and gore, but Rowan kept swinging his blades, holding his position at the tunnel mouth as soldier after soldier poured in. The scout leader, Bas, had let them in, Luca had told Rowan. The other demi-Fae who had conspired with Bas wanted the power the creatures offered—wanted a place in the world. From the devastation in the bleeding boy's eyes, Rowan knew that Bas had already met his end. He hoped Luca hadn't been the one to do it.

The soldiers kept coming, highly trained men who were not afraid of the demi-Fae, or of the little magic that they bore. They were armed with iron and did not differentiate between young and old, male and female, as they hacked and slaughtered.

Rowan was not drained, not in the least. He had fought for longer and in worse conditions. But the others were flagging, especially as soldiers continued flooding the fortress. Rowan yanked his sword from the gut of a falling soldier, dagger already slicing across the neck of the next, when growling shook the stones of the fortress. Some of the demi-Fae froze, but Rowan nearly shuddered with relief as twin wolves leapt down the staircase and closed their jaws around the necks of two Adarlanian soldiers.

Great wings flapped, and then a glowering, dark-eyed male was in front of him, swinging a sword older than the occupants of Mistward. Vaughan merely nodded at him before taking up a position, never one to waste words.

Beyond him, the wolves were nothing short of lethal, and did not bother to shift into their Fae forms as they took down soldier after soldier, leaving those that got through to the male waiting behind them. That was all Rowan had to see before he sprinted for the stairs, dodging the stunned and bloodied demi-Fae.

Darkness had not fallen, which meant she had to still be breathing, she had to still be holding the line, but—

A mountain cat skidded to a halt on the stairwell landing and shifted. Rowan took one look at Gavriel's tawny eyes and said, "Where is she?"

Gavriel held out an arm. As if to stop him. "She's in bad shape, Rowan. I think—"

Rowan ran, shoving aside his oldest friend, shouldering past the other towering male who now appeared—Lorcan. Even *Lorcan* had answered his call. The time for gratitude would come later, and the dark-haired demi-Fae didn't say anything as Rowan rushed to the battlement gates. What he saw beyond almost drove him to his knees.

The wall of flame was in tatters, but still protecting the barrier. But the three creatures . . .

Aelin was standing in front of them, hunched and panting, sword limp in her hand. They advanced, and a feeble blue flame sprang up before them. They swiped it away with wave of their hands. Another flame sprang up, and her knees buckled.

The shield of flame surged and receded, pulsing like the light around her body. She was burning out. Why hadn't she retreated?

Another step closer and the things said something that had her raising her head. Rowan knew he could not reach her, didn't even have the breath to shout a warning as Aelin gazed into the face of the creature before her.

She had lied to him. She had wanted to save lives, yes. But she had gone out there with no intention of saving her own.

He drew in a breath—to run, to roar, to summon his power, but a wall of muscle slammed into him from behind, tackling him to the grass. Though Rowan shoved and twisted against Gavriel, he could do nothing against the four centuries of training and feline instinct that had pinned him, keeping him from running through those gates and into the blackness that destroyed worlds.

The creature took Aelin's face in its hands, and her sword thudded to the ground, forgotten.

Rowan was screaming as the creature pulled her into its arms. As she stopped fighting. As her flames winked out and darkness swallowed her whole.

53

There was blood everywhere.

As before, Celaena stood between the two bloody beds, reeking breath caressing her ear, her neck, her spine. She could feel the Valg princes roving around her, circling with predators' gaits, devouring her misery and pain bit by bit, tasting and savoring.

There was no way out, and she could not move as she looked from one bed to the other.

Nehemia's corpse, mangled and mutilated. Because she had been too late, and because she had been a coward.

And her parents, throats slit from ear to ear, gray and lifeless. Dead from an attack they should have sensed. An attack *she* should have sensed. Maybe she *had* sensed it, and that was why she had crept in that night. But she had been too late then as well.

Two beds. Two fractures in her soul, cracks through which the abyss had come pouring in long before the Valg princes had ever seized her. A claw scraped along her neck and she jerked away, stumbling toward her parents' corpses.

The moment that darkness had swept around her, snuffing out her exhausted flame, it began eating away at the reckless rage that had compelled her to step out of the barrier. Here in the dark, the silence was complete—eternal. She could feel the Valg slinking around her, hungry and eager and full of cold, ancient malice. She'd expected to have the life sucked from her instantly, but they had just stayed close in the dark, brushing up against her like cats, until a faint light had formed and she'd found herself between these two beds. She was unable to look away, unable to do anything but feel her nausea and panic rise bit by bit. And now . . . Now . . .

Though her body remained unmoving on the bed, Nehemia's voice whispered, *Coward.*

Celaena vomited. A faint, hoarse laugh sounded behind her.

She backed up, farther and farther from the bed where Nehemia lay. Then she was standing in a sea of red—red and white and gray, and—

She now stood like a wraith in her parents' bed, where she had lain ten years ago, awakening between their corpses to the servant woman's screaming. It was those screams she could hear now, high and endless, and—*Coward.*

Celaena fell against the headboard, as real and smooth and cold as she remembered it. There was nowhere else for her to go. It was a memory—these were not real things.

She pressed her palms against the wood, fighting her building scream. *Coward.* Nehemia's voice again filled the room. Celaena squeezed her eyes shut and said into the wall, "I know. I know."

She did not fight as cold, claw-tipped fingers stroked at her cheeks, at her brow, at her shoulders. One of the claws severed clean through her long braid as it whipped her around. She did not fight as darkness swallowed her whole and dragged her down deep.

The darkness had no end and no beginning.

It was the abyss that had haunted her steps for ten years, and she free-fell into it, welcomed it.

There was no sound, only the vague sense of going toward a bottom that might not exist, or that might mean her true end. Maybe the Valg princes had devoured her, turning her into a husk. Maybe her soul was forever trapped here, in this plunging darkness.

Perhaps this was hell.

The blackness was rippling now, shifting with sound and color that she passed through. She lived through each image, each memory worse than the next. Chaol's face as he saw what she truly was; Nehemia's mutilated body; her final conversation with her friend, the damning things she'd said. *When your people are lying dead around you, don't come crying to me.*

It had come true—now thousands of slaves from Eyllwe had been slaughtered for their bravery.

She tumbled through a maelstrom of the moments when she had proved her friend right. She was a waste of space and breath, a stain on the world. Unworthy of her birthright.

This was hell—and looked like hell, as she saw the bloodbath she'd created on the day she rampaged through Endovier. The screams of the dying—the men she'd cut apart—tore at her like phantom hands.

This was what she deserved.

She went mad during that first day in Endovier.

Went mad as the descent slowed and she was stripped and strapped between two blood-splattered posts. The cold air nipped at her bare breasts, a bite that was nothing compared to the terror and agony as a whip cracked and—

She jerked against the ropes binding her. She scarcely had time to draw in a breath before the crack sounded again, cleaving the world like lightning, cleaving her skin.

"Coward," Nehemia said behind her, and the whip cracked. "Coward." The pain was blinding. "Look at me." She couldn't lift her head, though. Couldn't turn. *"Look at me."*

She sagged against her ropes, but managed to look over her shoulder.

Nehemia was whole, beautiful and untouched, her eyes full of damning hatred. And then from behind her emerged Sam, handsome and tall. His death had been so similar to Nehemia's, and yet so much worse, drawn out over hours. She had not saved him, either. When she beheld the iron-tipped whip in his hands, when he stepped past Nehemia and let the whip unfurl onto the rocky earth, Celaena let out a low, quiet laugh.

She welcomed the pain with open arms as he took a deep breath, clothes shifting with the movement as he snapped the whip. The iron tip—oh gods, it ripped her clean open, knocked her legs out from underneath her.

"Again," Celaena told him, the word little more than a rasp. *"Again."*

Sam obeyed. There was only the thud of leather on wet flesh as Sam and Nehemia took turns, and a line of people formed behind them, waiting for what they deserved as payment for what she had failed to do.

Such a long line of people. So many lives that she had taken or failed to protect.

Again.

Again.

Again.

She had not walked past the barrier expecting to defeat the Valg princes.

She had walked out there for the same reason she had snapped that day in Endovier.

But the Valg princes had not killed her yet.

She had felt their pleasure as she begged for the whipping. It was their sustenance. Her mortal flesh was nothing to them—it was the agony within that was the prize. They would draw this out forever, keep her as their pet.

There was no one to save her, no one who could enter their darkness and live.

One by one, they groped through her memories. She fed them, gave them everything they wanted and more. Back and back, sorting through the years as they plunged into the dark, twining together. She did not care.

She had not looked into the Valg prince's eyes expecting to ever again see sunrise.

She did not know how long she fell with them.

But then there was a rushing, roaring below—a frozen river. Whispers and foggy light were rising to meet them. No, not rising—this was the bottom.

An end to the abyss. And an end to her, perhaps, at last.

She didn't know if the Valg princes' hissing was from anger or pleasure as they slammed into that frozen river at the bottom of her soul.

54

Trumpets announced his arrival. Trumpets and silence as the people of Orynth crowded the steep streets winding up to the white palace that watched over them all. It was the first sunny day in weeks—the snow on the cobblestone streets melting quickly, though the wind still had a final bite of winter to it, enough so that the King of Adarlan and his entire massive party were bundled in furs that covered their regalia.

Their gold and crimson flags, however, flapped in the crisp wind, the golden poles shining as brightly as the armor of their bearers, who trotted at the head of the party. She watched them approach from one of the balconies off the throne room, Aedion at her side running a constant commentary about the state of their horses, armor, weapons—about the King of Adarlan himself, who rode near the front on a great black warhorse. There was a pony beside him, bearing a smaller figure. "His sniveling son," Aedion told her.

The whole castle was miserably quiet. Everyone was dashing

around, but silently, tensely. Her father had been on edge at breakfast, her mother distracted, the whole court snarly and wearing far more weapons than usual. Only her uncle seemed the same—only Orlon had smiled at her today, said she looked very pretty in her blue dress and golden crown, and tugged one of her freshly pressed curls. No one had told her anything about this visit, but she knew it was important, because even Aedion was wearing clean clothes, a crown, *and* a new dagger, which he'd taken to tossing in the air.

"Aedion, Aelin," someone hissed from inside the throne room—Lady Marion, her mother's dearest friend and handmaiden. "On the dais, *now*." Behind the lovely lady peeked a night-black head of hair and onyx eyes—Elide, her daughter. The girl was too quiet and breakable for her to bother with usually. And Lady Marion, *her* nursemaid, coddled her own daughter endlessly.

"Rat's balls," Aedion cursed, and Marion went red with anger, but did not reprimand. Proof enough that today was different—dangerous, even.

Her stomach shifted. But she followed Lady Marion inside, Aedion at her heels as always, and preched on her little throne set beside her father's. Aedion took up his place flanking her, shoulders back and head high, already her protector and warrior.

The whole of Orynth was silent as the King of Adarlan entered their mountain home.

She hated the King of Adarlan.

He did not smile—not when he stalked into the throne room to greet her uncle and parents, not when he introduced his eldest son, Crown Prince Dorian Havilliard, and not when they came to the great hall for the largest feast she'd ever seen. He'd only looked at her twice so far: once during that initial meeting, when he'd stared at her long and hard enough that her father had demanded to know what he found so interesting about his daughter, and their whole court had tensed. But she hadn't broken his dark stare. She hated his scarred, brutish face and furs. Hated the way he ignored his dark-haired son, who stood like a pretty doll beside him, his manners so elegant and graceful, his pale hands like little birds as they moved.

The second time the king had looked at her had been at this table, where she now sat a few seats down, flanked by Lady Marion on the side closest to the king and Aedion on the other. There were daggers on Lady Marion's legs beneath her dress—she knew because she kept bumping into them. Lord Cal, Marion's husband, sat beside his wife, the steel on him gleaming.

Elide, along with all the other children, had been sent upstairs. Only she and Aedion—and Prince Dorian—were allowed here. Aedion puffed with pride and barely restrained temper when the King of Adarlan viewed her a second time, as if he could see through to her bones. Then the king was swept into conversation with her parents and uncle and all the lords and ladies of the court who had placed themselves around the royal family.

She had always known her court took no chances, not with her and not with her parents or uncle. Even now, she noticed the eyes of her father's closest friends darting to the windows and doorways as they maintained conversation with those around them.

The rest of the hall was filled with the party from Adarlan and the outer circles of Orlon's court, along with key merchants from the city who wanted to make ties with Adarlan. Or something like that. But her attention was on the prince across from her, who seemed utterly ignored by his father and his own court, shoved down near the end with her and Aedion.

He ate so beautifully, she thought, watching him cut into his roast chicken. Not a drop moved out of place, not a scrap fell on the table.

She had decent manners, while Aedion was hopeless, his plate littered with bones and crumbs scattered everywhere, even some on her own dress. She'd kicked him for it, but his attention was too focused on the royals down the table.

So both she and the Crown Prince were to be ignored, then. She looked at the boy again, who was around her age, she supposed. His skin was from the winter, his blue-black hair neatly trimmed; his sapphire eyes lifted from his plate to meet hers.

"You eat like a fine lady," she told him.

His lips thinned and color stained his ivory cheeks. Across from her, Quinn, her uncle's Captain of the Guard, choked on his water.

The prince glanced at his father—still busy with her uncle—before replying. Not for approval, but in fear. "I eat like a prince," Dorian said quietly.

"You do not need to cut your bread with a fork and knife," she said. A faint pounding started in her head, followed by a flickering warmth, but she ignored it. The hall was hot, as they'd shut all the windows for some reason.

"Here in the North," she went on as the prince's knife and fork remained where they were on his dinner roll, "you need not be so formal. We don't put on airs."

Hen, one of Quinn's men, coughed pointedly from a few seats down. She could almost hear him saying, *Says the little lady with her hair pressed into careful curls and wearing her new dress that she threatened to skin us over if we got dirty.*

She gave Hen an equally pointed look, then returned her attention to the foreign prince. He'd already looked down at his food again, as if he expected to be neglected for the rest of the night. And he looked lonely enough that she said, "If you like, you could be my friend." Not one of the men around them said anything, or coughed.

Dorian lifted his chin. "I have a friend. He is to be Lord of Anielle someday, and the fiercest warrior in the land."

She doubted Aedion would like that claim, but her cousin remained focused down the table. She wished she'd kept her mouth closed. Even this useless foreign prince had friends. The pounding in her head increased, and she took a drink of her water. Water—always water to cool her insides.

Reaching for her glass, however, sent spikes of red-hot pain through her head, and she winced. "Princess?" Quinn said, always the first to notice.

She blinked, black spots forming. But the pain stopped.

No, not a stop, but a pause. A pause, then—

Right between her eyes, it ached and pressed at her head, trying to get in. She rubbed her brows. Her throat closed up, and she reached for the water, thinking of coolness, of calm and cold, exactly as her tutors and the court had told her. But the magic was churning in her gut—burning up. Each pulse of pain in her head made it worse.

"Princess," Quinn said again. She got to her feet, legs wobbling. The blackness in her vision grew with each blow from the pain, and she swayed. Distantly, as if she were underwater, she heard Lady Marion say her name, reach for her, but she wanted her mother's cool touch.

Her mother turned in her seat, face drawn, her golden earrings catching in the light. She stretched out an arm, beckoning. "What is it, Fireheart?"

"I don't feel well," she said, barely able to get the words out. She gripped her mother's velvet-clad arm, for comfort and to keep her buckling knees from giving out.

"What feels wrong?" her mother asked, even as she put a hand to her forehead. A flicker of worry, then a glance back at her father, who watched from beside the King of Adarlan. "She's burning up," she said softly. Lady Marion was suddenly behind her, and her mother looked up to say, "Have the healer go to her room." Marion was gone in an instant, hurrying to a side door.

She didn't need a healer, and she gripped her mother's arm to tell her as much. Yet no words would come out as the magic surged and burned. Her mother hissed and jerked back—smoke rising from her dress, from where she had gripped her. "Aelin."

Her head gave a throb—a blast of pain, and then . . .

A wriggling, squirming inside her head.

A worm of darkness, pushing its way in. Her magic roiled, thrashing, trying to get it out, to burn it up, to save them both, but—*"Aelin."*

"Get it out," she rasped, pushing at her temples as she backed away from the table. Two of the foreign lords grabbed Dorian from the table and swept him from the room.

Her magic bucked like a stallion as the worm wriggled farther in. *"Get it out."*

"Aelin." Her father was on his feet now, hand on his sword. Half the others were standing too, but she flung out a hand—to keep them away, to warn them.

Blue flame shot out. Two people dove in time to avoid it, but everyone was on their feet as the vacated seats went up in flames.

The worm would latch into her mind and never let go.

She grabbed at her head, her magic screaming, so loud it could shatter the world. And then she was burning, a living column of turquoise flame, sobbing as the dark worm continued its work and the walls of her mind began to give.

Above her own voice, above the shouting in the hall, she heard her father's bellow—a command to her mother, who was on her knees, hands outstretched toward her in supplication. *"Do it, Evalin!"*

The pillar of flame grew hotter, hot enough that people were fleeing now.

Her mother's eyes met her own, full of pleading and pain.

Then water—a wall of water crashing down on her, slamming her to the stones, flowing down her throat, into her eyes, choking her.

Drowning her. Until there was no air for her flame, only water and its freezing embrace.

The King of Adarlan looked at her for a third time—and smiled.

The Valg princes enjoyed that memory, that terror and pain. And as they paused to savor it, Celaena understood. The King of Adarlan had used his power on her that night. Her parents could not have known that the person responsible for that dark worm, which had vanished as soon as she'd lost consciousness, was the man sitting beside them.

There was another one of them now—a fourth prince, living inside Narrok, who said, "The soldiers have almost taken the tunnel. Be ready to move soon." She could feel him hovering over her, observing. "You've found me a prize that will interest our liege. Do not waste her. Sips only."

She tried to summon horror—tried to feel anything at the thought of where they would take her, what they would do to her. But she could feel nothing as the princes murmured their understanding, and the memory tumbled onward.

Her mother thought it was an attack from Maeve, a vicious reminder of whatever debt she owed, to make them look vulnerable. In the hours afterward, as she'd lain in the ice-cold bath adjacent to her bedroom, she had used her Fae ears to overhear her parents and their court debating it from the sitting room of their suite.

It had to be Maeve. No one else could do anything like that, or know that such a demonstration—in front of the King of Adarlan, who already loathed magic—would be detrimental.

She did not want to talk, even once she was again capable of walking and speaking and acting like a princess. Insisting some normalcy might help, her mother made her go to a tea the next afternoon with

Prince Dorian, carefully guarded and monitored, with Aedion sitting between them. And when Dorian's flawless manners faltered and he knocked over the teapot, spilling on her new dress, she'd made a good show of having Aedion threaten to pummel him.

But she didn't care about the prince, or the tea, or the dress. She could barely walk back to her room, and that night she dreamt of the maggot invading her mind, waking with screams and flames in her mouth.

At dawn, her parents took her out of the castle, headed for their manor two days away. Their foreign visitors might have caused too much stress, the healer said. She suggested Lady Marion take her, but her parents insisted they go. Her uncle approved. The King of Adarlan, it seemed, would not stay in the castle with her magic running rampant, either.

Aedion remained in Orynth, her parents promising he would be sent for when she was settled again. But she knew it was for his safety. Lady Marion went with them, leaving her husband and Elide at the palace—for their safety, too.

A monster, that was what she was. A monster who had to be contained and monitored.

Her parents argued the first two nights at the manor, and Lady Marion kept her company, reading to her, brushing her hair, telling her stories of her home in Perranth. Marion had been a laundress in the palace from her childhood. But when Evalin arrived, they had become friends—mostly because the princess had stained her new husband's favorite shirt with ink and wanted to get it cleaned before he noticed.

Evalin soon made Marion her lady-in-waiting, and then Lord Lochan had returned from a rotation on the southern border. Handsome Cal Lochan, who somehow became the dirtiest man in the castle and constantly needed Marion's advice on how to remove various stains. Who one day asked a bastard-born servant to be his wife—and not just wife, but Lady of Perranth, the second-largest territory in Terrasen. Two years later, she had borne him Elide, heir of Perranth.

She loved Marion's stories, and it was those stories she clung to in the quiet and tension of the next few days, when winter still gripped the world and made the manor groan.

The house was creaking in the brisk winds the night her mother walked into her bedroom—far less grand than the one in the palace, but still lovely. They only summered here, as the house was too drafty for winter, and the roads too perilous. The fact that they'd come . . .

"Still not asleep?" her mother asked. Lady Marion rose from beside the bed. After a few warm words, Marion left, smiling at them both.

Her mother curled up on the mattress, drawing her in close. "I'm sorry," her mother whispered onto her head. For the nightmares had also been of drowning—of icy water closing over her head. "I am so sorry, Fireheart."

She buried her face in her mother's chest, savoring the warmth.

"Are you still frightened of sleeping?"

She nodded, clinging tighter.

"I have a gift, then." When she didn't move, her mother said, "Don't you wish to see it?"

She shook her head. She didn't want a gift.

"But this will protect you from harm—this will keep you safe always."

She lifted her head to find her mother smiling as she removed the golden chain and heavy, round medallion from beneath her nightgown and held it out to her.

She looked at the amulet, then at her mother, eyes wide.

The Amulet of Orynth. The heirloom honored above all others of their house. Its round disk was the size of her palm, and on its cerulean front, a white stag had been carved of horn—horn gifted from the

Lord of the Forest. Between his curling antlers was a burning crown of gold, the immortal star that watched over them and pointed the way home to Terrasen. She knew every inch of the amulet, had run her fingers over it countless times and memorized the shape of the symbols etched into the back—words in a strange language that no one could remember.

"Father gave this to you when you were in Wendlyn. To protect you."

The smile remained. "And before that, his uncle gave it to him when he came of age. It is a gift meant to be given to people in our family—to those who need its guidance."

She was too stunned to object as her mother slipped the chain over her head and arranged the amulet down her front. It hung almost to her navel, a warm, heavy weight. "Never take it off. Never lose it." Her mother kissed her brow. "Wear it, and know that you are loved, Fireheart—that you are safe, and it is the strength of this"—she placed a hand on her heart—"that matters. Wherever you go, Aelin," she whispered, "no matter how far, this will lead you home."

~

She had lost the Amulet of Orynth. Lost it that very same night.

She could not bear it. She tried begging the Valg princes to put her out of her misery and drain her into nothing, but she had no voice here.

Hours after her mother had given her the Amulet of Orynth, a storm had struck.

It was a storm of unnatural darkness, and in it she felt that wriggling, horrific *thing* pushing against her mind again. Her parents remained unconscious along with everyone else in the manor, even though a strange smell coated the air.

She had clutched the amulet to her chest when she awoke to the pure dark and the thunder—clutched it and prayed to every god she knew.

But the amulet had not given her strength or courage, and she had slunk to her parents' room, as black as her own, save for the window flapping in the gusting wind and rain.

The rain had soaked everything, but—but they had to be exhausted from dealing with her, and from the anxiety they tried to hide. So she shut the window for them, and carefully crawled into their damp bed so that she did not wake them. They didn't reach for her, didn't ask what was wrong, and the bed was so cold—colder than her own, and reeking of copper and iron, and that scent that did not sit well with her.

It was to that scent that she awoke when the maid screamed.

Lady Marion rushed in, eyes wide but clear. She did not look at her dead friends, but went straight to the bed and leaned across Evalin's corpse. The lady in-waiting was small and delicately boned, but she somehow lifted her away from her parents, holding her tightly as she rushed from the room. The few servants at the manor were in a panic, some racing for help that was at least a day away—some fleeing.

Lady Marion stayed.

Marion stayed and drew a bath, helping her peel away the cold, bloody nightgown. They did not talk, did not try. Lady Marion bathed her, and when she was clean and dry, she carried her down to the cold kitchen. Marion sat her at the long table, bundled in a blanket, and set about building the hearth fire.

She had not spoken today. There were no sounds or words left in her, anyway.

One of the few remaining servants burst in, shouting to the empty house that King Orlon was dead, too. Murdered in his bed just like—

Lady Marion was out of the kitchen with her teeth bared before the man could enter. She didn't listen to gentle Marion slapping him, ordering him to get out and find help—find *real* help and not useless news.

Murdered. Her family was—dead. There was no coming back from death, and her parents . . . What had the servants done with their . . . their . . .

Shaking hit her so hard the blanket tumbled away. She couldn't stop her teeth from clacking. It was a miracle she stayed in the chair.

It couldn't be true. This was another nightmare, and she would awaken to her father stroking her hair, her mother smiling, awaken in Orynth, and—

The warm weight of the blanket wrapped around her again, and Lady Marion scooped her into her lap, rocking. "I know. I'm not going to leave—I'm going to stay with you until help comes. They'll be here tomorrow. Lord Lochan, Captain Quinn, your Aedion—they're all going to be here tomorrow. Maybe even by dawn." But Lady Marion was shaking, too. "I know," she kept saying, weeping quietly. "I know."

The fire died down, along with Marion's crying. They held on to each other, rooted to that kitchen chair. They waited for the dawn, and for the others who would help, somehow.

A clopping issued from outside—faint, but the world was so silent that they heard the lone horse. It was still dark. Lady Marion scanned the kitchen windows, listening to the horse slowly circling, until—

They were under the table in a flash, Marion pressing her into the freezing floor, covering her with her delicate body. The horse headed toward the darkened front of the house.

The front, because—because the kitchen light might suggest to whoever it was that someone was inside. The front was better for sneaking in . . . to finish what had begun the night before.

"Aelin," Marion whispered, and small, strong hands found her face, forcing her to look at the white-as-snow features, the bloodred lips. "Aelin, listen to me." Though Marion was breathing quickly, her voice was even. "You are going to run for the river. Do you remember the way to the footbridge?"

The narrow rope and wood bridge across the ravine and the rushing River Florine below. She nodded.

"Good girl. Make for the bridge, and cross it. Do you remember the empty farm down the road? Find a place to hide there—and do not come out, do not let yourself be seen by *anyone* except someone you recognize. Not even if they say they're a friend. Wait for the court—they will find you."

She was shaking again. But Marion gripped her shoulders. "I am going to buy you what time I can, Aelin. No matter what you hear, no matter what you see, don't look back, and don't stop until you find a place to hide."

She shook her head, silent tears finding their way out at last. The front door groaned—a quick movement.

Lady Marion reached for the dagger in her boot. It glinted in the dim light. "When I say run, you run, Aelin. Do you understand?"

She didn't want to, not at all, but she nodded.

Lady Marion brushed a kiss to her brow. "Tell my Elide . . ." Her voice broke. "Tell my Elide that I love her very much."

A soft thud of approaching footsteps from the front of the house. Lady Marion dragged her from under the table and eased open the kitchen door only wide enough for her to squeeze through.

"Run *now*," Lady Marion said, and shoved her into the night.

The door shut behind her, and then there was only the cold, dark air and the trees that led toward the path to the bridge. She staggered into a run. Her legs were leaden, her bare feet tearing on the ground. But she made it to the trees—just as there was a crash from the house.

She gripped a trunk, her knees buckling. Through the open window, she could see Lady Marion standing before a hooded, towering man, her daggers out but trembling. "You will not find her."

The man said something that had Marion backing to the door—not to run, but to block it.

She was so small, her nursemaid. So small against him. "She is a *child*," Marion bellowed. She had never heard her scream like that—with rage and disgust and despair. Marion raised her daggers, precisely how her husband had shown her again and again.

She should help, not cower in the trees. She had learned to hold a knife and a small sword. She should help.

The man lunged for Marion, but she darted out of the way—and then leapt on him, slicing and tearing and biting.

And then something broke—something broke so fundamentally she knew there was no coming back from it, either for her or Lady Marion—as the man grabbed the woman and threw her against the edge of the table. A crack of bone, then the arc of his blade going for her stunned form—for her head. Red sprayed.

She knew enough about death to understand that once a head was severed like that, it was over. Knew that Lady Marion, who had loved her husband and daughter so much, was gone. Knew that this—this was called sacrifice.

She ran. Ran through the barren trees, the brush ripping her clothes, her hair, shredding and biting. The man didn't bother to be quiet as he flung open the kitchen door, mounted his horse, and galloped after her. The hoofbeats were so powerful they seemed to echo through the forest—the horse had to be a monster.

She tripped over a root and slammed into the earth. In the distance, the melting river was roaring. So close, but—her ankle gave a bolt of agony. Stuck—she was stuck in the mud and roots. She yanked at the roots that held her, wood ripping her nails, and when that did nothing, she clawed at the muddy ground. Her fingers burned.

A sword whined as it was drawn from its sheath, and the ground reverberated with the pounding hooves of the horse. Closer, closer it came.

A sacrifice—it had been a sacrifice, and now it would be in vain.

More than death, that was what she hated most—the wasted sacrifice of Lady Marion. She clawed at the ground and yanked at the roots, and then—

Tiny eyes in the dark, small fingers at the roots, heaving them up, up. Her foot slipped free and she was up again, unable to thank the Little Folk who had already vanished, unable to do anything but *run*, limping now. The man was so close, the bracken cracking behind, but she knew the way. She had come through here so many times that the darkness was no obstacle.

She only had to make it to the bridge. His horse could not pass, and she was fast enough to outrun him. The Little Folk might help her again. She only had to make it to the bridge.

A break in the trees and the river's roar grew overpowering. She was so close now. She felt and heard, rather than saw, his horse break through the trees behind her, the whoosh of his sword as he lifted it, preparing to cleave her head right there.

There were the twin posts, faint on the moonless night. The bridge. She had made it, and now she had only yards, now a few feet, now—

The breath of his horse was hot on her neck as she flung herself between the two posts of the bridge, making a leap onto the wood planks.

Making a leap onto thin air.

She had not missed it—no, those were the posts and—

He had cut the bridge.

It was her only thought as she plummeted, so fast she had no time to scream before she hit the icy water and was pulled under.

That.

That moment Lady Marion had chosen a desperate hope for her kingdom over herself, over her husband and the daughter who would wait and wait for a return that would never come.

That was the moment that had broken everything Aelin Galathynius was and had promised to be.

Celaena was lying on the ground—on the bottom of the world, on the bottom of hell.

That was the moment she could not face—had not faced.

For even then, she had known the enormity of that sacrifice.

There was more, after the moment she'd hit the water. But those memories were hazy, a mix of ice and black water and strange light, and then she knew nothing more until Arobynn was crouched over her on the reedy riverbank, somewhere far away. She awoke in a strange bed in a cold keep, the Amulet of Orynth lost to the river. Whatever magic it had, whatever protection, had been used up that night.

Then the process of taking her fear and guilt and despair and twisting them into something new. Then the hate—the hate that had rebuilt her, the rage that had fueled her, smothering the memories she buried in a grave within her heart and never let out.

She had taken Lady Marion's sacrifice and become a monster, almost as bad as the one who had murdered Lady Marion and her own family.

That was why she could not, did not, go home.

She had never looked for the death tolls in those initial weeks of slaughter, or the years afterward. But she knew Lord Lochan had been executed. Quinn and his men. And so many of those children . . . such bright lights, all hers to protect. And she had failed.

Celaena clung to the ground.

It was what she had not been able to tell Chaol, or Dorian, or Elena: that when Nehemia arranged for her own death so it would spur her into action, that sacrifice . . . that worthless sacrifice . . .

She could not let go of the ground. There was nothing beneath it, nowhere else to go, nowhere to outrun this truth.

She didn't know how long she lay on the bottom of wherever this was, but eventually the Valg princes started up again, barely more than shadows of thought and malice as they stalked from memory to memory as if sampling platters at a feast. Little bites—sips. They did not even look her way, for they had won. And she was glad of it. Let them do what they wanted, let Narrok carry her back to Adarlan and throw her at the king's feet.

There was a scrape and crunch of shoes, then a small, smooth hand slid toward her. But it was not Chaol or Sam or Nehemia who lay across from her, watching her with those sad turquoise eyes.

Her cheek against the moss, the young princess she had been—Aelin Galathynius—reached a hand for her. "Get up," she said softly

Celaena shook her head.

Aelin strained for her, bridging that rift in the foundation of the world. "Get up." A promise—a promise for a better life, a better world.

The Valg princes paused.

She had wasted her life, wasted Marion's sacrifice. Those slaves had been butchered because she had failed—because she had not been there in time.

"Get up," someone said beyond the young princess. Sam. Sam, standing just beyond where she could see, smiling faintly.

"Get up," said another voice—a woman's. Nehemia.

"Get up." Two voices together—her mother and father, faces grave but eyes bright. Her uncle was beside them, the crown of Terrasen on his silver hair. "Get up," he told her gently.

One by one, like shadows emerging from the mist, they appeared. The faces of the people she had loved with her heart of wildfire.

And then there was Lady Marion, smiling beside her husband. "Get up," she whispered, her voice full of that hope for the world, and for the daughter she would never seen again.

A tremor in the darkness.

Aelin still lay before her, hand still reaching. The Valg princes turned.

As the demon princes moved, her mother stepped toward her, face and hair and build so like her own. "You are a disappointment," she hissed.

Her father crossed his muscular arms. "You are everything I hated about the world."

Her uncle, still wearing the antler crown long since burned to ash: "Better that you had died with us than shame us, degrade our memory, betray our people."

Their voices swirled together. "Traitor. Murderer. Liar. Thief. Coward." Again and again, worming in just as the King of Adarlan's power had wriggled in her mind like a maggot.

The king hadn't done it merely to cause a disruption and hurt her. He had also done it to separate her family, to get them out of the castle—to take the blame away from Adarlan and make it look like an outside attack.

She had blamed herself for dragging them to the manor house to be butchered. But the king had planned it all, every minute detail. Except for the mistake of leaving her alive—perhaps because the power of the amulet did indeed save her.

"Come with us," her family whispered. "Come with us into the ageless dark."

They reached for her, faces shadowed and twisted. Yet—yet even those faces, so warped with hatred . . . she still loved them—even if they loathed her, even if it ached; loved them until their hissing faded, until they vanished like smoke, leaving only Aelin lying beside her, as she had been all along.

She looked at Aelin's face—the face she'd once worn—and at her still outstretched hand, so small and unscarred. The darkness of the Valg princes flickered.

There was solid ground beneath her. Moss and grass. Not hell—earth.

The earth on which her kingdom lay, green and mountainous and as unyielding as its people. *Her* people.

Her people, waiting for ten years, but no longer.

She could see the snow-capped Staghorns, the wild tangle of Oakwald at their feet, and . . . and Orynth, that city of light and learning, once a pillar of strength—and her home.

It would be both again.

She would not let that light go out.

She would fill the world with it, with her light—her gift. She would light up the darkness, so brightly that all who were lost or wounded or broken would find their way to it, a beacon for those who still dwelled in that abyss. It would not take a monster to destroy a monster—but light, light to drive out darkness.

She was not afraid.

She would remake the world—remake it for them, those she had loved with this glorious, burning heart; a world so brilliant and prosperous that when she saw them again in the Afterworld, she would not be ashamed. She would build it for her people, who had survived this long, and whom she would not abandon. She would make for them a kingdom such as there had never been, even if it took until her last breath.

She was their queen, and she could offer them nothing less.

Aelin Galathynius smiled at her, hand still outreached. "Get up," the princess said.

Celaena reached across the earth between them and brushed her fingers against Aelin's.

And arose.

55

The barrier fell.

But the darkness did not advance over the ward-stones, and Rowan, who had been restrained by Gavriel and Lorcan in the grass outside the fortress, knew why.

The creatures and Narrok had captured a prize far greater than the demi-Fae. The joy of feeding on her was something they planned to relish for a long, long while. Everything else was secondary—as if they'd forgotten to continue advancing, swept up in the frenzy of feasting.

Behind them, the fighting continued, as it had for the past twenty minutes. Wind and ice were of no use against the darkness, though Rowan had hurled both against it the moment the barrier fell. Again and again, anything to pierce that eternal black and see what was left of the princess. Even as he started hearing a soft, warm female voice, beckoning to him from the darkness—that voice he had spent centuries forgetting, which now tore him to shreds.

"Rowan," Gavriel murmured, tightening his grip on Rowan's arm. Rain had begun pouring. "We are needed inside."

"No," he snarled. He knew Aelin was alive, because during all these weeks that they had been breathing each other's scents, they had become bonded. She was alive, but could be in any level of torment or decay. That was why Gavriel and Lorcan were holding him back. If they didn't, he would run for the darkness, where Lyria beckoned.

But for Aelin, he had tried to break free.

"Rowan, the others—"

"No."

Lorcan swore over the roar of the torrential rain. "She is *dead*, you fool, or close enough to it. You can still save other lives."

They began hauling him to his feet, away from her. "If you don't let me go, I'll rip your head from your body," he snarled at Lorcan, the commander who had offered him a company of warriors when he had nothing and no one left.

Gavriel flicked his eyes to Lorcan in some silent conversation. Rowan tensed, preparing to fling them off. They would knock him unconscious sooner than allow him into that dark, where Lyria's beckoning had now turned to screaming for mercy. It wasn't real. It wasn't real.

But Aelin *was* real, and was being drained of life with every moment they held him here. All he needed to get them unconscious was for Gavriel to drop his magical shield—which he'd had up against Rowan's own power from the moment he'd pinned him. He had to get into that dark, had to find her. *"Let go,"* he growled again.

A rumbling shook the earth, and they froze. Beneath them some huge power was surging—a behemoth rising from the deep.

They turned toward the darkness. And Rowan could have sworn that a golden light arced through it, then disappeared.

"That's impossible," Gavriel breathed. "She burned out."

Rowan didn't dare blink. Her burnouts had always been self-imposed, some inner barrier composed of fear and a lingering desire for normalcy that kept her from accepting the true depth of her power.

The creatures fed on despair and pain and terror. But what if—what if the victim let go of those fears? What if the victim walked through them—embraced them?

As if in answer, flame erupted from the wall of darkness.

The fire unfurled, filling the rainy night, vibrant as a red opal. Lorcan swore, and Gavriel threw up additional shields of his own magic. Rowan didn't bother.

They did not fight him as he shrugged off their grip, surging to his feet. The flame didn't singe a hair on his head. It flowed above and past him, glorious and immortal and unbreakable.

And there, beyond the stones, standing between two of those creatures, was Aelin, a strange mark glowing on her brow. Her hair flowed around her, shorter now and bright like her fire. And her eyes—though they were red-rimmed, the gold in her eyes was a living flame.

The two creatures lunged for her, the darkness sweeping in around them.

Rowan ran all of one step before she flung out her arms, grabbing the creatures by their flawless faces—her palms over their open mouths as she exhaled sharply.

As if she'd breathed fire into their cores, flames shot out of their eyes, their ears, their fingers. The two creatures didn't have a chance to scream as she burned them into cinders.

She lowered her arms. Her magic was raging so fiercely that the rain turned to steam before it hit her. A weapon bright from the forging.

He forgot Gavriel and Lorcan as he bolted for her—the gold and red and blue flames utterly hers, this heir of fire. Spying him at last, she smiled faintly. A queen's smile.

But there was exhaustion in that smile, and her bright magic flickered. Behind her, Narrok and the remaining creature—the one they had faced in the woods—were spooling the darkness into themselves, as if readying for attack. She turned toward them, swaying slightly, her skin deathly pale. They had fed on her, and she was drained after shredding apart their brethren. A very real, very final burnout was steadily approaching.

The wall of black swelled, one final hammer blow to squash her, but she stood fast, a golden light in the darkness. That was all Rowan needed to see before he knew what he had to do. Wind and ice were of no use here, but there were other ways.

Rowan drew his dagger and sliced his palm open as he sprinted through the gate-stones.

The darkness built and built, and she knew it would hurt, knew it would likely kill her and Rowan when it came crashing down. But she would not run from it.

Rowan reached her, panting and bloody. She did not dishonor him by asking him to flee as he extended his bleeding palm, offering his raw power to harness now that she was well and truly emptied. She knew it would work. She had suspected it for some time now. They were *carranam*.

He had come for her. She held his gaze as she grabbed her own dagger and cut her palm, right over the scar she'd given herself at Nehemia's grave. And though she knew he could read the words on her face, she said, "To whatever end?"

He nodded, and she joined hands with him, blood to blood and soul to soul, his other arm coming around to grip her tightly. Their hands clasped between them, he whispered into her ear, "I claim you, too, Aelin Galathynius."

The wave of impenetrable black descended, roaring as it made to devour them.

Yet this was not the end—this was not *her* end. She had survived loss and pain and torture; she had survived slavery and hatred and despair; she would survive this, too. Because hers was not a story of darkness. So she was not afraid of that crushing black, not with the warrior holding her, not with the courage that having one true friend offered—a friend who made living not so awful after all, not if she were with him.

Rowan's magic punched into her, old and strange and so vast her knees buckled. He held her with that unrelenting strength, and she harnessed his wild power as he opened his innermost barriers, letting it flow through her.

The black wave was not halfway fallen when they shattered it apart with golden light, leaving Narrok and his remaining prince gaping.

She did not give them a moment to spool the darkness back. Drawing power from the endless well within Rowan, she pulled up fire and light, embers and warmth, the glow of a thousand dawns and sunsets. If the Valg craved the sunshine of Erilea, then she would give it to them.

Narrok and the prince were shrieking. The Valg did not want to go back; they did not want to be ended, not after so long spent waiting to return to her world. But she crammed the light down their throats, burning up their black blood.

She clung to Rowan, gritting her teeth against the sounds. There was a sudden silence, and she looked to Narrok, standing so still, watching, waiting. A spear of black punched into her head—offering one more vision in a mere heartbeat. Not a memory, but a glimpse of the future. The sounds and smell and look of it were so real that only her grip on Rowan kept her anchored in the world. Then it was gone, and the light was still building, enveloping them all.

The light became unbearable as she willed it into the two Valg who had now dropped to their knees, pouring it into every shadowy corner of them. And she could have sworn that the blackness in Narrok's eyes faded. Could have sworn that his eyes became a mortal brown, and that gratitude flickered just for a moment. Just for a moment; then she burned both demon and Narrok to ash.

The remaining Valg prince crawled only two steps before he followed suit, a silent scream on his perfect face as he was incinerated. When the light and flames receded, all that remained of Narrok and the Valg were four Wyrdstone collars steaming in the wet grass.

56

A few days after the unforgivable, despicable slave massacre, Sorscha was finishing up a letter to her friend when there was a knock on her workroom door. She jumped, scrawling a line of ink down the center of the page.

Dorian popped his head in, grinning, but the grin faltered when he saw the letter. "I hope I'm not interrupting," he said, slipping in and shutting the door. As he turned, she balled up the ruined paper and chucked it into the rubbish pail.

"Not at all," she said, toes curling as he nuzzled her neck and slipped his arms around her waist. "Someone might walk in," she protested, squirming out of his grip. He let her go, but his eyes gleamed in a way that told her when they were alone again tonight, he might not be so easy to convince. She smiled.

"Do that again," he breathed.

So Sorscha smiled again, laughing. And he looked so baffled by it that she asked, "What?"

"That's the most beautiful thing I've ever seen," he said.

She had to look away, go find something to do with her hands. They worked together in silence, as they were prone to doing now that Dorian knew his way around the workroom. He liked helping her with her tonics for other patients.

Someone coughed from the doorway, and they straightened, Sorscha's heart flying into her throat. She hadn't even noticed the door opening—or the Captain of the Guard now standing in it.

The captain walked right in, and Dorian stiffened beside her.

"Captain," she said, "are you in need of my assistance?"

Dorian said nothing, his face unusually grim—those beautiful eyes haunted and heavy. He slipped a warm hand around her waist, resting it on her back. The captain quietly shut the door, and seemed to listen to the outside hall for a moment before speaking.

He looked even graver than her prince—his broad shoulders seeming to sag under an invisible burden. But his golden-brown eyes were clear as they met Dorian's. "You were right."

Chaol supposed it was a miracle in itself that Dorian had agreed to do this. The grief on Dorian's face this morning had told him he could ask. And that Dorian would say yes.

Dorian made Chaol explain everything—to both of them. That was Dorian's price: the truth owed to him, and to the woman who deserved to know what she was risking herself for.

Chaol quietly, quickly, explained everything: the magic, the Wyrdkeys, the three towers . . . all of it. To her credit, Sorscha didn't fall apart or doubt him. He wondered if she was reeling, if she was upset with Dorian for not telling her. She revealed nothing, not with that healer's training and self-control. But the prince watched Sorscha as if he could read her impregnable mask and see what was brewing beneath.

The prince had somewhere to be. He kissed Sorscha before he left, murmuring something in her ear that made her smile. Chaol hadn't suspected to find Dorian so . . . happy with his healer. Sorscha. It was an embarrassment that Chaol had never known her name until today. And from the way Dorian looked at her, and she him . . . He was glad that his friend had found her.

When Dorian had gone, Sorscha was still smiling, despite what she'd learned. It made her truly stunning—it made her whole face open up.

"I think," Chaol said, and Sorscha turned, brows high, ready to get to work. "I think," he said again, smiling faintly, "that this kingdom could use a healer as its queen."

She did not smile at him, as he'd hoped. Instead she looked unfathomably sad as she returned to her work. Chaol left without further word to ready himself for his experiment with Dorian—the only person in this castle, perhaps in the world, who could help him. Help them all.

Dorian had raw power, Celaena had said, power to be shaped as he willed it. That was the only thing similar enough to the power of the Wyrdkeys, neither good nor evil. And crystals, Chaol had once read in Celaena's magic books, were good conduits for magic. It hadn't been hard to buy several from the market—each about as long as his finger, white as fresh snow.

Everything was nearly ready when Dorian finally arrived in one of the secret tunnels and took a seat on the ground. Candles burned around them, and Chaol explained his plan as he finished pouring the last line of red sand—from the Red Desert, the merchant had claimed—between the three crystals. Equidistant from one another, they made the shape Murtaugh had drawn on the map of their continent. In the center of the triangle sat a small bowl of water.

Dorian pinned him with a stare. "Don't blame me if they shatter."

"I have replacements." He did. He'd bought a dozen crystals.

Dorian stared at the first crystal. "You just want me to . . . focus my power on it?"

"Then draw a line of power to the next crystal, then the next, imagining that your goal is to freeze the water in the bowl. That's all."

A raised brow. "That's not even a spell."

"Just humor me," Chaol said. "I wouldn't have asked if this wasn't the only way." He dipped a finger in the bowl of water, setting it rippling. Something in his gut said that maybe the spell required nothing more than power and sheer will.

The prince's sigh filled the stone hall, echoing off the stones and vaulted ceiling. Dorian gazed at the first crystal, roughly representing Rifthold. For minutes, there was nothing. But then Dorian began sweating, swallowing repeatedly.

"Are you—"

"I'm fine," Dorian gasped, and the first crystal began to glow white.

The light grew brighter, Dorian sweating and grunting as if he were in pain. Chaol was about to ask him to stop when a line shot toward the next crystal—so fast it was nearly undetectable save for the slight ripple in the sand. The crystal flashed bright, and then another line shot out, heading south. Again, the sand rippled in its wake.

The water remained fluid. The third crystal glowed, and the final line completed the triangle, making all three crystals flash for a moment. And then . . . slowly, crackling softly, the water froze. Chaol shoved back against his horror—horror and awe at how much Dorian's control had grown.

Dorian's skin was pasty and gleamed with sweat. "This is how he did it, isn't it?"

Chaol nodded. "Ten years ago, with those three towers. They were all built years before so that this could happen precisely when his invading forces were ready, so no one could strike back. Your father's spell must be far more complex, to have frozen magic entirely, but on a basic level, this is probably similar to what occurred."

"I want to see where they are—the towers." Chaol shook his head, but Dorian said, "You've told me everything else already. Show me the damn map."

With a wipe of his hand, a god destroying a world, Dorian knocked down a crystal, releasing the power. The ice melted, the water rippling and sloshing against the bowl. Just like that. Chaol blinked.

If they could knock out one tower . . . It was such a risk. They needed to be sure before acting. Chaol pulled out the map Murtaugh had marked, the map he didn't dare to leave anywhere. "Here, here, and here," he said, pointing to Rifthold, Amaroth, and Noll. "That's where we know towers were built. Watchtowers, but all three had the same traits: black stone, gargoyles . . ."

"You mean to tell me that the clock tower in the garden is one of them?"

Chaol nodded, ignoring the laugh of disbelief. "That's what we think."

The prince leaned over the map, bracing a hand against the floor. He traced a line from Rifthold to Amaroth, then from Rifthold to Noll. "The northward line cuts through the Ferian Gap; the southern cuts directly through Morath. You told Aedion that you thought my father had sent Roland and Kaltain to Morath, along with any other nobles with magic in their blood. What are the odds that it's a mere coincidence?"

"And the Ferian Gap . . ." Chaol had to swallow. "Celaena said she'd heard of wings in the Gap. Nehemia said her scouts did not come back, that something was brewing there."

"Two spots for him to breed whatever army he's making, perhaps drawing on this power as it makes a current through them."

"Three." Chaol pointed to the Dead Islands. "We had a report that something strange was being bred there . . . and that it's been sent to Wendlyn."

"But my father sent Celaena." The prince swore. "There's no way to warn them?"

"We've already tried."

Dorian wiped the sweat from his brow. "So you're working with them—you're on their side."

"No. I don't know. We just share information. But this is all information that helps us. You."

Dorian's eyes hardened, and Chaol winced as a cool breeze swept in.

"So what are you going to do?" Dorian asked. "Just . . . knock down the clock tower?"

Destroying the clock tower was an act of war—an act that could endanger the lives of too many people. There would be no going back. He didn't even want to tell Aedion or Ren, for fear of what they'd do. They wouldn't think twice before incinerating it, perhaps killing everyone in this castle in the process. "I don't know. I don't know what to do. You were right about that."

He wished he had something more to say to Dorian, but even small talk was an effort now. He was closing in on candidates to replace him as Captain of the Guard, sending more trunks to Anielle every week, and he could barely bring himself to look at his own men. As for Dorian . . . there was so much left between them.

"Now's not the time," Dorian said quietly, as if he could read Chaol's mind.

Chaol swallowed. "I want to thank you. I know what you're risking is—"

"We're all risking something." There was so little of the friend he'd grown up with. The prince glanced at his pocket watch. "I need to go." Dorian stalked to the stairs, and there was no fear in his face, no doubt, as he said, "You gave me the truth today, so I'll share mine: even if it meant us being friends again, I don't think I would want to go back to how it was before—who *I* was before. And this . . ." He jerked his chin toward the scattered crystals and the bowl of water. "I think this is a good change, too. Don't fear it."

Dorian left, and Chaol opened his mouth, but no words came out. He was too stunned. When Dorian had spoken, it hadn't been a prince who looked at him.

It had been a king.

57

Celaena slept for two days.

She hardly remembered what had happened after she incinerated Narrok and the Valg prince, though she had a vague sense of Rowan's men and the others having the fortress under control. They'd lost only about fifteen in total, since the soldiers had not wanted to kill the demi-Fae but to capture them for the Valg princes to haul back to Adarlan. When they subdued the surviving enemy soldiers, locking them in the dungeon, they'd come back hours later to find them all dead. They'd carried poison with them—and it seemed they had no inclination to be interrogated.

Celaena stumbled up the blood-soaked steps and into bed, briefly stopping to frown at the hair that now fell just past her collarbones thanks to the razor-sharp nails of the Valg princes, and collapsed into a deep sleep. By the time she awoke, the gore was cleaned away, the soldiers were buried, and Rowan had hidden the four Wyrdstone collars somewhere in the woods. He would have flown them out to the sea and dumped them there, but she knew he'd stayed to look after her—and did not trust his friends to do anything but hand them over to Maeve.

Rowan's cadre was leaving when she finally awoke, having lingered to help with repairs and healing, but it was only Gavriel who bothered to acknowledge her. She and Rowan were heading into the woods for a walk (she'd had to bully him into letting her out of bed) when they passed by the golden-haired male lingering by the back gate.

Rowan stiffened. He'd asked her point-blank what had happened when his friends had arrived—if any of them had tried to help. She had tried to avoid it, but he was relentless, and she finally told him that only Gavriel had shown any inclination. She didn't blame his men. They didn't know her, owed her nothing, and Rowan had been inside, in harm's way. She didn't know why it mattered so much to Rowan, and he told her it was none of her business.

But there was Gavriel, waiting for them at the back gate. Since Rowan was stone-faced, she smiled for both of them as they approached.

"I thought you'd be gone by now," Rowan said.

Gavriel's tawny eyes flickered. "The twins and Vaughan left an hour ago, and Lorcan left at dawn. He said to tell you good-bye."

Rowan nodded in a way that made it very clear he knew Lorcan had done no such thing. "What do you want?"

She wasn't quite sure they had the same definition of *friend* that she did. But Gavriel looked at her from head to toe and back up again, then at Rowan, and said, "Be careful when you face Maeve. We'll have given our reports by then."

Rowan's stormy expression didn't improve. "Travel swiftly," he said, and kept walking.

Celaena lingered, studying the Fae warrior, the glimmer of sadness in his golden eyes. Like Rowan, he was enslaved to Maeve—and yet he thought to warn them. With the blood oath, Maeve could order him to divulge every detail, including this moment. And punish him for it. But for his friend . . .

“Thank you,” she said to the golden-haired warrior. He blinked, and Rowan froze. Her arms ached from the inside out, and her cut hand was bandaged and still tender, but she extended it to him. “For the warning. And for hesitating that day.”

Gavriel looked at her hand for a moment before shaking it with surprising gentleness. “How old are you?” he asked.

“Nineteen,” she said, and he loosed a breath that could have been sadness or relief or maybe both, and told her that made her magic even more impressive. She debated saying that he would be less impressed once he learned of her nickname for him, but winked at him instead.

Rowan was frowning when she caught up to him, but said nothing. As they walked away, Gavriel murmured, “Good luck, Rowan.”

Rowan brought her to a forest pool she’d never seen before, the clear water fed by a lovely waterfall that seemed to dance in the sunlight. He took a seat on a broad, flat, sun-warmed rock, pulling off his boots and rolling up his pants to dip his feet in the water. She winced at every sore muscle and bone in her body as she sat. Rowan scowled, but she gave him a look that dared him to order her back to bed rest.

When her own feet were in the pool and they had let the music of the forest sink into them, Rowan spoke. “There is no undoing what happened with Narrok. Once the world hears that Aelin Galathynius fought against Adarlan, they will know you are alive. *He* will know you are alive, and where you are, and that you do not plan to cower. He will hunt you for the rest of your life.”

“I accepted that fate from the moment I stepped outside the barrier,” she said quietly. She kicked at the water, the ripples spreading out across the pool. The movement sent shuddering pain through her magic-ravaged body, and she hissed.

Rowan handed her the skein of water he'd brought with him but hadn't touched. She took a sip and found it contained the pain-killing tonic she'd been guzzling since she'd awoken that morning.

Good luck, Rowan, Gavriel had said to his friend. There was a day coming, all too soon, when she would also have to bid him farewell. What would her parting words be? Would she be able to offer him only a blessing for luck? She wished she had something to give him—some kind of protection against the queen who held his leash. The Eye of Elena was with Chaol. The Amulet of Orynth—she would have offered him that, if she hadn't lost it. Heirloom or no, she would rest easier if she knew it was protecting him.

The amulet, decorated with the sacred stag on one side . . . and Wyrdmarks on the other.

Celaena stopped breathing. Stopped seeing the prince beside her, hearing the forest humming around her. Terrasen had been the greatest court in the world. They had never been invaded, had never been conquered, but they had prospered and become so powerful that every kingdom knew to provoke them was folly. A line of uncorrupted rulers, who had amassed all the knowledge of Erilea in their great library. They had been a beacon that drew the brightest and boldest to them.

She knew where it was—the third and final Wyrdkey.

It had been around her neck the night she fell into the river.

And around the neck of every one of her ancestors, going back to Brannon himself, when he stopped at the Sun Goddess's temple to take a medallion from Mala's High Priestess—and then destroyed the entire site to prevent anyone from tracing his steps.

The medallion of cerulean blue, with the gold sun-stag crowned with immortal flame—the stag of Mala Fire-Bringer. Upon leaving Wendlyn's shores, Brannon had stolen those same stags away to Terrasen and installed them in Oakwald. Brannon had placed the third sliver of Wyrdkey inside the amulet and never told a soul what he had done with it.

The Wyrdkeys weren't inherently bad or good. What they were depended on how their bearers used them. Around the necks of the kings and queens of Terrasen, one of them had been unknowingly used for good, and had protected its bearers for millennia.

It had protected her, that night she fell into the river. For it had been Wyrdmarks she'd seen glowing in the frozen depths, as if she had summoned them with her watery cries for help. But she had lost the Amulet of Orynth. It had fallen into that river and—no.

No. It couldn't have, because she wouldn't have made it to the riverbank, let alone survived the hours she lay here. The cold would have claimed her. Which meant she'd had it when . . . when . . . Arobynn Hamel had taken it from her and kept it all these years, a prize whose power he had never guessed the depth of.

She had to get it back. She had to get it away from him and make sure that no one knew what lay inside. And if she had it . . . She didn't let herself think that far.

She had to hurry to Maeve, retrieve the information she needed, and go home. Not to Terrasen, but to Rifthold. She had to face the man who had made her into a weapon, who had destroyed another part of her life, and who could prove to be her greatest threat.

Rowan said, "What is it?"

"The third Wyrdkey." She swore. She could tell no one, because if anyone knew . . . they would head straight to Rifthold. Straight to the Assassins' Keep.

"Aelin." Was it fear, pain, or both in his eyes? "Tell me what you learned."

"Not while you are bound to her."

"I am bound to her *forever*."

"I know." He was Maeve's slave—worse than a slave. He had to obey every command, no matter how wretched.

He leaned over his knees, dipping a large hand in the water. "You're right. I don't want you to tell me. Any of it."

"I hate that," she breathed. "I hate her."

He looked away, toward Goldryn, discarded behind them on the rock. She'd told him its history this morning as she scarfed down enough food for three full-grown Fae warriors. He hadn't seemed particularly impressed, and when she showed him the ring she'd found in the scabbard, he had nothing to say other than "I hope you find a good use for it." Indeed.

But the silence that was building between them was unacceptable. She cleared her throat. Perhaps she couldn't tell him the truth about the third Wyrdkey, but she could offer him another.

The truth. The truth of her, undiluted and complete. And after all that they had been through, all that she still wanted to do . . .

So she steeled herself. "I have never told anyone this story. No one in the world knows it. But it's mine," she said, blinking past the burning in her eyes, "and it's time for me to tell it."

Rowan leaned back on the rock, bracing his palms behind him.

"Once upon a time," she said to him, to the world, to herself, "in a land long since burned to ash, there lived a young princess who loved her kingdom . . . very much."

And then she told him of the princess whose heart had burned with wildfire, of the mighty kingdom in the north, of its downfall and of the sacrifice of Lady Marion. It was a long story, and sometimes she grew quiet and cried—and during those times he leaned over to wipe away her tears.

When she finished, Rowan merely passed her more of the tonic. She smiled at him, and he looked at her for a while before he smiled back, a different smile than all the others he'd given her before.

They were quiet for some time, and she didn't know why she did it, but she held out a hand in front of her, palm facing the pool beneath.

And slowly, wobbling, a droplet of water the size of a marble rose from the surface to her cupped palm.

"No wonder your sense of self-preservation is so pathetic, if that's all the water you can conjure." But Rowan flicked her chin, and she knew he understood what it meant, to have summoned even a droplet to her hand. To feel her mother smiling at her from realms away.

She grinned at Rowan through her tears, and sent the droplet splashing onto his face.

Rowan tossed her into the pool. A moment later, laughing, he jumped in himself.

After a week of regaining her strength, she and the other injured demi-Fae had recovered enough to attend a celebration thrown by Emrys and Luca. Before she and Rowan headed downstairs to join the festivities, Celaena peered in the mirror—and stopped dead.

The somewhat shorter hair was the least of the changes.

She was now flushed with color, her eyes bright and clear, and though she'd regained the weight she'd lost that winter, her face was leaner. A woman—a woman was smiling back at her, beautiful for every scar and imperfection and mark of survival, beautiful for the fact that the smile was real, and she felt it kindle the long-slumbering joy in her heart.

She danced that night. The morning after, she knew it was time.

When she and Rowan had finished saying their good-byes to the others, she paused at the edge of the trees to look at the crumbling stone fortress. Emrys and Luca were waiting for them at the tree line, faces pale in the morning light. The old male had already stuffed their bags full of food and supplies, but he still pressed a hot loaf into Celaena's hands as they looked at each other.

She said, "It might take a while, but if—*when* I reclaim my kingdom, the demi-Fae will always have a home there. And you two—and Malakai—will have a place in my household, should you wish it. As my friends."

Emrys's eyes were gleaming as he nodded, gripping Luca's hand. The young man, who had opted to keep a long, wicked scratch bestowed in battle down his face, merely stared at her, wide-eyed. A part of her heart ached at the shadows that now lay in his face. Bas's betrayal would haunt him, she knew. But Celaena smiled at him, ruffled his hair, and made to turn away.

"Your mother would be proud," Emrys said.

Celaena put a hand on her heart and bowed in thanks.

Rowan cleared his throat, and Celaena gave them one last parting smile before she followed the prince into the trees—to Doranelle, and to Maeve, at last.

58

"Just be ready to leave for Suria in two days," Aedion ordered Ren as the three of them gathered at midnight in the apartment where Ren and Murtaugh had stayed, still unaware of who it belonged to. "Take the southern gate—it'll be the least monitored at that hour."

It had been weeks since they'd last met, and three days since a vague letter had arrived for Murtaugh from Sol of Suria, a friendly invitation to a long-lost friend to visit him. The wording was simple enough that they all knew the young lord was feeling them out, hinting at interest in the "opportunity" Murtagh had mentioned in an earlier letter. Since then, Aedion had combed every path northward, calculating the movements and locations of every legion and garrison along the way. Two more days; then perhaps this court could begin to rebuild itself.

"Why does it feel like we're fleeing, then?" Ren paused his usual pacing. The young Lord of Allsbrook had healed up just fine, though he'd now converted some of the great room into his own personal training space to rebuild his strength. Aedion wondered just how thrilled their queen would be to learn about *that*.

"You *are* fleeing," Aedion drawled, biting into one of the apples he'd picked up at the market for Ren and the old man. "The longer you stay here," he went on, "the bigger the risk of being discovered and of all our plans falling apart. You're too recognizable now, and you're of better use to me in Terrasen. There's no negotiating, so don't bother trying."

"And what about you?" Ren asked the captain, who was seated in his usual chair.

Chaol frowned and said quietly, "I'm going to Anielle in a few days." To fulfill the bargain he'd made when he sold his freedom to get Aelin to Wendlyn. If Aedion let himself think too much about it, he knew he might feel bad—might try to convince the captain to stay, even. It wasn't that Aedion liked the captain, or even respected him. In fact, he wished Chaol had never caught him in that stairwell, mourning the slaughter of his people in the labor camps. But here they were, and there was no going back.

Ren paused his pacing to stare down the captain. "As our spy?"

"You'll need someone on the inside, regardless of whether I'm in Rifthold or Anielle."

"I have people on the inside," Ren said.

Aedion waved a hand. "I don't care about your people on the inside, Ren. Just be ready to go, and stop being a pain in my ass with your endless questions." He would chain Ren to a horse if he had to.

Aedion was about to turn to go when feet thundered up the stairs. They all had their swords drawn as the door flew open and Murtaugh appeared, panting and grasping the doorframe. The old man's eyes were wild, his mouth opening and closing. Behind him, the stairwell revealed no sign of a threat, no pursuit. But Aedion kept his sword out and angled himself into a better position.

Ren rushed to Murtaugh, slipping an arm under his shoulders, but the old man planted his heels in the rug. "She's alive," he said, to Ren, to Aedion, to himself. "She's—she's truly alive."

Aedion's heart stopped. Stopped, then started, then stopped again. Slowly, he sheathed his sword, calming his racing mind before he said, "Out with it, old man."

Murtaugh blinked and let out a choked laugh. "She's in Wendlyn, and she's alive."

The captain stalked across the floor. Aedion might have joined him had his legs not stopped working. For Murtaugh to have heard about her . . . The captain said, "Tell me everything."

Murtaugh shook his head. "The city's swarming with the news. People are in the streets."

"Get to the point," Aedion snapped.

"General Narrok's legion did indeed go to Wendlyn," Murtaugh said. "And no one knows how or why, but Aelin . . . Aelin was there, in the Cambrian Mountains, and was part of a host that met them in battle. They're saying she's been hiding in Doranelle all this time."

Alive, Aedion had to tell himself—alive, and not dead after the battle, even if Murtaugh's information about her whereabouts was wrong.

Murtaugh was smiling. "They slaughtered Narrok and his men, and she saved a great number of people—with magic. Fire, they say—power the likes of which the world has not seen since Brannon himself."

Aedion's chest tightened to the point of hurting. The captain was just staring at the old man.

It was a message to the world. Aelin was a warrior, able to fight with blade or magic. And she was done with hiding.

"I'm riding north today. It cannot wait as we had planned," Murtaugh said, turning toward the door. "Before the king tries to keep the news from spreading, I need to let Terrasen know." They trailed him down the stairs and into the warehouse below. Even from inside,

Aedion's Fae hearing picked up the rising commotion in the streets. The moment he entered the palace, he would have to consider his every step, every breath. Too many eyes would be on him now.

Aelin. His Queen. Aedion slowly smiled. The king would never suspect, not in a thousand years, who he'd actually sent to Wendlyn—that his own Champion had destroyed Narrok. Few had ever known about the Galathyniuses' deeply rooted distrust of Maeve—so Doranelle *would* be a believable place to hide and raise a young queen all these years.

"Once I get out of the city," Murtaugh said, going to the horse he'd tied inside the warehouse, "I'll send riders to every contact, to Fenharrow and Melisande. Ren, you stay here. I'll take care of Suria."

Aedion gripped the man's shoulder. "Get word to my Bane—tell them to lie low until I return, but keep those supply lines with the rebels open at any cost." He didn't let go until Murtaugh gave him a nod.

"Grandfather," Ren said, helping the man into the saddle. "Let me go instead."

"You stay here," Aedion ordered, and Ren bristled.

Murtaugh murmured his agreement. "Gather what information you can, and then you'll come to me when I'm ready."

Aedion didn't give Ren time to refuse as he hauled open the warehouse door for Murtaugh. Brisk night air poured in, bringing with it the ruckus from the city. Aelin—Aelin had done this, caused this clamor of sound. The stallion pawed and huffed, and Murtaugh might have galloped off had the captain not surged to grab his reins.

"Eyllwe," Chaol breathed. "Send word to Eyllwe. Tell them to hold on—tell them to prepare." Perhaps it was the light, perhaps it was the cold, but Aedion could have sworn there were tears in the captain's eyes as he said, "Tell them it's time to fight back."

Murtaugh Allsbrook and his riders spread the news like wildfire. Down every road, over every river, to the north and south and west, through snow and rain and mist, their hooves churning up the dust of each kingdom.

And for every town they told, every tavern and secret meeting, more riders went out.

More and more, until there was not a road they had not covered, until there was not one soul who did not know that Aelin Galathynius was alive—and willing to stand against Adarlan.

Across the White Fangs and the Ruhnns, all the way to the Western Wastes and the red-haired queen who ruled from a crumbling castle. To the Deserted Peninsula and the oasis-fortress of the Silent Assassins. Hooves, hooves, hooves, echoing through the continent, sparking against cobblestones, all the way to Banjali and the riverfront palace of the King and Queen of Eyllwe, still in their midnight mourning clothes.

Hold on, the riders told the world.

Hold on.

Dorian's father was in a rage the likes of which he'd not seen before. Two ministers had been executed this morning, for no worse crime than attempting to calm the king.

A day after the news arrived of what Aelin had done in Wendlyn, his father was still livid, still demanding answers.

Dorian might have found it funny—so typically Celaena to make such a flamboyant return—had he not been utterly petrified. She had drawn a line in the sand. Worse than that, she'd defeated one of the king's deadliest generals.

No one had done that and lived. Ever.

Somewhere in Wendlyn, his friend was changing the world. She was fulfilling the promise she'd made him. She had not forgotten him, or any of them still here.

And perhaps when they figured out a way to destroy that tower and free magic from his father's yoke, she would know her friends had not forgotten her, either. That *he* had not forgotten her.

So Dorian let his father rage. He sat in on those meetings and shut down his revulsion and horror when his father sent a third minister to the butchering block. For Sorscha, for the promise of keeping her safe, of someday, perhaps, not having to hide what and who he was, he kept on his well-worn mask, offered banal suggestions about what to do regarding Aelin, and pretended. One last time.

When Celaena got back, when she returned as she'd sworn she would . . .

Then they would set about changing the world together.

59

It took a week for Celaena and Rowan to reach Doranelle. They traveled over the rough, miserable mountains where Maeve's wild wolves monitored them day and night, then down into the lush valley through forests and fields, the air heavy with spices and magic.

The temperature grew warmer the farther south they traveled, but breezes kept it from being too unpleasant. After a while, they began spotting pretty stone villages in the distance, but Rowan kept them away, hidden, until they crested a rocky hill and Doranelle spread before them.

It took her breath away. Even Orynth could not compare to this.

They had called it the City of Rivers for a reason. The pale-stoned city was built on a massive island smack in the center of several of them, the waters raging as the tributaries from the surrounding hills and mountains blended. On the island's north end, the rivers toppled over the mouth of a mighty waterfall, its basin so huge that the mist floated into the clear day, setting the domed buildings, pearlescent spires, and blue rooftops shining. There were no boats moored to the city edges, though there were two elegant stone bridges spanning the river—heavily guarded. Fae moved across the bridges, and carts loaded with everything from vegetables to hay to wine. Somewhere, there had to be fields and farms and towns to supply them. Though she'd bet Maeve had a stronghold of goods stocked up.

"I assume you normally fly right in and don't deign to use the bridges," she said to Rowan, who was frowning at the city, not looking very much like a warrior about to return home. He nodded distantly. He'd fallen silent in the past day—not rude, but quiet and vague, as if he were rebuilding the wall between them. This morning, she'd awoken in their hilltop camp to find him staring at the sunrise, looking for all the world as if he'd been having a conversation with it. She hadn't had the nerve to ask if he'd been praying to Mala Fire-Bringer, or what he would even ask of the Sun Goddess. But there had been a strangely familiar warmth wrapped around the camp, and she could have sworn that she felt her magic leap in joyous response. She didn't let herself think about it.

Because for the past day, she, too, had been lost in herself, busy gathering her strength and clarity. She hadn't been able to talk much, and even now, focusing on the present required an immense effort. "Well," she said, taking an exaggerated breath and patting Goldryn's hilt, "let's go see our beloved aunt. I'd hate to keep her waiting."

It took them until nightfall to reach the bridge, and Celaena was glad: there were fewer Fae to witness their arrival, even though the winding, elegant streets were now full of musicians and dancing and vendors selling hot food and drinks. There had been plenty of that in Adarlan, but here there was no empire weighing on them, no darkness or cold or despair. Maeve had not sent aid ten years ago—and while the Fae danced and drank mulled cider, Celaena's people had been butchered and burned. She knew it wasn't their fault, but as she headed across the city, toward the northern edge by the waterfall, she couldn't bring herself to smile at the merriment.

She reminded herself that *she* had danced and drunk and done whatever she pleased while her own people had suffered for ten years, too. She was in no position to resent the Fae, or anyone except the queen who ruled over this city.

None of the guards stopped them, though she did note shadows trailing them from the rooftops and alleys, a few birds of prey circling above. Rowan didn't acknowledge them, though she caught his teeth glinting in the golden lamplight. Apparently, the escort wasn't making the prince too happy, either. How many of them did he know personally? How many had he fought beside, or ventured with to unmapped lands?

They saw no sign of his friends, and he made no comment about whether or not he expected to see them. Even though his gaze was straight ahead, she knew he was aware of every sentry watching them, every breath issued nearby.

She didn't have the space left in her for doubt or fear. As they walked, she played with the ring tucked into her pocket, turning it over and over as she reminded herself of her plan and of what she needed to accomplish before she left this city. She was as much a queen as Maeve. She was the sovereign of a strong people and a mighty kingdom.

She was the heir of ash and fire, and she would bow to no one.

They were escorted through a shining palace of pale stone and sky-blue gossamer curtains, the floors a mosaic of delicate tiles depicting various scenes, from dancing maidens to pastorals to the night sky. Throughout the building, the river itself ran in tiny streams, sometimes gathering in pools freckled with night-blooming lilies. Jasmine wove around the massive columns, and lights of colored glass hung from the arched ceilings. Enough of the palace was open to the elements to suggest that the weather here was always this mild. Music played from distant rooms, but it was faint and placid compared to the riot of sound and color in the city outside the mammoth marble palace walls.

Sentries were everywhere. They lurked just out of sight, but in her Fae body she could smell them, the steel and the crisp scent of whatever soap they must use in the barracks. Not too different from the glass castle. But Maeve's stronghold had been built from stone—so much stone, everywhere, all of it pale and carved and polished and gleaming. She knew Rowan had private quarters in this palace, and that the Whitethorn family had various residences in Doranelle, but they saw nothing of his kin. He'd told her on their journey that there were several other princes in his family, with his father's brother ruling over them. Fortunately for Rowan, his uncle had three sons, keeping him free of responsibility, though they certainly tried to use Rowan's position with Maeve to their advantage. As scheming and sycophantic as any royal family in Adarlan, she supposed.

After an eternity of walking in silence, Rowan led her onto a wide veranda overhanging the river. He was tense enough to suggest he was scenting and hearing things she couldn't, but he offered no warning. The waterfall beyond the palace roared, though not loud enough to drown out conversation.

Across the veranda sat Maeve on her throne of stone.

Sprawled on either side of the throne were the twin wolves, one black and one white, monitoring their approach with cunning golden eyes. There was no one else—no smell of Rowan's other friends lurking nearby as they crossed the tiled floor. She wished Rowan had let her freshen up in his suite, but . . . she supposed that wasn't what this meeting was about, anyway.

Rowan kept pace with her as she stalked to the small dais before the carved railing, and when they stopped, he dropped to his knees and bowed his head. "Majesty," he murmured.

Her aunt did not even glance at Rowan or bid him to rise. She left her nephew kneeling as she turned her violet, starry eyes to Celaena and gave her that spider's smile.

"It would seem that you have accomplished your task, Aelin Galathynius."

Another test—using her name to elicit a reaction.

She smiled right back at Maeve. "Indeed."

Rowan kept his head down, eyes on the floor. Maeve could make him kneel there for a hundred years if she wished. The wolves beside the throne didn't move an inch.

Maeve deigned a glance at Rowan and then gave Celaena that little smile again. "I will admit that I am surprised that you managed to gain his approval so swiftly. So," Maeve said, lounging in her throne, "show me, then. A demonstration of what you have learned these months."

Celaena clenched the ring in her pocket, not lowering her chin one millimeter. "I would prefer to first retrieve the knowledge you're keeping to yourself."

A feminine click of the tongue. "You don't trust my word?"

"You can't believe I'd give you everything you want with no proof you can deliver your side of the bargain."

Rowan's shoulders tensed, but his head remained down.

Maeve's eyes narrowed slightly. "The Wyrdkeys."

"How they can be destroyed, where they are, and what else you know of them."

"They cannot be destroyed. They can only be put back in the gate."

Celaena's stomach twisted. She'd known that already, but hearing the confirmation was hard, somehow. "How can they be put back in the gate?"

"Don't you think they would already have been restored to their home if anyone knew?"

"You said you knew about them."

An adder's smile. "I *do* know about them. I know they can be used to create, to destroy, to open portals. But I do not know how to put them back. I never learned how, and then they were taken by Brannon across the sea and I never saw them again."

"What did they look like? What did they *feel* like?"

Maeve cupped her palm and looked at it, as if she could see the keys lying there. "Black and glittering, no more than slivers of stone. But they were not stone—they were like nothing on this earth, in any realm. It was like holding the living flesh of a god, like containing the breath of every being in every realm all at once. It was madness and joy and terror and despair and eternity."

The thought of Maeve possessing all three of the keys, even for brief moment, was horrifying enough that Celaena didn't let herself fully contemplate it. She just said, "And what else can you tell me about them?"

"That's all I can recall, I'm afraid." Maeve settled back in her throne.

No—no, there had to be *some* way. She couldn't have spent all these months in a fool's bargain, couldn't have been tricked *that* badly. But if Maeve did not know, then there were other bits of information to extract; she would not walk out of here empty-handed.

"The Valg princes—what can you tell me of them?"

For a few heartbeats, Maeve remained silent, as if contemplating the merits of answering more than she'd originally promised. Celaena wasn't entirely sure that she wanted to know why Maeve decided in her favor as the queen said, "Ah—yes. My men informed me of their presence." Maeve paused again, no doubt dredging up the information from some ancient corner of her memory. "There are many different races of Valg—creatures that even your darkest nightmares would flee from.

They are ruled by the princes, who themselves are made of shadow and despair and hatred and have no bodies to occupy save those that they infiltrate. There aren't many princes—but I once witnessed an entire legion of Fae warriors devoured by six of them within hours."

A chill went down her spine, and even the wolves' hackles rose. "But I killed them with my fire and light—"

"How do you think Brannon won himself such glory and a kingdom? He was a discarded son of nobody, unclaimed by either parent. But Mala loved him fiercely, so his flames were sometimes all that held the Valg princes at bay until we could summon a force to push them back."

She opened to her mouth to ask the next question, but paused. Maeve wasn't the sort to toss out random bits of information. So Celaena slowly asked, "Brannon wasn't royal-born?"

Maeve cocked her head. "Didn't anyone ever tell you what the mark on your brow means?"

"I was told it was a sacred mark."

Maeve's eyes danced with amusement. "Sacred only because of the bearer who established your kingdom. But before that, it was nothing. Brannon was born with the bastard's mark—the mark every unclaimed, unwanted child possessed, marking them as nameless, nobody. Each of Brannon's heirs, despite their noble lineage, has since been graced with it—the nameless mark."

And it had burned that day she'd dueled with Cain. Burned in front of the King of Adarlan. A shudder went down her spine. "Why did it glow when I dueled Cain, and when I faced the Valg princes?" She knew Maeve was well informed about the shadow-creature that had lived inside Cain. Perhaps not a Valg prince, but something small enough to be contained by the Wyrdstone ring he'd worn instead of a collar. It had recognized Elena—and it had said to both of them, *You were brought here—all of you were. All the players in the unfinished game.*

"Perhaps your blood merely recognized the presence of the Valg and was trying to tell you something. Perhaps it meant nothing."

She didn't think so. Especially when the reek of the Valg had been in her parents' bedroom the morning after they'd been murdered. Either the assassin had been possessed, or he'd known how to use their power to keep her parents unconscious while he slaughtered them. All bits of information to be pieced together later, when she was away from Maeve. If Maeve let her walk out of here.

"Are fire and light the only way to kill the Valg princes?"

"They are hard to kill, but not invincible," Maeve admitted. "With the way the Adarlanian king compels them, cutting off their heads to sever the collar might do the trick. If you are to return to Adarlan, that will be the only way, I suspect."

Because in Adarlan, magic was still locked up by the king. If she faced one of the Valg princes again, she'd have to kill it by blade and wits. "If the king is indeed summoning the Valg to his armies, what can be done to stop them?"

"The King of Adarlan, it seems, is doing what I never had the nerve to do while the keys were briefly in my possession. Without all three keys, he is limited. He can only open the portal between our worlds for short periods, long enough to let in perhaps one prince to infiltrate a body he has prepared. But with all three keys, he could open the portal at will—he could summon all the Valg armies, to be led by the princes in their mortal bodies, and . . ." Maeve looked more intrigued than horrified. "And with all three keys, he might not need to rely on magically gifted hosts for the Valg. There are countless lesser spirits amongst the Valg, hungry for entrance to this world."

"He'd have to make countless collars for them, then."

"He would not need to, not with all three keys. His control would be absolute. And he would not need living hosts—only bodies."

Celaena's heart stumbled a beat, and Rowan tensed from his spot on the ground. "He could have an army of the dead, inhabited by the Valg."

"An army that does not need to eat or sleep or breathe—an army that will sweep like a plague across your continent, and others. Maybe other worlds, too."

But he would need all three keys for it. Her chest tightened, and though they were in the open air, the palace, the river, the stars seemed to push in on her. There would be no army that she could raise to stop them, and without magic . . . they were doomed. She was doomed. She was—

A calming warmth wrapped around her, as if someone had pulled her into an embrace. Feminine, joyous, infinitely powerful. *This doom has not yet come to pass*, it seemed to whisper in her ear. *There is still time. Do not succumb to fear yet.*

Maeve was watching her with a feline interest, and Celaena wondered what it was that the dark queen beheld—if she, too, could sense that ancient, nurturing presence. But Celaena was warm again, the panic gone, and though the feeling of being held disappeared, she still could have sworn the presence lingered nearby. There *was* time—the king still did not have the third key.

Brannon—he had possessed all three, yet had chosen to hide them, rather than put them back. And somehow, suddenly, that became the greatest question of all: why?

"As for the locations of the three keys," Maeve said, "I do not know where they are. They were brought across the sea, and I have not heard of them again until these past ten years. It would seem that the king has at least one, probably two. The third, however . . ." She looked her up and down, but Celaena refused to flinch. "You have some inkling of its whereabouts, don't you?"

She opened her mouth, but Maeve's fingers clenched the arm of her throne—just enough to make Celaena glance at the stone. So much stone here—in this palace and in the city. And that word Maeve had used earlier, *taken* . . .

"Don't you?" Maeve pressed.

Stone—and not a sign of wood, save for plants and furniture . . .

"No, I don't," said Celaena.

Maeve cocked her head. "Rowan, rise and tell me the truth."

His hands clenched, but he stood, his eyes on his queen as he swallowed. Twice. "She found a riddle, and she knows the King of Adarlan has at least the first key, but doesn't know where he keeps it. She also learned what Brannon did with the third—and where it is. She refused to tell me." There was a glimmer of horror in his eyes, and his fists were trembling, as if some invisible force had compelled him to say it. The wolves only watched.

Maeve tutted. "Keeping secrets, Aelin? From your aunt?"

"Not for all the world would I tell you where the third key is."

"Oh, I know," Maeve purred. She snapped her fingers, and the wolves rose to their feet, shifting in flashes of light into the most beautiful men she'd ever beheld. Warriors from the size of them, from the lethal grace with which they moved; one light and one dark, but stunning—perfect.

Celaena went for Goldryn, but the twins went for Rowan, who did nothing, didn't even struggle as they gripped his arms, forcing him again to his knees. Two others emerged from the shadows behind them. Gavriel, his tawny eyes carefully empty, and Lorcan, face stone-cold. And in their hands . . .

At the sight of the iron-tipped whip each bore, Celaena forgot to breathe. Lorcan didn't hesitate as he ripped Rowan's jacket and tunic and shirt from him.

"Until she answers me," Maeve said, as if she had just ordered a cup of tea.

Lorcan unfurled the whip, the iron tip clinking against the stones, and drew back his arm. There was nothing merciful on his rugged face, no glimmer of feeling for the friend on his knees.

"Please," Celaena whispered. There was a crack, and the world fragmented as Rowan bowed when the whip sliced into his back. He gritted his teeth, hissing, but did not cry out.

"*Please*," Celaena said. Gavriel sent his whip flying so fast Rowan had only a breath to recover. There was no remorse on Gavriel's lovely face, no sign of the male she'd thanked weeks ago.

Across the veranda, Maeve said, "How long this lasts depends entirely on you, niece."

Celaena did not dare drag her gaze away from Rowan, who took the whipping as if he had done this before—as if he knew how to pace himself and how much pain to expect. His friends' eyes were dead, as if they, too, had given and received this manner of punishment.

Maeve *had* harmed Rowan before. How many of his scars had she given him? "Stop it," Celaena growled.

"Not for all the world, Aelin? But what about for Prince Rowan?"

Another strike, and blood was on the stones. And the sound—that sound of the whip . . . the sound that echoed in her nightmares, the sound that made her blood run cold . . .

"Tell me where the third Wyrdkey is, Aelin."

Crack. Rowan jerked against the twins' iron grip. Was this why he had been praying to Mala that morning? Because he knew what to expect from Maeve?

She opened her mouth, but Rowan lifted his head, teeth bared, his face savage with pain and rage. He knew she could read the word in his eyes, but he still said, "*Don't*."

It was that word of defiance that broke the hold she'd kept on herself for the past day, the damper she'd put on her power as she secretly spiraled down to the core of her magic, pulling up as much as she could gather.

The heat spread from her, warming the stones so swiftly that Rowan's blood turned to red steam. His companions swore and near-invisible shields rippled around them and their sovereign.

She knew the gold in her eyes had shifted to flame, because when she looked to Maeve, the queen's face had gone bone-white.

And then Celaena set the world on fire.

60

Maeve was not burning, and neither were Rowan or his friends, whose shields Celaena tore through with half a thought. But the river was steaming around them, and shouting arose from the palace, from the city, as a flame that did not burn or hurt enveloped everything. The entire island was wreathed in wildfire.

Maeve was standing now, stalking off the dais. Celaena let a little more heat seep through her hold on the flame, warming Maeve's skin as she moved to meet her aunt. Wide-eyed, Rowan hung from his friends' arms, his blood fizzing on the stones.

"You wanted a demonstration," Celaena said quietly. Sweat trickled down her back, but she gripped the magic with everything she had. "One thought from me, and your city will burn."

"It is stone," Maeve snapped.

Celaena smiled. "Your people aren't."

Maeve's nostrils flared delicately. "Would you murder innocents, Aelin? Perhaps. You did it for years, didn't you?"

Celaena's smile didn't falter. "Try me. Just try to push me, *Aunt*, and see what comes of it. This was what you wanted, wasn't it? Not for me to master my magic, but for you to learn just how powerful I am. Not how much of your sister's blood flows in my veins—no, you've known from the start that I have very little of Mab's power. You wanted to know how much I got from Brannon."

The flames rose higher, and the shouts—of fright, not pain—rose with them. The flames would not hurt anyone unless she willed it. She could sense other magics fighting against her own, tearing holes into her power, but the conflagration surrounding the veranda burned strong.

"You never gave the keys to Brannon. And you didn't journey with Brannon and Athril to retrieve the keys from the Valg," Celaena went on, a crown of fire wreathing her head. "You went to steal them for yourself. You wanted to keep them. Once Brannon and Athril realized that, they fought you. And Athril . . ." Celaena drew Goldryn, its hilt glowing bloodred. "Your beloved Athril, dearest friend of Brannon . . . when Athril fought you, you killed him. You, not the Valg. And in your grief and shame, you were weakened enough that Brannon took the keys from you. It wasn't some enemy force who sacked the Sun Goddess's temple. It was Brannon. He burned any last trace of himself, any clue of where he was going so *you* would not find him. He left only Athril's sword to honor his friend—in the cave where Athril had first carved out the eye of that poor lake creature—and never told you. After Brannon left these shores, you did not dare follow him, not when he had the keys, not when his magic—*my* magic—was so strong."

It was why Brannon had hidden the Wyrdkey in his household's heirloom—to give them that extra ounce of power. Not against ordinary enemies, but in case Maeve ever came for them. Perhaps he had not put the keys back in the gate because he wanted to be able to call upon their power should Maeve ever decide to install herself as mistress of all lands.

"That was why you abandoned your land in the foothills and left it to rot. That was why you built a city of stone surrounded by water: so Brannon's heirs could not return and roast you alive. That was why you wanted to see me, why you bargained with my mother. You wanted to know what manner of threat I would pose. What would happen when Brannon's blood mixed with Mab's line." Celaena opened her arms wide, Goldryn burning bright in one hand. "Behold my power, Maeve. Behold what I grapple with in the deep dark, what prowls under my skin."

Celaena exhaled a breath and extinguished each and every flame in the city.

The power wasn't in might or skill. It was in the control—the power lay in controlling *herself*. She'd known all along how vast and deadly her fire was, and a few months ago, she would have killed and sacrificed and slaughtered anyone and anything to fulfill her vow. But that hadn't been strength—it had been the rage and grief of a broken, crumbling person. She understood now what her mother had meant when she had patted her heart that night she'd given her the amulet.

As every light went out in Doranelle, plunging the world into darkness, Celaena stalked over to Rowan. One look and a flash of her teeth had the twins releasing him. Their bloodied whips still in hand, Gavriel and Lorcan made no move toward her as Rowan sagged against her, murmuring her name.

Lights kindled. Maeve remained where she stood, dress soot-stained, face shining with sweat. "Rowan, come here." Rowan stiffened, grunting with pain, but staggered to the dais, blood trickling from the hideous wounds on his back. Bile stung Celaena's throat, but she kept her eyes on the queen. Maeve barely gave Celaena a glance as she seethed, "Give me that sword and *get out*." She extended a hand toward Goldryn.

Celaena shook her head. "I don't think so. Brannon left it in that cave for anyone *but* you to find. And so it is mine, through blood and fire and darkness." She sheathed Goldryn at her side. "Not very pleasant when someone doesn't give you what you want, is it?"

Rowan was just standing there, his face a mask of calm despite his wounds, but his eyes—was it sorrow there? His friends were silently watching, ready to attack should Maeve give the word. Let them try.

Maeve's lips thinned. "You will pay for this."

But Celaena stalked to Maeve again, took her hand, and said, "Oh, I don't think I will." She threw her mind open to the queen.

Well, part of her mind—the vision Narrok had given her as she burned him. He had known. Somehow he had seen the potential, as if he'd figured it out while the Valg princes sorted through her memories. It was not a future etched in stone, but she did not let her aunt know that. She yielded the memory as if it were truth, as if it were a plan.

The deafening crowd echoed through the pale stone corridors of the royal castle of Orynth. They were chanting her name, almost wailing it. Aelin. *A two-beat pulse that sounded through each step she made up the darkened stairwell. Goldryn was heavy at her back, its ruby smoldering in the light of the sun trickling from the landing above. Her tunic was beautiful yet simple, though her steel gauntlets—armed with hidden blades—were as ornate as they were deadly.*

*She reached the landing and stalked down it, past the towering, muscled warriors who lurked in the shadows just beyond the open archway. Not just warriors—*her *warriors. Her court. Aedion was there, and a few others whose faces were obscured by shadow, but their teeth gleamed faintly as they gave her feral grins. A court to change the world.*

The chanting increased, and the amulet bounced between her breasts with each step. She kept her eyes ahead, a half smile on her face as she emerged at last onto the balcony and the cries grew frantic, as overpowering as the frenzied crowd outside the palace, in the streets, thousands gathered and chanting her name. In the courtyard, young priestesses of Mala danced to each pulse of her name, worshipping, fanatic.

With this power—with the keys she'd attained—what she had created for them, the armies she had made to drive out their enemies, the crops she had grown, the shadows she had chased away . . . these things were nothing short of a miracle. She was more than human, more than queen.

Aelin.

Beloved. Immortal. Blessed.

Aelin.

Aelin of the Wildfire. Aelin Fireheart. Aelin Light-Bringer.

Aelin.

She raised her arms, tipping back her head to the sunlight, and their cries made the entirety of the White Palace tremble. On her brow, a mark—the sacred mark of Brannon's line—glowed blue. She smiled at the crowd, at her people, at her world, so ripe for the taking.

Celaena pulled back from Maeve. The queen's face was pale.

Maeve had bought the lie. She did not see that the vision had been given to Celaena not to taunt her but as a warning—of what she might become if she did indeed find the keys and keep them. A gift from the man Narrok had once been.

"I suggest," Celaena said to the Fae Queen, "that you think very, very carefully before threatening me or my own, or hurting Rowan again."

"Rowan belongs to me," Maeve hissed. "I can do what I wish with him."

Celaena looked at the prince, who was standing so stalwart, his eyes dull with pain. Not from the wounds on his back, but from the parting that had been creeping up on them with each step that took them closer to Doranelle.

Slowly, carefully, Celaena pulled the ring from her pocket.

It was not Chaol's ring that she had been clutching these past few days.

It was the simple golden ring that had been left in Goldryn's scabbard. She had kept it safe all these weeks, asking Emrys to tell story after story about Maeve as she carefully pieced together the truth about her aunt, just for this very moment, for this very task.

Maeve went as still as death while Celaena lifted the ring between two fingers.

"I think you've been looking for this for a long time," Celaena said.

"That does not belong to you."

"Doesn't it? I found it, after all. In Goldryn's scabbard, where Brannon left it after grabbing it off Athril's corpse—the family ring Athril would have given you someday. And in the thousands of years since then, you never found it, so . . . I suppose it's mine by chance." Celaena closed her fist around the ring. "But who would have thought you were so sentimental?"

Maeve's lips thinned. "Give it to me."

Celaena barked out a laugh. "I don't have to give you a damn thing." Her smile faded. Beside Maeve's throne, Rowan's face was unreadable as he turned toward the waterfall.

All of it—all of it for him. For Rowan, who had known exactly what sword he was picking up that day in the mountain cave, who had thrown it to her across the ice as a future bargaining chip—the only protection he could offer her against Maeve, if she was smart enough to figure it out.

She had only realized what he'd done—that he'd known all along—when she'd mentioned the ring to him weeks ago and he'd told her he hoped she found some use for it. He didn't yet understand that she had no interest in bargaining for power or safety or alliance.

So Celaena said, "I'll make a trade with you, though." Maeve's brows narrowed. Celaena jerked her chin. "Your beloved's ring—for Rowan's freedom from his blood oath."

Rowan stiffened. His friends whipped their heads to her.

"A blood oath is eternal," Maeve said tightly. Celaena didn't think his friends were breathing.

"I don't care. Free him." Celaena held out the ring again. "Your choice. Free him, or I melt this right here."

Such a gamble; so many weeks of scheming and planning and secretly hoping. Even now, Rowan did not turn.

Maeve's eyes remained on the ring. And Celaena understood why—it was why she'd dared try it. After a long silence, Maeve's dress rustled as she straightened, her face pale and tight. "Very well. I've grown rather bored of his company these past few decades, anyway."

Rowan faced her—slowly, as if he didn't quite believe what he was hearing. It was Celaena's gaze, not Maeve's, that he met, his eyes shining.

"By my blood that flows in you," Maeve said. "Through no dishonor, through no act of treachery, I hereby free you, Rowan Whitethorn, of your blood oath to me."

Rowan just stared and stared at her, and Celaena hardly heard the rest, the words Maeve spoke in the Old Language. But Rowan took out a dagger and spilled his own blood on the stones—whatever that meant. She had never heard of a blood oath being broken before, but had risked it regardless. Perhaps not in all the history of the world had one ever been broken honorably. His friends were wide-eyed and silent.

Maeve said, "You are free of me, Prince Rowan Whitethorn."

That was all Celaena needed to hear before she tossed the ring to Maeve, before Rowan rushed to her, his hands on her cheeks, his brow against her own.

"Aelin," he murmured, and it wasn't a reprimand, or a thank-you, but . . . a prayer. "Aelin," he whispered again, grinning, and kissed her brow before he dropped to both knees before her.

And when he reached for her wrist, she jerked back. "You're free. You're free now."

Behind them, Maeve watched, brows high. But Celaena could not accept this—could not agree to it.

Complete and utter submission, that's what a blood oath was. He would yield everything to her—his life, any property, any free will.

Rowan's face was calm, though—steady, assured. *Trust me.*

I don't want you enslaved to me. I won't be that kind of queen.

You have no court—you are defenseless, landless, and without allies. She might let you walk out of here today, but she could come after you tomorrow. She knows how powerful I am—how powerful we are together. It will make her hesitate.

Please don't do this—I will give you anything else you ask, but not this.

I claim you, Aelin. To whatever end.

She might have continued to silently argue with him, but that strange, feminine warmth that she'd felt at the campsite that morning wrapped around her, as if assuring her it was all right to want this badly enough that it hurt, telling her that she could trust the prince, and more than that—more than anything, she could trust herself. So when Rowan reached for her wrist again, she did not fight him.

"Together, Fireheart," he said, pushing back the sleeve of her tunic. "We'll find a way together." He looked up from her exposed wrist. "A court that will change the world," he promised.

And then she was nodding—nodding and smiling, too, as he drew the dagger from his boot and offered it to her. "Say it, Aelin."

Not daring to let her hands shake in front of Maeve or Rowan's stunned friends, she took his dagger and held it over her exposed wrist. "Do you promise to serve in my court, Rowan Whitethorn, from now until the day you die?" She did not know the right words or the Old Language, but a blood oath wasn't about pretty phrases.

"I do. Until my last breath, and the world beyond. To whatever end."

She would have paused then, asked him again if he really wanted to do this, but Maeve was still there, a shadow lurking behind them. That was why he had done it now, here—so Celaena could not object, could not try to talk him out of it.

It was such a Rowan thing to do, so pigheaded, that she could only grin as she drew the dagger across her wrist, leaving a trail of blood in its wake. She offered her arm to him.

With surprising gentleness, he took her wrist in his hands and lowered his mouth to her skin.

For a heartbeat, something lightning-bright snapped through her and then settled—a thread binding them, tighter and tighter with each pull Rowan took of her blood. Three mouthfuls—his canines pricking against her skin—and then he lifted his head, his lips shining with her blood, his eyes glittering and alive and full of steel.

There were no words to do justice to what passed between them in that moment.

Maeve saved them from trying to remember how to speak as she hissed, "Now that you have insulted me further, get out. All of you." His friends were gone in an instant, padding off for the shadows, taking those wretched whips with them.

Celaena helped Rowan to his feet, letting him heal the wound on her wrist as his back knitted together. Shoulder to shoulder, they looked at the Fae Queen one last time.

But there was only a white barn owl flapping off into the moonlit night.

They hurried out of Doranelle, not stopping until they found a quiet inn in a small, half-forgotten town miles away. Rowan didn't even dare to swing by his quarters to collect his belongings, and claimed he had nothing worthwhile to take, anyway. His friends did not come after them, did not try to bid them good-bye as they slipped across the bridge and into the night-veiled lands beyond. After hours of running, Celaena tumbled into bed and slept like the dead. But at dawn, she begged Rowan to retrieve his needles and ink from his pack.

She bathed while he readied what he needed, and she scrubbed herself with coarse salt in the tiny inn bathroom until her skin gleamed. Rowan said nothing as she walked back into the bedroom, hardly gave her more than a passing glance as she removed her robe, bare to the waist, and laid on her stomach on the worktable he'd ordered brought in. His needles and ink were already on the table, his sleeves had been rolled up to the elbows, and his hair was tied back, making the elegant, brutal lines of his tattoo all the more visible.

"Deep breath," he said. She obeyed, resting her hands under her chin as she played with the fire, weaving her own flames among the embers. "Have you had enough water and food?"

She nodded. She'd devoured a full breakfast before getting into the bath.

"Let me know when you need to get up," he said. He gave her the honor of not second-guessing her decision or warning her of the oncoming pain. Instead, he brushed a steady hand down her scarred back, an artist assessing his canvas. He ran strong, callused fingers along each scar, testing, and her skin prickled.

Then he began the process of drawing the marks, the guide he would follow in the hours ahead. Over breakfast, he'd already sketched a few designs for her approval. They were so perfect it was as if he'd reached into her soul to find them. It hadn't surprised her at all.

He let her use the bathing room when he'd finished with the outline, and soon she was again facedown on the table, hands under her chin. "Don't move from now on. I'm starting."

She gave a grunt of acknowledgment and kept her gaze on the fire, on the embers, as the heat of his body hovered over hers. She heard his slight intake of breath, and then—

The first prick stung—holy gods, with the salt and iron, it hurt. She clamped her teeth together, mastered it, welcomed it. That was what the salt was for with this manner of tattoo, Rowan had told her. To remind the bearer of the loss. Good—good, was all she could think as the pain spiderwebbed through her back. Good.

And when Rowan made the next mark, she opened her mouth and began her prayers.

They were prayers she should have said ten years ago: an even-keeled torrent of words in the Old Language, telling the gods of her parents' death, her uncle's death, Marion's death—four lives wiped out in those two days. With each sting of Rowan's needle, she beseeched the faceless immortals to take the souls of her loved ones into their paradise and keep them safe. She told them of their worth—told them of the good deeds and loving words and brave acts they'd performed. Never pausing for more than a breath, she chanted the prayers she owed them as daughter and friend and heir.

For the hours Rowan worked, his movements falling into the rhythm of her words, she chanted and sang. He did not speak, his mallet and needles the drum to her chanting, weaving their work together. He did not disgrace her by offering water when her voice turned hoarse, her throat so ravaged she had to whisper. In Terrasen she would sing from sunrise to sunset, on her knees in gravel without food or drink or rest. Here she would sing until the markings were done, the agony in her back her offering to the gods.

When it was done her back was raw and throbbing, and it took her a few attempts to rise from the table. Rowan followed her into the nearby night-dark field, kneeling with her in the grass as she tilted her face up to the moon and sang the final song, the sacred song of her household, the Fae lament she'd owed them for ten years.

Rowan did not utter a word while she sang, her voice broken and raw. He remained in the field with her until dawn, as permanent as the markings on her back. Three lines of text scrolled over her three largest scars, the story of her love and loss now written on her: one line for her parents and uncle; one line for Lady Marion; and one line for her court and her people.

On the smaller, shorter scars, were the stories of Nehemia and of Sam. Her beloved dead.

No longer would they be locked away in her heart. No longer would she be ashamed.

61

The War Games came.

All the Ironteeth Clans were granted time to rest the day before, but none took it, instead squeezing in last-minute drills or going over plans and strategies.

Officials and councilors from Adarlan had been arriving for days, come to monitor the Games from the top of the Northern Fang. They would report back to the King of Adarlan about what the witches and their mounts were like—and who the victor was.

Weeks ago, after Abraxos had made the Crossing, Manon had returned to the Omega to grins and applause. Her grandmother was nowhere to be seen, but that was expected. Manon had not accomplished anything; she had merely done what was expected of her.

She saw and heard nothing of the Crochan prisoner in the belly of the Omega, and no one else seemed to know anything about her. She was half tempted to ask her grandmother, but the Matron didn't summon her, and Manon wasn't in the mood to be beaten again.

These days her own temper was fraying as the Clans closed in tight, kept to their own halls, and hardly spoke to each other. Whatever unity they'd shown on the night of Abraxos's crossing was long gone by the time the War Games arrived, replaced by centuries' worth of competition and blood feuding.

The Games were to take place in, around, and between the two peaks, including the nearest canyon, visible from the Northern Fang. Each of the three Clans would have its own nest atop a nearby mountain peak—a literal nest of twigs and branches. In the center of each lay a glass egg.

The eggs were to be their source of victory and downfall. Each Clan was to capture the eggs of the two enemy teams, but also leave behind a host to protect their own egg. The winning Clan would be the one who gained possession of the two other eggs by stealing them from the nests, where they could not be touched by their guardians, or from whatever enemy forces carried them. If an egg shattered, it meant automatic disqualification for whoever carried it.

Manon donned her light armor and flying leathers. She wore metal on her shoulders, wrists, and thighs—any place that could be hit by an arrow or sliced at by wyverns or enemy blades. She was used to the weight and limited movement, and so was Abraxos, thanks to the training she'd forced the Blackbeaks to endure these past few weeks.

Though they were under strict orders not to maim or kill, they were allowed to carry two weapons each, so Manon took Wind-Cleaver and her best dagger. The Shadows, Asterin, Lin, and the demon-twins would wield the bows. They were capable of making kill shots from their wyverns now—had taken run after run at targets in the canyons and made bulls-eyes each time. Asterin had swaggered into the mess hall that morning, well aware that she was lethal as all hell.

Each Clan wore braided strips of dyed leather across their

brows—black, blue, yellow—their wyverns painted with similar streaks on their tails, necks, and sides. When all the covens were airborne, they gathered in the skies, presenting the entirety of the host to the little mortal men in the mountains below. The Thirteen rode at the head of the Blackbeak covens, keeping perfect rank.

"Fools, for not knowing what they've unleashed," Asterin murmured, the words carried to Manon on the wind. "Stupid, mortal fools."

Manon hissed her agreement.

They flew in formation: Manon at the head, Asterin and Vesta flanking behind, then three rows of three: Imogen framed by the green-eyed demons, Ghislaine flanked by Kaya and Thea, the two Shadows and Lin, then Sorrel solo in the back. A battering ram, balanced and flawless, capable of punching through enemy lines.

If Manon didn't bring them down, then the vicious swords of Asterin and Vesta got them. If that didn't stop them, the six in the middle were a guaranteed death trap. Most wouldn't even make it to the Shadows and Lin, who would be fixing their keen eyes on their surroundings. Or to Sorrel, guarding their rear.

They would take out the enemy forces one by one, with hands and feet and elbows where weapons would ordinarily do the job. The objective was to retrieve the eggs, not kill the others, she reminded herself and the Thirteen again. And again.

The Games began with the ringing of a mighty bell somewhere in the Omega. The skies erupted with wings and claws and shrieks a heartbeat later.

They went after the Blueblood egg first, because Manon knew the Yellowlegs would go for the Blackbeak nest, which they did immediately. Manon signaled to her witches and one third of her force doubled back, falling behind home lines, putting up a solid wall of teeth and wings for the Yellowlegs to break against.

The Bluebloods, who had probably done the least planning in favor of all their various rituals and prayers, sent their forces to the Blackbeaks as well, to see if extra wings could break that iron-clad wall. Another mistake.

Within ten minutes, Manon and the Thirteen surrounded the Blueblood nest—and the home guard yielded their treasure.

There were whoops and hoots—not from the Thirteen, who were stone-faced, eyes glittering, but from the other Blackbeaks, the back third of whom peeled off, circled around, and joined Manon and her returning force to smash the Bluebloods and Yellowlegs between them.

The witches and their wyverns dove high and low, but this was as much for show as it was to win, and Manon did not yield them one inch as they pushed from the front and behind, an aerial vise that had wyverns nearly bucking off their riders in panic.

This—*this* was what she had been built for. Even battles she'd waged on a broom hadn't been this fast, brilliant, and deadly. And once they faced their enemies, once they added in an arsenal of weapons . . . Manon was grinning as she placed the Blueblood egg in the Blackbeak nest on the flat mountaintop.

Moments later, Manon and Abraxos were gliding over the fray, the Thirteen coming up from behind to regroup. Asterin, the only one who'd kept close the entire time, was grinning like mad—and as her cousin and her wyvern swept past the Northern Fang and its gathered observers, the golden-haired witch sprang up from her saddle and took a running leap right off the wing.

The Yellowlegs witch on the wyvern below didn't see Asterin until she'd landed on her, a hand on her throat where a dagger would have been. Even Manon gasped in delight as the Yellowlegs witch lifted her hands in surrender.

Asterin let go, lifting her arms to be gathered up into the claws of her own wyvern. After a toss and a harrowing fall, Asterin returned to her own saddle, swooping until she was again beside Manon and Abraxos. He swung toward Asterin's blue wyvern, swiping with his wing—a playful, almost flirtatious gesture that made the female mount shriek in delight.

Manon raised her brows at her Second. "You've been practicing, it seems," she called.

Asterin grinned. "I didn't claw my way to Second by sitting on my ass."

Then Asterin was swooping low again, but still within formation, a wing-beat away. Abraxos roared, and the Thirteen fell into formation around Manon, four covens flanking them behind. They just had to capture the Yellowlegs egg and bring it back to the Blackbeak nest, and it would be done.

They dodged and soared over fighting covens, and when they reached the Yellowlegs line, the Thirteen pulled up—and back, sending the other four covens behind them shooting in like an arrow, punching a line through the barrier that the Thirteen then swept through.

Closest to the Northern Fang, the Yellowlegs nest was circled by not three but four covens, a good chunk of the host to keep behind the lines. They rose up from the nest—not individual units, but as one—and Manon smiled to herself.

They raced for them, and the Yellowlegs held, held . . .

Manon whistled. She and Sorrel went up and down respectively, and her coven split in three, exactly as they'd practiced. Like the limbs of one creature, they struck the Yellowlegs lines—lines where every coven had mixed, now next to strangers and wyverns with whom they had never ridden closely before. The confusion got worse as the Thirteen scattered them and pushed them about. Orders were shouted, names were screamed, but the chaos was complete.

They were closing in on the nest when four Blueblood covens swept in out of nowhere, led by Petrah herself on her mount, Keelie. She was nearly free-falling for the nest, which had been left wide open while the Blackbeaks and the Yellowlegs fought. She'd been waiting for this, like a fox in its hole.

She swept in, and Manon dove after her, swearing viciously. A flash of yellow and a shriek of fury, and Manon and Abraxos were back-flapping, veering away as Iskra flashed past the nest—and slammed right into Petrah.

The two heirs and their wyverns locked talons and went sprawling, crashing through the air, clawing and biting. Shouts rose from the mountain and from the airborne witches.

Manon panted, righting her spinning head as Abraxos leveled out above the nest, swooping back in to seal their victory. She was about to nudge him to dive when Petrah screamed. Not in fury, but pain.

Agonizing, soul-shredding pain, the likes of which Manon had never heard, as Iskra's wyvern clamped its jaws on Keelie's neck.

Iskra let out a howl of triumph, and her bull shook Keelie—Petrah clinging to the saddle.

Now. Now was the time to grab the egg. She nudged Abraxos. "*Go,*" she hissed, leaning in, bracing for the dive.

Abraxos did not move, but hovered, watching Keelie fight to no avail, wings barely flapping as Petrah screamed again. Begging—begging Iskra to stop.

"*Now,* Abraxos!" She kicked him with her spurs. He again refused to dive.

Then Iskra barked a command to her wyvern . . . and the beast let go of Keelie.

There was a second scream then, from the mountain. From the Blue-blood Matron, screaming for her daughter as she plummeted down to the rocks below. The other Bluebloods whirled, but they were too far away, their wyverns too slow to stop that fatal plunge.

But Abraxos was not.

And Manon didn't know if she gave the command or thought it, but that scream, that mother's scream she'd never heard before, made her lean in. Abraxos dove, a shooting star with his glistening wings.

They dove and dove, for the broken wyvern and the still-living witch upon it.

Keelie was still breathing, Manon realized as they neared, the wind tearing at her face and clothes. Keelie was still breathing, and fighting like hell to keep steady. Not to survive. Keelie knew she would be dead any moment. She was fighting for the witch on her back.

Petrah had passed out, twisted in her saddle, from the plunge or the loss of air. She dangled precariously, even as Keelie fought with her last heartbeats to keep the fall smooth and slow. The wyvern's wings buckled and she yelped in pain.

Abraxos hurtled in, wings spread as he made one pass and then a second, the canyon appearing too fast below. By the time he finished the second glide, almost close enough to touch that bloodstained leathery hide, Manon understood.

He couldn't stop Keelie—she was too heavy and he too small. Yet they could save Petrah. He'd seen Asterin make that jump, too. She had to get the unconscious witch out of the saddle.

Abraxos roared at Keelie, and Manon could have sworn that he was speaking some alien language, bellowing some command, as Keelie made one final stand for her rider and leveled out flat. A landing platform.

My Keelie, Petrah had said. Had smiled as she said it.

Manon told herself it was for an alliance. Told herself it was for show.

But all she could see was the unconditional love in that dying wyvern's eyes as she unbuckled her harness, stood from the saddle, and leapt off Abraxos.

62

Manon hit Keelie and the beast screamed, but held on as Manon hauled herself against the wind and into the saddle where Petrah dangled. Her hands were stiff, her gloves making her even clumsier as she sliced with a blade through the leathers, one after another. Abraxos roared his warning. The canyon mouth loomed closer.

Darkness have mercy on her.

Then Manon had Petrah free, the Blueblood heir a dead weight in her arms, her hair whipping Manon's face like a thousand small knives. She lashed a length of leather around herself and Petrah. Once. Twice. She tied it, lacing her arms through Petrah's. Keelie kept steady. The canyon lips closed around them, shadow everywhere. Manon bellowed at the weight as she hauled the witch up out of the stirrups and the saddle.

Rock rushed past, but a shadow blotted out the sun, and there was Abraxos, diving for her, plummeting, small and sleek. He was the only wyvern she'd seen bank at that speed in this canyon.

"Thank you," she said to Keelie as she flung herself and Petrah into the air.

They fell for a heartbeat, twisting and dropping too fast, but then Abraxos was there, his claws outstretched. He swept them up, banking along the side of the canyon and over the lip, rising into the safety of the air.

Keelie hit the floor of the canyon with a crash that could be heard across the mountains.

She did not rise again.

The Blackbeaks won the War Games, and Manon was crowned Wing Leader in front of all those frilly, sweating men from Adarlan. They called her a hero, and a true warrior, and more nonsense like that. But Manon had seen her grandmother's face when she had set Petrah down on the viewing platform. Seen the disgust.

Manon ignored the Blueblood Matron, who had gotten on her knees to thank her. She did not even see Petrah as she was carried off.

The next day, rumor had it, Petrah would not rise from bed. They said she had been broken in her soul when Keelie died.

An unfortunate accident brought on by uncontrollable wyverns, the Yellowlegs Matron had claimed, and Iskra had echoed. But Manon had heard Iskra's command to kill.

She might have called Iskra out, might have challenged her, if Petrah hadn't heard that command, too. The vengeance was Petrah's to claim.

She should have let the witch die, her grandmother screamed at her that night as she struck Manon again and again for her lack of obedience. Lack of brutality. Lack of discipline.

Manon did not apologize. She could not stop hearing the sound made as Keelie hit the earth. And some part of her, perhaps a weak and undisciplined part, did not regret ensuring the animal's sacrifice had not been in vain.

From everyone else, Manon endured the praise heaped on her and accepted the bows from every gods-damned coven no matter their bloodline.

Wing Leader. She said it to herself, silently, as she and Asterin, half of the Thirteen trailing behind them, approached the mess hall where the celebration was to be held.

The other half were already there, scouting ahead for any possible threat or trap. Now that she was Wing Leader, now that she had humiliated Iskra, others would be even more vicious—to put her down and claim her position.

The crowd was merry, iron teeth glinting all around and ale—real, fresh ale brought in by those awful men from Adarlan—sloshing in mugs. Manon had one shoved into her hand, and Asterin yanked it away, drank a mouthful, and waited a moment before she gave it back.

"They're not above poisoning you," her Second said, winking as they made their way to the front of the room where the three Matrons were waiting. Those men at the Games had held a small ceremony, but this was for the witches—this was for Manon.

She hid her smile as the crowd parted, letting her through.

The three High Witches were seated in makeshift thrones, little more than ornate chairs they'd found. The Blueblood Matron smiled as Manon pressed two fingers to her brow. The Yellowlegs Matron, on the other end, did nothing. But her grandmother, seated in the center, smiled faintly.

A snake's smile.

"Welcome, Wing Leader," her grandmother said, and a cry went up from the witches, save for the Thirteen—who stayed cool and quiet. They did not need to cheer, for they were immortal and infinite and gloriously, wonderfully deadly.

"What gift can we give you, what crown can we bestow, to honor what you shall do for us?" her grandmother mused. "You have a fine blade, a fearsome coven"—the Thirteen all allowed a hint of a smirk—"what else could we give you that you do not possess?"

Manon bowed her head. "There is nothing I wish for, save the honor which you have already given me."

Her grandmother laughed. "What about a new cloak?"

Manon straightened. She could not refuse, but . . . this was her cloak, it had always been.

"That one is looking rather shabby," her grandmother went on, waving her hand to someone in the crowd. "So here is our gift to you, Wing Leader: a replacement."

There were grunts and curses, but the crowd gasped—in hunger, in anticipation—as a brown-haired, shackled witch was hauled forward by three Yellowlegs cronies and forced to her knees before Manon.

If her broken face, shattered fingers, lacerations, and burns did not give away what she was, then the bloodred cloak she wore did.

The Crochan witch, her eyes the solid color of freshly tilled earth, looked up at Manon. How those eyes were so bright despite the horrors written on her body, how she didn't collapse right there or start begging, Manon didn't know.

"A gift," said her grandmother, extending an iron-tipped hand toward the Crochan. "Worthy of my granddaughter. End her life and take your new cloak."

Manon recognized the challenge. Yet she drew her dagger, and Asterin stepped in close, eyes on the Crochan.

For a moment, Manon stared down at the witch, her mortal enemy. The Crochans had cursed them, made them eternal exiles. They deserved to die, each and every one of them.

But it was not her voice that said those things in her head. No, for some reason, it was her grandmother's.

"At your leisure, Manon," her grandmother cooed.

Choking, her lips cracked and bleeding, the Crochan witch looked up at Manon and chuckled. "Manon Blackbeak," she whispered in what might have been a drawl had her teeth not been broken, her throat ringed with bruises. "I know you."

"Kill the bitch!" a witch shouted from the back of the room.

Manon looked into her enemy's face and raised her brows.

"You know what we call you?" Blood welled as the Crochan's lips peeled into a smile. She closed her eyes as if savoring it. "We call you the White Demon. You're on our list—the list of all you monsters to kill on sight if we ever run into you. And you . . ." She opened her eyes and grinned, defiant, furious. "You are at the *top* of that list. For all that you have done."

"It's an honor," Manon said to the Crochan, smiling enough to show her teeth.

"Cut out her tongue!" someone else called.

"End her," Asterin hissed.

Manon flipped the dagger, angling it to sink into the Crochan's heart.

The witch laughed, but it turned into a cough that had her heaving until blue blood splattered on the floor, until tears were leaking from her eyes and Manon caught a glimpse of the deep, infected wounds on her chest. When she lifted her head, blood staining the corners of her mouth, she smiled again. "Look all you want. Look at what they did to me, your sisters. How it must pain them to know they couldn't break me in the end."

Manon stared down at her, at her ruined body.

"Do you know what this is, Manon Blackbeak?" the Crochan said. "Because I do. I heard them say what you did during your Games."

Manon wasn't sure why she was letting the witch talk, but she couldn't have moved if she wanted to.

"This," the Crochan said for all to hear, "is a reminder. My death—my *murder* at your hands, is a reminder. Not to them," she breathed, pinning Manon with that soil-brown stare. "But to you. A reminder of what they made you to be. They *made* you this way.

"You want to know the grand Crochan secret?" she went on. "Our great truth that we keep from you, that we guard with our lives? It is not where we hide, or how to break your curse. You have known all this time how to break it—you have known for five hundred years that your salvation lies in your hands alone. No, our great secret is that we pity you."

No one was speaking now.

But the Crochan did not break Manon's stare, and Manon did not lower her dagger.

"We pity you, each and every one of you. For what you do to your children. They are not born evil. But you force them to kill and hurt and hate until there is nothing left inside of them—of you. That is why you are here tonight, Manon. Because of the threat you pose to that monster you call grandmother. The threat you posed when you chose mercy and saved your rival's life." She gasped for breath, tears flowing unabashedly as she bared her teeth. "They have made you into monsters. *Made*, Manon. *And we feel sorry for you.*"

"Enough," the Matron said from behind. But the whole room was silent, and Manon slowly raised her eyes to her grandmother's.

In them, Manon beheld a promise of the violence and pain that would come if she disobeyed. Beyond that, there gleamed nothing but satisfaction. As if the Crochan had spoken true, but only the Blackbeak Matron knew she had done so.

The Crochan's eyes were still bright with a courage Manon could not comprehend.

"Do it," the Crochan whispered. Manon wondered if anyone else understood that it was not a challenge, but a plea.

Manon angled her dagger again, flipping it in her palm. She did not look at the Crochan, or her grandmother, or anyone as she gripped the witch by the hair and yanked back her head.

And then spilled her throat on the floor.

Legs dangling off a cliff edge, Manon sat on a plateau atop a peak in the Ruhnns, Abraxos sprawled at her side, smelling the night-blooming flowers on the spring meadow.

She'd had no choice but to take the Crochan's cloak, to dump her old one atop the body once it fell, once the witches gathered around to rip her apart.

They have made you into monsters.

Manon looked at her wyvern, the tip of his tail waving like a cat's. No one had noticed when she left the celebration. Even Asterin was drunk on the Crochan's blood, and had lost sight of Manon slipping through the crowd. She told Sorrel, though, that she was going to see Abraxos. And her Third, somehow, had let her go alone.

They'd flown until the moon was high and she could no longer hear the shrieks and cackles of the witches in the Omega. Together they sat on the last of the Ruhnns, and she gazed across the endless flat expanse between the peaks and the western sea. Somewhere out there, beyond the horizon, was a home that she had never known.

Crochans were liars and insufferably preachy. The witch had probably enjoyed giving her little speech—making some grand last stand. *We feel sorry for you.*

Manon rubbed at her eyes and braced her elbows on her knees, peering into the drop below.

She would have dismissed her, wouldn't have thought twice about it, if it hadn't been for that look in Keelie's eyes as she fell, fighting with every last scrap of strength to save her Petrah. Or for Abraxos's wing, sheltering Manon against icy rain.

The wyverns were meant to kill and maim and strike terror into the hearts of their enemies. And yet . . .

And yet. Manon looked toward the star-flecked horizon, leaning her face into a warm spring breeze, grateful for the steady, solid companion lounging behind her. A strange feeling, that gratitude for his existence.

Then there was that other strange feeling that pushed and pulled at her, making her replay the scene in the mess hall again and again.

She had never known regret—not true regret, anyway.

But she regretted not knowing the Crochan's name. She regretted not knowing who the new cloak on her shoulders had belonged to—where she had come from, how she had lived.

Somehow, even though her long life had been gone for ten years . . .

Somehow, that regret made her feel incredibly, heavily mortal.

63

Aedion let out a low whistle and offered Chaol the bottle of wine between them on the rooftop of Celaena's apartment. Chaol, not feeling at all like drinking, shook his head.

"I wish I had been there to see it." He gave Chaol a wolfish smile. "I'm surprised you're not condemning me for saying that."

"Whatever creatures the king sent with Narrok, I do not think they were innocent men," Chaol said. "Or really men at all anymore."

She had done it—had made such a statement that even days later, Aedion was still celebrating. Quietly, of course.

Chaol had come here tonight planning to tell Aedion and Ren what he knew of the spell the king had used and how they might destroy it. But he hadn't yet. He still wondered what Aedion would do with that knowledge. Especially once Chaol left for Anielle in three days.

"When she gets home, you need to lie low in Anielle," Aedion said, swigging from the bottle. "Once it comes out who she was all these years."

And it would, Chaol knew. He was already preparing to get Dorian and Sorscha out of the castle. Even if they had done nothing wrong, they had been her friends. If the king knew that Celaena was Aelin, it could be just as deadly as if he discovered that Dorian had magic. When she came home, everything would change.

Yes, Aelin would come home. But not to Chaol. She would come home to Terrasen, to Aedion and Ren and the court that was regathering in her name. She would come home to war and bloodshed and responsibility. Part of him still could not fathom what she'd done to Narrok, the battle cry she'd issued from across the sea. He could not accept that part of her, so bloodthirsty and unyielding. Even as Celaena, it had been hard to swallow at times, and he had tried to look past it, but as Aelin . . . He'd known, since the moment he figured out who she was, that while Celaena would always pick him, Aelin would not.

And it would not be Celaena Sardothien who returned to this continent. It would take time, he knew—for it to stop hurting, to let go. But the pain wouldn't last forever.

"Is there . . ." Aedion clenched his jaw as if debating saying the rest. "Is there anything you want me to tell her, or give her?" At any moment, any time, Aedion might have to flee to Terrasen and to his queen.

The Eye of Elena was warm at his neck, and Chaol almost reached for it. But he couldn't bring himself to send her that message, or to let go of her that completely—not yet. Just as he couldn't bring himself to tell Aedion about the clock tower.

"Tell her," Chaol said quietly, "that I had nothing to do with you. Tell her you barely spoke to me. Or Dorian. Tell her I am fine in Anielle, and that we are all safe."

Aedion was quiet long enough that Chaol got up to leave. But then the general said, "What would you have given—just to see her again?"

Chaol couldn't turn around as he said, "It doesn't matter now."

Sorscha rested her head on the soft spot between Dorian's shoulder and chest, breathing in the smell of him. He was already sleeping deeply. Almost—they had almost taken things over the edge tonight, but she had again hesitated, again let that stupid doubt creep in when he asked her if she was ready, and though she wanted to say yes, she had said no.

She lay awake, stomach tight and mind racing. There was so much she wanted to do and see with him. But she could feel the world shifting—the wind changing. Aelin Galathynius was alive. And even if Sorscha gave everything to Dorian, the upcoming weeks and months would be trying enough for him without having to worry about her.

If the captain and the prince decided to act on their knowledge, if magic was freed . . . it would be chaos. People might go as mad from its sudden return as they'd gone from its departure. She didn't want to think what the king would do.

Yet no matter what happened tomorrow, or next week, or next year, she was grateful. Grateful to the gods, to fate, to herself for being brave enough to kiss him that night. Grateful for this little bit of time she'd been given with him.

She still thought about what the captain had said all those weeks ago—about being queen.

But Dorian needed a true queen if he was to survive this. Someday, perhaps, she'd have to face the choice of letting him go for the greater good. She was still quiet, and small. If she could hardly stand up to Amithy, how could she ever be expected to fight for her country?

No, she could not be queen, for there were limits to her bravery, and to what she could offer.

But for now . . . for now, she could be selfish for a little longer.

For two days, Chaol continued to plan an escape for Dorian and Sorscha, Aedion working with him. They hadn't objected when he'd explained—and there had even been a hint of relief in the prince's eyes. They would all go tomorrow, when Chaol left for Anielle. It was the perfect excuse to get them out of the castle: they wanted to accompany their friend for a day or two before bidding him farewell. He knew Dorian would try to return to Rifthold, that he'd have to fight him on it, but at least they could both agree that Sorscha was to get out. Some of Aedion's own belongings were already at the apartment, where Ren continued to gather resources for them all.

Just in case. Chaol had turned in his formal suggestions for his replacement to the king, and the announcement would be made tomorrow morning. After all these years, all that planning and hoping and working, he was leaving. He hadn't been able to bring himself to leave his sword to his replacement, as he should have done. Tomorrow—he only had to get through tomorrow.

But there was no way Chaol could prepare for the summons he received from the King of Adarlan to meet him in his private council chamber. When he arrived, Aedion was already inside, surrounded by fifteen guards Chaol did not recognize, all wearing those tunics with the royal wyvern embroidered with black thread.

The King of Adarlan was grinning.

Dorian heard within minutes that Aedion and Chaol had been summoned to his father's private council room. As soon as he heard, he ran—not for Chaol, but to Sorscha.

He almost collapsed with relief when he found her in her workroom. But he willed strength to his knees as he crossed the room in a few strides and grabbed her hand. "We're getting out. Now. You are getting out of this castle right now, Sorscha."

She pulled back. “What happened? Tell me, what—”

“We’re going *now*,” he panted.

“Oh, I don’t think so,” someone purred from the open doorway.

He turned to find Amithy—the old healer—standing there, arms crossed and smiling faintly. Dorian could do nothing as half a dozen unfamiliar guards appeared behind her and she said, “The king wants to see you both in his chambers. Immediately.”

64

In the council room high in the glass castle, Aedion had already marked the exits and considered what furniture he could use as a defense or as a weapon. They'd taken his sword when they'd come for him in his rooms, though they hadn't shackled him. A lethal mistake. The captain wasn't shackled, either; in fact, the fools had left him armed. The captain was doing his best to look vaguely confused as the king watched them from his glass throne.

"What an interesting night this has turned out to be. What interesting information my spies have brought me," the king said, looking from Aedion to Chaol to Dorian and his woman.

"My most talented general is found to be sneaking around Rifthold in the dead of night—after spending so much of my gold on parties he does not even bother attending. And he has somehow, despite years of animosity, become close with my Captain of the Guard. While my son"—Aedion did not envy the smile the king gave the Crown Prince—"has apparently been dabbling with the rabble. Again."

To his credit, Dorian snarled and said, "Consider your words carefully, Father."

"Oh?" The king raised a thick, scarred brow. "I had it on good authority that you were planning to run away with this healer. Why would you ever do such a thing?"

The prince's throat bobbed, but he kept his head high. "Because I can't stand the thought of her spending another minute in this festering shithole that you call a court." Aedion couldn't help but admire him for it—for yielding nothing until the king showed his hand. Smart man—brave man. But it might not be enough to get them out of this alive.

"Good," the king said. "Neither can I."

He waved a hand, and before Aedion could bark a warning, the guards separated the prince and the girl. Four held Dorian back, and two forced Sorscha to kneel with a kick behind the knees.

She cried out as she hit the marble, but went silent—the whole room went silent—as a third guard pulled a sword and placed it lightly on the back of her slender neck.

"*Don't you dare*," Dorian growled.

Aedion looked to Chaol, but the captain was frozen. These were not his guards. Their uniforms were those of the men who had hunted Ren. They had the same dead eyes, the same vileness, that had made him not at all regret killing their colleagues in the alley. He'd taken down six that night with minimal damage—how many could he cut down now? His gaze met the captain's, and the captain flicked his eyes to the guard who held Aedion's sword. That would be one of his first moves—get Aedion a sword so they could fight.

Because they would fight. They would fight their way out of this, or to their deaths.

The king said to Dorian, "I would choose your next words carefully, Prince."

Chaol couldn't start the fight, not with that sword resting on Sorscha's neck. That was his first goal: get the girl out alive. Then Aedion. Dorian, the king wouldn't kill—not here, not in this way. But Aedion and Sorscha had to get away. And that could not happen until the king called off the guard. Then Dorian spoke.

"Let her go and I'll tell you anything." Dorian took a step toward his father, palms out. "She has nothing to do with—with whatever this is. Whatever you think has happened."

"But you do?" The king was still smiling. There was a carved, round bit of familiar black stone resting on the small table beside the king. From the distance, Chaol couldn't see what it was, but it made his stomach turn over regardless. "Tell me, *son*: why were General Ashryver and Captain Westfall meeting these months?"

"I don't know."

The king clicked his tongue, and the guard raised his sword to strike. Chaol started forward as Sorscha sucked in a breath.

"No—stop!" Dorian flung out a hand.

"Then answer the question."

"I am! You bastard, I *am*! I don't know why they were meeting!"

The guard's sword still remained up, ready to fall before Chaol could move an inch.

"Do you know that there has been a spy in my castle for several months now, Prince? Someone feeding information to my enemies and plotting against me with a known rebel leader?"

Shit. *Shit.* He had to mean Ren—the king knew who Ren was, had sent those men to hunt him down.

"Just tell me who, Dorian, and you can do whatever you wish with your friend."

The king didn't know, then—if it was he or Aedion or both of them who had been meeting with Ren. He didn't know how much they'd learned about his plans, his control over magic. Aedion was somehow still keeping his mouth shut, somehow still looking ready for battle.

Aedion, who had survived for so long without hope, holding together his kingdom as best he could . . . who would never see the queen he so fiercely loved. He deserved to meet her, and she deserved to have him serve in her court.

Chaol took a breath, preparing himself for the words that would doom him.

But it was Aedion who spoke.

"You want a spy? You want a traitor?" the general drawled, and flung his replicated black ring on the floor. "Then here I am. You want to know why the captain and I were meeting? It was because your stupid bastard of a boy-captain figured out that I'd been working with one of the rebels. He's been blackmailing information out of me for months to give to his father to offer *you* when the Lord of Anielle needed a favor. And you know what?" Aedion grinned at them all, the Northern Wolf incarnate. If the king was shocked about the ring, he didn't show it. "All you monsters can burn in hell. Because my queen is coming—and she will spike you to the walls of your gods-damned castle. And I can't wait to help her gut you like the pigs you are." He spat at the king's feet, right on top of the fake ring that had stopped bouncing.

It was flawless—the rage and the arrogance and the triumph. But as he stared each of them down, Chaol's heart fractured.

Because for a flicker, as those turquoise eyes met with his, there was none of that rage or triumph. Only a message to the queen that Aedion would never see. And there were no words to convey it—the love and the hope and the pride. The sorrow at not knowing her as the woman she had become. The gift Aedion thought he was giving her in sparing Chaol's life.

Chaol nodded slightly, because he understood that he could not help, not at this point—not until that sword was removed from Sorscha's neck. Then he could fight, and he might still get them out alive.

Aedion didn't struggle as the guards clapped shackles around his wrists and ankles.

"I've always wondered about that ring," the king said. "Was it the distance, or some true strength of spirit that made you so unresponsive to its suggestions? But regardless, I am so glad that you confessed to treason, Aedion." He spoke with slow, deliberate glee. "So glad you did it in front of all these witnesses, too. It will make your execution that much easier. Though I think . . ." The king smiled and looked at the fake black ring. "I think I'll wait. Perhaps give it a month or two. Just in case any last-minute guests have to travel a long, long way for the execution. Just in case someone gets it into her head that she can rescue you."

Aedion snarled. Chaol bit back his own reaction. Perhaps the king had never had anything on them—perhaps this had only been a ruse to get Aedion to confess to something, because the king knew that the general would offer up his own life instead of an innocent's. The king wanted to savor this, and savor the trap that he had now set for Aelin, even if it cost him a fine general in the process. Because once she heard that Aedion was captured, once she knew the execution date . . . she would run to Rifthold.

"After she comes for you," Aedion promised the king, "they'll have to scrape what's left of you off the walls."

The king only smiled. Then he looked to Dorian and Sorscha, who seemed to be hardly breathing. The healer remained on the floor and did not lift her head as the king braced his massive forearms on his knees and said, "And what do you have to say for yourself, girl?"

She trembled, shaking her head.

"That's *enough*," Dorian snapped, sweat gleaming on his brow. The prince winced in pain as his magic was repressed by the iron in his system. "Aedion confessed; now let her go."

"Why should I release the true traitor in this castle?"

Sorscha couldn't stop shaking as the king spoke.

All her years of remaining invisible, all her training, first from those rebels in Fenharrow, then the contacts they'd sent her family to in Rifthold . . . all of it ruined.

"Such interesting letters you send to your friend. Why, I might not ever have read them," the king said, "if you hadn't left one in the rubbish for your superior to find. See—you rebels have your spies, and I have mine. And as soon as you decided to start using my son . . ." She could feel the king smirking at her. "How many of his movements did you report to your rebel friends? What secrets of mine have you given away over the years?"

"Leave her alone," Dorian growled. It was enough to set her crying. He still thought she was innocent.

And maybe, maybe he could get out of this if he was surprised enough by the truth, if the king saw his son's shock and disgust.

So Sorscha lifted her head, even as her mouth trembled, even as her eyes burned, and stared down the King of Adarlan.

"You destroyed everything that I had, and you deserve everything that's to come," she said. Then she looked at Dorian, whose eyes were indeed wide, his face bone-white. "I was not supposed to love you. But I did. I do. And there is so much I wish . . . I wish we could have done together, seen together."

The prince just stared at her, then walked to the foot of the dais and dropped to his knees. "Name your price," he said to his father. "Ask it of me, but let her go. Exile her. Banish her. Anything—say it, and it will be done."

She began shaking her head, trying to find the words to tell him that she hadn't betrayed him—not her prince. The king, yes. She had reported his movements for years, in each carefully written letter to her "friend." But never Dorian.

The king looked at his son for a long moment. He looked at the captain and Aedion, so quiet and so tall—beacons of hope for their future.

Then he looked again at his son, on his knees before the throne, on his knees for her, and said, "No."

"No."

Chaol thought he had not heard it, the word that cleaved through the air just before the guard's sword did.

One blow from that mighty sword.

That was all it took to sever Sorscha's head.

The scream that erupted out of Dorian was the worst sound that Chaol had ever heard.

Worse even than the wet, heavy thud of her head hitting the red marble.

Aedion began roaring—roaring and cursing at the king, thrashing against his chains, but the guards hauled him away, and Chaol was too stunned to do anything other than watch the rest of Sorscha's body topple to the ground. And then Dorian, still screaming, was scrambling through the blood toward it—toward her head, as if he could put it back.

As if he could piece her together.

65

Chaol hadn't been able to move a muscle from the moment the guard cut off Sorscha's head to the moment Dorian, still kneeling in a pool of her blood, stopped screaming.

"That is what awaits traitors," the king said to the silent room.

And Chaol looked at the king, at his shattered friend, and drew his sword.

The king rolled his eyes. "Put away your sword, Captain. I've no interest in your noble antics. You're to go home to your father tomorrow. Don't leave this castle in disgrace."

Chaol kept his sword drawn. "I will not go to Anielle," he growled. "And I will not serve you a moment longer. There is one true king in this room—there always has been. And he is not sitting on that throne."

Dorian stiffened.

But Chaol went on. "There is a queen in the north, and she has already beaten you once. She will beat you again. And again. Because what she represents, and what your son represents, is what you fear most: hope. You cannot steal it, no matter how many you rip from their homes and enslave. And you cannot break it, no matter how many you murder."

The king shrugged. "Perhaps. But maybe I can start with you." He flicked his fingers at the guards. "Kill him, too."

Chaol whirled to the guards behind him and crouched, ready to fight a path out for himself and Dorian.

Then a crossbow snapped and he realized there had been others in the room—hidden behind impossibly thick shadows.

He had only enough time to twist—to see the bolt firing for him with deadly accuracy.

Only enough time to see Dorian's eyes widen, and the whole room plunge into ice.

The arrow froze midflight and dropped to the floor, shattering into a hundred pieces.

Chaol stared at Dorian in mute horror as his friend's eyes glowed a deep, raging blue, and the prince snarled at the king, "*Don't you touch him.*"

The ice spread across the room, up the legs of the shocked guards, freezing over Sorscha's blood, and Dorian got to his feet. He raised both hands, and light shimmered along his fingers, a cold breeze whipping through his hair.

"I knew you had it, boy—" the king started, standing, but Dorian threw out a hand and the king was blasted into his chair by a gust of frozen wind, the window behind him shattering. Wind roared into the room, drowning out all sound.

All sound except Dorian's words as he turned to Chaol, his hands and clothes soaked with Sorscha's blood. "Run. And when you come back . . ." The king was getting to his feet, but another wave of Dorian's magic slammed into him, knocking him down. There were tears staining Dorian's bloody cheeks now. "When you come back," the prince said, "*burn this place to the ground.*"

A wall of crackling black hurtled toward them from behind the throne.

"*Go*," Dorian ordered, turning toward the onslaught of his father's power.

Light exploded from Dorian, blocking out the wave, and the entire castle shook.

People screamed, and Chaol's knees buckled. For a moment, he debated making a stand with his friend, right there and then.

But he knew that this had been the other trap. One for Aedion and Aelin, one for Sorscha. And this one—this one to draw out Dorian's power.

Dorian had known it, too. Known it, and still walked into it so Chaol could escape—to find Aelin and tell her what had happened here today. Someone had to get out. Someone had to survive.

He looked at his friend, perhaps for the last time, and said what he had always known, from the moment they'd met, when he'd understood that the prince was his brother in soul. "I love you."

Dorian merely nodded, eyes still blazing, and lifted his hands again toward his father. Brother. Friend. King.

As another wave of the king's power filled the room, Chaol shoved through the still-frozen guards and fled.

Aedion knew everything had gone to hell as the castle shuddered. But he was already on his way to the dungeons, bound from head to toe.

It had been such an easy choice to make. When the captain had been about to take the fall for both of them, he'd thought only of Aelin, what it would do to her if her friend died. Even if he never got to see her, it was still better than having to face her when he explained that the captain was dead.

From the sound of it, it seemed the prince was providing a distraction so the captain could flee—and because there was no way in hell the prince would let his father go unpunished for that woman's death. So Aedion Ashryver let himself be led into the darkness.

He did not bother with prayers, for himself or for the captain. The gods had not helped him these past ten years, and they would not save him now.

He did not mind dying.

Though he still wished he'd gotten a chance to see her—just once.

Dorian slammed into the marble floor, where the puddle of Sorscha's blood had now melted.

Even as his father sent a wave of blinding, burning black power crashing onto him, filling his mouth and his veins; even as he screamed, all he could see was that moment—when the sword cut through flesh and tendon and bone. He could still see her wide eyes, her hair glimmering in the light as it, too, was severed.

He should have saved her. It had been so sudden.

But when the arrow had fired at Chaol . . . that was the death he could not endure. Chaol had drawn his line—and Dorian was on his side of it. Chaol had called him his king.

So revealing his power to his father did not frighten him.

No, to save his friend, dying did not scare him one bit.

The blast of power receded, and Dorian was left panting on the stones. He had nothing left.

Chaol had gotten away. It was enough.

He reached out an arm toward where Sorscha's body lay. His arm burned—maybe it was broken, or maybe it was his father's power still branding him—but he reached for her nonetheless.

By the time his father stood over him, he'd managed to move his hand a few inches.

"Do it," Dorian rasped. He was choking—on blood and the gods knew what.

"Oh, I don't think so," his father said, digging a knee into his chest. "It won't be death for you, my gifted son."

There was something dark and gleaming in his father's hands.

Dorian fought like hell against the guards now pinning his arms, trying to drag up any ounce of power as his father brought the collar of Wyrdstone toward his neck.

A collar, like the ones worn by those *things* Chaol had said were in the Dead Islands.

No—no.

He was screaming it—screaming it because he'd seen that creature in the catacombs, and heard what was being done to Roland and Kaltain. He had seen what a mere ring could do. This was an entire collar, with no visible keyhole . . .

"Hold him still," his father barked, digging his knee in deeper.

The breath was sucked from his chest, and his ribs groaned in agony. But there was nothing Dorian could do to stop it.

He wrenched his arm from one of the guards—wrenched it free and reached, bellowing.

He had just touched Sorscha's limp hand when cool stone gripped his throat, there was a faint click and hiss, and the darkness swept in to tear him apart.

Chaol ran. He did not have the time to take anything except what he had on him as he sprinted like hell for Dorian's rooms. Fleetfoot was waiting, as she had been all night, and he scooped her over a shoulder and hauled her to Celaena's room and into the secret passage. Down and down they went, the dog unusually obedient.

Three blasts shook the castle, shaking dust from the stones above. He kept running, knowing each blast meant Dorian was alive a bit longer, and dreading the silence to come.

Hope—that was what he carried with him. The hope of a better world that Aedion and Sorscha and Dorian had sacrificed themselves for.

He made one stop, with Fleetfoot still gripped over his shoulder.

With a silent prayer to the gods for their forgiveness, Chaol hurtled into the tomb to grab Damaris, shoving the sacred blade through his belt and stuffing a few handfuls of gold into his cloak pockets. And though the skull-shaped knocker didn't move, he told Mort precisely where he would be. "Just in case she comes back. In case . . . in case she doesn't know."

Mort remained stationary, but Chaol had the sense he'd been listening all the same as he grabbed the satchel containing Dorian and Celaena's magic books and fled to the passage that would take him to the sewer tunnel. A few minutes later, he was raising the heavy iron grate over the sewer stream. The outside beyond was wholly dark and still.

As he heaved Fleetfoot back into his arms to swing them both around the wall and onto the stream bank beyond, the castle went silent. There were screams, yes, but silence lurked beneath them. He did not want to know if Dorian was alive or dead.

He couldn't decide which was worse.

When Chaol got to the hidden apartment, Ren was pacing. "Where's—"

There was blood on him, he realized. The spray from Sorscha's neck. Chaol didn't know how he found the words, but he told Ren what had happened.

"So it's just us?" Ren asked quietly. Chaol nodded. Fleetfoot was sniffing around in the apartment, having made her inspection and decided Ren wasn't worth eating—even after Ren had protested that the dog might draw too much attention. She was staying; that was nonnegotiable.

A muscle feathered in Ren's jaw. "Then we find a way to free Aedion. As soon as possible. You and me. Between your knowledge of the castle and my contacts, we can find a way." Then he whispered, "You said Dorian's woman was—was a healer?" When Chaol nodded, Ren looked like he was about to be sick, but he asked, "Was she named Sorscha?"

"You were the friend she sent those letters to," Chaol breathed.

"I kept pressing her for information, kept . . ." Ren covered his face and took a shuddering breath. When his eyes at last met Chaol's, they were bright. Slowly, Ren held out a hand. "You and me, we'll find a way to free them. Both Aedion and your prince."

Chaol didn't hesitate as he gripped the rebel's outstretched hand.

66

"Morath," Manon said, wondering if she'd heard right. "For battle?"

Her grandmother turned from the desk, eyes flashing. "To serve the duke, just as the king ordered. He wants the Wing Leader in Morath with half the host ready to fly at a moment's notice. The others are to stay here under Iskra's command to monitor the north."

"And you—where will you be?"

Her grandmother hissed, rising. "So many questions now that you're Wing Leader."

Manon bowed her head. They had not spoken of the Crochan. Manon had gotten the message: next time, it would be one of the Thirteen on her knees. So she kept her head down as she said, "I only ask because I would not be parted with you, Grandmother."

"Liar. And a pathetic one." Her grandmother turned back to the desk. "I shall remain here, but come to you in Morath during the summer. We have work to finish here."

Manon lifted her chin, her new red cloak pooling around her, and asked, "And when shall we fly to Morath?"

Her grandmother smiled, iron teeth shining. "Tomorrow."

Even under the cover of darkness, the warm spring breeze was full of new grass and snow-melted rivers, only disrupted by the booming of wings as Manon led the host south along the Fangs.

They kept to the shadows of the mountains, shifting ranks and dipping out of sight to prevent anyone from getting an accurate count of their numbers. Manon sighed through her nose, and the wind ripped the sound away, just as it streamed her long red cloak behind her.

Asterin and Sorrel flanked her, silent like the rest of the covens for the long hours they'd flown down the mountains. They would cross Oakwald where Morath's mountains were closest, then rise above the cover of the cloud line for the rest of the journey. Unseen and as quiet as possible—that was how the king wanted them to arrive at the duke's mountain fortress. They flew all night down the Fangs, swift and sleek as shadows, and the earth below quivered in their wake.

Sorrel was stone-faced, monitoring the skies around them, but Asterin was smiling faintly. It was not a wild grin, or one that promised death, but a calm smile. To be aloft and skimming the clouds. Where every Blackbeak belonged. Where Manon belonged.

Asterin caught her stare and smiled wider, as if there wasn't a host of witches flying behind them and Morath lying ahead. Her cousin turned her face into the wind, breathing it in, exultant.

Manon did not let herself savor that beautiful breeze or open herself to that joy. She had work to do; they all did. Despite what the

Crochan had said, Manon had not been born with a heart, or a soul. She did not need them.

Once they fought the king's war, when his enemies were bleeding out around them . . . only then would they ride to reclaim their broken kingdom.

And she would go home at last.

67

The rising sun was staining the Avery River with gold as the cloaked man strode onto a rickety dock in the slums. Fishermen were heading out for the day, revelers were stumbling in for the night, and Rifthold was still asleep—unaware of what had happened the night before.

The man pulled out a lovely blade, its eagle pommel glinting in the first light of dawn. For a long moment, he stared at the sword, thinking of all that it had once embodied. But there was a new sword at his side—an ancient king's blade, from a time when good men had served noble rulers and the world had prospered for it.

He would see that world reborn, even if it took his last breath. Even if he had no name now, no position or title save Oath-Breaker, Traitor, Liar.

No one noticed when the sword was jettisoned over the river, its pommel catching the sun and burning like golden fire, a flash of light before it was swallowed by the dark water, never to be seen again.

68

It turned out that the "submission" part of a blood oath was something Rowan liked to interpret as it suited him. During their two-week trek to the nearest port in Wendlyn, he bossed Celaena around even more—seeming to believe that now he was part of her court, it entitled him to certain nonnegotiable rights regarding her safety, her movements, and her plans.

She was starting to wonder, as they approached the docks at the end of the cobblestone street, if she had made a teensy mistake in binding him to her forever. They'd been arguing for the past three days about her next move—about the ship she'd hired to take her back to Adarlan.

"This plan is absurd," Rowan said for the hundredth time, stopping in the shadows of a tavern by the docks. The sea air was light and crisp. "Going back alone seems like suicide."

"One, I'm going back as Celaena, not Aelin—"

"Celaena, who did not accomplish the king's mission, and who they are now going to hunt down."

"The King and Queen of Eyllwe should have gotten their warning by now." She'd sent it the first time they'd gone into town while investigating the murder of those poor people. Though letters were nearly impossible to send into the empire, Wendlyn had certain ways of getting around that. And as for Chaol . . . well, that was another reason why she was here, on this dock, about to get onto this ship. She had awoken this morning and slipped the amethyst ring off her finger. It had felt like a blessed release, a final shadow lifted from her heart. But there were still words left unsaid between them, and she needed to make sure he was safe—and would remain that way.

"So you're going to get the key from your old master, find the captain, and then what?"

Complete submission to her indeed. "Then I go north."

"And I'm supposed to sit on my ass for the next gods know how many months?"

She rolled her eyes. "You're not exactly inconspicuous, Rowan. If your tattoos don't attract attention, then the hair, the ears, the *teeth* . . ."

"I have another form, you know."

"And, *just like I said*, magic doesn't work there anymore. You'd be trapped in that form. Though I do hear that Rifthold rats are particularly delicious, if you want to eat them for months."

He glared at her, then scanned the ship—even though she knew he'd snuck out of their room at the inn last night to inspect it already. "We're stronger together than apart."

"If I'd known you would be such a pain in the ass, I never would have let you swear that oath."

"Aelin." At least he wasn't calling her "Majesty" or "My Lady." "Either as yourself or as Celaena, they will try to find you and kill you. They are probably already tracking you down. We could go to Varese right now and approach your mother's mortal kin, the Ashryvers. They might have a plan."

"My chance at success in getting the Wyrdkey out of Rifthold lies in stealth as Celaena."

"Please," he said.

But she merely lifted her chin. "I am going, Rowan. I will gather the rest of my court—*our* court—and then we will raise the greatest army the world has ever witnessed. I will call in every favor, every debt owed to Celaena Sardothien, to my parents, to my bloodline. And then . . ." She looked toward the sea, toward home. "And then I am going to rattle the stars." She put her arms around him—a promise. "Soon. I will send for you soon, when the time is right. Until then, try to make yourself useful." He shook his head, but gripped her in a bone-crushing embrace.

He pulled back far enough to look at her. "Perhaps I'll go help repair Mistward."

She nodded. "You never told me," she said, "what you were praying to Mala for that morning before we entered Doranelle."

For a moment, it looked like he wouldn't tell her. But then he quietly said, "I prayed for two things. I asked her to ensure you survived the encounter with Maeve—to guide you and give you the strength you needed."

That strange, comforting warmth, that presence that had reassured her . . . the setting sun kissed her cheeks as if in confirmation, and a shiver went down her spine. "And the second?"

"It was a selfish wish, and a fool's hope." She read the rest of it in his eyes. *But it came true.*

"Dangerous, for a prince of ice and wind to pray to the Fire-Bringer," she managed to say.

Rowan shrugged, a secret smile on his face as he wiped away the tear that escaped down her cheek. "For some reason, Mala likes me, and agreed that you and I make a formidable pair."

But she didn't want to know—didn't want to think about the Sun Goddess and her agenda as she flung herself on Rowan, breathing in his scent, memorizing the feel of him. The first member of her court—the court that *would* change the world. The court that would rebuild it. Together.

She boarded the boat as night fell, herded into the galley with the other passengers to keep them from learning the route through the reef. With little fuss they set sail, and when they were at last allowed out of the galley, she emerged onto the deck to find dark, open ocean around them. A white-tailed hawk still flew overhead, and it swooped low to brush its star-silvered wing against her cheek in farewell before it turned back with a sharp cry.

In the moonless light, she traced the scar on her palm, the oath to Nehemia.

She would retrieve the first Wyrdkey from Arobynn and track down the others, and then find a way to put the Wyrdkeys back in their Gate. She would free magic and destroy the king and save her people. No matter the odds, no matter how long it took, no matter how far she had to go.

She lifted her face to the stars. She was Aelin Ashryver Galathynius, heir of two mighty bloodlines, protector of a once-glorious people, and Queen of Terrasen.

She was Aelin Ashryver Galathynius—and she would not be afraid.

ACKNOWLEDGMENTS

This book would not exist without my friends. Especially my best friend, Jaeger copilot, and *anam cara*, Susan Dennard.

It's to her that I owe the biggest debt, for the entire days spent brainstorming and figuring out the right way to tell the story, for holding my hand as I walked down the dark paths of this book, for being the voice in my head telling me to keep going, keep going, keep going. There was no one else that this book could have been dedicated to; no one else who challenges and uplifts and inspires me so greatly. So, thank you, Soozyface, for being the kind of friend I was so sure didn't exist in this world. Love you, dude.

I also owe a huge debt to my brilliant and immensely talented friend Alex Bracken, for the genius feedback, for the bajillion-page e-mails, and for being so, so incredibly supportive. I cannot tell you how grateful I am that our paths crossed all those years ago—what an insane journey it's been.

And none of this would ever have happened without my lovely and badass agent, Tamar Rydzinski, who has been with me from the very beginning, and whose tireless work has made this series reality. I'm so honored to call you my agent, but even more honored to call you my friend.

To the incredible worldwide team at Bloomsbury—how can I ever fully convey what a joy it is to work with you all? Thank you, thank you, thank you for all that you do for me and Throne of Glass. To my editor, Margaret Miller—this book would be a hot mess without you. To Cat Onder, Cindy Loh, and Rebecca McNally—you guys are the absolute best. To Erica Barmash, Hali Baumstein, Emma Bradshaw, Kathleen Farrar, Cristina Gilbert, Courtney Griffin, Alice Grigg, Natalie Hamilton, Bridget Hartzler, Charli Haynes, Emma Hopkin, Linette Kim, Lizzy Mason, Jenna Pocius, Emily Ritter, Amanda Shipp, Grace Whooley, and Brett Wright: thank you from the bottom of my heart for all your hard work, enthusiasm, and dedication.

To the team at Audible and to the Throne of Glass audiobook narrator, Elizabeth Evans, thank you for making Celaena's world come to life in a whole new way, and for giving her a voice. And thank you to Janet Cadsawan, whose beautiful Throne of Glass jewelry line continues to blow my mind.

To the lovely Erin "Ders" Bowman, for the cheerleading and the unfailing encouragement, for the video chats, and the epic (non-writing) retreats. Hero Squad Forever.

To Mandy Hubbard, Dan Krokos, Biljana Likic, Kat Zhang, and the Publishing Crawl gang—thanks so much for being some of the bright lights.

To my parents—my number-one fans—for the many adventures that so often serve as inspiration for these books. To my family, for the love and support, and for pushing this series on your friends and book clubs. Love you all. To my wonderful Grandma Connie—I miss you and wish you were here to read this.

To the readers who have picked up and championed this series—words cannot express my gratitude. I am truly blessed to have you all as fans. You make the hard work worth it.

To my dog, Annie: you can't read (though it wouldn't surprise me if you secretly could), but I want it written here—for eternity—that you're the best canine companion anyone could hope for. Thanks for the cuddles, for sitting in my lap while I'm trying to write, and for giving me someone to talk to all day. Sorry I play the music so loudly when you're trying to snooze. Love you, love you, love you forever and ever and ever.

And to my husband, Josh: You get last billing here, but that's because you're first in my heart. I'll never stop being grateful that I get to share this wild journey with you.